SUN CHILD OF THE MOOR

TRICIA D. WAGNER

LYRIDAE BOOKS

For my mother, Margaret Ann Snead,
who has known about the Sylphic Kingdom
far longer than I have.
And for my father, Billy Joe Snead,
who taught me how to reach it
by means of stories.

ALSO BY TRICIA D. WAGNER

*The Strider and the Regulus, The Star of Atlantis
& The Shepherd of the Stars*

A starry-eyed boy.
A cryptic map. A mythical treasure.
What perils await in the chasing of dreams?

"As Swift lives up to his name and his family legacy, young adults receive a fast-paced fantasy that will appeal not just on the adventure or fantasy levels, but in matters of the heart as the young struggle for independence and action in the face of parental restrictions.
Tricia D. Wagner's attention to pairing psychological struggle with the adventure of finding a promised treasure creates a story that pulls on the emotions of young readers as it satisfies their desire for action and adventure."
- D. Donovan, Senior Reviewer, *Midwest Book Review*

"Wagner has a beautiful and poetic writing style which serves to enhance the descriptive detail she provides to her novels. This gives her books a whimsical and otherworldly quality that supports the fantastical elements within them. Readers who appreciate thoughtful narratives that focus on the human condition within the context of charming and memorable stories will quickly fall for this series and its immersive quality.
The medical and scientific elements found within this book help readers puzzle out the question of what is true in Swift's world alongside the legend and lore. This is a satisfying series that will speak to young adult readers and adults alike."
- Mary R. Lanni, MLIS, Reviewer, *Reedsy Discovery*

PRAISE FOR TRICIA D. WAGNER

"*SUN CHILD OF THE MOOR* IS A VIVID STORY THAT INTERSECTS FANTASY AND PHYSICAL STRUGGLES THAT PLAY OUT ON INTERNAL AND EXTERNAL FIELDS. LIBRARIES AND READERS WILL FIND THAT THIS STORY GOES BEYOND THE ANTICIPATED COMING-OF-AGE OF A YOUNG MAN WHO IS FACED WITH UNCOMMON DANGER TO DELVE INTO THE NATURE OF WIELDING POWERFUL GROWTH IN A SOCIALLY RESPONSIBLE, AWARE MANNER.
THIS FANTASTIC LITERARY ADVENTURE AND ITS LIVELY, ENGAGING ACTION WILL ENCOURAGE DISCUSSION AND DEBATE IN READER CIRCLES ABOUT THE CONSEQUENCES OF SPECIAL ABILITIES, AND THE CONTRAST BETWEEN IMAGINATION AND REALITY, MAKING *SUN CHILD OF THE MOOR* A TOP RECOMMENDATION ABOVE MANY OTHER ACTION-PACKED FANTASIES."
- **D. DONOVAN, SENIOR REVIEWER,** *MIDWEST BOOK REVIEW*

"*SUN CHILD OF THE MOOR* IS A WELL-WRITTEN, BEAUTIFULLY POETIC, FANTASTICAL TALE. IT IS FILLED WITH MAGICAL REALISM THAT EXPERTLY BLENDS MAGIC WITH REALITY IN A COMPELLING AND BELIEVABLE WAY. SYLPHIC FOLKLORE IS UNIQUE TO THIS BOOK AND HOLDS THE POWER OF BELIEVABILITY THANKS TO WAGNER'S MASTERFUL WRITING.
THE FAMILIAR INTERACTIONS IN *SUN CHILD OF THE MOOR* ARE REMINISCENT OF *A WRINKLE IN TIME*, MAKING IT A DELIGHTFULLY IMMERSIVE TALE OF LOVE AND PERSONAL GROWTH THAT IS WELL SUITED TO YOUNG ADULT AND OLDER READERS WHO ENJOY EXPLORING THE WORLD'S UNLIMITED POSSIBILITIES THROUGH A MAGICAL LENS."
- **MARY R. LANNI, MLIS,** *REEDSY DISCOVERY*

He ne'er is crowned with immortality
who fears to follow where airy voices lead.

- John Keats

---

*B*astian stared at the dark wall alongside his closet, where the shape of a goblin loomed.

His earliest memories, from just beyond babyhood, were of struggling to lie still in night's dark, aching for sleep to take hold and dampen his fright.

But now, at almost thirteen—Bastian was far too old to fear the dark.

Unless there was a legitimate reason. Unless in the dark, something really was waiting.

It had to be a plain shadow, just there. A shadow cast by the moving boxes, stacked nearly to the ceiling. Because goblins don't lurk beside closets.

Of course they don't.

Goblins aren't real.

And yet—there stood a dark something, more solid than shadow. A dark something breathing, it seemed.

Lucas, Bastian's closest older brother, lay across the room, fast asleep. Lucas, born deaf, rarely awoke to Bastian's disturbances. He said the shapes Bastian saw in the darkness either were eerie moon shadows cast through the window—some illusion...

...or they were signs of Bastian's descent into madness.

Well, Bastian wasn't going mad. Of course not.

But it really seemed something monstrous was standing right there.

The something—thick-looking and massive—bore two defined shoulders. The shape was darker than the deepest night, like a black hole devouring starlight. A suffocating void. A fanged blankness. Something claw-fingered, it seemed. Something biding its time until came the moment to strike.

Bastian had to do something.

He could wake Lucas. Should he?

Bastian slipped out of his sheets.

Watching the thing, he edged closer to Lucas' bed.

In the middle of the room, though, he stopped.

He shouldn't wake Lucas. When Lucas, together with their oldest brother, Rhys, caught Bastian seeing or hearing odd things, they tore into him. It was all in good fun, but inside the jabs lay the not-too-subtle message that it was time for their youngest brother to let go of his imaginative games.

Bastian watched the dark wall.

A shadow arm separated from the rest and unsheathed a jagged, obsidian blade.

Bastian rushed to Lucas. Shook him.

Lucas turned over.

Bastian pointed at the goblin standing alongside the closet, its blade glinting darkly in the sheen of the full, gentle moon.

Lucas looked where Bastian was pointing, then signed, "There's nothing. Go back to bed."

Bastian could hardly breathe as the creature came away from the wall, as it moved into a blue shaft of moonlight.

It was a goblin, unmistakably.

Its tusked face was greasy and rippled in terrible folds. A thick ring pierced its nose. Of all the shadow shapes Bastian had glimpsed, nothing ever had seemed this threatening, or this real.

It opened its eyes, showing irises flickering like fireplace embers.

"I'm not kidding," signed Bastian. "It's standing right there."

Lucas sat up some and squinted where Bastian was looking.

The goblin lifted its blade and stepped toward them.

"It's coming." Bastian backed away, signing, "Run."

Lucas turned on a lamp.

The goblin's shadowy form, its black blade, its fiery eyes—they all vanished.

Bastian sank into a crouch.

Lucas tapped him on the shoulder. "Are you even awake?" he signed.

Bastian watched the emptiness where a goblin had stood, only seconds ago.

"See, there's nothing," signed Lucas.

And there was nothing. There was a legitimate, undeniable nothing.

That mortifying nothingness seemed suddenly worse than a goblin.

Lucas smirked. "If you want to be sure, I can wake Rhys to come check."

Rhys had lost patience with Bastian's "night terrors" years ago, when Bastian would wake up in the middle of shouting and running, usually into Rhys' room.

But these visions weren't night terrors.

They were Sylphic.

When Bastian was small and had last lived in England, he'd many times heard the legends of the Sylphic Kingdom—tales of its brave Moor Folk and wicked goblins, its shining faeries, its dragons. He'd heard the stories so often, so vividly, they seemed as real as his toys, as concrete as his brothers.

Even after Bastian and his family had moved away from England, to San Francisco—where few seemed to know the Sylphic legends, he still ran across them.

It felt as though Sylphic myths were a part of him; that he'd carried them to San Francisco like luggage.

Or maybe they'd followed him there.

Now that Da's professorship had moved them to England once again, Sylphic legends were all Bastian could think about.

The legends still refused to leave him, it seemed, because the chalet he and his family were soon to move into, nestled inside the forests of Dartmoor, was last owned by Malachi Daoine Kingfisher—the story-teller who'd first recorded the legends of the Sylphic Kingdom.

Bastian stood, steadying himself on the bookcase separating Lucas' bed from his own.

"Don't tell Rhys," he signed. "Okay?"

"It's fine—I won't," Lucas signed, wrapping himself in his covers. "Just try and go to sleep."

Bastian moved back to his own bed and sat on its edge. "I promise you," he signed, "I'm not crazy."

"I didn't say you were," Lucas signed back. "I'm not surprised, actually, that you're having night terrors. This is a weird flat in a creepy borough. And you trained with Master Sayre today. I'm betting he went on and on about the legends."

Master Sayre, Bastian's new Ryudo martial arts teacher, did speak of Sylphic legends often. The way he talked of them, so seriously—it did make them seem all the more believable. But he certainly didn't mean any harm.

"It's a bit cruel," signed Lucas, "the way Master Sayre insists on speaking to you about Sylphic frights, given your wild imagination."

"Nothing about Master Sayre could ever be cruel," signed Bastian.

Master Sayre was a rare and true friend.

In San Francisco, Bastian had enjoyed hanging around with the kids on his baseball team, and at school. And of course he'd had Rhys and Lucas.

But his friendship with Master Sayre felt different. Though Bastian had only known his new master for a few meager weeks, their connection felt somehow deeper.

With Master Sayre beside him, Bastian felt stronger. Older. More himself.

Lucas signed, "Still, you should tell him to give the Sylphic legends a rest."

Bastian glanced at the wall by the closet—empty, but heavy with the memory of that tusked, goblin face. "I don't think the problem is Master Sayre's storytelling."

Though older than Da, Master Sayre seemed like a young man—but for a white padlock of a short beard standing starkly against his suntanned skin. His dark eyes seemed to see to the soul, and he spoke to Bastian as though he were an equal—not just some new kid he had to train.

It wasn't that they were never cross with each other. Everyone gets cross from time to time. And on the Ryudo pitch, Master Sayre was a merciless coach.

But in his steady way, he seemed to care for Bastian the way Granddadda had. He said he perceived greatness in Bastian and was determined to see him reach his potential.

It seemed Master Sayre held a readiness to do anything for Bastian. To spend every spare minute coaching him. To live or to die for him.

And the feeling was mutual.

"When we're finally settled in our middle-of-nowhere chalet," signed Lucas, "where nothing interesting or important could possibly happen, my guess is your nightmares will stop."

The charmed chalet awaiting them indeed stood in the middle of nowhere. The Dartmoor forests surrounding it were incredible, with their great stretches of moors and wide, starry skies; their ancient knots of woods and spacious vales.

But for all their beauty, compared to the scene in San Francisco, there'd be next to nothing to do.

Bastian lay back and signed, "Do you really think it will be that bad—living in Dartmoor?"

"We'll likely be bored to tears," signed Lucas. "Although, I do have some good memories of England. Moving back here feels more like returning to a home than leaving one."

Mum and Da swore to their three boys that they'd love living so close to nature—that unmatched fun awaited in the chance to ramble over Devon like banshees, building forts inside thickets, stalking frogs, sailing rafts of bark and reeds along the winding Windrush.

When Mum and Da talked like that, it seemed they hadn't noticed that Bastian and Lucas were both in secondary school now—and that Rhys had just graduated.

Bastian and his brothers had been truly sorry to leave San Francisco—although tedium wasn't Bastian's primary concern. Dartmoor's forests were so thick with shadows, and its wilds were so dark at night—even spangled with stars as they were.

"I'll miss San Francisco," signed Bastian. "My baseball team. Our friends. The city lights."

"Mum says Kingfisher Chalet is the home she and Da will grow old in," signed Lucas. "So I guess we'd better get used to it."

Bastian's family would never have discovered Kingfisher Chalet, a lofty stone mansion tucked deeply inside Dartmoor's Wystan Woods, except that an obscure realtor firm had sent a package—rumpled and spilling open—stuffed with pictures of the place.

Mum and Da were so taken by the chalet's beauty that they looked into it immediately. They'd all been thrilled to discover that it was being sold at a deep discount for having suffered some wear, the owner having abandoned it. And not only that—it was well within driving distance of Da's new job.

When they toured it, they'd found the chalet sound and very charming—just in need of a little care.

Its grounds, though, had truly gone badly untended and were swamped with weeds.

Mum and Da, stricken by both love and pity, had made an offer the very same day they visited.

The Dartmoor locals had spoken sadly of Malachi Daoine King-fisher's strange disappearance, more than a decade ago. It'd seemed a general relief to the village that a structure so important to English lore would be cared for once again.

Bastian glanced at the closet, at the packing boxes heaped around it.

"Settling down anyplace will be better than always worrying about whether we'll move again," he signed. "And Kingfisher Chalet will be a thousand times better than this flat."

Their Exeter flat, cramped with its piles of clothes and towers of boxes, was tiny and stunk of rotten water. Da's new university had offered it as free temporary housing, so Bastian's parents hadn't shopped around.

They should have.

Closing on Kingfisher Chalet had taken longer than they'd planned, and this neighborhood was scary. This was the same borough they'd lived in right after Bastian was born, but it was nothing like anyone in his family remembered.

Most of the businesses nearby had shut down, making the streets feel abandoned. And all the other houses on the block stood vacant.

Except one.

Down the street, there lived a boy who harassed them daily, shouting at Bastian, "Hey bastard," making raunchy signs at Lucas and casting threats and stupid insults. Bastian saw red when the boy got after Lucas like that, but he never managed to muster enough nerve to stand up to the boy. He'd just sort of freeze where he stood, unable to say or do anything.

Lucas caught Bastian's attention and signed, "What did your night terror look like this time?"

"It was a Sylphic goblin," signed Bastian.

Just picturing the creature's face quickened his heart.

"Was the goblin bucktoothed?" Lucas bit his lip and crossed his eyes.

Bastian smirked.

"Did it have ugly stubble," Lucas signed, "like what Rhys won't shave off and swears is a beard?"

Bastian laughed out loud.

Lucas—grinning—signed, "Sweet dreams." He flashed his brows, then clicked off the lamp.

Bastian, smiling, closed his eyes. Lucas always knew how to lighten things. He always knew exactly what to say to help Bastian ease away from his fears. And he understood what not to say. He knew how to keep a brother's humiliating secret.

By smiling in the darkness, Bastian felt he was smoothing off its edges, like maybe it wasn't so threatening. He breathed deeply and grew warm, his muscles finally relaxing.

A growl pierced the stillness.

Bastian sucked a hard breath that he couldn't let out.

For there, straight above him, gripping a jagged black blade, stood a swear-to-god goblin.

Bastian tried to cry out, but his voice hitched. He tried to move, but his body felt stony. Staring at the thing's fiery eyes jolted him to try to jump up and run—but he only managed to kick his covers into a knot.

"Lucas," he signed to the darkness.

The goblin lifted its blade.

Bastian grasped the bookshelf and tried to bring it down on the goblin, but it wouldn't budge.

The goblin let a blood-chilling roar, then plunged the blade straight into Bastian's chest.

Bastian twisted beneath the agony of a sharp coldness rushing into him; an electric, icy current flooding his body.

A flash brightened the window, shattering it. A sound like dissonant chimes blared.

In through the busted window, a streak of fire streamed.

Flames shrouded the goblin. Even the blade ignited, shards of fire twisting down its sheath and metal, smoldering across Bastian's chest.

Bastian shrieked. Thrashed. Down came the bookshelf.

It struck the goblin's shoulder but slid right off and crashed to the floor.

The goblin, its skin smoking, pulled out the knife.

The lamp snapped on, and suddenly Lucas was standing over Bastian.

Bastian couldn't draw breath. An aching cold was searing his heart, like a metallic pool of poison was spreading.

Lucas signed, "Hold tight," then raced off.

Seconds later, Mum and Da were by Bastian, sitting him up, rubbing his chest, his back, coaching him to take slow breaths.

A thick mist, cold and fresh like what follows a spring rain, seeped in through the broken window.

As the mist bathed his face, Bastian found he could draw air, though scantly. Looking down, he discovered his skin unburned, his chest uncut.

Rhys hurried in, carrying an asthma inhaler.

Lucas, standing alongside, was holding Mum's phone. He was signing to his telephone interpreter, "Call an ambulance."

2

Bastian jogged across a Ryudo pitch deep in the woods behind his family's chalet in Dartmoor, his eyes on a bundle of aspen trunks bound by a rope Master Sayre was hacking at with his axe.

The pitch was littered with racquetballs—Ryudo mortars Bastian had cast at targets or dodged, painted electric orange for easier retrieval in the woods.

Master Sayre was standing high on a rise, his gaze fixed on Bastian. He was holding back the last axe strike, waiting for the optimal moment to release the trunks, setting them to tear down the rise toward Bastian in an accelerating rush.

Anytime Bastian asked Master Sayre how he managed to set the logs spinning so fast—faster than seemed natural and aimed perfectly at him, he'd just reply that some things can't be explained through pedantic processes; that at times, we must accept what verges on the non-natural.

The rushing aspens were among the last obstacles Bastian would have to deal with in trying to close in on his Ryudo target—the broad trunk of an old English oak standing recessed in the woodland at the top of the rise.

He tightened his grip on his racquetball.

Master Sayre laid the last blow to the rope, setting the logs loose.

Bastian leapt into a sprint, racing right at them.

A head-on confrontation, he'd learned, was the sole way to deal with them. Turning aside or stopping would end in a pulverizing.

Bastian tripped over the first few, then managed to leap among the spaces between them until he finally broke past.

He sprinted, straining to reach within striking distance of the oak but had to cut back as something like tree roots—maybe actual tree roots—lifted out of the hillside.

Though most of the obstacles on Master Sayre's course were rigged in ways Bastian could figure out, this one stymied him. Something more than ropes and mechanics had to be at play—something "non-natural." Though, Bastian couldn't imagine what that could be.

He raced among the roots, barely avoiding tripping. Upon reaching their far side, he angled off, running until he had a clear sightline to the oak's thick trunk, standing among a tangling of branches.

The instant he found his shot, he pitched his mortar.

The mortar sailed over the top of the rise and struck the oak square, hard enough to leave an imprint of orange.

Master Sayre, from the hilltop, hollered and punched the air. He jogged down to Bastian.

When Bastian first had entered into training with Master Sayre, the idea of casting the Ryudo mortars the great distances, of keying in on targets that were impossibly small, or far, or mired with obstacles, seemed beyond his reach. He'd pitched in baseball leagues all his life, and he'd made a good start with Ryudo in San Francisco.

But Master Sayre was renowned, internationally, for his teaching, and Ryudo with him demanded every bit of Bastian's skill—and then some.

Bastian, staring at the glorious streak of orange marring the distant tree, dropped to kneeling. He gripped his chest, quelling a sharp ache.

This pain—burning, even stabbing at times—had eased since the dreadful night, a year ago, when he'd suffered the night terror of the goblin. But at moments like this, after running a challenging Ryudo course, or after any excitement, really, it still ached fiercely.

Master Sayre tried to help him sit straight.

Bastian, cradling his chest, pushed Master Sayre away. "I can deal."

It was mortifying, the way Master Sayre was watching him, obviously knowing Bastian couldn't deal.

"This asthma isn't your fault," said Master Sayre. "You can let go of that shame."

This ache, termed "asthma" by his doctor, loomed as a constant, sometimes dangerous threat.

It seemed tied to all darkness—a portent of something deadly approaching; something seething in shadows. Something Bastian couldn't see, much less deal with.

"It's no wonder you're struggling," said Master Sayre, steadying him. "The weeds are coming up quite early. It's no surprise that working this hard might induce a reaction. But chin up. Pain often is a pathway to healing. I'm watching you grow more skilled by the day."

This pain seemed far more complex than any asthmatic reaction, than any trouble with nightmares or weeds. Though, he himself had to admit that he'd advanced significantly in Ryudo, despite the pain. And the night terrors had markedly lightened over the last year.

By no means, though, were they gone.

Bastian could assuredly say he'd never again seen anything like the goblin that'd appeared in the creepy Exeter flat, but he had sensed other odd things.

He'd seen trees sparkling in the forest, even when no sunlight could reach them. He'd heard the woodlands faintly peal with strange music —something like pipes and flutes and drums, sometimes windchimes. From almost anyplace, he could catch the sound of distant ocean waves crashing.

And wherever he went, the smell of rain and freshly cut grass seemed to hang as a heady mist, even on clear, sunny days. When he concentrated on the sensations, it was like he was sensing the bustle of a country far off.

And though very rare, when his imagination was particularly active, he'd sometimes sight, at the edge of the forest, a shadow shaped like a goblin. Or he might think—for a second—on a walk in the darker tracks of Dartmoor's woods, that he'd glimpsed a pair of fiery eyes.

Master Sayre knelt before him. "Try to steady your breathing."

"It's just—what I saw—or thought I saw—last year." Bastian cradled his chest. "When this pain strikes, the memory of it—everything comes rushing back."

Master Sayre settled his hand on Bastian's shoulder. "Through reliving our fears, may we overcome them."

"What happened to me, though—it wasn't just fear." Bastian pushed to kneeling, mirroring Master Sayre. "It was a hallucination. Why couldn't I just wake up?"

"Freezing in confrontation happens to even the bravest of us," said Master Sayre. "And Ryudo—the Way of the Dragon—has markedly strengthened your nerve."

Bastian studied Master Sayre.

"You just said, 'confrontation.'"

Whenever the goblin nightmare came up, Master Sayre typically digressed into folklore.

But at rare times, like this, it seemed he was on the brink of acknowledging that something more sinister than asthma and night terrors, more threatening than a bully's rock cast through a window, had befallen Bastian that horrific night.

"What I meant to say," said Master Sayre, adjusting his legs beneath him, "is that we, all of us, might lose our daring when fear strikes."

Bastian didn't remove his gaze from Master Sayre's. "But you said— 'confrontation.'"

Master Sayre seemed to be watching Bastian carefully, as though wisely choosing his words.

As though guarding something.

"Our fears," said Master Sayre, "they may surprise us with what forms they take. Standing bravely in the face of anything that might present itself—this is key."

And this was the whole point of Ryudo. To learn to stand one's ground despite opposition of all kinds.

It was a challenging athletic art form to say the least, geared to help an athlete develop strength and agility and aim.

But it also helped one build tolerance for fear, and find the determination to carry out an objective, despite overwhelming odds.

Bastian tightened his hand against his chest at the ache sharpening.

Master Sayre eased Bastian's hand down and pressed his own palm against Bastian's chest.

Beneath the strong pressure, the ache eased. It even seemed to Bastian that his lungs opened a touch, delivering him an almost-full breath.

"See now," said Master Sayre. "As terribly as that pain troubles you, you are healing."

Bastian stared into the forest, along a track dark and thick enough that its shadows seemed primed to shift goblin-esque.

"Part of me wishes that goblins truly were real," said Bastian.

At this point, after learning Master Sayre's geometric aiming methods; his techniques for accessing power and strength and control from within his own musculature and frame; for studying and using the wind, the humidity, the light, even, to drive home his mortar—he hardly ever missed a target.

"If I saw a Sylphic goblin now," said Bastian, "after training for a whole year with you—I know I wouldn't freeze."

"While I appreciate your confidence," said Master Sayre, "and though I certainly am watching you attain near-champion level, I must caution you—don't go looking for trouble."

Bastian eyed him. "What kind of trouble could I look for?"

"Nothing in particular." Master Sayre sat back some. "But no matter how much strength you may be building, I assure you—you'd rather that Sylphic goblins weren't real."

"Goblins might not be real," said Bastian, "but plenty of dreadful things are."

He found his gaze drawn to the ancient oak with its splash of orange, darkening beneath mounding clouds.

"That night," said Bastian, "when I faced—whatever that was, I was less afraid for myself than I was at the thought of something bad happening to Lucas. The rock that flew through the window—it landed an inch from his head. I was terrified that something more, something worse, might be coming."

Master Sayre, listening closely, settled back to sitting on his heels.

"I never again want to feel so helpless." Bastian sent Master Sayre a prompting look. "And I want to understand everything about what happened that night."

"When challenges rise, do you not think that I, too, want you ready to meet them?"

At face value, that sounded supportive.

But Master Sayre was hedging. It was obvious he was keeping something back.

Bastian held his gaze. "If you knew something more about that night, you would tell me—right?"

Master Sayre gently smiled. "I suppose you can read me handily by now. You're not wrong that there's a great deal of truth waiting to be discovered."

He reached into his jacket pocket and drew out a small box. "I've been keeping this for you, for a good while."

Master Sayre glanced toward the western horizon, where the sliver of the setting crescent moon was dipping low against the Earth.

"And the time's about right for you to have it." He met Bastian's eyes. "This is something that amounts to real knowledge."

"Real knowledge." Bastian rested his gaze on the box.

"Full understanding is something we often must wait for," said Master Sayre. "But you'll not be waiting much longer, I expect." He handed Bastian the box. "Think of this as an early birthday present."

Bastian opened it.

Inside lay a viewing device.

It was silver and tarnished and intricately made, with the impressions of vines sculpted along its length. Its far lens stretched to the diameter of a large marble, and the casing around it flared like the mouth of a moonflower.

"Can you guess what that is?" asked Master Sayre.

"A Sylphic scope," murmured Bastian.

He held it up, looking closely at the fine etching of leaves and curling stalks in the metal.

He'd heard of such things. Scopes like this were said to have been fashioned by a Sylphic prince of ancient days as tools by which mortals could learn to see Sylphic things.

Bastian stared up at Master Sayre. "You said Sylphic relics, if any ever existed, have all been destroyed or lost."

Master Sayre pointed to a card lying in the box.

Bastian opened it.

There, he found scribbled the name of a bookshop on Bloomsbury Street, in Exeter, and a title: *Moor Folk of the English Highlands*, by M.D. Kingfisher.

Bastian sat high on his knees. "You can't be serious."

Moor Folk of the English Highlands was a rare book—a one-and-only original, said to have been handwritten by its renowned author, with artwork painted directly on its pages.

It was the ultimate authority on the Sylphic Kingdom and the tales and ways of the Moor Folk—the mythical people fabled to trek in secrecy through England's ancient woodlands and rugged moors, its wildest places.

"This book—is it a copy or something?" asked Bastian. "Surely, it can't be *the* book Kingfisher wrote." He ran his thumb along the elegant scope. "And this—is it a model?"

"Both are authentic pieces of Sylphic lore, long lost and lately found. For reasons of"—Master Sayre rubbed his cheek—"well, for security's sake, I couldn't deliver the book to you. So it's waiting for you in Exeter, to be claimed by your own hands. It's the safest way. And you must bring it straight back to your chalet—the safest place."

"Safe?" asked Bastian. "Isn't *Moor Folk of the English Highlands* just a rare book of faerie stories? I mean, thank you, I'll love having it—Kingfisher's brilliant. But why on Earth would it not have been safe for you to bring it to me?"

"I'll just say"—Master Sayre seemed to force a smile—"the sooner you retrieve the book, the better. I'd like you to pick it up no later than tomorrow. For it holds teachings on—"

A bank of clouds suddenly bubbling in from the north arrested Master Sayre's gaze.

With the way the coming storm was spreading and blotting the setting sun, the heart of each rolling cloud appeared green and sickly. And at their advancing, the woods starkly dimmed.

"The book holds enchantments," mumbled Master Sayre, his eyes on the sky, "ones that..."

"Enchantments?" asked Bastian.

Master Sayre stood.

Bastian stared with him at the north, at monstrous clouds building impossibly fast.

The woods darkened almost to black, and the storm seemed to swallow the day's warmth.

Bastian stood before Master Sayre. "You'd started to say that this book holds teachings. Is there something I need to know?"

Master Sayre seemed to be listening intently, like he was trying to hear something far off.

And—there was a sound. It was a distant echo, shrill and broken, like people shouting from a beach or an amusement park, panicked.

"Elemental hell," Master Sayre murmured. "She's done it."

"Sorry, what?" asked Bastian.

Master Sayre, his face pale, finally focused on Bastian. "You must race home. At once."

"But—you were adamant that I should run the Ryudo course twice today." Bastian glanced at the blistering clouds. "I don't care about a bit of rain."

"We must forgo that second run." Master Sayre led him quickly across the Ryudo pitch.

"But the great Ryudo master—your master—you told me he's already arrived in England. You said the more practice I can get in, the better off I'll be to train with him."

Master Sayre seemed not to be listening. "Lucas is waiting for you, in the park near your chalet, yes? Find him at once, then sprint home. The storm coming promises to be fierce."

Bastian glanced back at his target oak, its orange smear barely visible in the deepening dusk. "Shouldn't I find my mortar before I go?"

"Leave the mortar. Get to your chalet. Stay there until this storm passes."

Bastian paused at that. Master Sayre was obsessive when it came to the care of equipment. He'd never before let Bastian just leave a mortar in the woods.

"Can we practice tomorrow?" asked Bastian.

Master Sayre hurried on, toward a narrow crossing in the Windrush stream at the edge of the pitch.

Bastian ran to catch up with him. "Can't we talk for a second about...whatever it was you were going to tell me? And what did you mean—Kingfisher's book holds 'enchantments?'"

"Kingfisher's book," said Master Sayre, "it's of Sylphic history. And enchantments, yes." He splashed into the crossing. "It's about Moor Folk. Elemental Spirits. But most importantly—it speaks of the Sun Child."

"Slow down." Bastian slogged through the crossing after him.

"Urgent business will keep me away for some time." Master Sayre, upon reaching the stream's far bank, finally stopped and faced Bastian. "Retrieve that book. Study it. Learning the lore of the Sun Child, understanding Sylphic histories—this will help you make sense of... well, something that I must indeed soon tell you."

He glanced aside at the dark northern forest.

"Why can you not tell me now?" asked Bastian.

"A momentous event is about to take place," said Master Sayre. "One that's been long foretold in Sylphic legends. Something wonderful. Something terrible. But"—he glanced at Bastian's chest—"it involves a precise timing. I can't tell you anything until a certain prophesy is fulfilled."

Never before had Master Sayre spoken about Sylphic legends so explicitly, as though he had no doubt they were real.

Thunder struck—less of an echo of lightning and more of a shock of a firecracker blast someplace close.

Master Sayre pulled Bastian to walk on. "The moment will come swiftly for telling you everything. But until that moment arrives, because of the prophecy—I can't."

A strike of anger washed over Bastian. Despite the constraints surrounding whatever it was Master Sayre had to reveal, the truth was —he had been keeping secrets.

Bastian pulled away from him. "So, there are things you've not told me. Sylphic things."

He'd suffered—profoundly—for a whole year, since that dreadful night in Exeter. And worse, he'd had to endure the mortification of laying out what he thought he'd seen while his parents, his brothers, and his doctor exchanged patronizing smiles and assured him he'd imagined that goblin, that blade.

Master Sayre hurried back to him. "There are indeed many things you must learn. But now isn't the time." He glanced from Bastian to the black clouds. "Now, go. Find Lucas. I'll contact you when I can."

"You're really leaving?" Bastian stared at him. "Just when you've started dealing honestly with me?"

"I wish I could offer you the insights you crave." Master Sayre held Bastian's shoulder. "To have seen what you have and to not understand —yes, how difficult."

Bastian glanced away. "With my brothers, my parents, this has been a matter of shame."

"You've been so patient." Master Sayre guided him on. "But you must remain so for a bit longer."

The wind rose, and the sky rumbled.

Master Sayre angled off and ran toward the northern woods.

Slowing, he glanced back. "Do as I say, lad. It's imperative that you and Lucas race to your chalet and remain there." The look on him was dread. "It's the safest place."

3

____

astian skipped into a sprint and made for a small park cut from the forest, near their chalet, where Lucas was practicing football drills.

The storm darkening the north was beautiful and wild. It smelled not of rain, but of smoke and static electricity. Bastian never had seen anything like it, and it provoked a feeling of terror, precisely like what he'd felt that awful night in Exeter. It felt Sylphic.

Despite the feeling of dread those boiling clouds were calling up in Bastian's heart, he found he couldn't draw his gaze off them. For this—whatever it was—an electric storm, strange and furious, unearthly—it was dead real and unfolding before him.

Master Sayre had seemed truly to think Bastian's nightmare had been somehow real. And whatever this storm might bring, it was something he clearly didn't want Bastian to see.

After a year, though, of wondering what really had happened that night—after enduring such pain, so much pity and judgment from others who thought him disturbed, Bastian was starving for the truth.

And something even deeper than shame was urging him to want to stand this ground. Despite Master Sayre's warnings, Bastian felt at the level of blood and bone that he needed to see this.

He hurried into the park and found Lucas racing toward him, kicking his football.

"Can you believe this storm?" Bastian signed.

Lucas caught up his football. "It's going to drench us," he signed. "Let's beat it."

Bastian glanced at the green thunderheads, darkening to steel with the setting of the red-beaming sun.

The sounds in the storm—frantic yelling, so distant—had clarified.

Dissonant chords of music, too, were rising and tangling with the wind.

"The sky looks so cool, doesn't it?" signed Bastian.

"It looks weird," signed Lucas. "And the wind's up, but I smell no rain. This is freaky."

Bastian hooked the ball away from Lucas and held it tight under his foot. "Let's stay out. Watch the storm build."

"The thunder—I can feel it getting stronger," signed Lucas. "And the air pressure's changing. Storms have been harsh lately, and this one feels scary. We need to get home."

The sound of screaming heightened, sending chills racing across Bastian's skin.

But for all the storm's terror, in it, truths waited. Frightful ones perhaps, but still truths. And had not Master Sayre been coaching him hard, strengthening him to face his fears?

Lucas stared up at the blackening sky. "This seems even dangerous. Like there's something more sinister in it than ordinary weather."

Bastian pulled the ball further back and signed, "Don't tell me you now think you're sensing Sylphic things."

"I meant like a tornado or fierce lightning or something." Lucas swept the ball from beneath Bastian's foot and kicked it toward the trail leading home.

Bastian sprinted and captured the football. "Check this out," he signed. "I've almost nailed this trick." He cast up the football, spun, and caught it—barely—on the top of his foot.

Lucas stood before him. "If we don't go now, we'll get soaked."

Bastian picked up the football. "I'm not scared of a little rain." He glanced at the sky. "Besides, look—it seems to be moving off."

Lucas watched the sweeping clouds. "Maybe."

"You've got a match tomorrow," signed Bastian. "Don't you want to be ready? I'll help you drill."

He dropped the ball, then glanced at the far end of the field—well away from the trail leading home.

"I bet you can't get the ball past me and through those two tall pines."

Lucas studied the pines a moment, then shouldered Bastian back and wedged the ball away.

Bastian chased him across the football park as light drained from the sky.

When they reached the field's far edge, a strong shudder of thunder halted them both. Through an opening in the forest to the west, they together watched the sun blare fiery underneath a bank of low, heavy clouds.

Bastian pulled out his Sylphic scope and trained it northward, on the storm swelling over the forest.

Through its lens, the dark sky appeared a touch brighter. The scope was rendering the clouds somewhat translucent, and inside them, sediment, like ash, was swirling.

The sun vanished beneath the horizon, leaving just a weak glow in the west.

The park's field light buzzed, shuddering on. It sputtered a beam of weak light over the grass.

Lucas tapped Bastian's arm, then signed, "What's that you're holding?"

Bastian handed him the scope. "An early birthday gift, from Master Sayre," he signed. "It's supposed to reveal Sylphic things, usually invisible."

Lucas took it and peered through. "A kaleidoscope, cool. It looks old." He handed it back.

Through the Sylphic scope, Bastian studied the thicket edging the north side of the park.

There, the shadows between the trees appeared to be taking on a material quality.

Bastian carefully aimed the scope along the tree line, studying its every gap, every branch.

For it seemed like something was about to unveil itself.

In the west, the lingering twilight wholly faded. Beyond the field light's weak glow, the falling night shrouded the forest in absolute blackness.

The twisting storm closing in seemed to tighten itself around the clearing, like a constrictor snake coiling.

The wind suddenly died, leaving the park strangled in stillness.

"What's going on?" signed Lucas. "Are we in the storm's eye?"

From the north, the wind picked up again—a raging gale weighted with panicked cries. The air pressed a feeling of claustrophobia, giving Bastian the sense that he'd been driven with his brother to the center of a trap.

The field light snapped off.

Darkness swarmed in. No glow from any failing sunset could reach them. No stars or moonlight could pierce the thick clouds.

Hyperventilation struck. Bastian couldn't even see Lucas standing beside him.

The fear teeming was bad, but worse, he felt foolish for not heeding Master Sayre's directive. It was awful to think Master Sayre had been withholding insights. But perhaps he'd had a reason. Now Bastian found himself in the grip of a storm that seemed not made by the Earth —and he'd led Lucas here.

The field light snapped on with a flash, then hummed low, like the shire was in a brownout.

The wind shifted, and the pressure changed, popping Bastian's ears.

Lucas found Bastian's shoulder and gripped it.

Bastian frantically scanned the darkness around them through the scope, but it showed him nothing.

Lucas tugged him back, and they together raced toward the trail in the woods leading home.

In the center of the clearing, Lucas tripped. Bastian held up and ran back to him.

He found Lucas kneeling and tightening an undone shoelace.

Bastian again swept the scope along the length of the northern tree line.

It showed only the darkness of the forest—until its lens landed on a foggy stretch hazed by the low-glowing field light.

From the vapor—a figure emerged. A figure advancing out of the northern woods.

His build, his gait, Bastian would've recognized anyplace.

It was the bully who'd lived by them, a year ago, in that decrepit neighborhood in Exeter.

Bastian nudged Lucas with his knee.

Lucas looked up, then slowly stood.

The bully was as frightful as ever, his face marred with a pain-loving sneer. And yet—something about him was changed.

It was the eyes. They seemed what Master Sayre might call "non-natural."

Through the scope, the bully's eyes looked as though they were casting flashes of fire. His body—sinewy, muscular—seemed to be shifting in and out of the shape of a goblin.

Bastian tightened his fist. Tonight, he'd see the payoff of his Ryudo training. Tonight, though swathed in darkness, he'd confront this. That boy wouldn't touch him, or Lucas.

"That can't be who I think it is," Lucas signed.

The goblin boy came fast. "Hey, bastard."

Bastian stood in front of Lucas.

An ear-shattering lightning bolt singed the near woods. The wind picked up and went icy.

Dizzied by electricity, his ears ringing, his lungs drawing air as cold as a midwinter's frost, Bastian couldn't move.

The boy rushed him and shoved him back.

Lucas pushed Bastian behind him and signed to the boy, "Leave us alone."

Lucas didn't look frightened at all. He seemed oblivious to the thing's ember eyes.

"What was that you said to me, gimp?" The goblin boy jabbed Lucas' shoulders.

"Don't touch him," shouted Bastian.

The goblin boy stared around Lucas at Bastian, hungrily.

Lucas closed in on the boy.

The boy cocked his arm and punched Lucas twice in the face.

Lucas wavered a moment, then steadied. He signed and mouthed, "Back off."

The goblin boy laughed at Lucas. "Well, aren't you smart, to be able to talk at all."

Bastian drew as big a breath as he could, then stood and ran at the boy, slamming into him.

The Sylphic scope dropped from Bastian's hand and rolled.

The boy's eyes, fixing on it, shifted to a darker red, as though inside his skull, an old fire was strengthening. He dove for the scope.

Bastian slid to the ground and kicked it out of his reach.

The boy knelt and punched him in the chest.

Bastian shrieked at the pain. The goblin boy seemed to know Bastian was hurt—he seemed to know precisely where a strike would be the most agonizing.

Bastian managed to get his foot near the scope. He knocked it to Lucas.

Lucas snatched it up.

The goblin boy, his eyes on Bastian, clenched his fist.

Lucas tried to rush the boy but stalled at a swift kick to the stomach. He reeled, then volleyed the scope back to Bastian.

The goblin boy rammed Lucas and hauled him onto his shoulders.

Bastian lunged for the boy's legs but missed.

The boy carried Lucas to a rubbish bin at the edge of the field and threw him against it.

Lucas struck its metal face first and fell to the ground.

He didn't move. A line of blood spilled down his temple.

The boy shifted his red eyes onto Bastian.

He clenched his fist, and in his hand a black knife materialized, as though conjured from the dark of the storm.

Bastian tried to get to his feet, but he couldn't even sit upright.

The boy stood over him, his dark blade leaching black smoke.

Terror took Bastian. This terror—exactly this terror—was what he'd felt in Exeter.

"The scope." The boy's red eyes flashed. "Give it to me."

Bastian focused the way Master Sayre had taught him. He stilled his mind. He gathered what energy would come. He gathered nerve.

The boy aimed the blade at Bastian's chest. "I said—give it."

Bastian tightened his fist. "Get lost, or you'll be sorry."

The boy thrust the knife.

Bastian twisted, marginally dodging its strike and sending the blade plunging into the turf.

The goblin boy tugged at it, but it seemed lodged.

Bastian heaved himself up and knocked the boy back.

The knife came loose and dropped onto the grass.

Bastian jumped at the goblin boy and worked him to the ground. He locked the boy's legs in place with his own and held down his arms.

With the degree of agony Bastian was in, he was well-aware that he had no chance of keeping the boy pinned. But at catching sight of Lucas, still not moving, Bastian's hold—his arms and legs clenching the goblin boy—was a death grip.

With a last shred of strength, Bastian stretched out his foot and tried to hook the blade.

The instant his shoe touched it, it evaporated.

The goblin boy fought free of Bastian's grip and knocked him flat on his back. He cocked his fist and punched him again in the chest, calling up a snap, like he'd cracked Bastian's ribs.

Light flared and levitated around them.

The goblin boy scattered away from Bastian.

The light seemed a product of the pain, and in that anguish Bastian could scarcely breathe.

A new light, a gray-blue light flashing in the forest, seemed to startle the boy. The flare shifted to the sharp, electric color of lightning —but it lingered beyond what any storm's electricity might produce.

The goblin boy, gazing at it, wholly stilled. He seemed full of dread.

Without giving Bastian another look, he raced off and disappeared among trees in the misted northern forest.

Bastian lay on his back, barely breathing, his punched chest throbbing like an open cut.

The electric glow in the woods dimmed as the storm clouds dispersed, letting down starlight.

Bastian fought to gain his bearings, to breathe, to move.

After a few minutes, he found that he could, and he sat up.

Lucas, lying by the rubbish bin, wasn't stirring. His face was a mask of blood.

Bastian crawled to him. He shook Lucas by the shoulder.

Lucas opened his eyes.

"You're bleeding," signed Bastian.

Lucas signed, "You're not kidding." He wiped his face on his sleeve.

"Does it feel like you've broken any bones?" signed Bastian.

Lucas pulled himself to leaning against the rubbish bin. "No."

"There's a bad cut on your head." Bastian doubled and struggled to breathe.

Lucas blotted blood off his forehead, his mouth. "I think I'm in one piece. But are you?"

"My chest hurts," signed Bastian. "He had a knife."

"Wait, he cut you?"

"I don't know," Bastian signed. "There was definitely a knife."

"Let me look," Lucas signed.

Bastian sucked a breath, then lifted his shirt.

"There's no blood," signed Lucas. "It must be the asthma. Are you sure he had a knife?"

"Positive," signed Bastian.

"What was he doing here anyway?" signed Lucas. "To have come all the way from Exeter—"

"I'm not sure that was the boy from Exeter," signed Bastian. "The face—it was different."

"He didn't look any different to me," signed Lucas. "I'd know him anyplace."

"His eyes, though," signed Bastian. "Did you not see his eyes? They looked fiery."

A roar sounded from the woods and strengthened until the ground shook.

Bastian steadied himself until it passed. "Did you feel that?"

Lucas glanced at the sky. "Feel what?"

Bastian signed, "Let's get out of here."

He helped Lucas to his feet.

When he let go, though, Lucas collapsed back to sitting.

"You can't walk, can you?" signed Bastian. "I'll run home and bring Rhys."

Lucas gripped Bastian's ankle. "No chance I'm letting you out of my sight with that bozo around. I just need a minute."

Bastian stared into the dark trees, where it seemed shadows were shifting. "This is my fault. We should've run home before the storm hit."

"It was a bully that clobbered us, not a storm," signed Lucas. "You couldn't have known he was in the shire."

"No, but I might've known something was coming." Bastian lowered his gaze to meet Lucas' eyes. "When the storm rose, Master Sayre told me to run straight home."

"Master Sayre couldn't have known this would happen either," signed Lucas.

Within the mist in the northern woods, Bastian glimpsed a pale flash of silver. He aimed his scope at it.

The light blared, then clarified into a strong, person-shaped shine rushing among the trees. Three more flashes flared, further back in the forest.

The lit figure stopped. Raised a bright bow. Lifted onto it a bright arrow.

Bastian had spotted hazy, odd lights in the woods before—but never had he known them to look like a person.

The lit figure let the arrow fly.

A shriek rang.

Then all the lights in the woodland snapped out like snuffed candle flames.

"Why did he want that kaleidoscope?" signed Lucas.

Bastian lowered the scope—heavy and cold.

It was not a kaleidoscope. It was a Sylphic instrument known only to legends.

The thing that'd come for him and Lucas tonight was something non-natural—far more treacherous than any plain bully.

And the dark woods had shaken with unexplainable sounds and mysterious lights, all of which had been some manner of real.

"But he probably didn't even care what it was," signed Lucas. "He just cared that it was yours. Like always, he just wanted to pulverize us."

Bastian slipped the scope inside his jacket pocket.

Lucas carefully pushed to his knees.

It was painful, watching him try to move. He was covered in blood —one side of his face, his neck, and a streak down the front of his shirt was dark with it.

The goblin, or whatever non-natural thing that'd been—it seemed he'd assaulted Lucas simply because he was in the way. It was Bastian he'd come at with the knife. It was Bastian whom he clearly wanted to incapacitate. Or kill.

But Bastian wasn't incapacitated. His chest ached from the strikes, but besides that, he was basically untouched. He'd faced down the goblin boy and arrived on the other side of the fight breathing.

But why had he not been able to stand his ground between the goblin boy and Lucas? He should've taken every strike that'd fallen on his brother.

Lucas stood all the way up. He steadied himself.

Bastian supported him around the waist and signed, "We'll go easy."

4

Bastian and Lucas sat together on the exam table in their doctor's office, in Exeter.

The doctor settled a mask over Bastian's nose and mouth for a breathing treatment.

Bastian, his eyes closed, whispered to himself, *"The moment will come swiftly for telling you everything"*—Master Sayre's words.

What could he have to tell? And at what moment?

The doctor removed Bastian's mask. "I didn't catch that?"

Bastian opened his eyes. "Oh." He hadn't realized he'd spoken aloud. "Nothing."

The doctor reset Bastian's mask, then stood before Lucas. He again studied Lucas' bruised face and the cut forehead he'd stitched.

"This one's going to be fine," said the doctor. "He's a bit worse for wear, but I don't see any injury time won't mend." He glanced at Mum's belly, swollen with eight months of pregnancy. "You've surely got plenty on your mind. I'm glad I can set you at ease about these lads."

The doctor glanced at Lucas, then gestured to a sucker jar.

Lucas hopped off the table and dug into it.

"Lucas," Mum signed. "Act your age."

Lucas let go of the handful he'd grabbed and drew out just one.

Bastian again concentrated on recalling Master Sayre's words.

Master Sayre had said he could tell Bastian nothing *"until a certain prophecy was fulfilled."*

"What prophecy?" whispered Bastian from within his mask.

Mum's expression shifted to worry. She clearly had heard that.

"About Bastian," she said. "Are you sure he has no injuries from the fight?"

The doctor glanced up from the notes he was typing. "There's not a mark on him, inside or out."

"But what can be done about these asthma attacks? You can imagine what Lucas looked like coming home last night—but I was honestly more worried about Bastian. There was little we could do to get his pain under control. He ended up falling asleep with it. I think it was the worst asthma attack he's had since that first one."

"It's very common, and treatable, this childhood asthma that Bastian deals with," said the doctor.

"Yes, but we're talking about chest pain," said Mum. "Does that not seem quite different, quite more serious, than childhood asthma?"

"I assure you, there's nothing at all wrong with your lad." The doctor glanced at Bastian. "It's not that I doubt what he's reporting. It's just that—with adolescents, these complaints are sometimes..." He rubbed his cheek.

Lucas grinned around the sucker at Bastian and signed, "I knew your madness would eventually take hold."

Bastian shielded his hand from Mum's eyes and signed, "Bite me."

Lucas quietly laughed.

"Bastian practices Ryudo," said Mum. "Since the school term has ended, he's been in the thick of practice every single day, for some hours."

Master Sayre had told Bastian that Ryudo, though a relatively young martial art, had its roots in the Sylphic Kingdom. Some even believed it'd been developed by Sylphic beings of some sort—forest children, maybe. Or a Sun Child.

Bastian pulled the card from his pocket and studied the title of the book written on it—*Moor Folk of the English Highlands.*

This book spoke of the Sun Child, Master Sayre had said. Maybe there was some connection between Ryudo and this book.

"The thought has crossed my mind"—Mum glanced at Bastian— "could the Ryudo training be agitating his condition?"

"Of course it isn't." Bastian pushed aside the mask. "Why would you think that? Ryudo is helping me."

"Sweetheart, you come home from practice very often in pain. You can't think I've not noticed."

"After I practice, there's less pain than before I practice." Bastian glanced at Lucas, at his busted lip and stitched head. "I can't give up Ryudo."

Though Bastian hadn't prevented Lucas from coming away from the fight bloodied, it was partly his clear thinking, sharpened by Ryudo —the strength and focus he'd built—that'd delivered him and Lucas from something worse happening.

Bastian met the doctor's gaze. "Ryudo is very important to me."

The doctor settled the mask again over Bastian's face. "How often does he normally practice?"

"Every single day," said Mum. "I spoke with his teacher last week and confessed that I sometimes feel he might be pushing Bastian a touch too hard."

"You did what?" Bastian went again for the mask.

The doctor eased him with a glance. "Exercise strengthens lungs. And Ryudo offers excellent exercise. Aside from the asthma, Bastian's in exceptional shape."

Mum, wincing, rubbed at the side of her hip. "I just don't understand why he struggles so profoundly."

She looked pained, as she often had, since the stronger twinges of discomfort had set in last week, telling them the baby was well on his way.

That day, Da had seated Bastian and his brothers, gathering them to allow a moment of talk about the impending birth. He'd done his best to settle their trepidation, saying the change of having a new child in the family—though perhaps difficult at times—would be quite positive.

He'd finished by touching quickly on the mechanics of birth, saying little more than, "A messy business, that. Lots of water and blood. Any questions?"

"Rhys, when he was Bastian's age, also dealt with asthma," said Mum. "But he never suffered to this extent."

Her eyes seemed to be tearing, but it wasn't clear whether it was her worry over Bastian, or her own pain—maybe the baby kicking—that was distressing her.

"How are you, by the way?" the doctor asked her. "Are you in a little pain now yourself?"

"A very little," said Mum. "Nothing to worry over."

The doctor knelt by her and felt her belly.

Bastian was glad the doctor had noticed Mum's pain.

Her pregnancy, though it'd gone all right, was high risk. In fact, her age put her in the category of a "geriatric mother," which Rhys had enjoyed to no end. When Mum and Da had first announced the pregnancy, Rhys had pretended not to believe it. He kept asking them—*at your ages, are you sure?*

Lucas had confessed a worry that he, or any of them, might get lost in a family with so many brothers. Rhys had pointed out that Lucas wouldn't be bothered by the baby's crying, which was an advantage, and Lucas had agreed that was true. He'd grown downright thrilled, though, when Da proposed he should teach the baby to sign as his first language.

Bastian felt no apprehension over the coming new brother. Just a strong sense of peace. Mum and Da often praised Bastian for his accepting and openhearted nature when encountering a new situation. But the truth was, the idea of the new baby wasn't all that difficult to accept.

When Bastian contemplated gaining a younger brother, a sense of wholeness settled. Despite that the baby had been a surprise to all of them, Bastian often felt that, at his coming, their family would at last be complete.

"Do you not think," said Mum, glancing between the doctor and Bastian, "that easing up on Ryudo might help Bastian manage the asthma?"

"I'm not going to ease up," Bastian said from within the mask. "If you make Master Sayre ease up, I'll just practice more on my own."

Mum watched the doctor.

"It's possible that something might be aggravating his condition," said the doctor. "But I'm not convinced it's Ryudo." He studied Bastian. "Has anything happened that's out of the ordinary? I mean, granted, in the last year, you've moved across an ocean. And the scrap you lads got into was no day at the beach. But have there been any other disruptions?"

Bastian discretely threaded the card for the bookshop deeply into his pocket, alongside the Sylphic scope. "No."

"That isn't true," Lucas signed, dropping Bastian a knowing look.

Having a close brother was mostly wonderful, but the downside was—nothing could ever be hidden.

The odd sights and sounds that caught Bastian's attention often, the smells and sensations that he never could manage to ignore, had strengthened over time. And Lucas knew it.

Bastian had confided in Lucas that last night he'd seen lights in the woods; the boy's eyes glowing. Lucas, though, had seen nothing but a strong storm and a plain bully. He'd sensed nothing at all that one might call Sylphic.

Even now, very distantly, Bastian couldn't deny that pipes and flutes were softly sounding, that drums were distantly pealing, all of it interspersed with sea waves.

And this was no mere impression of sound, so low Bastian could believe he was imagining it. This was actual music.

Lucas could probably read all over Bastian's face that he was hearing things.

"You should be honest with him," signed Lucas.

"Honest?" signed the doctor.

But how could Bastian bear, again, the humiliation of confessing that he was sensing things that would seem impossible? Though he knew Sylphic things were—to some degree—real, he certainly couldn't admit it.

Bastian shook his head. "There's nothing."

The doctor looked carefully at Lucas and signed, "Is there something I should know?"

Bastian subtly signed to Lucas, "Please."

"I just meant," signed Lucas, "well, our granddadda passed away about a year ago, right after we moved here. Bastian was especially close to him."

Bastian closed his eyes in relief.

"I'm so sorry." The doctor faced Bastian. "Your granddadda. Tell me about him."

"He was very brave," said Bastian, signing. "He was a Royal Marine who saw conflict. A hero."

If Granddadda had seen him last night, unable to do a thing while someone bloodied Lucas—Bastian couldn't lift his eyes for the shame flooding him.

The doctor glanced at Mum. "How did their granddadda die?"

"He carried a wound from the war, since he was a young man," said Mum. "It caused problems at the end."

"What kind of wound?"

"Shrapnel," said Mum. "Lodged in the...chest."

The doctor's knotted brow eased. So did Mum's.

"The agony of grief does strike each of us differently," said the doctor. "Sometimes it truly can seem like physical pain."

He removed Bastian's treatment mask.

"Given some time," he signed, "I think you'll have two lads fit to take on any bully." He caught Lucas' glance and signed, "Right?"

Lucas answered the doctor's high-five.

Bastian couldn't look at any of them. He only could rest his gaze on his pocket, where lay a Sylphic scope—a relic of legends sought by an assailant straight out of a nightmare who wanted to pierce him with some sort of non-natural, vanishing blade, whose eyes had glowed the fire-red of a goblin's.

5

Mum and Bastian stood together at the checkout counter in the bookshop on Bloomsbury Street—just a few blocks from the doctor's office, while Lucas browsed the isles, sunlit from high windows.

A cheery, frazzled clerk whose upside-down name badge read *Esmerelda* pushed a box onto the counter. On it lay an illustration—a colorful painting of the cover belonging to the rare book hidden within.

The painting was masterfully done. On one side crouched a goblin so realistic it sent a rush of adrenaline flashing, bringing a chill to Bastian's face.

But opposite the goblin, across a beautifully rendered stream, knelt a Sylphic boy who looked about Bastian's age—a forest child maybe, with a faerie perched on his hand. The boy was dressed in a light armor of metal plates and red leather.

With the two of them facing the goblin, it didn't seem so fierce. In fact, it seemed frightened. From the picture alone, Bastian could perceive that the Sylphic boy was powerfully brave. It seemed he'd have the courage and skill to stave off any goblin.

Bastian lifted the lid off the box.

And there it was.

Moor Folk of the English Highlands, by M.D. Kingfisher.

A whispered sound—voices, low and snickering, lifted from a curtained room behind the counter.

The clerk rushed to it and yanked the curtain more tightly closed.

In gazing at Kingfisher's actual book—a renowned relic of Sylphic lore—Bastian could scarcely draw breath. Maybe it wouldn't matter that Master Sayre wasn't around to tell him the honest truth about Sylphic legends. This book perhaps could.

Mum opened the book's cover and read the price, scribbled in pencil. "Goodness." She glanced at Bastian. "I had no idea the book would cost so much. Did Master Sayre tell you what we'd have to pay for it?"

The room darkened as low clouds swept the sun from the skylighted windows.

With how fast the clouds were moving, this seemed like the same sort of storm that'd risen last night—the storm that'd assembled so quickly and violently; the storm that'd driven Master Sayre away; the storm out of which the goblin boy had appeared.

"We don't have to pay for it," said Bastian, over a rumbling of thunder. "Master Sayre bought this for me, as an early birthday present."

"Is that the case?" Mum asked Esmerelda. "Has this book been paid for?"

A peal of thunder lifted, hardly audible at first but rising strongly enough to set the light fixtures to shaking.

The clerk, Esmerelda, had hazel eyes that were somewhat dazzling. She gazed past Mum and Bastian, as though the storm, darkening the windows, was capturing her. Disturbing her.

"I must say," said Mum, "this price seems quite inflated, even for a book this rare."

Esmerelda didn't respond to mum. She only watched Bastian in an odd way as Mum explained further that Master Sayre had claimed to have bought the book already.

"You see, my son's been saving his allowance for any books on Sylphic legends he might find." Mum tried to draw Esmerelda's gaze. "But paying this much for a single book is really out of the question. I'm sure Master Sayre was honest that he meant this as a gift—do you have no record of its purchase?"

Esmerelda rested her gaze on the book. She glanced up at Bastian, training her brilliant eyes hard on his.

Bastian slipped his fingers into the box. He lifted out the book.

Mum adjusted her purse on her shoulder. She seemed a bit put out that Esmerelda wasn't paying any mind to her.

But Mum didn't press her questions further. She seemed to be growing captivated as Bastian thumbed through the book.

Bastian found within its gilded pages text that was artistically penned. And alongside the writing lay illustrations that indeed looked hand-painted.

The book's opening page read—

Open your eyes to England's wilds, and may you spy flickering fires and find Moor Folk resting nigh the hearth, their cozy homes thatched smartly to let ribbons of starlight drift in.

Follow the light, that you, like I, might boldly fight for the Sylphic Kingdom.

"Fight for the Sylphic Kingdom," Bastian whispered to himself. "What fight?"

He pulled the book closer and turned the page.

There, the book read—

Moor Folk are as old as England's hills, and the blood of the sun, the rivers, and the highlands runs inside their veins.

Moor Folk are clever and not often seen. But be not deceived—no flower that's ever bloomed, no leaf you've touched, no drop of rain you've ever tasted, nor any good thing growing, could come without the tender care of Moor Folk.

It seemed as though wind, whispering through pine trees and old oaks, was spinning right out of Dartmoor's forests and through these pages, washing Bastian with freshness.

Bastian glanced up at Esmerelda.

She was staring at him, wide-eyed, her hazel irises brightening like metal liquifying in a crucible.

"Payment has surely been made," said Mum to her. "Can you not check? Or—if not, do you perhaps offer a payment plan?"

Esmerelda glanced at Bastian's hand, readying to turn the page, then met his eyes in an eager way.

Bastian flipped the page to find another picture—one of the Sylphic boy from the cover, standing in his light armor before a bright coral sunset.

The text beneath the painting read—

*In the music of the faeries and the voices of the streams, the prophecy of
the Sun Child has been sung.*

At reading those words, a sensation stirred in Bastian's chest.
Though keen, it was not painful. More, it was a tingling, like what sets
in when sensation slowly returns to a hand or foot after pinching a
nerve.

"Prophecy." Bastian glanced up, meeting Esmerelda's gaze.

She flashed her brows.

Bastian read on in a whisper—

*"May he waken, our Sun Child—heart beating with bravery, mind
forged of dauntlessness, defender of the Sylphic Kingdom."*

A deep darkness swept the windows as though dusk had rapidly
fallen. With it, the tingling in Bastian's chest shifted sharp.

Esmerelda smacked the book's cover closed and crammed it back in
its box.

The instant the book was concealed, the darkness lifted in a slow
spread, like a fit of asthma easing.

Bastian stared at the windows—the color of the sky beyond them
now eerie.

It very much seemed that the darkness had been something
Sylphic. Lucas, standing in an aisle, seemed captivated by the weird
quality of the light now suddenly slanting in.

Esmerelda leaned close to Bastian and spoke in the merest whisper,
"Leave it boxed until you've reached home."

"Perhaps we should speak to Master Sayre," said Mum, wincing
and pressing her hip.

"And hurry," Esmerelda whispered, just to Bastian. "Your protection won't last."

"Protection?" he whispered back.

"Perhaps Master Sayre intended to pay but forgot." Mum bent to
capture Esmerelda's glance. "How do you suggest we resolve this?"

"Let's just buy it and go." Bastian pulled out his wallet and dumped
money onto the counter.

"That's not nearly enough, love," said Mum.

Esmerelda held Bastian's gaze with her stunning eyes. "Once it
crosses the border of your chalet, it'll be safe."

"I'll pay this much," said Bastian, to Mum. "Will you pay for the rest? Keep my allowance until I've paid you back. Let's just go."

"Well"—Mum let go of a sigh—"consider it an early birthday gift from me and Da." She fished out her credit card and handed it to Esmerelda.

Esmerelda, seeming lost, held up the card a moment, then tossed it back to Mum. She snatched Bastian's cash, shoved the boxed book into his hands, then backed off from the counter. She stood closely in front of the curtain—rustling with movement.

She kept her eyes trained on Bastian as he followed Mum and Lucas out the door.

6

Bastian clutched his boxed book as he peered out the windscreen of Mum's car.

Whatever darkness had descended over the bookshop hadn't returned, and the evening shone brightly.

Silver haze was weaving through the Dartmoor wilderness, its striking moors blued by distance. The haze seemed to shroud every shadow and lent a sense of enchantment to the woodland scrolling past.

A gentle wind, salt-tanged, shifted in through the window, as though having traveled thickly inland from the sea. And chimes—clear, though distant—were ringing.

Master Sayre had spoken of sunlit mists as Sylphic in nature. He said they were believed to carry powers of protection.

Of course, if these mists were Sylphic, there could very well be wicked things—goblins, or who knew what else, obscured within.

But a strong feeling of goodness was descending with the sensation of drawing the briny cool of the salty vapor into his lungs. And the way the mist seemed to be carrying the sunlight as though borne on the surface of a river—it seemed there could be nothing sinister in it.

Mum glanced at Bastian. "Why don't you have another look at your book? You can read me a bit out of it if you'd like."

Bastian was desperate to take out the book and study it—but Esmerelda's instructions had been explicit. He must leave it boxed.

"I'd rather wait until we get home," he told Mum, "so I can sit outside to read it."

And though it might've been a coincidence, the darkness that'd fallen while they were in the bookshop had seemed to dissipate when Esmerelda secured the lid back over the book.

Mum lent him a smile. "That sounds lovely."

Esmerelda—how odd she was. But there'd been something familiar about her that felt trustworthy. And she'd spoken with such authority about the *Moor Folk of the English Highlands*, and so directly to him—it was like she knew, very well, both the book and Bastian himself. And her counsel that his chalet was a safe place agreed with Master Sayre's.

Bastian lifted the Sylphic scope and peered at the landscape.

The sloping fields scrolling past glittered, bearded as they were with hoary grasses shimmering with early spring's dew. It wasn't difficult to imagine that such sparkling could be the leavings of Moor Folk, having visited them.

And the mist—was it possible that it was an actual protective Sylphic charm?

The seeds brightening in the wind looked not unlike how Bastian imagined sprites would appear, airborne and sprinting in their games.

Or the glistening clouds coasting over the highlands—they seemed slightly like companies of faeries cascading over the hilltops.

Mum turned the car, bringing them alongside a river within whose shallows Bastian had many times imagined naiads and rain angels and dryads consorting.

He tried to envision what the movements of naiads would look like, sliding over the riverbed on their sleek, watery feet.

And how regal willow dryads would appear, standing along the riverbanks as they tended to the solemn business of tree talk and water meanderings.

But best and most importantly of all, in the shadows of the riverside's gnarled oak trees, Bastian often imagined ranging forest children —bare-chested and crossed with bandoleers and bows, looking after everyone and keeping safe and free the magnificent Sylphic Kingdom of Moor Folk.

Bastian glanced back, beyond Lucas—mobbed by grocery sacks, toward the rear of the car.

Last weekend, Mum had picked up Bastian, Lucas, and Rhys after they'd ridden too far to make it home before a hard storm hit.

There, his bike hung, along with his brothers' bikes.

"Could you please pull over?" asked Bastian. "I want to bike home from here."

If Mum would let him, he could ride through these magnificent, misted woods. And perhaps—using his scope—he'd catch sight of something Sylphic.

"With all these weeds as high as your shoulder?" asked Mum. "I think not." She rubbed the edge of her belly.

As much as he wanted to negotiate getting to ride his bike the rest of the way to Kingfisher Chalet, he didn't push back. The look of pain on Mum seemed to have intensified since they'd left the doctor's office. He ought to stay with her.

A glance down at his boxed book brought Master Sayre's words to mind. *"Learning the lore of the Sun Child, understanding Sylphic histories—this will help you make sense of...well, something that I must soon tell you."*

Maybe he could open the box just for a second, just to thumb through and see if he could gather a hint of what Master Sayre might've been talking about.

Perhaps Esmerelda's instructions to hold off on reading the book had been more of a suggestion than a directive. It was, after all, possible the storm that'd risen when they were at the bookshop hadn't been anything Sylphic.

And besides, they were nearly home. Kingfisher Chalet was waiting just on the other side of the river crossing they were coming up on. It was just up the road to the west, and then north a few miles.

As Bastian felt of the edges of the box's lid, the tingling in his chest again rose as a pleasant thrill.

Had not Master Sayre told him to learn what this book held as quickly as possible? Master Sayre needed him to understand something kept here about the Sylphic Kingdom.

Probably, quite a bit could be discovered by opening the book for a mere minute.

He carefully slipped the lid off the box.

A gentle sound of water rose, like a stream's merry chattering, and with it came the soft smell of rain.

He shifted in his seat, sinking into the lovely sensations.

Lucas kicked his seat.

Bastian turned.

"Are you hearing things?" signed Lucas. "Because I am." He feigned to be listening.

"Don't be mean," signed Bastian.

"Seriously, I think I hear something," signed Lucas. "It sounds like…"

Bastian fully faced him. "What?" he signed. "If you're going to make fun of me, then let's have it."

Lucas, his face deadpan, signed, "I just heard a faerie fart."

Bastian let out a laugh he couldn't help.

He signed to Lucas, "You look terrible, by the way."

Lucas grinned. "I look amazing."

He pointed to his face, then signed, "These are battle scars. I hope they take weeks to heal."

Lucas' left eye was bruised all around, and the cut on his lip was fresh and wet red. His cheeks—all busted capillaries—were flushed brightly and seemed swollen. And the stitched cut on his forehead was thick.

He certainly would get his wish that the injuries would last a while.

"Hey, thanks for not spilling to the doctor," signed Bastian.

Lucas shrugged. "It's nothing."

"I wish I could've stopped the boy from laying into you. I wish he'd done that to me instead of you."

"He was too much for me," signed Lucas. "How could you be expected to do anything?"

The sun burst out of a bank of dark clouds, drenching the car in warm light.

The timbre of the twilight reflected beautifully in the book's silver title.

Bastian rested against the back of his seat. He lifted the book out of the box and held still.

Nothing changed. No storm clouds raced in. No darkness descended.

Bastian glanced at Mum, who seemed lost in thought. Lucas was settling into reading a comic.

Bastian watched out the windows as he opened the book.

Everything remained bright. There was no change in the lovely smell of the sea on the wind.

He angled the pages into a stream of silvery twilight and silently read from where he'd left off—

In the music of the faeries and the voices of the streams, the prophecy of the Sun Child has been sung.

May he waken, our Sun Child—heart beating with bravery, mind forged of dauntlessness, defender of the Sylphic Kingdom.

Bastian flipped through the pages and found, at almost each place he paused, writings about the lore of Sun Children.

Master Sayre had recounted to Bastian their legendary deeds. According to him, many Sun Children had been artists and inventors, developing amazing devices—like the Sylphic scope.

And they were brilliant in battle, for they were first and foremost defenders and warriors. Adventurers.

Bastian had always pictured Sun Children as having the same sort of character as Granddadda.

He pictured them brave, like Granddadda.

Bastian read on—

Though the coming Sun Child's arrival is far off, I must write urgently. For beneath these peaceful trees awakening to spring, an unmatched wickedness seethes, threatening all who love peace, be we Moor Folk of the Sylphic Lands, or people, mortal born.

There was strange thing about Sun Children, which Master Sayre had once told him.

Sun Children—though they were Sylphic creatures—were born into human families.

Sun Children were mortals with lineage in the Sylphic Kingdom, or spontaneously gifted with Sylphic blood—perhaps chosen to bear the title; chosen to play out the Sun Child's destiny.

Early on, in hearing those tales, Bastian had pressed Master Sayre on whether he actually believed any part of Moor Folk lore—about Sun Children or anything else.

Master Sayre had only replied that plenty of folk believed Sun Children to be "a fact sure as dawn," and that the Sylphic Kingdom was due for one.

Mum's wincing, how she was tightly cradling her belly, drew Bastian to look at her.

He watched as she rubbed at her side, where the baby's elbow or knee was probably protruding in an uncomfortable way.

Master Sayre had said: *"The moment will come swiftly for telling you everything. But until that moment arrives, because of the prophecy—I can't."*

As Bastian contemplated those words, a thought dawned.

What if the secret Master Sayre was guarding had something to do with Sun Children?

"A momentous event is about to take place," Master Sayre had said. *"One that's been long foretold. Something wonderful. Something terrible."*

Bastian stared at Mum and found himself unable to blink.

Because—what if the Sun Child predicted was his own coming brother, very soon to be born?

"Love?" Mum glanced at him. "Are you okay?"

Bastian lowered his gaze to her belly. The fact was, this baby did feel entirely different and special, being such a surprise and coming about right after they'd moved into a chalet that was allegedly Sylphic.

And here, right here in Kingfisher's book, were details about a prophecy—a prophecy Master Sayre had intended Bastian to receive.

A prophecy foretelling the birth of a Sun Child.

"Bastian?" Mum studied him. "Is something wrong?"

Bastian glanced up at her eyes.

Mum was bright. Sharp-minded. Lovely.

With the singed-sugar scent she carried from the kitchen, with the cheery twilight calling roses from her cheeks and making her hair shine, she seemed not at all far off from how Kingfisher described Moor Folk —wise, beautiful, merry, and brave.

Maybe all that brilliance came from carrying a Sun Child.

Mum cast him a gentle look and stroked the back of his neck. "Would you like to talk?"

Bastian rested his gaze on the horizon, on a copse of conifers that Moor Folk, apparently, had nurtured to their towering heights.

Tales of the magnificent Sylphic Kingdom and the courageous feats of those defending it—the possibility of the great Sun Child myth playing out in his own family, a brother of his carrying bravery like a banner—it felt strange and wonderful and entirely feasible.

Bastian thumbed a few pages further into his book.

He stopped at an illustration of what seemed to be a company of forest children clasping bows. Bandoleers holding arrows crossed their bare chests.

They were standing shoulder-to-shoulder, their gazes downcast at their hands on their bows, as though readying for a fight.

May the battle be won, and may all Moor Folk find joy, for their hearts are knit of peace and mirth. May they laugh and tell stories of valor and raise toasts with goblets brimming with berry wine.

May they spend twilights sitting on the dappled caps of toadstools in a cold radiance of silver moonshine, composing music, fashioning artworks, weaving poetry, and conjuring wonders lovely enough to call forth tears from rabbits, and clever enough to summon foxes from dens.

If a fight—a battle of some kind—were in fact coming, of course Master Sayre would want the brother of the Sun Child to be well-trained in Ryudo.

Bastian had sort of—though poorly—protected Lucas.

Could it be that Master Sayre was preparing him to protect the Sun Child?

Bastian placed his palm on Mum's belly.

The unborn baby arched into it.

"It's as though he trusts me already," Bastian whispered.

Mum settled her palm beside Bastian's. "I daresay he does."

Their hands were met by a tiny, gliding phantom foot.

The effect was alien and wonderful.

Mum pressed her hip and drew a sharp breath.

The unborn child sank away.

"Are *you* okay?" Bastian drew back his hand.

Mum forced a smile. "A bit of discomfort is to be expected in the final month."

At watching Mum's smile touch her eyes, Bastian relaxed. He settled again into reading—

Though Moor Folk are dauntless, their greatest test is yet to come. Though they fight with valor, I fear many will be lost. It is the foretold Sun Child who shall take my place in battle and defeat our foe. Or— may it not be—the Sun Child shall fail and usher in our doom.

May the faeries have seen well, and may the Child wake before the darkness strikes. Else worlds will waste away.

Bastian rubbed at his chest, tingling yet more strongly.

"You know," said Mum, watching him closely, "it's okay if you're troubled by what happened last night."

Suddenly—there was something in the road.

It was something muscled. Something massive. Something with flaming red eyes.

Bastian pointed. "Mum, look out!"

Mum tore her gaze back to the road and slammed on the brakes.

The book and its box flew from Bastian's lap onto the floorboard.

Mum slowed the car to a crawl as they crept toward—nothing.

"What did you see?" asked Mum.

Bastian stared through the windscreen at the empty road.

A goblin, undoubtedly, had been standing right there in the middle of the road, facing the car. And now it was just—gone.

"Bastian?" Mum, easing the car along slowly, captured his glance. "What did you see?"

"What did *you* see?" he asked her.

She shook her head. "I didn't see anything."

Last night, the goblin boy had tried to take from Bastian the Sylphic scope—a relic created by a Sun Child and probably important to the coming fight.

And now, Bastian was holding a book full of secret teachings and Sylphic enchantments; details about Moor Folk; about prophecies; about battles; about Sun Children.

It was probable that the goblin would want this book, too.

Mum held his gaze. "Can you not tell me what was in the road?"

Bastian scanned the road's edge. "I'm not sure I can say."

She quickened the car to again drive at a normal pace. "Did you perhaps see the flash of an animal crossing?"

"It definitely wasn't an animal." Bastian searched the floorboard among grocery sacks until he found *Moor Folk of the English Highlands.*

Its box and lid, though, were wedged under his seat.

"Are you certain you saw anything?" Mum aimed the air conditioning vent more toward her face. "Please tell me you weren't messing around."

"Of course I wasn't—I'd never do something like that." He reached under the seat and fingered closer the box and its lid.

Lucas leaned forward, between them. "I saw something," he signed.

Bastian sat straight and stared at Lucas.

"The thing in the road looked like a person," signed Lucas. "A big, tall person."

"You saw that?" Bastian signed.

Lucas nodded.

A frightened look crossed Mum's face as she murmured, "A person."

Esmerelda's words rang in Bastian's mind—"*Once it crosses the border of your chalet, it'll be safe.*" And Master Sayre's words—that Kingfisher Chalet was the safest place.

The light shafting through the car's windows darkened as they drove into a thick stretch of forest.

Every shadowy swatch between trees seemed to hold the potential for a muscled goblin to materialize.

Bastian scrambled to snatch the box and its lid from the floor.

He snagged the box but knocked the lid out of reach.

"Love, what's the matter?" asked Mum.

"Drive, just drive," he said. "Get us home." He glanced out the windscreen.

Again—there, right in the middle of the road, the goblin stood.

It was holding high a jagged black sword, its tip pointed at the sun, across which gray clouds were racing.

"Mum..." Bastian eased up the lid from the side of his seat. "It's there."

Mum squinted. "What's there?" She touched the brakes. "Where?"

"There," Lucas reached, signing frantically. "There! There!"

Bastian crammed the lid on the box.

The steering wheel jerked out of Mum's hands, on its own.

The car swerved around the goblin and veered toward the road's shoulder.

Bastian snatched the wheel and pulled the car back into their lane.

The car barreled toward a left-hand curve.

Mum pumped the brakes, but the curve came too sharp, too fast.

The car skidded across the other lane and swiped a hedge bordering the road. The two right-hand wheels slipped off the pavement's edge.

Mum screamed. Groceries from the back seat flew into the front. The car struck a tall boulder, jetting from the road's shoulder.

The car spun, ricocheted, and skidded sideways into the ditch.

It rocked into stillness inside a cloud of dust, smoke, and steam.

7

Bastian unbelted and looked out every window. Lucas leaned between them and cleared spilled groceries off Mum.

Mum didn't seem able to lift her head.

She just sat collapsed whispering, "No...no..."

Bastian fished her phone out of her purse and called Da.

Mum murmured to Bastian, "Are you hurt?" She glanced back at Lucas. "Are we hurt?"

Lucas reached into the front seat and held her hand.

"Such pain"—Mum clenched her belly—"it's wrong."

"What pain?" asked Bastian. "What hurts?"

"It's the baby," signed Mum.

She reached for the phone.

Bastian, glancing out the windows, gave it to her.

The goblin was nowhere in sight.

Bastian signed to Lucas, "Are you okay?"

Lucas signed back, "I think so."

When Da answered the call, Mum doubled and cried out.

"Helena?" Da's voice rang. "Bastian? Are you there?"

Bastian pried the phone from Mum's hand. He told Da where they were and answered his panicked questions.

"I don't know if she's injured," Bastian told him. "She's in lots of pain. Lucas and I are okay."

"The baby," whispered Mum.

"Mum's worried about the baby," said Bastian. "No, the car's definitely not drivable. There was something in the road—we skidded off and nailed a big rock. The front looks jacked up."

"Hey, Bastian?" Da had given the phone to Rhys. "Listen, just stay calm."

An engine's roar blared through the phone—Da's car revving.

Mum tipped toward Bastian, resting her head on his shoulder.

Bastian tried to see her face. "Mum?"

"We'll be there in five minutes," said Rhys. "No—Da says two."

"Mum?" Bastian shook her. "Mum's falling asleep or something."

"Get her to talk to you," shouted Da. "Can she say what's wrong?"

"Mum? Are you hurt?"

She didn't speak. She just sat very still, very tense.

Bastian stared at her belly, waiting for the water, the blood.

"What do we do if she blows?"

Mum's held breath broke in a quiet laugh.

"Just hold tight," said Rhys. "We've called an ambulance, but Da thinks we can get to you faster. We're nearly there."

Bastian watched the road.

Minutes of stillness passed.

Minutes of Mum weeping, of Lucas stroking her hair, signing, "It's all right...it's all right."

Finally, the rumbling of a motor approached.

Da's car swept a corner and lurched to a stop by the ditch.

He and Rhys jumped out.

Da jerked open Mum's door. "An ambulance is on its way." He reached in and unbelted her.

"The baby." She scooted to him. "We must go."

Da said, "The medics will better know how to—"

"They'll see to Bastian and Lucas," said Mum. "You're taking me. Now."

Da helped her to his car and eased her to lying down in the backseat.

Rhys wrenched open Lucas' door, then Bastian's.

A soft sound rose, a distant shivering—like if tiny lily-of-the-valley bells could ring. And all around, on every hilltop, it seemed figures were standing, like gathering troops silhouetted against the blazing twilight.

Whenever Bastian looked directly at any one of them, though, their forms faded.

Bastian clutched his boxed book. If Mum was about to deliver the Sun Child, perhaps all these figures—Moor Folk, maybe—were approaching to greet their new member. Or—what if the accident had injured the baby? The bells sounded sort of mournful.

"Da," Rhys said. "Bastian seems dazed. He isn't answering me."

"I'm not dazed." Bastian climbed out.

He walked around the car's smashed front and stood beside Lucas, staring at Mum.

"I've never seen her cry like that," signed Lucas.

Rhys signed, "She's going to be okay."

The shivery ringing strengthened as though it were advancing—slipping over the hills with the mist.

Bastian, gripping his boxed book, studied the horizon at all points.

There was no sign of any goblin. There were just the vague figures.

According to Esmerelda, to Master Sayre, he needed to get the book over the threshold of his chalet. Perhaps there, with the book safe from the goblin, he and his family would be safe, too.

Or—perhaps they wouldn't. The book was an authentic Sylphic relic that the goblin, by all reckoning, wanted. Gripping the book suddenly felt less like holding a shield and more like holding a target.

Bastian bowed his head over it.

"Lad?" Da was standing before him, ducking to meet his eyes.

Mum cried out.

"I'm fine." Bastian looked over Da's shoulder at her. "Take her."

Da glanced at Rhys. "Keep him calm until the medics arrive."

"I don't need medics," said Bastian. "I need to go home."

"I can't predict how long we'll be," said Da, signing.

"Go," signed Rhys.

Bastian glanced around at the hills—hills that were sparkling with bright silhouettes and ringing with wind chimes; hills that were trilling with pipes and flutes and sounding with drums and swelling with melodies played in poignant keys.

Rhys and Lucas guided Bastian to the side of the road.

They stood together, staring at the dust cloud left in the wake of Da's car disappearing.

Rhys seated Bastian and Lucas on the road's shoulder. "Did either of you get knocked around?"

"We were belted in," signed Lucas. "But the impact seemed to jar Bastian."

"I really don't need an ambulance." Bastian glanced at the back of the car. "Our bikes are tied on—let's just bike home."

Lucas pointed, then signed, "I see flashing lights."

An ambulance rounded the corner and pulled up beside them. Two medics hustled out.

One opened the tall rear doors of their vehicle, while the other approached Rhys.

"Who was in the accident?" asked the medic.

"These two." Rhys stood away from Bastian and Lucas.

The medic, hardly older than Rhys, crouched before Lucas. "Lad, can you speak?"

He glanced over Lucas' face, looked at the stitches.

"Or...what happened, here?"

Lucas signed, "None of this is from the crash."

Rhys translated, then added, "He's telling the truth."

"Then where'd you get so bloodied up?" asked the medic.

"Street fight," signed Lucas, standing, letting the second medic guide him to sit on the tail of the ambulance. "You should see the other guy."

Rhys translated.

The medic cracked a smile as he knelt before Bastian. "And what about you?"

"I'm fine." Bastian let the medic examine his head and neck. "Can we please just go home?"

"Are you in any pain?" The medic shone a light in Bastian's eyes.

With the music drifting out of the evening's growing mist—mist stricken silver by the low sun; mist swelling over the heights and back-lighting the pale figures—something wonderful seemed to be pressing in.

Perhaps all those ethereal figures were forest children, come to watch over Bastian and his brothers.

"Any difficulty moving? Standing?" the medic asked Bastian.

Every hill on every stretch of horizon in every direction was ringing with music.

The medic held Bastian's shoulder. "Lad? Can you answer me?"

Bastian met his eyes. "We were belted in."

"Can you tell me what happened?" the medic asked.

"There was something in the road," Bastian said. "Mum lost control of the car."

"Did the car strike something in the road?"

"The car swerved," said Bastian. "When we stopped, she was in awful pain. Maybe labor. Da took her. I tried to keep us on the road, but—" He glanced at the wreckage.

"Is he okay?" asked Rhys.

"I believe so." The medic guided Bastian to sit in the back of the ambulance beside Lucas. "He's in a bit of shock, but that's to be expected. We'll check him well over."

"I really don't need to be checked over." Bastian glanced at his boxed book. "I just need to get home."

The medic cuffed Bastian's arm to a machine.

Lucas signed, "Is this cool or what?" He stood and moved further back into the ambulance.

"Are you dizzy?" the medic asked Bastian. "Or nauseous?"

"No. Are you going to make me go to the hospital? Because I don't need to go."

The medic turned to Rhys. "We can take them if you'd like an eye on them. But I'm not finding any injuries. This one's struggling a bit with asthma, I see."

"I've got my inhaler," said Bastian. "Can't we just bike home?"

"Home isn't that far," said Rhys. "They'd rest better at home."

"Is there no one you can call to come collect you?" asked the medic.

"There's no need," said Bastian.

The instant the medic unhooked him, Bastian hopped off the tail of the ambulance and climbed down the ditch, to their bikes tied to the back of the car.

Lucas followed him.

"Watch for headaches, nausea, and disorientation."

The medic handed Rhys something to sign.

"Don't hesitate to call us back."

Bastian and Lucas rolled their bikes up onto the dirt road as the ambulance drove off.

Rhys opened the car's back door.

Bean sacks and bread and grain boxes and vegetables spilled out.

"We ought to take what we can manage." Rhys lifted a couple of sacks and tied them to his handlebars.

Lucas gathered groceries from the front floorboards.

Bastian leaned against the wrecked car and studied the picture on his boxed book.

Marvelous.

The Sylphic boy carried such a confident expression despite that he was crouched eye-to-eye with a goblin.

The stream dividing them lay streaked with bold colors reflecting the handsome sunset.

On the tips of the Sylphic boy's fingers perched the faerie, her silver eyes bejeweling her angel's face. Platinum-golden wisps of hair whorled about her head like a whelk, and fallen strands played around her sweetly angled ears.

"Bastian?" Lucas signed.

A perfect, pinched nose peaked between the faerie's apricot cheeks. Her wings were just silver suggestions of wings—ephemeral master-pieces of wind-woven metallic threads tipped with gems at points that lifted to sharpness along their longitudes.

She was balancing on her toes, her hands lifted a touch, as though she'd just lighted there and might shoot off again like a spark.

Lucas tapped Bastian's hand, then signed, "Maybe you'd better sit for a minute."

The goblin crouching opposite the forest child was muscled and sinewy. Its horns pierced the sunset-splashy sky, and its batty wings hung from its shoulders like a cloak. It held in its clawed hand a blue jag of lightning.

Lucas lowered Bastian's boxed book and signed, "Look at me."

Bastian clutched the box to his chest and signed, "This might make me a better Ryudo champion. Better, all around, when it comes to things like car crashes."

Lucas took the boxed book from him and laid it on the seat of the car.

Bastian signed on, "I mean, would a Ryudo champion worth his meddle have let a car wreck like this? Especially with his mum inside. His mum, pregnant with...I should've thought faster. I should've kept us on the road. Why didn't I?"

He lowered his gaze and kept signing.

"I mean, would a true Ryudo champion have let that bully lay into you?"

Lucas snapped in Bastian's face.

Bastian startled and looked up.

"Are you sure you didn't hit your head or something?" Lucas signed.

Bastian slid the book into his rucksack and lifted it, along with a few grocery sacks. He strapped everything onto his bike and walked it to Rhys, waiting on the road behind the steaming car.

Bastian turned just in time to catch Lucas signing to Rhys, "Something's wrong with him."

"Nothing's wrong," Bastian signed back. "The medic said so."

"Since you're struggling with that asthma," said Rhys, climbing onto his bike, "let's have you lead. If you get dizzy, or if the going gets too difficult, just stop."

Bastian walked his bike ahead.

Lucas caught him by the arm, then signed, "That was brave, by the way—how you jumped to action, to steer."

"I let the car go off the road," Bastian signed back. "What if Mum... the baby—"

Rhys rested his hand on Bastian's shoulder. "This could've been way worse."

Bastian mounted his bike and guided his brothers toward a trail opening into the forest thicket—a shortcut to Kingfisher Chalet.

He angled down a brambly path shimmering with a coursing mist that seemed to be carrying quiet chimes; a mist glowing brightly silver, despite how the forest was darkening in the blue of the deepening twilight.

8

Bastian set a quick pace, leading Rhys and Lucas down a forest path winding toward home.

The mist swirling through their spokes glowed more brightly than it seemed it should in sunlight this low, which certainly made it feel Sylphic.

And the mist seemed to hold a strain of sweet music, barely detectable. Inside it, Bastian found he could breathe easily.

At every place where a clearing offered a sightline to the distant hills, he slowed a touch and scouted the heights for signs of anything Sylphic.

He caught no further glimpse of the figures he'd seen standing against the misted heights. Even the Sylphic scope showed him nothing.

Bastian angled off the path and led his brothers into a thickly grown stretch of pines leading to the wide river. At the far edge of the thicket lay a rickety bridge that cars couldn't manage but was perfect for bikes.

During winter, the river lay motionless—a frozen jelly pan of translucent white, its edges dusted with sugared snow.

Now in early April, it was alive with melt water and roiling with carp and pike, the wildness of its rush calling up a shining veil of mist. The intensity of the current—high and fast with runoff from storms—sculpted the water into what seemed almost a living thing that reared, each smooth ripple crowned with a blue diamond gleam of sunshine.

The strong river, glinting between the bridge's planks as Bastian rode, seemed to be drawing a division.

Behind them to the west, a crashed car steamed. A goblin roved. While ahead to the east, a fleet of drifting clouds were letting down sunbeams, and the sweet music the mist carried was strengthening.

Not to mention, Kingfisher Chalet lay just around the next bend.

Kingfisher Chalet seemed as alive and as strong as the river, as the forest, with how it sprouted from its sweeping garden meadow; with how its rounded windows glinted in pairs, cherished by shutters painted the blue of the North Atlantic and thrown open, wide, like interested eyes.

Light sconces, buried at the bases of shrubs and tucked among tree roots, splashed cones of light like faerie fire upon the chalet's garden trees and cobbled walls.

The thought of seeing *Moor Folk of the English Highlands* securely enclosed inside Kingfisher Chalet, the thought of finally learning what secrets it held, pushed Bastian to pedal harder.

And he couldn't shake Esmerelda's final words: *"Your protection won't last."*

Bastian glanced around as he rode into the deep tracks of forest on the river's far side.

He still found no sign of any vague, shining figures. He saw no shadows taking the shapes of goblins. No ember-like eyes shone from any dark corridor.

He climbed a wooded hill and cut through a thicket of ripening winter gooseberry bushes. He pressed on into a thin crop of budding saplings and rode out onto the lane leading to their chalet.

In the distance, the thatched roof of the chalet was standing tall above the canopy of greening trees.

Its roofline was angular and oddly high—higher than the ceilings on the second floor appeared to reach.

Bastian had caught the irregularity the day they'd moved in, but with no access point to any attic, Mum and Da had assured him that the high roof was an artistic feature, stuffed with insulation. A circular garret rising on the north end of the peak—like a castle's citadel, also inaccessible—was, they'd said, a plain old hot air vent.

Rhys, squinting at the chalet, sped up and took the lead.

As Bastian drew nearer to the edge of their yard, the shivery sounds ringing through the countryside faltered.

The air felt less fresh here than the misted air of the forest had, and he found himself having to labor some to breathe. And an aching seemed to be setting in, head to toe—a soreness that seemed to have come from the car crash. He slowed his bike.

The strengthening pain brought back the shock of the accident strongly—the peal of Mum's scream, the screeching of the tires, the awful crunch of their car striking the rock, the rake of bending metal, the smell of burnt rubber and oil.

And the terrible sight of Mum—how she'd gripped her belly; how she'd cried in the back of Da's car.

"Bloody bindweed," Rhys muttered, circling back.

He stopped his bike behind a pile of pine mulch bags and weed poison heaped at the corner of the front yard.

Bastian eased his bike to a stop beside Rhys. "What?"

"It's too late," Rhys signed, peering over the pile. "She's seen us."

Lucas braked beside Bastian. "Who?"

Whoever it was, they'd made Rhys' face go gray, like the shadows dropping from the wych elms had swathed him; like he'd seen something terrible, something wicked.

Like a goblin.

Bastian peeked over the mulch heaps.

Climbing their front porch steps was—not a goblin, but possibly worse.

It was their neighbor, Lady Agatha Marrowight.

Bastian felt his face go gray, too.

Kingfisher Chalet was set apart from all other homes, including Lady Marrowight's gothic, black manor, by the Wystan Woods—an expansive swath of Devon's forests that local lore had it was visited by Moor Folk more often than people.

Yet Lady Marrowight kept turning up.

When Bastian and his family had first moved into Kingfisher Chalet, he and his brothers often had stumbled upon Lady Marrowight walking the woods. She'd trap them in chats about where they'd been born, and where they'd lived in San Francisco and Exeter, and how they liked this shire, and why, exactly, had they moved to Dartmoor, and what Kingfisher Chalet was like.

Mum and Da called her "harmless," but something about her was definitely off, and Bastian and his brothers did their best to avoid her. Lately, though, she'd started showing up at the door.

Lady Marrowight, standing beneath the chalet's broad eave, had her gaze fixed on the heaps of mulch currently serving as a foxhole for Bastian and his brothers. The chalet's shade left her colorless against Mum's pink and orange honeysuckle florets spiraling up wooden trellises edging the front porch.

Though Lady Marrowight looked rather normal, and might even seem pretty, when viewed objectively, her brand of beauty was odd. She appeared neither old nor young, but dry; a last autumn leaf, still a kind of green, but spent and persistently clinging.

She carried none of Mum's kindness and warmth but seemed drawn from dark woods, from dagger-stoned caves, from strong storms.

And she didn't keep herself cared for, the way Mum did. Lady Marrowight always looked in need of a bath, her tangly black hair hanging in knots or twisted up into a disheveled bun.

A drab, gray walking jumper sheathed her skeletal figure beneath a drabber, grayer, ankle-length cardigan that gaudily set off her clown-yellow tennis shoes.

Lucas signed, "Why's she here?"

Lady Marrowight pulled from beneath her cardigan a twisted stick. It was too short for a walking stick, and too polished to be something she'd just picked up.

The head of it looked a bit snaky, and many times when he'd spotted her out walking, Bastian had noticed her wielding it like a short sword.

"It seems you two handled the ride okay," Rhys signed. "Are you feeling all right? Bastian—is the asthma getting to you?"

Breathing was definitely more difficult here, but Bastian could hardly think on that. All he could think about was Mum.

"Has Da texted you?" signed Bastian.

Rhys pulled out his phone. "Nothing yet," he signed. "I'm sure it'll be a while."

"What if something bad is happening to Mum?" signed Lucas. "I mean—why hasn't Da called?"

"They certainly will call us, as soon as they know anything," signed Rhys.

"Mum might be having the baby right now, though," signed Bastian. "Maybe the shock of the crash, of having almost hit something in the road, triggered labor."

"What was it she almost hit?" signed Rhys.

Bastian focused on Lucas. "You said you saw something. What do you think it was?"

"I only saw a dark flash," signed Lucas. "It was like—ahead of us—a person had darted into the road."

"It was bigger than a person," Bastian signed. "Massive, actually. Muscled. Its eyes sort of blazed in its face."

"Something muscled and massive," signed Rhys, "with fiery eyes—please don't tell me you think Mum nearly hit a goblin on the way home from Exeter."

"Look, it doesn't matter what was in the road," signed Lucas. "Mum called her pain 'wrong.' Something terrible might've happened to her in the crash. Something terrible might've happened to the baby. Or at the very least, Bastian's right—Mum might be in labor."

If Mum were on the verge of giving birth to the Sun Child, Bastian felt he should give Rhys and Lucas fair warning.

He lifted his hands to tell them what he'd discovered about the Sun Child in *Moor Folk of the English Highlands*—but he lowered them again. To Rhys and Lucas, the notion would seem beyond cracked.

Rhys glanced at Lady Marrowight staring their way, her arms crossed.

"Let's get rid of her," he signed. "Then we can wait this out in peace."

He biked to their driveway and angled into it, Bastian and Lucas lagging behind.

"If you're here to see Mum, she's not home," said Rhys to the Lady.

Bastian glanced at a stone walk edging the chalet, leading to the back kitchen door—offering escape.

Every shred of instinct was driving him to want to race down it, around the house, and safely in—but it seemed cruel to leave Rhys to deal with Lady Marrowight alone.

He drew his bike slightly nearer to Rhys.

Though Rhys was speaking to Lady Marrowight, she wasn't looking at him.

Rather, she was leering at Bastian, her hard stare seeming to make the air frigid, too thick to breathe easily.

Bastian bore it as well as he could, but a moment was all he could stand of her steely gaze fixed on him.

He glanced toward the chalet and calculated his evasive maneuver.

Slowly, he backed his bike into the driveway, then slunk off it.

He lifted two sacks from his handlebars and took off running along the walk.

"Bastian don't leave your bike like that," Rhys called after him.

Lucas, sharing Bastian's approach, whipped past, rumbling his bike over the weedy lawn.

Bastian sprinted for the back porch, but his toe caught on the edge of a flagstone, and he lost hold of a sack, sending oranges rolling.

He scrambled to collect the fruit but stopped at the shock of the sight of a boy peering from the blind of a tree—a boy crouching on a high branch of an evergreen growing against the chalet.

The boy was bare-chested, and his eyes—wild and cheery, Sylphic-seeming—shone from his angular face.

He looked a great deal like one of the forest children painted in *Moor Folk of the English Highlands*.

Bastian blinked, and the Sylphic boy was gone.

The soft music lifted once again—a whisper of songbirds. The sound mingled with a fresh atmosphere, like rain on tender earth, that made breathing easier.

Bastian crept nearer to the evergreen. He scanned the yard for the Sylphic boy.

The yard was mobbed in the weeds that since winter had erupted from the grass.

As aggressive as they were, they seemed less like plants and more like the tentacles of some great, green subterranean leviathan with a mean appetite for little garden statues.

Figurines and gazing globes that Kingfisher had left behind lay scattered about the lawn. On the north side of the yard, a broad, hoary apple tree rocked gently in the wind.

A marble fountain at the lawn's center, studded with fantastical creatures dancing around its scalloped rim, held at its apex a large stone angel with silvery flared wings.

There were plenty of places here for someone to hide.

Bastian studied the high hill rising at the eastern end of the yard.

Its rounded crest was crowned with rowan berry trees whose twirling limbs netted the brilliance of the sunrise and caught the smolder of the sunset, their allure giving credence to the occasionally reported sightings of Moor Folk near Kingfisher Chalet.

He scanned the hill's wooly foot, blanketed by mats of tangled thyme that sparked with white flowers, shaped like stars.

There was nothing Sylphic anyplace in sight.

Bastian explored the earth beside the evergreen.

At its base, a faint footprint—bigger than his own, shimmered like the iridescent trail of wet left by a snail.

He pressed the ground. His thumb went right in.

A human footprint in soil this soft should be deeper.

Bastian glanced up to find Lady Marrowight staring past Rhys and fixing on him.

Bastian tried to run off, but he couldn't stand up. The thickness of the air seemed to constrict, and he could barely draw breath. He couldn't even blink. All he could do was stare at Lady Marrowight and remain kneeling where he was, stone still.

"We've had quite an adventure," Rhys said to Lady Marrowight. "We're a little tired and should go in and rest. Is there any message you'd like me to pass along to Mum?"

Lady Marrowight pulled her gaze off Bastian and stared at Rhys.

Clear of the constraint, Bastian found he could breathe and move. He flew along the stone walk to the back door.

He raced up the back porch, slung himself inside the kitchen, and slammed the door.

He clung to the counter, taking lovely, whole breaths while the chalet flushed him with warmth.

9

*I*nside the coziness of the kitchen, the soft music swelled, mingling with distant sea waves and a scent, like soft rainclouds.

It seemed Master Sayre and Esmerelda had been right. Here, Bastian felt wholly safe.

Here hung gingerbread-style cupboards that looked to have been baked on spiced cookie sheets. Sunshine glittered through the latticed windows, small and bay, from whose sills potted herbs spilled tendrils of new growth. Antique cooking bits n' bobs hung from the creamy walls, and shelves of baking spices sweetened the mild pungency of the morning's tea bags abandoned in unwashed teacups in the sink.

Bastian peered out into the back yard, looking again for the Sylphic boy.

He'd been shirtless, wearing just shabby trousers. There'd been something crossing his chest—a bandoleer, maybe.

Naga, their chummy silver tomcat, uncoiled from where he'd been sleeping on the kitchen island in a topsy-turvy cyclone of whiskers and belly fur. He jumped onto the counter and peered out the window with Bastian.

Naga had come with Kingfisher Chalet, and his affectionate nature, directed particularly at Bastian, endeared him to the whole family. His eyes were silvery blue, like Bastian's, and kisses from Naga could mend anything.

"Psst—"

Bastian spun.

Lucas, kneeling by the front window, waved him over.

Bastian hurried to him and knelt.

Outside, Lady Marrowight was chattering relentlessly at Rhys.

"Why is she still talking to him?" asked Bastian. "He told her we all needed to come in and rest."

"What's she saying?" signed Lucas.

Lady Marrowight's words, though muffled by the windowpane, were clear.

Bastian translated as the Lady shared with Rhys her prickly thoughts on how shabby Kingfisher Chalet looked, how wrecked were its grounds, and how they might've done better to just stay in Exeter.

"Your brother, the youngest, suffers from a weak chest, I understand," said Lady Marrowight.

She swatted around her face as though fending off a swarm of invisible insects.

Rhys shrugged. "Bastian manages all right."

All Bastian—all any of them—wanted was to see Mum safe.

Instead, they were staring at Lady Marrowight, saying rude and intrusive things, swatting weirdly at nothing, her thin shadow darkening the planters Mum had dressed.

Watching her made Bastian's insides twist until he felt positively homesick for Mum.

"Something's seriously wrong with Lady Marrowight," Lucas signed. "Just because she lives in that monstrosity of a manor—because she's got a lot of money—she thinks she owns everybody."

Lady Marrowight did have a lot of money—old money. But she seemed not to know what to do with it.

Her manor, as ostentatious as an old French chateaux, wasn't all that pristine itself, lashed together as its aged marble walls were with iron ties.

Behind her manor stretched an enormous vale whose edges produced vines of black roses that choked granite sculptures of fantastical creatures. Birds didn't nest, nor even sing, from Marrowight Manor, and gnarly traps kept forest animals at bay.

The traps were thought to be a danger to pets as well. Several neighbors had lost a dog or cat last seen wandering near Marrowight Manor.

One apparent victim was a fluffy, snow-white Samoyed puppy, whose owner, Mr. Brighton, used to walk him by Kingfisher Chalet. The puppy had crawled under Lady Marrowight's hedgerow in midwinter, never to be seen again.

"We should rescue Rhys from her," signed Lucas.

"We really should," signed Bastian.

Neither of them moved.

"I've brought something for your brother, for his breathing," said Lady Marrowight, digging into a pouch hanging from her shoulder. "It's a concoction of my own making."

She offered Rhys a weird, wide smile as she drew out a small bottle.

"A drop or two of this in his tea should fix everything."

Rhys just looked at the bottle. "Thanks, but we've got it well under control." He glanced around. "To be straight, the source of the trouble is these weeds. They get the best of him. You've lived in Dartmoor a long while—have you any idea how we might get rid of them? We've cut them back, we've rooted them, we've tried poison— no matter what, they just keep coming back. I bet you've got them, too."

"There's nothing to be done."

Lady Marrowight swiped her hand in the air so hard, she almost struck Rhys.

"The best thing you and your lot could do is clear out. Go back to Exeter. Or better yet, California."

"The doctor says Bastian will outgrow the sensitivity," said Rhys.

The corner of Lady Marrowight's mouth lifted. "I doubt it."

Lucas faced Bastian. "Hey, did we remember to grab your Kingfisher book? Or is it still in Mum's car?"

Bastian, glancing back at the kitchen, realized his book had not been in the grocery bags. He'd placed it in his rucksack—still hooked to his bike.

He raced out the front door and jumped the porch rail. He untangled his rucksack from his bike's handlebars, toppling an apple sack.

He yanked out his boxed book.

"What have you there?" asked Lady Marrowight, her voice chilling.

Bastian froze as apples rolled.

The gentle sounds he'd been hearing—birdsong and a hum of crashing waves—ceased, and the smell of rain vanished. Instead, a reek of mildew rose.

Lady Marrowight looked down her nose and met Bastian's eyes. *"Moor Folk of the English Highlands."*

She reached her long-nailed fingers toward the book, then jerked them back.

Lucas slipped out the front door and down the porch stairs. He stood beside Bastian.

Lady Marrowight swatted at nothing. "I'll take that book off your hands"—she glanced at Rhys—"if you'd rather your young brother not read rubbish."

"That won't be necessary." Rhys slipped between Bastian and the Lady and gathered up the spilled apples.

Bastian peered alongside the chalet for any sign of the Sylphic boy. His fingers itched to open his book and search out descriptions of forest children.

"If you've had an adventurous day," said Lady Marrowight, "will you not invite me in for tea to tell me about it?"

"There are bats in the thatching," signed Lucas. "We could brew her bat stew."

Rhys stifled a grin. "Look, we're quite tired. Our Mum might be having a baby as we speak. We're anxiously waiting to hear from her and Da."

"Mammal birth," she said. "There's nothing nastier." She laid into a discourse on its horrors.

Lucas glanced off, avoiding reading her lips. Rhys stood squirming, rubbing at his neck.

Bastian focused on the picture on his book's box.

In gazing at the Sylphic boy and faerie painted there, the ache of sickness over Mum's absence, the thickness of the air, lightened.

The beaming sun burst out of the clouds, turning the sky copper and slipping down its western trail behind the pale green canopies of a stand of silver birches.

Lady Marrowight flipped up her hood. "The sun will go, each night it will go. And a babe born in darkness might rain down misery." She held Bastian's glance. "Your meddling in folklore could affect a newborn child in a repugnant way."

Rhys and Lucas glanced off, concealing smirks.

"I expect the baby will be all right," said Bastian, laboring to breathe.

Rhys climbed the porch. "Come on, lads. Let's get all this inside. Take a load each."

Lady Marrowight pointed her sharp-nailed finger at the goblin on the box's cover. "If you don't wish to wake the terrors that lurk in the shadows, you'd best give that book to me."

Lucas nudged Bastian with his shoulder, then signed, "Can you believe this nutjob?"

Lady Marrowight fixed on Lucas. "Is this one trying to speak, or is he just flapping his hands?"

The ache in Bastian's chest clenched.

Lady Marrowight glanced at Rhys, disappearing into the chalet with a heavy load of groceries.

She arched her thin brows and stared at Lucas. "Can he manage to read and write at all?"

Lucas lowered his gaze, like he was struggling to shake off the insult.

Bastian wanted to scream at Lady Marrowight. Hit her. Shove her off the walk and shout at her to get lost.

He battled to find his voice, to tell her that Lucas was smarter than every other student in his class. And he was the best footballer. And the funniest kid he knew. But he could do nothing but stare at her.

Lucas signed, "I wish you'd leave us the hell alone."

"Did he really say something?" asked Lady Marrowight, glancing at Bastian.

Bastian whispered, "He said that we need to go in now."

Lady Marrowight keyed in on Lucas. "Well aren't you smart, to be able to talk at all."

Heat flashed into Bastian's face. That was exactly what the goblin boy had said last night, just before he'd punched Lucas.

Bastian grabbed Lucas' arm and tugged him away from her.

Movement flitted alongside the chalet.

Again, there stood the Sylphic boy—by all counts, a forest child.

He lifted an arrow out of a dark leather quiver affixed to the back of his bandoleer.

Lady Marrowight swatted the air, then locked eyes with Bastian. "Give in to night's sleep, little one."

Bastian tried to back away from her, but couldn't. Lucas seemed likewise frozen.

Lady Marrowight leaned closely to Bastian and whispered, "For ahead lie dark days when no dreamer shall wake."

Though the words were nonsensical, a sense of dreaminess did wash.

Bastian struggled to keep his eyes open. His arm loosened on his boxed book.

The Sylphic boy seemed to be fitting another arrow to his bowstring.

The impression of the Sylphic boy, though somewhat vague, was so real. Wonderfully real. But Lady Marrowight, towering over Bastian, muttering words that felt cold, seemed not just real, but terribly so.

Of the two of them, Lady Marrowight seemed the stronger.

Lady Marrowight's eyes widened as she watched Bastian's fingers slacken from the box.

An arrow streamed in, then burst into flames.

Bastian jolted as if roused from a daydream. He clenched the box to his chest.

Ashes drifted through Lady Marrowight's swatting fingers.

Rhys opened the front door. "Lads. Seriously. Inside. Now." He held the door wide for Lucas and Bastian as they hurried through. "Lady Marrowight, we'll tell Mum you stopped—"

But she was already halfway down the drive.

She went on swatting at nothing, her cardigan billowing, until she disappeared into the woodland path severing their properties.

10

*B*astian sat at the dining room table, staring at Rhys' phone. Da had sent a quick text a few hours earlier saying they were getting settled in the hospital and would know more soon.

Rhys and Lucas had gone up to bed, but Bastian could do nothing but watch the window for headlights; for massive and muscular shapes moving against the night sky.

He wanted to believe that the bookshop clerk had been right—that the book was safe now. That he and his brothers were.

But he didn't feel safe.

And if an instant of security visited him, any inkling of peace, his stomach turned—for they still had no idea what was going on with Mum and the baby.

Bastian pulled his gaze down from the window and opened *Moor Folk of the English Highlands*.

Throughout the evening, he'd tried to read some, but all he could do was fixate on the opening page. Here was drawn a detailed and masterful rendition of a dragon coiling around the words: *May this book lend aid, shielding, and guidance.*

It seemed an outlandish notion—that a mere book, or even the ordinary walls of a stone chalet, might offer protection from things that were extraordinary.

But he wanted it to be true. He needed it to be true.

And if only that shield might extend now to Mum and the baby.

But he had to shake himself out of this paralysis. Master Sayre had instructed him not just to bring the book here to Kingfisher Chalet, but to learn its teachings.

He turned past the dragon and its words of hopeful protection. He paged through the book until a drawing of the Sylphic scope caught his eye.

May the Sylphic scope, fashioned by Kellyn Woodthrush, open the eyes of those destined to see. Peer through it at skies, woods, and hills. Though at first, it will show mere magnifications of common things, in time, its bearer may see anew—it may show things Sylphic.

Bastian drew from his pocket the Sylphic scope Master Sayre had given him.

Master Sayre had mentioned that it was about time for Bastian to have this. But why now? That specific comment made it seem all the more likely that the secret he was guarding had something to do with the coming new baby.

Bastian read on—

To newly born eyes, the Sylphic Kingdom will appear as nothing more than hints of silvered motion—like starry shadows gliding past a pool of moon. With practice peering into dark haunts, it may be that Sylphic forms will grow clear. One might spy wings glistening on the backs of faeries, faces of dryads in trees, naiads splashing in rivers, and forest children ranging with their quivers of arrows across the high moors.

The idea of aiming the scope into Dartmoor's dark places seemed pointless. Bastian knew exactly what the darkness held.

But this passage suggested that, in the dark, more than just danger waited. Dartmoor's darkness might keep Moor Folk. Forest children. Faeries. And in the dark, truths might also be found.

Bastian lifted the scope to his eye and aimed it toward the night-blackened window.

The scope showed him nothing.

He aimed it higher, at the sky's wash of stars.

Through the scope, the stars looked rather normal, though hazed.

He laid down the scope and again picked up the book.

Persist, and may the day come when the Sylphic Kingdom can be seen with unaided eyes. By this relic, may those gifted with insight into Sylphic Lands gain knowledge that will bring to pass triumph.

The phone rang.

Bastian snatched it up. "Da?"

"My lad." There was relief in Da's voice, though he sounded tired. "Are your brothers with you?"

"No, why? What's going on with Mum? Is she okay?"

"Mum's fine. She isn't in labor, and the pain's under control. She's trying to get a little rest."

"And what about the baby?"

"The baby's fine, too."

Bastian took a deep breath and let it go.

"What happened to her?"

"Pregnant women sometimes experience ligament pain," said Da. "The crash apparently triggered it. It isn't abnormal, nor dangerous, though it's terribly agonizing. It's just one of the body's processes, preparing for birth."

Bastian closed his eyes and dropped against the back of his chair.

"Where are Rhys and Lucas?" asked Da.

"Gone to bed."

"You should go to bed, too," said Da. "We'll likely come home soon. There's no reason to wait up."

Considering the degree of pain Mum had been in, and with how close she was to having the baby, bringing her home seemed like a mistake.

"There's no need to rush home," said Bastian. "We're all right. If Mum's in any pain at all, she should stay where she is."

"Mum is, of course, dreadfully worried about you and Lucas."

"Tell her we're fine," said Bastian. "She should stay at the hospital. With the nurses and doctors, okay? Tell her."

"We certainly shall stay if her obstetrician suggests it," said Da. "However he's planning to release Mum following about an hour more of observation. And speaking of doctors, there's an A&E doctor we met who's almost as big of a Kingfisher enthusiast as you are."

Bastian straightened.

"Could you believe that?" asked Da. "He knows the Sylphic legends, he said, by heart."

Bastian had met many people who loosely knew the Sylphic legends. But aside from Master Sayre, he'd never met anyone truly knowledgeable about them. Maybe this doctor could shed some light on the more cryptic passages in *Moor Folk of the English Highlands*.

If Mum spent the night at the hospital in Exeter, she might be in the care of this doctor—someone who knew about Sun Children.

And if Mum stayed where she was—and if Bastian and his brothers visited tomorrow—he might meet this doctor.

"Tell Mum to stay at the hospital, and goodnight," said Bastian. "Tomorrow, Rhys can drive Lucas and me back to Exeter. We can take care of anything Mum needs."

"What Mum needs, lad, is for you to rest. Try and get some sleep, all right?"

"That A&E doctor," said Bastian, "tell him I said Sylphic legends are the coolest. Say I want to talk to him sometime."

"If I see him again, I certainly shall. For now, though, please rest. Do that for Mum, okay?"

BASTIAN CLIMBED the stairs to the lamplit bedroom he shared with Lucas—a large room ringed with short shelves Da had fitted to accommodate their growing collections of natural treasures: winged seeds, heart-shaped stones, leaf samplings, shriveled mushrooms, pressed flowers, and acorns sporting all styles of caps.

Lucas was well asleep.

Bastian lay down in the darkness, one hand clutching his book, the other holding Woodthrush's Sylphic scope.

He tried to relax, but he couldn't keep his eyes closed. Because when he closed his eyes, he could think about nothing but the massive, muscled goblin that'd stood in the middle of the road, his dark, gleaming sword pointed at the sky.

Bastian willed himself to think of something else, but the only other thought that would visit him was of Lady Marrowight.

He rubbed at his chest, at the ache that'd been a nuisance since she'd laid into them with her meanness. He all over again felt the ice in her stare; the jab of her insults.

Relief finally came from visualizing biking to Marrowight Manor and having it out with her.

He studied Lucas, who seemed to be having no trouble resting. That Lucas had shaken off Lady Marrowight's insults so easily made the problem seem all the worse. Lucas might be growing used to this—hateful people taking dirty shots.

Bastian turned on a dim reading light and angled it away from Lucas. Inside its golden glow, he opened his book to a section entitled: *Legends of the Sun Child.*

On the first page, there rested a sketch—lifelike—of a boy somewhere around his age with a mop of curly hair and a clever grin.

The caption read: *Aubrey Gyrfalcon, the first Sun Child.*

Bastian startled at a pair of underwear landing squarely on the open pages of his book.

Lucas pushed to an elbow and signed, "Do you know if Da called?"

Bastian gingerly unloaded the underwear onto the floor. "Mum's okay," he signed. "The baby is, too. They're coming home soon—though, I think they should stay at the hospital."

"How's that book?" signed Lucas.

"Wonderful, I think," signed Bastian. "I haven't been able to focus enough to read much."

"Did Rhys talk to you before he went to bed?"

"No," signed Bastian. "Why?"

"He came across a news article you'll like. There were reports today of people seeing figures appearing and vanishing on tors throughout Dartmoor. Ask him to show you tomorrow."

Figures appearing and vanishing. That was exactly what Bastian had seen.

"Can you believe so many people claimed to have seen that?" signed Lucas. "And can you believe this sort of stuff makes the news?"

"I know you don't believe any of it," signed Bastian.

Though Lucas often ribbed him for his obsession with Sylphic legends, he seemed, at times, to envy Bastian's engagement with them. Probably, he was more captivated than he let on.

And now, after having seen something unexplainable in the road today, he might be even a bit more interested.

Lucas glanced at Bastian's book. "You're wanting to read a bit to me, aren't you?"

"You'd only make fun of me," signed Bastian.

Lucas, grinning, snuggled into the quilt their grandmamma had stitched for him, cut from squares of his favorite stage-curtain red.

"Tomorrow's your birthday," he signed, "so why shouldn't I let you have some fun?"

"Actually," signed Bastian, "this section about the Sun Child does seem pretty captivating."

Lucas shrugged and signed, "Bring on the Sun Child."

Bastian propped the book on a pillow. Signing, he read—

"Long ago, before the tallest peak in England was shorn to softness by sea winds and summer rains, it was known as the Golden Moor. No one in those ancient days ever ascended that high hill, though its top seemed fertile and warm, with sunlight shimmering from the green.

"Its slopes, you see, were steep, and when the misty rains would come, they'd slick and turn as treacherous as icy stones. None, in fact, ever ventured up the Golden Moor, save beasts, and birds, and one brave boy named Aubrey Gyrfalcon."

Bastian turned the gilded page.

Lucas twisted to his side, facing Bastian more fully.

Bastian read on—

"Aubrey was the child of the Sun Devaa, who reigns over England's Sylphic Kingdom, and Caelia, a mortal maiden of the seaside who'd fled into the wilds during a violent storm. Caelia almost died, but stars scattered rumors of the passage of a woman of unrivaled kindness.

"When the Sun Devaa found her, he fell deeply in love. He healed her and crowned her his queen.

"The baby born to them was the first Sun Child—partly star, partly mortal, and heir to the silver throne set upon the Golden Moor. Aubrey Gyrfalcon was a wise child who carried sunlight in his heart and the blue of shining seas within his eyes.

"Now and then, a human child with royal lineage from the people native to the Golden Moor is born a Sun Child. To this imperial ancestry, Sun Children owe their uncommon intelligence, bravery, and compassion. Sun Children carry a destiny to love and defend the Sylphic Kingdom."

Bastian glanced up at Lucas. "Do you think these stories of Sun Children might be based in any truth?"

Lucas just stared at him, on his face—a slight cringe.

"I'll take that as a 'no.'" Bastian turned the page.

"One warm summer night, in a village cobbled with stones as bright as honey, near the brink of the Golden Moor, another Sun Child was born. His name was Kellyn Woodthrush.

"Though Kellyn was born to mortal parents, he was no ordinary mortal boy. He was distantly descended from Aubrey Gyrfalcon and had inherited the sun blood of his forbearers.

"Kellyn grew in peace inside his lowland home, dreaming of valorous feats.

"One starry night, a wise woman in his village cast an enchantment on Kellyn. 'Sun Child, wake up. For the fate of the world depends on your courage.'"

Bastian laid the book in his lap.

Lucas, watching him, seemed very engaged.

"Imagine that," Bastian signed. "A child, Sylphic and powerful, born into an ordinary family."

"I see what you're thinking," signed Lucas, looking at him with a slight smile that was jeering. "You're wondering if our new brother is going to be a Sun Child."

Bastian worked to keep his expression neutral. "That isn't what I was thinking." Signing, he read on—

"On the day of his coming-of-age, Kellyn's ancient blood woke, and he spied on the gleaming heights figures of Moor Folk. Kellyn packed a satchel of bread and beans, kissed his mother and father goodbye, and ventured to climb the Golden Moor.

"While he was on his way to the highlands, the villagers stopped Kellyn and cautioned him not to go, warning him that wicked Elemental Spirits haunted those hills.

"For they believed that the shining beauty Kellyn had seen was a bait set to draw fools who'd find themselves stunned blind or cast into stone or captured and held for dark purposes."

"Was Kellyn Woodthrush stunned blind or set in stone or captured?" signed Lucas, yawning largely, using his toes to drag comic books from beneath his bed. "Read just the ending."

Bastian closed the book. "When you treat a story carelessly, it sucks the fun out of it."

"You mean—since I don't actually believe any of this, I'm sucking the fun out of it."

In signing the tale to Lucas, the way Bastian had often done since he was small and first learning to sign stories, *Moor Folk of the English Highlands* felt like just a collection of imagined legends.

Bastian set the book on the shelf beside his Rudyard Kipling collection, and next to a model galley ship with sly, triangular sails.

"Come on, don't be a poor sport," signed Lucas. "How does the chapter end?"

Bastian signed, "Da said we should try and get some sleep." He turned off the lamp.

As he lay down, he listened for the gentle stirrings he'd grown used to at night—whispers of winds that seemed to hold chanted words, calming chimes, far-off birdcalls, lullabies of pan flutes and pipes, songs of crashing waves.

Often, the Sylphic sounds he heard seemed stronger at night.

But now, there were none.

Lucas, it seemed, had gone straight to sleep again, almost the moment the light went off.

In that unsettling, absolute stillness, Bastian felt utterly alone.

If only Lucas could lend these legends the credence they deserved.

It would be so relieving if even one other person in his family were willing to acknowledge that Sylphic legends harbored at least some bit of truth.

A slight, high-pitched ringing sounded.

Bastian sat up some.

The sound was clear, but distant. It was unlike any Sylphic sound he'd yet heard.

He sat up all the way.

The ringing—high-pitched and weak at first, strengthened. It wasn't soothing but seemed sharp and irregular, like a cry of pain.

Bastian glanced around the dark room.

Nothing Sylphic, nothing goblin-like, seemed near.

He climbed out of bed and peered out the window.

He could see nothing Sylphic—no glowing mist, no lit figures, no red eyes seething from the woodland.

He pushed open the window.

A swirl of energetic wind seemed to sweep in an echo of voices—crying voices. And then there was a sharp, pealing sound—metallic, like a blade drawn from a steel scabbard. And following that, a clamor of terrible screaming.

Bastian jumped as the bedroom door squealed.

It was Da, striding in. He toed aside a microscope and moved a half-built rocket to a shelf.

"Where's Mum?" asked Bastian.

"She's comfortably settled in bed," said Da.

"How long have you been home?"

"Not long. We wanted to let you sleep if you were sleeping. But I thought I heard somebody bumping around in here."

"Why'd you bring Mum home?" Bastian sat on his bed.

"Mum's not sick, you know," said Da. "Pregnancy and childbirth are normal, healthy things. Even the pain that struck her today is quite common."

The sounds of crying—of screaming—through the window grew stronger. They sounded like they were coming from the north, from where Marrowight Manor loomed. The commotion seemed to set off the pain more sharply in Bastian's chest. It was as though other mothers, other families, other sons, were in agony or grieving; as though others were being stunned cold by goblins or injured by terrible words.

The screaming suddenly ceased.

Thick clouds sailed in and vanquished the stars.

The coming storm brought a darkness so thick, it seemed breathing out in the black night had to be impossible.

"Are you sore anyplace from the car crash?" asked Da.

Bastian waited, his eyes on the window. He listened.

He heard nothing.

The silence was more blood-curdling than the screaming had been. It seemed that at any second, whatever had called up those cries might swoop in and lash him.

Da flipped on the reading lamp. "Let's have a look at you."

Lucas sat up and rubbed his eyes.

Da angled Bastian's face away from the window. "Have you dealt with any headache tonight?"

"I'm fine," said Bastian. "The medic said I was fine."

"Rhys tells me you've seemed all right," said Da, "but is there anything you've not mentioned?"

"I'm a little stiff, I guess, but that's all."

Lucas signed, "Has the baby come?"

"No—it won't be long now, though," said Da, signing. "The obstetrician predicts he'll arrive in the next several days."

A misty breeze lilted in through the window.

This was an old sensation—one of the first Bastian had experienced.

It was as though the night air were ferrying the sweet fragrance of dilating moon flowers and a tinge of the briny sea. Its gentleness soothed the aching in his chest and seemed to fend back the fear of whatever had summoned those cries of pain.

Da shut the window. "Is something else bothering you, lad? You do seem quite dazed."

"Lady Marrowight came by earlier," said Bastian, signing.

Da chuckled. "Ah, yes. Rhys said you three had to shake her off."

"I hate the way she makes me feel," said Bastian, signing. "And you wouldn't believe what she said to Lucas."

Da faced Lucas and signed, "What did she say?"

"It doesn't matter," signed Lucas. "She's bonkers."

"Being bonkers isn't any excuse for being cruel," said Bastian.

"No, indeed," said Da. "We'll have to have a word, the next time we see her, won't we?"

Bastian shrugged. "If I can muster the nerve even to speak to her. When she insulted him, I"—he met Da's eyes—"I froze."

Da crouched beside Bastian's bed. "I'm so thankful, my lad, that you were with Mum today. You were magnificent, she said, taking the wheel when she lost control. You're a quick thinker and so smart. Because of your deftness, your fine judgment, she's sleeping, safe. And your new brother is well on his way."

The expression on Da was sheer pride.

Bastian didn't have the heart to tell him how wrong he was. That it was luck that'd saved them, or some force beyond his control. That he knew exactly what'd stood in the road, and if he could've just dealt with it in the park the night before, the accident could never have happened. That if he could've just handled the goblin in Exeter, Lucas wouldn't have had stitches placed in his forehead today, the car wouldn't be wrecked, and Mum—pregnant—wouldn't have gone through the trauma of a bad accident.

Da patted Bastian's chest. "Let's all try to get some sleep, shall we?"

"How can we sleep now, knowing the baby might come any minute?" signed Lucas. "I still haven't decided on the first sign I'll teach him."

"There's plenty of time for such planning," said Da, signing.

Bastian glanced at the light in the hallway, spilling from Mum's lamp. "Do you think the baby really could come tonight?"

"He may." Da snugged the quilt—blue and elaborately stitched, softened by patches from Bastian's beloved granddadda's shirts—around him. "And that's all the more reason that you must try to sleep."

Bastian raised to his elbows. "Can I ask you something? Even if it's sort of wild."

Da sat on the edge of the bed, making the springs squeak.

"What would happen," asked Bastian, "if our baby turned out to be a bit...different?"

"I expect he will be different," said Da, signing. "So far, no two of you have turned out anything alike."

Lucas, grinning, let his comic book flop onto his belly and signed, "Bastian believes we're destined to get a Sun Child."

Da lifted a brow.

Bastian glanced at Lucas. "You saying it makes it seem mad."

"Because—it is mad," signed Lucas.

Da eased Bastian to lying back down. "Whether he's a Sun Child or not, the baby will certainly need you."

Some small part in Bastian's chest warmed at those words. Da might discredit the Sylphic legends, but at least he wasn't making fun.

"There'll be baths and feedings," said Da. "And babies insist on being walked all the time."

"And there'll be crying, and messes, and the baby will get into everything," signed Lucas. "Not to mention, if he is a Sun Child, there's no telling what the diapers will be like."

Da chuckled as he rose.

He flicked off the light and left, closing the door softly behind him.

Bastian lay awake in the dun silence, thinking of how tiny the baby's foot had felt, inside Mum. A sense of wonder washed.

Lady Marrowight, then, drifted to mind.

Lady Marrowight, speaking hatefully. Lady Marrowight's mad stare fixing on him. Lady Marrowight, warning of dark days ahead.

The sense of wonder morphed into a fit of cold sweat, and the ache in his chest again deepened.

At times, the pain seemed to be coming from a material substance—like there was actual ice or cold metal in his chest.

He trolled *Moor Folk of the English Highlands* back off the shelf, along with a flashlight. He shone the beam on its cover.

He touched the faerie's wings, the Sylphic boy's muscled arm.

If the baby did turn out to be a Sun Child, that would mean Bastian himself would actually be connected to the Sylphic Kingdom. If that happened, he could teach his new brother its legends.

His new brother, a Sun Child, would certainly believe them. Even if no one else ever would.

He tossed his covers over his head and lit the page he'd last read.

Undaunted by the warnings of peril, compelled by the sunlight rushing in his blood, Kellyn Woodthrush braved the Golden Moor and scaled its fearsome heights. He found the Moor desolate, but for whispers lilting through mist—offers to teach him the art of seeing Moor Folk.

Posing for hours at the crown of the Moor, breathing slowly, his arms crossing his chest, his eyes wide open—just so—Kellyn waited and watched.

Day after day, night after night, he practiced his forms for seeing Moor Folk. And gradually, between the shades of sleeping trees, visions emerged. Spiritual and smoke they were at first, but Kellyn grew to be so skilled a seer that the Moor Folk assumed solid forms and would sit with him, whispering their wisdom and histories.

Finally, the Sun Devaa himself appeared on the Golden Moor and revealed to Kellyn that he was a Sun Child, destined to wage a great battle.

The battle that Kingfisher now described as coming seemed every bit as dreadful as what Kellyn Woodthrush had faced.

And the thought of the new baby at its front sent a chill zipping down Bastian's spine.

Yet the idea of the Sun Child, his own brother, destined for adventure and bravery, entrusted to save the Sylphic Kingdom from something terrible—it was thrilling.

Bastian flipped further in.

On almost every page lay an odd emblem—an eye, embellished with swirls. It seemed like a hieroglyph, although it was possible that it was more decorative than meaningful.

He explored further on, reaching a page heavily worn and marked by a crack in the spine.

There lay a picture of the goblin from the cover. And beside it scrolled a caption: *Kek—Goblin King, enemy of Moor Folk.*

Bastian hurried on to a centerfold where lay a map that showed Kingfisher Chalet, drawn at the western edge of a woodland.

He sat tall, a sense of importance striking from seeing drawn in this book the very place he now called home.

North of Kingfisher Chalet squatted a marbled gray and black square with spires shaped like hornet stingers—a good semblance of Marrowight Manor. To the east were scattered cottages and streams along many paths he'd never explored.

One sketched path, though, was familiar. It meandered through a thicket of trees labeled: *The Wystan Woods.*

These he knew well, and not just by the division they drew between Kingfisher Chalet and Marrowight Manor.

The Wystan Woods also stretched south and east of Kingfisher Chalet, and the path through them led to the Ryudo pitch and finished at a wide pool—the Natterjack Lagoon—a favorite haunt of his, named for the striped, green-on-green Natterjack toads that bubbled from its waters like plague and rasped like a choir of hobgoblins.

The lagoon's gathered waters were emerald and still, ever keeping a mystical peace.

The page beside the map read—

The waters flowing through Dartmoor carry wonders, not the least of which are budding flowers, sprouting toads, and hatching roe.

A Keeper of a Sun Child would do well to explore them, for here grows the prize of pygmyweed—a water plant that serves Sun Children as a charm of protection.*

**The Keeper of the Sun Child is a champion, a sentry, a guide who bears the task of awakening the light in the Sun Child's blood, teaching the Child about England's Sylphic Kingdom, and preparing the Child for the coming battle: The Day of the Dark Sun. May the Keeper find the Sun Child valiant, and may the Sylphic Kingdom shine beneath a dawning night of stars.*

Perhaps this task—being a Sun Child's Keeper—was what Master Sayre had been training Bastian for.

Tomorrow, Bastian would turn fourteen, which was plenty old enough to be good for such a task. And he'd invested years upon years into hard-core Ryudo training.

He closed the book, but he couldn't put it down. He found his eyes drawn to the painting of the Sylphic boy on its cover.

He studied the boy's expression—dauntless under the fiery stare of that goblin.

The Sylphic Kingdom, the Moor Folk, Ryudo, this book—they were all about courage.

In the starry blue deepness of the night, Bastian resolved to look after the baby, to do whatever he must to awaken the light in his new brother's blood.

In trying to handle a fight, Bastian had not done right by Lucas. But as *Keeper of the Sun Child*, he'd be a champion, a sentry, a guide behind the scenes.

Perhaps he'd be better at that.

He flipped to the first page of a colorful section he'd passed earlier —one of rites, enchantments, and charms for awakening the blood of a Sun Child.

He straightened the page.

These, he'd master. And very soon, he'd deliver to the Sylphic Kingdom its champion, its Sun Child.

Clutching the book, Bastian drifted into a fitful sleep beneath visions of standing in a garb of light armor, gripping a sword, its tip dripping with the black blood of goblins, a baby Sun Child cradled in his arms.

11

In the rustic quiet that lingers before dawn sheers the night away, Bastian's bedroom window shifted from emptiness to a watery, beckoning blue.

Through the window, the new moon—a barely-detectable circle of deepness—seemed to cast a pallor of shade on the hill behind Kingfisher Chalet.

The moon was coasting skyward with a strong determination that Bastian could almost sense, though it was rising in a lightless, spent way. Yet for all that, the stars near to it shone on, brightly silver, from the bleak dawning sky.

The fresh hour was so starlit and dreamy, no one else in the chalet had stirred. Bastian rose and tiptoed down the stairs, taking care not to wake anyone.

The dusk of the waning night cast the empty rooms he passed as chasms, dark and deep. It distorted the stretch of the hallways, the slope of the stairs, making them feel curved and devious. And the shadows of bookshelves and chairs seemed like abysmal black pools of shade.

"If you don't wish to wake the terrors that lurk in the shadows..." Lady Marrowight's recalled words.

Bastian crept past corners that seemed to slant.

He hurried through the den, trying not to see the ottoman that, in the waning night's dark, seemed precisely the shape of a crouched goblin.

The dining room's angular shadows seemed to be watching for him to catch a toe on a rug; seemed to be waiting for the fall that would slow him—stop him—land him in the grip of something deadly.

He raced into the kitchen and threw open the back door. He stumbled into the quicksilver cradle of dawn.

The weedy, dark yard rested callow and windless. Soundless. The sky stretched vast and indigo, with the brighter stars gleaming on, though the east was steadily paling. Translucent billows of clouds floated above the horizon like the frozen exhalations of celestial blue whales cajoling beneath the rim of the Earth.

On the hilltop rising at the east end of the yard, there seemed to be a faint play of color—white and golden lights that seemed not to have any origin.

He wandered into the yard's center and settled on a patch of dewy grass. He watched the unearthly lights flicker in a mist weaving through the still rowan berry bushes.

Whether that strange haze was an effect of the early hour or Moor Folk drifting nearby—Moor Folk waiting, perhaps, as he was, for the birth of the Sun Child—he couldn't guess. All he knew was that he was on the brink of something extraordinary.

The shimmering mist rolled over the hilltop and cascaded down.

The fluid whiteness swayed like spirits dancing. Sunlight crept up the side of the planet, its gentleness outlining the barely-there glow of the new moon.

Though the fire of the day star was yet beneath the eastern trees, Bastian grew warm by its coming.

He heard, behind him, the soft click of the back door opening.

It was Mum coming outside. Warming her hands on an earthenware teacup, she leaned forward against the porch rail.

Somewhere in the Wystan Woods, a thrush nightingale trilled, calling for the dawn.

Well, that did it.

Mum dropped her cup, ceramic shards scattering.

The thrush cried again, and Mum sank to her knees.

Bastian rushed across the yard and up onto the porch.

Mum pushed to an elbow. "Get Da."

Bastian raced inside and bounded up the stairs. He threw open Da's door.

At just catching Bastian's glance, Da sprang out of bed.

Bastian ran into Rhys' room.

Rhys pushed to sitting up. "Is it Mum?"

Da, buttoning his shirt, hurried past. "Dress quickly."

Lucas, rubbing his eyes, stumbled into the hallway. Da handed him a suitcase and signed, "Straight to the car."

Bastian ran to his room and grabbed his rucksack and *Moor Folk of the English Highlands*. He started to pack it, but—Master Sayre had told him to bring it here, to his chalet, the safest place.

Should he leave it behind?

With the Sun Child actually coming, though, he couldn't possibly leave it behind.

He'd done what'd been asked of him—he'd brought it to Kingfisher Chalet. And now he felt in his bones that he needed to keep this book with him. He needed to read it, to understand it.

Bastian looked at the inscription in the opening of the book—

May this book lend aid, shielding, and guidance.

If there was anything enchanted about this book, anything protective, then bringing it to the hospital seemed imperative. Hospitals were places of healing, and births were joyous occasions, certainly. But Bastian couldn't shake the dread rising from the recognition that not every birth ended happily.

He'd wished last night that whatever protection the book held might extend to Mum and the baby. Maybe by keeping it close to them today, it actually could.

He crammed the book in his rucksack and ran downstairs and to the car.

Da helped Mum ease into the front seat as Bastian and his brothers filed into the back.

The instant they closed the doors, Da took off, hustling out of the driveway and down the lane.

The way leading to the hospital in Exeter wound close to Marrowight Manor—punching its spiny black turrets through the green woodland canopy. Just driving past the manor made Bastian shiver. Lucas seemed to be avoiding looking at it.

As they sped down the lane, Bastian jolted at Mum's every cry. He bit his lip, watching her breathe raggedly, Da's hand fluttering over her back, randomly patting her through fits of screaming.

"Maybe this is what happened yesterday," signed Lucas. "Lots of pain, but no labor."

Rhys signed back. "Da said Mum's water broke." He caught the gazes of both Bastian and Lucas. "Everything's going to be all right."

Da skidded the car to a stop at the hospital's entrance.

Bastian jumped out and opened Mum's door. Da greeted a midwife at the A&E entrance, who guided Mum to sit in a wheelchair and led them all inside. She took Mum away down a hall labeled: *Birthing Center*.

Bastian stood staring down the corridor after her until Rhys nudged him to come away.

He followed Rhys into a vacant waiting room, silent but for the buzzing of fluorescent bulbs.

"How long does it take to deliver a baby?" asked Bastian.

Lucas drew a comic book from his rucksack. "Not long. You didn't take long, I think."

"Bastian took ages." Rhys pulled out snack bundles Mum had packed weeks ago. "Mum was in labor for two full days, and when Bastian finally came, he was blue."

Bastian sat beside Lucas. "You don't remember the story? I almost died."

"I remember Bastian the blue baby, of course," signed Lucas. "But I didn't remember that it took two days." He dumped snacks and juice boxes onto his lap and shifted some into Bastian's. "I hope the baby does get on with it. If he hurries, I could still make football practice."

"Not a chance of that." Rhys concocted a rough pillow from all their jackets. "Best get cozy."

Urgent voices flooded the corridor.

"Mum." Bastian raced to the door and opened it.

A medical team rushed by, wheeling an occupied bed.

Not Mum.

They disappeared through a set of swinging doors, leading to the birthing center.

Bastian peered beyond the swinging doors into the distant hallway. There, he caught sight of a vague mist meandering. The vapor was carrying a slight glow—like the mist on the hilltop behind the chalet had.

As the swinging doors stilled, a snapping sound—shimmery—rose. It was like the tinkling of small bells. The shivery delicacy of it raised goosebumps on the nape of his neck.

A whisper curled through the corridor—"*Sun Child, wake up.*" Words from Kingfisher's book.

A tap on his shoulder made Bastian jump.

He turned.

Lucas, his mouth full of candy, signed. "What are you looking at?"

Bastian again faced the hallway. It was now nothing more than a dull, gray-green corridor, cloaked in quiet.

He signed back, "Nothing."

Hours later, there still was no baby.

Da hadn't come back to the waiting room—not even once. Bastian had grown so anxious, he'd taken up making hourly trips to the nurse's station to inquire after Mum.

The nurses would just smile and gently direct him back to the waiting room, assuring him Da would return the minute there was news.

Rhys and Lucas were now lounging together amidst a wreckage of empty snack boxes and foils, distracting themselves from hunger by exploring women's magazines.

Bastian, able to do nothing but stare at the clock ticking, sat toying with his Sylphic scope. He'd tried to read from *Moor Folk of the English Highlands*, several times, but he found himself incapable of studying it.

All he could think about was the memory of Mum's face in the car, tear-streaked.

Throughout the day, Lucas and Rhys had gathered a respectable collection of board games from various waiting rooms and had suggested a tournament.

But in trying to play, Bastian couldn't keep his attention off the clock, off the door, off the frenzied sounds of people hurrying along the corridor.

Lucas had tried to engage him in the magazines, and Rhys had even offered to let Bastian mess around on his phone—a privilege he allowed rarely.

But Bastian couldn't focus on any of it.

Rhys opened the last box of Maltesers and reached a handful to Bastian.

Bastian didn't look at him. "Something's wrong."

"We don't know that." Rhys gave Lucas a ration. "Remember what Da told us about labor," he said, signing. "It's usually unpredictable."

He pressed a fistful of candy against Bastian's hand.

Bastian didn't take it.

Instead, he stood and went to the waiting room door. He peered out, hoping to see Da coming through those swinging doors. He looked again for the shining mist. Listened for Sylphic sounds.

The peculiar haze was gone, and the hallway now stood in complete silence.

Untouched by any daylight, the corridor looked miserable—like a pathway delivering its unfortunate travelers to terrible endings.

The last time they'd been at this hospital was when Granddadda was sick. Everyone thought he'd just be here a day. But he'd never come home.

Bastian glanced back at his brothers. "People die in hospitals."

"Everything's all right." Rhys coaxed him back in. "You'll see."

"If things were all right, Da would've at least checked on us," said Bastian, signing. "We haven't seen him in seven hours."

Rhys guided him to sit down. "I know."

WHEN THE LIGHT streaming through the window into the waiting room shifted golden with evening, Bastian drew *Moor Folk of the English Highlands* out of his rucksack. So much time had passed, it seemed worthwhile to try studying it again.

He stretched out on his back, on the hard-carpeted floor, and held the book—open to the section on Sun Children—before him.

Special things were said to happen to Sun Children. Weird and wonderful things, like their chests brightening, as though a star were lighting them from within; shining birthmarks appearing and vanishing; their new voices speaking, calling faeries by name to be born into the Sylphic Kingdom.

And then, some coming-of-age rite of passage called "waking" happened to them at thirteen.

Bastian's own thirteenth birthday had been awful. It'd fallen just days after that first encounter with the goblin in Exeter.

He was too sick to celebrate—or, not sick, exactly. More, he was sad, with the ache in his chest sharp and new.

Bastian shuddered off the memory. He flipped the page and read—

The mothers of Sun Children often suffer greatly, for Sun Children never come until the stars rise.

Bastian rolled onto his knees. "Do you think Mum is suffering greatly?"

Rhys and Lucas, leaning together over a magazine on childbirth, didn't answer.

Bastian went to them. "Hey—is Mum suffering?"

"Of course she is," said Rhys, signing back. "Suffering's a normal part of getting a child."

Bastian held up his book. "Or a Sun Child."

Lucas rolled his eyes.

Rhys elbowed him and signed, "Go easy."

"All right, then," signed Lucas. "If the baby is a Sun Child, how would we know?"

"According to Kingfisher, there are signs." Bastian flipped back a few pages and read—

"A common sign of an infant Sun Child is a Sun Kiss—a small star, or moon, appearing and vanishing on the baby's face."

Lucas seemed to be having difficulty concealing a grin.

"There are also enchantments that can set the blood of a Sun Child to shine," said Bastian, signing. "That's called *sun dowsing*. One involves an apple switch and winter gooseberries, and I've seen that the crops in the woods are growing very ripe. I'm planning to try it."

"Those winter gooseberries are close to spoiling," said Rhys. "Even if you harvested them this morning, they'd go to rot before Mum and the baby could come home."

"They're ripening, sure, but they're not too far gone yet," said Bastian, signing. "In fact, as golden and swollen as they are, they're at the perfect stage for collecting. And Kingfisher says gooseberries can be frozen and still used for months in enchantments."

"So—you're now believing that you can brew magical spells—using frozen fruit?" signed Lucas. "Aren't you taking this a bit far?"

"It's good he's found a distraction," signed Rhys. "Even if it is a bit mad."

"This isn't mad," said Bastian, signing. "The ritual reads like a biology experiment or something."

Rhys and Lucas didn't meet his eyes.

Bastian felt legitimately ridiculous for admitting to his brothers that he was giving credence to Kingfisher's fantastical book. It was a bare fact, though, that every word in it was absolutely true.

Soon, his whole family would have to accept that a Sun Child had been born to them, and they'd all be better off if they were prepared. After all, the birth of the Sun Child meant that the Sylphic Kingdom was on the brink of battle between forces none of them could understand. And having a Sun Child in their family—it meant they'd be involved.

"The gooseberry charm is an older rite," said Bastian, signing.

Rhys and Lucas exchanged controlled expressions.

Bastian flipped further on a few pages carefully, treating the book like the academic text that it was. "According to this," he said, signing, "more recently, an enchantment's been developed that involves river stones and witch hazel. But that one would be difficult, because—"

Lucas reached and closed Bastian's book.

Bastian met his eyes. "Why wouldn't you want to know this?"

"It's just—I'm not sure it's all that helpful," signed Lucas.

Bastian glanced at Rhys. "Do you want to know it?"

Rhys gently drew the book out of Bastian's hands and set it aside. "Let's cool the fantasy talk for a bit."

Bastian dropped beside him into a chair.

Next to him, on the wall, hung a map of the hospital.

Bastian studied it, homing in on where their waiting room was located.

Just down the hall from here stood the A&E wing.

Maybe if he explored it, he'd find the A&E doctor Da had told him about—the doctor who knew Sylphic legends by heart.

The waiting room door swung.

Da, ruffle-haired and glassy-eyed, stepped in.

Bastian jumped up and rushed to him. "Mum—is she okay? Has the baby come?"

Da said nothing. He just pulled Bastian into a long hug.

Rhys stood.

So did Lucas, signing, "What's wrong?"

"This brother of yours is giving Mum some trouble," signed Da.

That was right in line with what *Moor Folk of the English Highlands* seemed to predict. Kingfisher had clearly described how Sun Children, at birth, often cause their mothers to suffer greatly.

Perhaps things were happening just as they should.

"Is she close?" asked Rhys.

"It's going to be a while yet, I'm afraid," said Da, signing.

That, too, seemed to make sense. Kingfisher had plainly written that Sun Children never were born until the stars were out.

Bastian cradled his chin. "What time do the stars normally brighten?"

Da eased past him and slumped into a seat. He buried his face in his hands.

Rhys stood closely behind Bastian and Lucas, his hands on their shoulders. "What can we do?"

Da eased to sitting straight. "That's exactly the problem."

He wasn't crying, but he looked like he might.

"There's nothing to do. Your Mum...she isn't handling the labor normally. It's put her in danger, in fact."

"That can't..." signed Lucas. "Mum was supposed to...the baby was safe, they said. He should've been born already."

"Indeed," said Da, signing. "The baby can't safely stay unborn much longer."

"Then they'll just take him surgically." Rhys held up a magazine. "Apparently loads of women end up with C-sections."

"That wouldn't be safe for Mum at this point," said Da, signing. "The obstetrician says the best thing we can do is wait for Mum to stabilize, for either surgery or birth."

"Stabilize..." Bastian pulled back. "Mum isn't stable?"

Da stood. "I must go to her."

Stabilize.

Bastian couldn't draw breath. Lucas, beside him, was crying.

Da handed his wallet to Rhys. "Look after them. I'll come back when there's news."

Rhys eased Bastian into a chair. "Deep breaths."

Da tipped Bastian's chin up. "We're still in the shorter days of spring. Watch the sunset while you wait, and presently, you'll see stars."

Lucas laid *Moor Folk of the English Highlands* open in Bastian's lap.

Bastian couldn't bear to meet the trouble on Rhys' face, nor the tears on Lucas. He couldn't muster the nerve to read anything more from Kingfisher about Sun Children, knowing his own was in peril. Knowing Mum wasn't stable.

He watched the sun slip, then swell into a molten disc of silvery red before it finally dropped beneath the sharp-edged horizon.

One-by-one, tiny white stars bloomed.

12

he next thing Bastian knew, he was inside a dream of walking with Mum across a high moor carpeted with spiraling ferns.

The sun, veiled by a shimmering, summery haze, hovered low. Cumulus clouds careened, scattering patches of silver beams over the blue pools of heather. The sharp scent of crushed wildflowers wove into the wind.

Bastian pulled Mum to kneeling. He laid *Moor Folk of the English Highlands* atop a tuft of butterwort and turned to an illustration of a baby.

The newborn Sun Child in the book was tiny. Perfect. Waves seeming to have escaped from the sea curled their crests into his hair.

Lights in the sky overhead—waking stars—brightened, one by one, until finally they blazed in a marvelous chorus that shone in the Sun Child's sapphire eyes.

Bastian and Mum together startled as the baby came to life on the page, cooing and twisting there like a marooned fish.

Bastian stroked the newborn's cheek—tiny and tan.

Nothing ever had felt so soft.

The baby took Bastian's finger into his mouth, gripping it between his tiny hands.

The body of the moon slid in front of the sun, and stars burst between clouds.

Daylight drained from everything, and color sped from the Earth.

The baby, set in steely tones, his oceanic hair luminous with streaks of moon, dozed in a rapid onset of night.

The shivering of wind chimes, of pan flutes and pipes, lifted. A quiet surging of the distant sea sang.

Bastian jolted awake in a cold sweat in the black waiting room.

Rhys and Lucas were slumped together, both fast asleep.

Bastian crept past them and went to the window.

Outside, the midnight starscape was glittering over the countryside.

That night sky, though beautiful with its billion-fold galaxies, struck him as confounding. That things had to be so complex, so dangerous, so despairing—it troubled him to the point where he felt he might collapse underneath so much sorrow.

He watched the stars sparkle as he drew deep breaths.

He touched Rhys' phone, plugged in under the window. On it, he found no message from Da.

For hours and hours more to have passed—long hours when all the stars were alight—with no word...it seemed the only explanation was that Mum still wasn't stable. That the Sun Child—unable to stay safely unborn for long—still hadn't come.

Bastian glanced at the chair he'd been resting in and considered trying to go back to sleep.

But how could he sleep now, knowing there'd still been no word from Da?

And if he did fall asleep again in this despairing waiting room, the nightmares that might visit would likely be of the worst sort—imaginings of the dreadful news that could come.

Bastian quietly walked to the hospital map. He traced the hallways that led to the A&E department.

Who knew, but that the doctor who'd spoken to Da about Sylphic legends was right there, just around the corner?

Hugging his book, feeling Woodthrush's Sylphic scope heavy in his pocket, he silently moved through the waiting room door.

The second his foot hit the corridor tiles, the shivery strains of bells, of chimes, sounded.

The sensations grew clearer as he followed a dimly lit hallway that led to the A&E wing.

Halfway there, he reached a wall of windows—the nursery where newborn babies were kept.

The newborns were all bundled in identical wrappings, like a row of battered bangers waiting to be fried. Each had a tiny, squashed face sculpted into either a slack look of relaxation or a ruddy, tearful mask of rage. The hair crowning them ranged from peachy white fuzz to dark, matted pelts.

All the newborns, even the fat ones, were smaller than Bastian imagined they'd be. He couldn't determine whether holding one would feel dense like an armload of puppy, or airy like a hollow-boned bird.

A nurse in the room with the babies caught Bastian's glance. She loosed the bindings off one of the newborns.

The unspun baby stretched, her miniature arms and legs unbending, her tiny hands opening like moonlit cereus blooms.

The baby's bassinet was identified with her mother's name.

Bastian followed the windows, checking the labels on each.

None of the babies belonged to his family.

As Bastian reached the hall's end, the soft chiming seemed to strengthen. There, an open door revealed a softly lit room labeled *Doctor's Lounge*.

Bastian crept to it.

Inside, a man—a doctor, presumably—illumined by a single low lamp, sat alone. He was wearing pale green scrubs and looked a bit wild with fair hair corkscrewing out of a knot on the top of his head. He was marking careful notes in a journal.

The shivery sounds seemed to be manifesting in a glow, barely shimmering from him.

To Rhys and Lucas, it would seem like a loony idea, that light could hover around a person. They'd say this was just an effect of Bastian's tiredness, or some byproduct of his imagination—a need for distraction.

But that seemed less probable than that it might be Sylphic.

Bastian drew Woodthrush's scope.

Through the scope, the lamp, the empty chairs, and the walls all looked ordinary, though somewhat magnified and hazed.

When he aimed the scope at the doctor, however, the pale shimmer shifted to bright silver tendrils that rose from him like twines of smoke.

Bastian lowered the scope.

He focused on the doctor and tried to speak, to introduce himself. But words wouldn't come.

The doctor glanced over his reading glasses and looked Bastian straight in the eyes. "Hello there."

Bastian tightened his arm around his book. It felt shameful to have been caught staring.

"You have family somewhere in this place, I'm guessing," said the doctor.

Bastian nodded.

"And you're supposed to be sleeping right now but can't." He capped his pen. "Really, though—how can anyone be expected to sleep here? Even our patients have a terrible time of it."

Bastian approached him. "It's my Mum."

"I see."

"And my brother," said Bastian.

"Oh."

The man's scrub pocket looked heavy with instruments.

"Are you a doctor?" asked Bastian.

"Yes, and I'm supposed to be getting some sleep, too."

Bastian squinted at the label stitched onto the front of the doctor's scrubs.

"You work in the Accident & Emergency wing?"

"That's right," said the doctor. "But I have a few patients not doing so well, and—you see, I can't rest either."

Bastian moved closer in, until he was standing right before the doctor. "But they're going to be all right—your patients?"

"I hope so."

Seen with plain eyes, the hint of shimmering on the doctor was barely detectable.

And yet he still seemed as radiant as how he'd appeared through the scope—in a way more felt than seen.

Bastian stared down at the cover of his book.

He touched the bright wing of the faerie, radiant in the very same way.

"What's that you've got?" asked the doctor.

Bastian, watching the doctor's expression, showed him the book.

"Would you look at that," said the doctor. "Some of my favorite people—or—stories are written of here."

It was him.

This had to be the A&E doctor Mum and Da had met. The doctor who loved Sylphic legends.

"You know Kingfisher's stories?" Bastian sat by him.

"I sure do. His stories, to me, feel alive. Like they're real. Know what I mean?"

Bastian went at the book, flipping pages. "My family and I—can you believe this? We actually live in Kingfisher's chalet." He pointed to the chalet drawn on the map.

"You don't say."

Anytime Bastian talked with Rhys and Lucas about Sylphic legends, he felt juvenile and never escaped suffering some shame about how deeply he believed them. In sitting next to this doctor, however, in examining *Moor Folk of the English Highlands* with him, Bastian felt somehow more grown up—like he was discussing this most important book with an appropriate measure of sincerity.

And he felt no shame.

"I think you met my mum and da yesterday," said Bastian. "They went to A&E after a car crash. We'd thought Mum might be in labor."

"Then you must be the Sylphic legend enthusiast and Ryudo champion I heard about."

"I'm no champion, but I do love Ryudo," said Bastian. "And yeah, I'm crazy about Sylphic legends."

His glance caught on a charm hanging from a leather strand fastened around the doctor's neck.

It was shaped like an eye, embellished with swirls.

"Hey, I've seen that emblem," said Bastian. "It appears beside a lot of the paintings in Kingfisher's book."

The doctor untangled it from his collar. "Know its meaning? It's called, 'The Eye of Ra.' Ra—as in Egypt's Sun. The sun is a key symbol in Sylphic legends. And the Eye of Ra is a counterpart to it. The Eye of Ra doesn't create light as the sun does, but rather it receives sunlight—it absorbs and reflects all that beauty and power."

"You mean like the moon?" asked Bastian. "The way the moon is sort of a counterpart to the sun?"

"One could say that, sure. Although, I tend to think a bit wilder. I like dragons, you see. And dragon fire—some mythologies say—is born from the sun; that it's a dark counterpart to the sun."

A dark rune, wild, seemed fitting for this man.

His face was open and kind but for all that, he seemed to have an edge, like some part of him, dormant, was fierce. With that almost-shimmer, with that emblem tied to him, he seemed in every way Sylphic.

Bastian's anxiety over what was happening with Mum and the baby, his grief over what might happen, the humiliation he carried for his fascination with legends—it all fell apart as he studied the doctor.

He felt a connection strong enough, even, to want to throw his arms around the man's neck and weep over the news that might come; strong enough that he felt he could cry and know it was okay.

And certainly, he was feeling bold enough, sitting beside this doctor, to confess how surely he knew Kingfisher's legends were swear-to-god real; that they told of genuine histories and dependable predictions.

Real Sylphic beings. Actual enchantments. Stories embodying great truths.

"Can I tell you a secret?" asked Bastian.

"If you'd like." The doctor laid aside his journal and pen.

"It's not a secret, exactly, though." He glanced at his book in his lap. "It's written right here, as clear as day. But...my brothers tear into me for thinking this way."

The doctor leaned in a touch. "Go on."

"It's just—do you know what the Sylphic legends say about Sun Children?"

The doctor folded his arms. "I think I have heard a few things about them."

"A Sun Child needs a Keeper, apparently," said Bastian. "The Sun Child foretold in this book is destined to fight in a battle—"

"—and the Keeper is to prepare and guide the Sun Child in that conflict," said the doctor.

"It may sound insane, I know," said Bastian. "But I kind of want to believe that's me and my brother. My brother—a Sun Child, who was supposed to be born tonight."

"Supposed to be born?"

"Da said he ought to have come easily," said Bastian. "He's my Mum's fourth, you see. Rhys has said that we have to look after her carefully, because at her age the baby might just fall out. Mum always slugged him when he said that."

The man cracked a smile.

"But Mum's had a problem of some kind. And now they can't do anything but wait. It's not safe, for her, for them to take the baby out. And it's not safe for the baby to stay unborn much longer."

Bastian drew a sharp breath.

"So they're just not doing anything." Another sharp breath—he rubbed at his chest. "It wasn't supposed to be this complex." He could do no more than whisper. "You're a doctor." A quick breath that delivered iciness. No air. "Why can't they fix this?"

"Let me see to you." The doctor placed his palm on the center of Bastian's chest.

Heat from the man's fingers washed him, through his hoodie even. Warmth swelled against his skin.

Bastian drew a deep breath that settled him.

Another moment of warmth bathing his chest, and the petrifying terrors he carried—his fright of the dark, of shadows, of fiery eyes blazing from the forest, of goblin blades, of what could've happened to Lucas, of what might happen to the baby, to Mum—they all lightened.

"You're dealing with a fair amount of fear, I see." The doctor drew back his hand. "It won't come off easily."

"Fear is what my life is all about, it seems," said Bastian, more to himself than to the doctor. "Fear of what's happened. Fear of what's coming."

The doctor held Bastian's gaze. "I can promise you—those helping your Mum and brother are doing absolutely everything they can."

Staring into the doctor's assuring eyes—it seemed, for a second, that things might be all right.

"All the myths about Sun Children," said Bastian, "all the descriptions—they line up so perfectly with this baby."

"Sometimes, if we're determined," said the doctor, watching him carefully, "we may perceive things the way we want them to be. Even if it isn't the truth."

"But the Sylphic legends..." Bastian pulled back.

He cringed a little at catching the childish sound that'd come into the tone of his voice with those words.

But he couldn't let this go. It was a fact that the Sylphic legends were true. And it was a fact that his coming brother was the Sun Child.

"It's just—the way the baby was such a surprise to us," said Bastian, "and how Mum became pregnant right after we moved into Kingfisher Chalet, not to mention how difficult this labor has been for her. And my Ryudo Master has spoken to me about secrets and prophecies—about how the Sylphic Kingdom is due for a Sun Child. It seems to make so much sense, and, to be honest, my older brothers and I—we could use a Sun Child."

"A Sun Child is a legendary champion who fights on behalf of an entire kingdom," said the doctor. "What could one do for your family?"

Bastian stared at his book. "Kingfisher writes a lot about courage—about brave deeds in battle, brave Moor Folk, brave Sun Children. If our family included a Sun Child, maybe nothing else bad could happen to us."

"So—you'd like someone to fight your battles for you?"

Bastian shrunk back a touch. Putting it that way sounded awful.

"It's just"—Bastian gestured to the Sylphic boy on the book's cover—"I'm no hero. You're precisely right that I'm overrun with fear. I'm worthless in any sort of confrontation. But, even though I'm not brave, here's the thing—"

He met the doctor's eyes.

"—I do want to be brave. I want protect others, in my own way. I think that I could be a Keeper."

The doctor cast him a sidelong glance. "How old are you?"

"Thirteen."

"It's unlikely you know, yet, your own bravery."

"Hang on," said Bastian. "I'm fourteen. I turned fourteen today. Or —yesterday, I guess. Fourteen's plenty old enough to know who I am in a fight, and anytime I try to stand up to something, I freeze."

He flipped pages to the illustration of Aubrey Gyrfalcon.

"It's sad, really—me, wanting to live through these stories." Bastian leaned closer to the book. "But that's exactly it. Sylphic legends make me feel courageous in ways I never otherwise do. When I read them, I like to imagine myself as a hero, as him—Aubrey Gyrfalcon, or Kellyn Woodthrush. It's like, for a moment, I am brave. Brave, like a Sun Child. Brave like a Keeper." He glanced at the doctor. "You're probably going to tell me I shouldn't get so lost in stories."

The doctor's face softened. "Stories exist precisely so we can get lost in them."

Bastian warmed a touch. "I can't help but dream about these legends a little."

The doctor settled back. "I don't buy that you lack courage. Look how you're facing your family's situation. You're awake because you're keeping watch—like forest children do. It requires courage to keep your eyes open when you'd rather not see." He tapped the book's cover. "Heroes are often the people who catch what others miss; those who listen for insights."

Bastian lowered the book. "Well, I'm certainly nothing like a forest child."

The doctor shed a vague smile. "There isn't much on this Earth like a forest child."

Bastian thumbed to the painting of the forest children. "They're great, aren't they?"

The doctor captured Bastian's glance. "Consider—at barely fourteen, you likely haven't been properly tested. As challenges come your way—whatever they are, however fierce—embrace them."

At those words, the glow around the doctor brightened a touch.

Shivers raced up Bastian's arms and sparkled at the nape of his neck as though sunlight were flushing in, bathing him.

The doctor settled his chin in his hand. "Now, what to do about this birthday of yours. Yesterday, you said it was? It seems it may have been quite overlooked."

"It doesn't matter," said Bastian. "With all that's going on, even I barely remembered."

"Well, we mustn't let a birthday go uncelebrated." He unclasped the leather band from around his neck. "Sylphic legends hold that brave acts yield more than just battle wins. Brave acts can open our eyes. Chase our fears. Teach us of our capability. Even build up our fortitude."

"You're sounding like my Ryudo master," said Bastian.

The doctor fixed the emblem of the Eye of Ra—counterpart to the sun—around Bastian's neck.

Bastian lifted the charm. "You're giving me this?"

"Such an enthusiast of Kingfisher as you are—it's fitting for you to have it," said the doctor. "When you see it, I'd like you to remember that somebody believes that you're brave."

"Do you really think that?"

"I do, and in time, you'll see it, too. Bravery is often discovered once we've learned to perceive the world with the proper perspective."

"Perceiving the world as it is—even that's proving difficult for me," said Bastian. "There's this odd thing—I sometimes hear what no one else seems to. I see and feel things my brothers don't—things that, rationally speaking, couldn't be there. My Ryudo master tells me I might have the raw stuff needed to peer into the Sylphic Kingdom. That sounds far-fetched, I know—though, it doesn't to me. But Master Sayre, I'll admit, is a bit far-fetched."

"In studying Ryudo, you'd know plenty about seeing beyond the surface," said the doctor, "about working with opportunities and understanding obstacles that are difficult to perceive. Through Ryudo, you'd know all about sharpening the capabilities within your own body to strike your target."

"How long have you studied Ryudo?" asked Bastian.

The doctor shrugged. "I've practiced long enough to note how strong that pitching arm of yours looks. You must be quite skilled."

"But the odd music, the sights," said Bastian. "We're not talking about improving my aim or my stamina. We're talking about hallucinations—sensing things everyone tells me aren't there."

"Any chance that your Ryudo master is right?" The doctor looked carefully at him. "That you're learning to sense things that are there?"

Suddenly, rushing past the doorway—Rhys. Then Rhys rushing back.

"Bloody bindweed, there you are." Rhys hung huffing to the doorframe. "Mum's out of danger."

"And the baby?" Bastian stood, sending his book sliding to the floor.

"He's arrived. Da came out to tell us, then hurried back to Mum. He said the doctor who helped her was *brilliant*. We're to wait just a bit longer." He glanced at the A&E doctor. "Sorry if my brother's disturbing you." He gestured for Bastian to come. "Da says we're to wait together."

"You're no doubt in for an adventure." The doctor lifted Bastian's book from the floor and handed it to him. "Keep that close. Study it carefully. It's been hard won."

Bastian received his book from the doctor—a man lightly glowing, sharing emblems of moonlight, of dragon fire, knowing Sylphic legends by heart, understanding Ryudo; a man seeming to represent that there were heroes at the ready, both in this world and in worlds Sylphic.

"This is just like the Sun Child myth," said Bastian. "A brilliant hero stepped in, and now Mum and my brother are safe."

"You might be surprised at what heroism actually looks like," said the doctor. "It's often less about being brilliant and more about being willing."

"That's easy for you to say," said Bastian. "You're in the business of brilliantly saving lives."

"Perhaps I am." The doctor tapped the emblem strung around Bastian's neck. "But we all might be in the business of saving worlds."

13

astian followed Rhys and Lucas down the corridor. The weight of his rucksack, with Woodthrush's Sylphic scope and *Moor Folk of the English Highlands* tucked inside, felt like a steady hand resting on his shoulder.

Rhys gestured to an almost-closed door.

Bastian tipped it open an inch.

From a railed bed, Mum waved. Beside her stretched a large window, the open curtains presenting a blazing panorama of the velvet night and its glittery splash of South England's spring stars.

Though Mum was smiling, gray shades rimmed her eyes.

She presented a tiny bundle. "Would you like to say 'hi?'"

Bastian drew near to her. To the baby nestling against her.

The baby wasn't flustered or sleeping like the babies in the nursery had been. He was just lying very still, staring at his brothers approaching, his fingers, no bigger than matchsticks, sprawling in the air.

Bastian touched his cheek—tiny and tan. "He's so small."

Da smiled. "He's fine-boned as a bird, though I daresay he'll grow like a weed. And with skin so golden—can you believe such a thing?"

Bastian eased away the corner of the blanket and studied the body of the baby, still wet from a bath.

The babies in the nursery had come in shades along a palette of pink or gray, but this newborn was positively bronzed.

Bastian cradled the baby's tiny feet.

Every bit of him seemed perfectly made, as though the dough of him had been pressed into the mold of an angel and baked in the sun until golden. His ears lay flush against his downy head and lifted into gently rounded points, like they'd been fashioned from a pair of turbinella seashells. Sapphire blue eyes shone from his round face.

"And by Jove—that shock of hair." Da cradled the baby's crown, heavy with curls. "Who would've imagined—long, light hair?"

Bastian pressed the tips of the baby's hair—fair wisps twisting like incense rings rising.

According to Kingfisher, Sun Children often had wild hair. He'd described it as like a crop of corkscrew willow or a pile of glittering wood-moss.

Bastian glanced at Rhys' dark hair, at the blonde on Lucas, and then considered his own twisting peaks and their chestnut shade.

The baby's hair was the color of a wheat field in autumn when the sun is on it. But there was a cast of white here, too. Molten daylight, maybe? The color registered nowhere.

Lucas touched the baby's tall pale hair, then glanced at Bastian and signed, "Do you think he's Sylphic?"

"I don't know," Bastian signed back. "He certainly seems extraordinary."

Mum lifted the baby against her shoulder. "He has your eyes, Bastian—like the sea in summer."

She trailed her fingers along the baby's slender back and kissed his fleecy skull. "Who among our ancestors have we to thank for contributing so beautiful a combination of sun and shade?"

Da squeezed Bastian's shoulder. "It seems Bastian has his Sun Child."

Mum lowered the baby into her lap and stroked his pale ringlets. "Quite."

Lucas pointed to the baby's face, wrinkling into a squeal. "He doesn't have any Sun Kiss."

Bastian held the baby's chin between his finger and thumb.

"Sun kisses are unpredictable," he signed. "They apparently show up only sometimes, then vanish."

"If you're actually expecting a Sun Child," signed Rhys, "you're in for a big disappointment."

Mum shushed the crying baby, who took her finger into his mouth.

Bastian startled at the recollection of his dream.

A hint of an herbal fragrance drifted—a poultice of berries and wildflowers, and the cool impression of petals.

Bastian looked around for a cup of tea or something that could be the source of the sensation, but he could pinpoint nothing.

"What will we call him?" signed Lucas.

"Cassian Julius," said Mum, fingerspelling the name of the Sun Child. "Cassian means 'curly headed'—it couldn't be more fitting. Julius, after your granddadda, of course."

"Cassian Julius Goldcrest," whispered Bastian. It was a perfect Sun Child's name. "Can I hold him?"

Mum smiled.

Bastian scooped Cassian's pooching bottom into one hand, cupped his curly head into the other, and lifted his featherweight frame.

"You're a natural at holding a newborn," said Mum. "Look at how peaceful he is."

Bastian shivered at the delight of feeling that Cassian might indeed trust him already.

"I couldn't ask for a better birthday present than him."

Mum cast him a sad look. "My dear one. Your poor birthday. Overlooked entirely in all this excitement."

"Not entirely," said Bastian.

He laid his hand on the soft head of the baby—from all calculations, a Sun Child—the key to peace in the Sylphic Kingdom. A Sun Child in need of a Keeper.

Bastian settled his finger inside Cassian's open palm.

Cassian grasped it, and his first brother-pact was made.

Bastian held him closely to his chest and promised without words to look after him, to be his champion, his sentry, and his guide.

He'd believe in this baby. He'd call up the sun in his new brother's blood. He'd shield him and prepare him for battle.

For this baby, he would be brave.

14

On the morning Cassian was to come home, the sun broke over the eastern hill singing like the clarion call of a silver trumpet. Dartmoor's entire bank of birds seemed to have swooped in for the occasion, chiming from every limb of the trees sprawling outside Bastian's window.

Bastian sat on his bed, *Moor Folk of the English Highlands* open across his lap.

On the page before him lay a painting of a gooseberry bush, heavy with green-golden orbs. Gooseberries were essential to the oldest ritual of dowsing a Sun Child, lighting the sun blood he carried.

Bastian flipped to the book's map and traced a northeastward-tending trail leading to the Windrush Stream, whose eastern banks held the most bountiful winter gooseberry crop he'd seen.

He stowed his book on his shelf. He slid Woodthrush's Sylphic scope inside his pocket and went downstairs.

In the kitchen, underneath Naga's watchful eye, he scribbled a note. He left the note there, beneath Naga's paw, telling his family he'd hiked to the Windrush Stream and would be back soon. He snugged on his jacket and hustled out.

He retrieved his bike from where it leaned against the back porch rail and pushed it up the eastern hill.

As he reached the hill's pinnacle, a murmuration of starlings broke wildly from the chalet's thatching.

They lifted into the sky high over the chalet and fanned out.

Bastian, watching them fly off, found his gaze lingering on the roof's peaked center point.

The oddly high roof gave the impression that the chalet was a place that kept secrets, and beginning today, it would. Today, as soon as Mum and Cassian came home, Kingfisher Chalet would serve as home to the Sun Child.

Jumping branches and scraping past shrubs, Bastian biked into a northern hook of the Wystan Woods, where Moor Folk enchantment was fabled to hang in the very wind.

The air, as sunny as a bright song, swept lacy and golden with spores and with pollen, with iridescent-winged insects and airborne seedlings.

Bastian reached the edge of a rise that sloped down to the twinkling Windrush Stream flowing fast and south, coursing to the Natterjack Lagoon.

This stream seeped down from a chain of steep, rocky tors that stood further north.

The tors weren't visible from this deeply inside the forest, but they could be felt in the chill of the water—as icy as the winds that raced over Dartmoor's highest reaches.

What was visible from where Bastian stood was the mouth of a cave that punched blackly into the forest and delivered the Windrush's waters to these warmer lowlands.

He'd never dared to go inside the cave, as dark as it was, deep and maintaining an aching cold.

Lucas, fascinated by the sense of adventure the cave offered, often had wanted to. Bastian never had indulged him, except for having once gathered the nerve to stand at the cave's mouth and shine in a light.

Just inside the cave's opening, a pair of boulders had stood, large and as spherical as Earths. They made the place seem holy in an ancient way, like a hidden cairn.

Crystals—blue and diamond white—their tips as keen as arrowheads, projected from among the stones on the cave's slippery floor and grew from its wet walls.

To take a single step into the cave's darkness was to risk a deep cut or dangerous fall.

Water droplets had tinkled darkly from the prism-studded ceiling, creating an unsettling music.

Its sonorous timbre had struck Bastian as toned like what he imagined the singing of naiads or mermaids or sirens might sound like—a mesmeric song drawing its hearers to haunts where they couldn't survive.

Bastian peered across the wide stream, distantly to the east. There, just beyond an aspen grove, the winter gooseberry bushes grew in a prickly thicket.

To the south, the cattails and reeds thinned enough to show a vein of the Windrush glittering in a rapid turn along a spacious plantation of birch trees, wherein nestled Sayre Cottage—a cozy forest home that Master and Mrs. Sayre had occupied as long as anyone in the shire remembered.

Bastian could see the silver smoke curling from the cottage's chimney, and a warmth of baking bread was drifting in the gentle wind.

The smoke cheerfully piping struck to life a hope that Master Sayre had returned.

But that seemed unlikely.

If he had, he certainly would've sought Bastian out. It was probably just Mrs. Sayre baking alone, biding the time until his return.

Bastian leaned his bike against a tree and eased down the grassy slope. He stood at the edge of the Windrush's stream, studying its shallows where the smooth waters were slipping softly over pebbles and stones.

The sun—shimmering through low clouds—was letting down shifting beams that brightened the shallows in a dazzling way.

But the band of water flowing from the mouth of that treacherous cave was a shadow country that the sun's warmth could not touch.

The wide stream, storm fed, was running swiftly and high—standing on the shallowest crossing stones would still bring icy water rushing up to his knees.

He studied the stream and pinpointed the best possible course—a series of larger bedrock stones that would hopefully let him avoid a misstep that would plunge him into the dangerous green depths.

Bastian took one step in, but then suddenly stopped.

For there, in the center of the stream, stood a girl—watching him.

Never before had Bastian spotted any kids wandering through the Wystan Woods. And this girl was young—maybe eight or nine.

He glanced around, looking for an adult or older kid who might be looking after her. But no one else was in sight.

Where the girl stood, the stream was running deep, the water nearly reaching her shoulders. Her skin was the pale, bloodless pallor of a fish's cold belly. Her hair hung tangled with sopping grasses and algae.

Around her forehead was clasped a silvery headband studded with a kite-shaped blue gemstone that seemed to flicker with sunlight, as though it'd been forged from the Windrush's waters.

"Hello?" Bastian called.

She didn't respond. She just stood still, her eyes wide and stark and locked on his, like she was as shocked at being discovered as Bastian was at discovering her.

She had to be lost. Or in trouble? In that deep place in the stream, she'd soon freeze. She could drown.

Bastian eased to the next crossing stone. "Are you all right?"

The girl just stared at him.

Maybe she, like Lucas, couldn't hear.

"You look frightened," he said, signing too. "Can you swim? Try to come this way. I'll help you."

A snaky pike fish twisted around the girl's shoulder.

She didn't even move.

"There are leaches in the Windrush," called Bastian. "And we've seen snakes around here. There could be swimming adders. You'd better climb out."

A silent slip into water, and the girl was gone.

Bastian tore off his jacket and stepped off the crossing stone.

He sucked an agonized breath at the shock of cold water sliding against his stomach, but he pressed on, making toward the sunlit, clearer patches. An adder in this stream would be unlikely, but the threat of leeches was legitimate. If he could stay out of the slow, stagnant stuff, he might fare better.

He reached the stream's center where a current twisted, sending clouds of blue mayflies zipping by on glassy wings and schools of minnows diving into the shadowy depths.

The girl was nowhere.

Bastian stepped off a shelf and into chest-deep water.

The boulder-strewn bed was jagging the stream's surface into bubbly crests that made catching a breath difficult.

Shivering, he trekked further upstream, fighting the current's tug.

He clung to slippery boulders as he moved through the deeper water, searching for any sign of the girl.

"Where are you?" Speaking was almost impossible for the chill. "Don't be afraid—I'll help you."

But doubt rose about whether he could help her. Currents in the deeper stretches of the Windrush were known to build strongly enough to grip a person the size of that child—or even his size—and hold them under.

When he reached the point where she'd gone in, he hung steady.

Minnows washed back in like slivers of night, and on the water's glassy surface, reflections of sparrowhawks streaked.

Suddenly, the magical sight of sky on water was disrupted by a nebulous impression on the stream's deep bed—the girl's pale face, her hair composed of streaming water grasses, her eyes like shining stones.

Bastian drew a deep breath and plunged in.

The girl, at the bottom of the stream, twisted and sped off.

Bastian fought the current after her.

She glanced back.

Her face, under the sunlit water, looked less pale-white and more silver—like the tense shine on the surface of a bubble. She was nearing the black mouth of the Natterjack Cave.

Bastian sputtered to the surface. He clung stiff to a boulder, gripped by the horrifying thought of the girl underwater for so long, not breathing.

During asthma attacks, his lungs sometimes tightened to the point where drawing a full breath was next to impossible.

His vision sometimes would blacken before the medicine kicked in, and there was nothing scarier or more painful than airlessness. He ached, imagining the girl feeling that.

He glanced at the shore, where he'd left his bike and rucksack. He had no phone. To find help, he'd have to ride someplace.

He started to swim on toward the bank—but stopped as the girl surfaced again, close to the cave, and hung still in the thick of the current.

She moved to standing higher, as though balancing on a water-logged boulder. Weeds and algae clung to her from the knees up, making a sort of short dress.

She seemed ghostly.

Sylphic.

Seeing this Sylphic girl—this being from the fraught country of cave water, of slithering pikes, of deathly cold and killing currents—her strangeness seemed to hint that the Sylphic realm tended more toward frightfulness than peace.

As enthralled as Bastian was with Sylphic legends, so immersed as he felt in this unearthly moment—he found himself wanting to believe that despite all her strangeness, the girl was a mere human child.

"Let me help you," he called. "Follow me out."

"Follow me in," she answered, her voice reverberant.

She dove and twisted toward the cave.

Bastian stayed where he was, clinging to the boulder and staring at the print she'd left in the water.

Kingfisher's book told that goblins lurked in the dark parts of woodlands, in rocky crags and in caves, in the deep haunts of mountains and tors—places heavy with shade, never touched by the sun.

The A&E doctor had made the point that if we're determined, we may perceive only what we wish to believe, even if it isn't the truth. Here, Bastian was perceiving nothing desirable; rather, things that legitimately terrified him.

Perhaps then, as alarming as the girl was, as dark as the cave looked, both might be harbingers of truth.

Bastian fought the water to swim toward where the girl had dived. He pulled under and caught sight of her silver legs kicking. He swam after her until the frigidness of the water, its dimness, the stream's bubble and churning—a clatter in his ears—arrested his progress.

The girl wheeled back to him and hung before him in the icy green water.

She closed her eyes and kissed him on the mouth.

Heat flushed his face and rushed down his limbs.

She pulled him to the surface, well inside the cave's darkness.

Bastian struggled to keep his face above the hard current and wouldn't have, had the girl not been gripping the front of his shirt.

"We thought all hope was lost." Her strange voice seemed to mix with the splash of cave water.

"Who are you?" asked Bastian.

"But insights they won, over stone, over blood. They learned the secret of chasing the dark." She moved closer to him. "It's your secret now. Listen. Open your eyes. For darkness carries not shadows, but messages."

She thrust him out of the water and onto a boulder.

"You must see."

Bastian held steady on the slick boulder, jagged crystals encircling it. He eased more to its center, gingerly avoiding their tips.

He glanced around, trying to gather a sense of what the girl wanted him to see. The sunny opening lay far behind him, and there was nothing before him but the cave's gaping throat and a murmur of water song.

"Draw Woodthrush's scope." The girl dipped back under the water and there hovered by his boulder, her face peering up at him as through a pane of dark glass.

His mouth felt on fire from her kiss, and despite having been in the freezing water, his body felt piping, like he'd been at Ryudo practice for a full sunny afternoon.

Bastian held the gaze of the girl as she sank into the depths of the water.

Finally, she disappeared into bleakness.

Bastian pulled his Sylphic scope from his pocket and scanned the water.

The scope showed him nothing—there was no sign of the girl or anything else, ordinary or Sylphic.

It showed nothing until he pointed it at the black throat of the cave, toward shadows that felt heavy and living.

From the cave's deep recession, a fleck of light glimmered—light Bastian couldn't see except through his scope.

It wasn't the silvery shine that'd risen when he'd aimed the scope at the A&E doctor. Rather, it was a harsh yellow light—a streetlamp piercing the dead of night, serving only to thicken the shadows and blind anyone standing beneath it.

The light grew more defined, its glare strengthening until it illumined a scene.

Bastian saw himself standing beside Lucas. They were in the football park behind their chalet, watching the sky from underneath the blare of its field light.

The field light snapped off.

Trembling lightning echoed, as though a strong storm were churning in the depths of the cave.

From the shadowy woods in the far distance, a pair of red eyes appeared. A bolt of lightning fired close, showing someone advancing.

It was the goblin boy.

"No." Bastian lowered the scope.

In looking at the interior of the cave with just his bare eyes, it seemed empty.

There was only the sound of its cavernous dripping. There were just its glossy black walls, its boulders and crystals.

Bastian smelled no storm but rather the cave's clay-tinged air. He felt no wind but the gentle draft coursing from the cave's pitch-black throat.

With trembling hands, he slid the scope back into his pocket. For how could he bear to relive the night the goblin boy had attacked him and Lucas?

Lucas unconscious and bloodied on the ground—Bastian could never handle seeing that again.

But at feeling this impulse to refuse to see, to avoid confronting something dreaded, he gripped his scope.

Because the Ryudo he practiced—the Ryudo at which he'd reached near-champion level, according to Master Sayre—was it not about keeping one's eyes open? And the A&E doctor had added the twist that Ryudo was about seeing when one would rather not see.

"*As challenges come your way,*" the A&E doctor had said, "*whatever they are, however fierce—embrace them.*"

In accepting his role as the Sun Child's Keeper, Bastian would certainly have to confront moments more terrible than this.

And he couldn't deny that it'd been a Sylphic creature—a naiad, maybe—who'd guided him here. A Sylphic creature who'd said there was something he must see.

Perhaps if he dared to look through the scope, he'd discover something critical. Some truth he was meant to understand.

He closed his hand around the emblem—the Eye of Ra, counterpart to the sun—that the doctor had given him. He drew his scope again from his pocket and looked through it toward the recess stretching at the back of the cave.

The park scene lay beneath an advancing, low storm.

In the distance between the park and the woods, a glow—like a coppery fire catching on a log's heartwood—erupted. It outlined the shape of the goblin boy.

Bastian watched the goblin boy approach.

He watched it strike Lucas. He watched his own struggle with the goblin boy. He watched himself take a punch to the chest.

The goblin boy rushed Lucas and lifted him. He threw Lucas against the rubbish bin.

Bastian watched himself lay frozen and airless as lighting tore up the sky and clarified the shape of the goblin boy and the blade that it gripped. And then he saw himself wrestling the goblin boy to the ground.

He watched as the goblin boy punched his chest hard—calling a great flash to leap from Bastian's body.

Bastian remembered that flash, but he thought it'd burst from the storm, or from something in the forest. Seeing the fight from this perspective, though, it was clear. The flash had come from him.

At its blare, the goblin boy raced off.

Bastian dropped to his knees at the sense of pain from that punch reigniting.

A burst like a blue flare of lightning lit the back of the cave, and then everything went pitch dark.

Bastian, arrested with the agony in his chest, collapsed sideways into the water. He felt for the girl, but she did not reappear.

He was with the current now, and it lifted him to the stream's surface. A moment more, and it delivered him to the reedy shallows edging the eastern bank.

He pushed to standing in the shin-deep water. He searched the stream for the girl, but she seemed far gone.

Drawing hard breaths, he climbed out onto the muddy bank. He wrung out his clothes—his trousers torn on one side from snagging on crystals at his fall.

He backed away from the water.

He trekked through the copse of thin aspens, toward the thicket holding gooseberry brambles.

15

_W_arm sunlight broke the clouds and draped Bastian in daylight.

In that blissful brightness, while standing in the middle of an open forest—cheery with the shining white tree trunks of aspens, Bastian found it difficult to believe what he'd just seen.

He'd encountered a naiad, or other Sylphic creature of some sort. Through his scope, he'd watched that most awful night play out before him—Lucas attacked by the goblin boy, fire-eyed.

Bastian lifted the scope and scanned the woods around him, searching for anything Sylphic, be it dreadful like the goblin or freakish like the naiad.

There were no red eyes, no shapes in the shadows, no goblins; no captivating creatures born from the water or bright figures racing through the trees.

But in a clearing, not far in among the aspen grove, a twisted staff as high as Bastian's shoulder, its shaft polished to glassy, pierced the earth.

As Bastian approached it, a sound like whispered singing bent the wind.

Patches of sage-blue lichen feathered the staff, and its bulbed crown split into prongs, like a casing for a lost ornament. Bastian reached his fingers toward it.

At his touch, the whispered singing ceased.

He drew the staff from the earth.

It smelled of leaf mold and felt sleek, as though tempered by a hand gripping it over long stretches of time.

Using the staff to make his way, he crossed through the aspen grove and moved into a wilder stretch of the Wystan Woods.

He pushed aside reeds and sedges and kicked through brome and moonwort, his steps flushing ground mice from clusters of winter tor grass. A few minutes of hiking brought him to the edge of the gooseberry glade.

As he stepped in, a thundercloud gobbled the sun. The trees all in chorus stretched skyward, wrested by storm wind.

The gale seemed to have come on too fast, the temperature plummeting too swiftly for this to have been spurred by any natural force. And although Bastian saw nothing Sylphic, terror pierced him. For every gust of wind seemed to flare the cold ache in his chest.

This violent wind, these dark clouds, even that girl—perhaps something more dangerous than a naiad—was it possible that they were all part of some Sylphic wickedness fighting to keep him from reaching the gooseberry glade; aiming to hinder him from calling forth the power in Cassian's blood?

He cast down the staff and fought the gale as he rushed through the glade. He ripped the taut gooseberry globes from their branches and fed them into the wet pockets of his cargo trousers. When his pockets were bulging, he took off back to the crossing in the Windrush's stream.

The storm let fly raindrops as sharp as daggers, as swift as spears. Foul wind washed from lowering green clouds, casting lightning.

Bastian splashed through the stream's crossing—vacant, it seemed, of anything Sylphic. He retrieved his soaked jacket from the bank and climbed to where he'd left his bike.

He rode wildly through the woods, taking cuts through thinly planted stretches that offered no trails, but a direct path toward home.

When he reached the crest of the hill overlooking Kingfisher Chalet, he eased to a stop.

From within those walls, M.D. Kingfisher had written *Moor Folk of the English Highlands*—a book about the strange Sylphic realm; about Sun Children; about wickedness and war.

The steep, thatched roof of Kingfisher Chalet, the choking vines encircling its round stones, the weeds snaking over its grounds all seemed to shed the same foreboding sense that the strong thunder carried.

The place seemed less like a forest chalet owned by a great story weaver and more a dark secret that slept in wait.

What'd spurred this cold wind to screech, that water child to find him, the most frightful night of his life to replay before him, Bastian did not understand.

Only one thing was certain: the Sylphic Kingdom was undeniably real, and he'd confronted forces powerful and straight from it.

He biked down the hill, cutting at an edge to keep from striking a slick rock or root that would throw him. He raced over the wet, weedy yard and skidded to a stop at the back porch.

He dropped his bike and sprinted up the porch steps and through the back door.

He rushed through the house. "Da? Rhys?"

No one answered.

A note in reply on the kitchen island told that his brothers and Da had left for the hospital and would be back soon with Mum and Cassian.

Bastian raced up to Cassian's nursery and peered out the window, its broad, panoramic glass showing the wide east.

As quickly as it'd risen, the storm calmed to nothing.

Hazy clouds now were stretching in gilded ribbons that floated peacefully across a vanilla afternoon sky, casting the nursery in a state of complete serenity, its walls sun-heated and as soft-seeming as cream.

Since Bastian had last visited the nursery, Mum had hung, over the crib, three photos.

They showed Bastian, Lucas, and Rhys each as babies, each set in a white oval frame, dropped from a billowing bow.

Bastian took down the picture of himself.

He was resting in the arms of a neighbor boy who'd once been his caretaker—Dom.

The two of them were seated on a bench in a springtime park. Bastian was gripping a baseball between his chubby hands and showing off a smile loaded, like a pirate's musketoon, with a single tooth.

Dom had taught Bastian to pitch before he learned to speak. Because of Dom's steady coaching, the day Bastian turned four, he'd been ready to join the San Francisco Little League baseball team. He'd pitched in leagues summer after summer, each season earning a place in a league more elite, until they'd moved back here.

He liked baseball, and he'd won loads of trophies for his pitching. But he liked far better the memory of the boy who'd taught him.

He lifted from Cassian's toy shelf a baseball he'd contributed.

He could remember, early on, being afraid of the ball. He could remember following the instinct prompting him to remain safe by avoiding it, rather than mastering the skill of remaining safe by catching it.

He rubbed his thumb across familiar scuff marks.

The memory of Dom teaching him to pitch, to catch, to stand his ground, worked on him like medicine.

Some of what he'd experienced of the Sylphic Kingdom, though startling, was wondrous. But not all of it had been.

Holding that scuffed ball, Bastian felt an inner strength—evidence, perhaps, of his capacity to handle the true nature of things.

He could feel as true the insight that rewards lie beyond challenges, no matter how mystifying, how terrifying those challenges might be.

From outside, car doors slammed.

Bastian pushed back the window's curtain.

Naga slipped into the nursery and jumped onto the windowsill.

Bastian stroked him as they together watched Rhys help Mum out of the car, while Da and Lucas unloaded the baby in his seat and Mum's suitcase.

Even at this height, from the shining ringlets on Cassian, Bastian recognized him as theirs.

A warm wind spinning through the window and drifting out again gave the impression that the chalet was taking deep breaths.

Bastian breathed deeply with it as he soaked in a final moment of life as he knew it—a life without a Sun Child to look after.

Beginning today, he was no longer the boy he'd always known himself to be.

Beginning today, he was a Keeper, responsible to wake the Sylphic lineage in Cassian's blood; to prepare him for the battle to come.

16

assian's first weeks were marked by unusually warm weather, and the last day of April dawned roasting.

Since Cassian's birth, Bastian had showed up at the Ryudo course every day, hoping to find Master Sayre, to talk to him about the Sun Child.

But there'd been no sign of him, which was troubling.

What could be keeping him away for almost a month, Bastian couldn't imagine.

Master Sayre had left the Ryudo course somewhat active, with many of the obstacles still cocked, still triggered by Bastian's appearance on the pitch.

No matter how unforgiving the heat, no matter how fierce the downpours, Bastian had dominated the course.

With every run, he felt more dexterous at handling the slithering tree roots. He felt faster and more capable at maintaining his pace, no matter how the slope of the ground shifted under his feet.

And since Cassian's birth, he hadn't once missed his target.

In these last weeks, though, it hadn't been only Master Sayre's absence that'd been troubling.

Before and after each run, Bastian would walk the woods, scope in hand, searching for anything Sylphic.

But the Sylphic sounds and sensations seemed to have withered, Bastian now finding them barely detectable.

It seemed odd, because Kingfisher had written that the moon, entering the final few days of its waning crescent phase, marked a season of overlap between the mortal and Sylphic worlds.

Today, the moon seemed to be at that point, or close to it, coasting over the zenith like a shard of fire, double horned, strung from the neck of the sky.

In exploring the woodland, Bastian occasionally thought he'd caught sight of an unexplainable shine, or a wisp of vapor that seemed to be moving independently of the wind.

But everything he saw—or thought he saw—was so vague, he couldn't ever be sure.

Each time he walked the woods, he made it a point to venture to the Windrush, to the mouth of its cave.

He'd never again caught a glimpse of any Sylphic girl, though.

He'd also checked Cassian daily to see if a sun kiss might be forming, but no hint of any mark had appeared.

He hadn't been able to find any explanation in *Moor Folk of the English Highlands* for why the Sylphic Kingdom might suddenly seem diminished, especially to someone in possession of a Sylphic scope; to the brother of the Sun Child; to a student of Sylphic legends who practiced Ryudo; to one who knew that when the moon waned the Sylphic realm might appear more concretely to mortals; to someone who'd already seen plenty of Sylphic things.

This final April day was the hottest Dartmoor ever had suffered, and Bastian had to cut his Ryudo practice short from sheer heat exhaustion.

The sun was so intense, he also had no choice but to forgo biking through the woods in search of Moor Folk, which pained him particularly.

According to Kingfisher, on days of strong sun, forest children couldn't resist ranging.

Bastian picked up his bike from the edge of the Ryudo pitch and started the ride home by the fastest trail.

It was some comfort to recognize that bypassing his search today for things Sylphic wouldn't be a complete loss.

For tomorrow, the moon waned even further—to almost its thinnest sliver.

For that occasion, he had preparations to make.

Tomorrow, he'd put the gooseberries he'd gathered and frozen to work, to dowse the light inside Cassian.

Tomorrow, he'd wake his Sun Child's true nature, unlocking Cassian's Sylphic abilities and instilling in him some kind of power needed for the battle Kingfisher foretold.

As Bastian biked, leaves skipping across the trails in a frolicky way gave him pause to wonder if something Sylphic might be driving them. The forest canopy, too, rocking in high, hot winds, was shimmering as though the sunlight caught in its boughs were material.

But in studying the woodland through the Sylphic scope as he rode, he found them ordinary.

Once home, Bastian settled at the dining room table with *Moor Folk of the English Highlands* open before him. He read a page written in elegant script holding careful instructions for thawing gooseberries and conducting the charm for sun dowsing.

This was the first of two methods laid out for lighting the blood in a Sun Child. Sun dowsing by either method was apparently complicated, though. The number of caveats Kingfisher had included for what darker Sylphic interferences might crop up were extensive, and it was clear that the charm might not work after trying just one method.

The technique involving gooseberries was the older of the two rites and considered the more reliable.

Mum's voice lifted, speaking to Rhys from the back porch.

They were talking about cutting Cassian's hair.

Bastian stood and hurried to the back door.

Cassian's curls had grown noticeably, every day, and now towering locks projected every which way—a clear characteristic of a Sun Child.

Almost since the day they'd brought Cassian home, Mum had been threatening to cut his hair, which Bastian so far had managed to talk her out of. When he'd rock Cassian to sleep, Bastian had developed a habit of picking bits of leaves and twigs out of those curls to keep them soft and tidy, so Mum would be less inclined to want to cut them.

Who knew but that hacking off his wondrous curls might stifle him in his development as the Sun Child?

Bastian stepped out on the porch to find Cassian strapped inside a baby pack fixed on Rhys' chest.

Mum was holding one of Cassian's ringlets taut in the crook of her haircutting shears.

Bastian abandoned his book on the porch swing. "What are you doing?"

Mum dropped the curl. "I'm sorry, love, but I simply must cut his hair."

"Please don't," said Bastian. "Kingfisher has written that children with Sylphic blood often have wild hair—this certainly seems the case with Cassian."

Mum and Rhys exchanged a look.

Bastian felt unforgivably foolish. But he had to speak up. He couldn't let Mum cut Cassian's hair now—not with the moon just on the verge of its deepest crescent stage; not with the gooseberry ritual all set for tomorrow.

Bastian closed in on them. "What if cutting his hair will somehow make him less of a Sun Child?"

"Are you hearing yourself?" asked Rhys.

"Imagine a battle happening," said Bastian, "with a champion not fit to fight."

"You can't seriously think there'll be a battle in Dartmoor," said Rhys.

Bastian glanced at a copse of oaks towering over the hilltop—oaks just like the ones painted in *Moor Folk of the English Highlands*, illustrating conflicts that'd happened in the past. Oaks drawn with branches supporting wounded forest children, arrows strung on their taut bowstrings.

"A battle here isn't that far-fetched," said Bastian.

"Um...if we're talking about in the legendary Sylphic Kingdom," said Rhys.

As humiliating as it was to seem so obsessed with something his family outright dismissed, Bastian couldn't drop this, not for a second. *Moor Folk of the English Highlands* was dense with critical, true information on Sun Children and how to wake their power, on protective charms, and on the battle foreseen.

The best way to understand any of its protective rites, the best way to make progress with either of the enchantments for sun dowsing, was to try them.

It certainly was mandatory to keep Cassian in his optimal state— wild hair and all—for those enchantments to work; for Bastian to clearly see what abilities or skills they might unlock in the baby.

"According to Kingfisher, and Master Sayre," said Bastian, "battles have happened in Dartmoor before."

"Look, Master Sayre might be willing to play along with your fantasies," said Rhys, "but I've about had it with the Sylphic Kingdom and the Sun Child. Maybe we should've given that book to Lady Marrowight after all."

Bastian moved closer to his book, lying on the porch swing.

"Just look how his fringe slumps right over his eyes." Mum bunched the baby's hair and let it fall. "What a mess."

"What does it matter if Cassian has wild hair?" asked Bastian.

"You could use a shearing yourself," said Rhys.

Mum again picked up the scissors.

Bastian hovered over the baby as Mum clipped his hair—barely.

The instant she finished, Bastian liberated Cassian from the pack tied to Rhys and held him.

A cloud skating over the sun shed a coolness that felt relieving, but Cassian didn't seem to think so. Encased in that shade, the baby's face scrunched like the cap of a penny bun mushroom, and he cried like his tiny heart would break.

"It isn't so bad," Bastian whispered to Cassian. "Your curls are still all there, mostly."

He pulled a glassy pacifier from his pocket, which Cassian rejected forthright. Bastian lifted the *Moor Folk of the English Highlands* from the swing.

"You'd do well to give those legends a rest," said Rhys, untangling himself from the baby carrier.

Bastian took the baby, along with the book, inside the house and found Cassian's teddy. Cassian gripped it as he lay against Bastian's chest in a fit of angry meditation, sucking on the teddy's golden ear.

Bastian slipped into a dark recess off the dining room that kept a rocking chair, encircled by an arc of bookcases. There, perhaps, he could study *Moor Folk of the English Highlands* without being scorned.

He squeezed into the chair with Naga sleeping, curled. He turned to a section on protective charms that could render a Sun Child's bedchamber impervious to Sylphic curses and conducive to dreaming— a vital experience for a Sun Child.

He read it to Cassian—

"There's no place safer for a Sun Child than his sleeping chamber. It must be warm and love-ridden, laced with the charm of Pygmyweed to deflect dark enchantments and stimulate dreaming. For the Sun Child dreams of feats of valor that serve as inspiration and insight.

"The prime orientation of a Sun Child's bedchamber is a matter of some debate. Flower faeries, dryads, and oakmen would have a window pointing due south, for none know better than they the benefits of all-day sun.

"English pookas maintain that a window facing the northwest will produce a child of fortitude. But the ancestry of the English pooka lies along the emerald coasts of Ireland, and their bias is clear.

"The Nymphic daughters of Oceanus hold that the windows of Sun Children ought to look full west, for in that way lies the cerulean blue coast of the Celtic Waters, beyond which churns the bluer blue of the North Atlantic, and nothing—not wind, nor storms, nor thirst, nor any passion—can match the power of the thrashing sea.

"The placement of the chamber is up to the discretion of the Sun Child's Keeper, although one would do well to mind that, more impor-tant than direction, all sources recommend that it be sun-bearing. And there's no question that protective charms must be placed."

Cassian's window faced southeast, and the rising sun could be seen in all seasons.

Good.

His nursery was certainly love-ridden, with as much rocking and story reading and play as any baby could ask for.

Bastian turned the page and studied a picture of the protective charm recommended—a weedy green stalk known to grow prolifically in shallow waters and calm streams—pygmyweed.

He read to Cassian—

"Pygmyweed makes an excellent bedchamber charm, for its flower decants protection and night visions that speak of the future, of the past, of Moor Folk, of wars, of heroism, of duty, and of love."

"The moon will be in its slimmest crescent phase tomorrow," Bastian whispered to the baby. "I'll dowse the sunlight in you, and I'll hunt along the stream and find you your pygmyweed. You won't have to be afraid of anything, then. Not clouds, not shade—"

Cassian kicked at the book, shuffling its pages, flipping them.

Upon reaching the page with the painting of the Goblin King, he quieted.

Bastian, too, staring at the picture, sat motionless. "Not even goblins."

Naga seemed to rouse at their sudden stillness. He eyed the picture as he climbed from the seat of the chair to its arm.

Beneath the picture lay a feasting song said to be chanted by lesser goblins.

In a whisper, Bastian read—

"Slick and slime and boiled grime
fill my plate at supper time.
Tongues of tadpoles burned on hot coals,
sweets of meats hooked out of worm holes,
dragon flies and damsel eyes
I mix with mud and bake in pies.
Fed to fight and blind the light,
I'll sink the sun and bring the night."

The song seemed childish and mild, given the ghastliness of the Sylphic Kingdom's wicked edge. Cassian, so little, even seemed to delight in its silliness.

Bastian never had ventured further into this section of Sylphic frights. But as warm and bright as was the sunlight streaming in from a high window, with Cassian kicking merrily in his arms, with Naga sitting tall beside him, leaning against his shoulder a touch, he felt perhaps he could handle it.

He flipped the page to reveal a sketch of a figure standing on a jagged cliff.

Naga bent near to it, his fur lifting until he was a round puff of a cat.

Bastian felt his heart pick up as he read the caption—*"Wight Witch."*

The wight witch was painted standing on a cliff's edge jetting from a rugged, high tor comprised of rocky spires. The wind looked fierce in that high place, blowing her hair and her dress. She was peering into a steaming cauldron, her crazed eyes seeming even deader than a goblin's.

The text alongside the drawing described wight witches as the most powerful of all Sylphic wickedness, for they were skilled in conjuring curses that no others in the Sylphic Kingdom could.

Goblins, as horrific and powerful as they were, served wight witches.

Lucas peered over Bastian's shoulder and signed, "What are you up to?"

Bastian slammed closed the book.

"Don't hide it," signed Lucas. "That picture looked cool—like something from a comic."

Bastian held the book closely.

"I won't make fun of it, I swear." Lucas lowered the book back into Bastian's lap. "That page looked interesting. Show me."

He really seemed intrigued. Or, at least not in the mood to tease.

Bastian opened the book and found the terrifying painting.

The witch, so realistic, so menacing, seemed to darken the whole room despite the trees, stirred by a gentle wind and sparkling outside the sunny window; despite Cassian's tiny, perfect foot wrinkling the page.

Maybe the lesser goblin song had seemed like child's play because goblins were mild compared to wight witches.

Lucas studied the painting a moment. "Cool." He scruffed the baby's curls. "Kingfisher was a great artist."

He left the reading nook.

Bastian studied Cassian—so loved, so perfect, his tiny body and newborn mind having so slight an understanding of fear or pain.

Even with his small face, crumpling now into sorrow, his blue eyes wetting with tears—it seemed there was so little that could truly trouble him.

Bastian drew him close and shushed him until his crying eased.

Though he doubted his own courage, he couldn't help wishing that the role of the Keeper was to stand between the Sun Child and what terrible things might appear in a battle. He couldn't bear the thought of this baby in any danger or pain.

Perched on the eaves outside, a thrush nightingale caroled a melody that seemed to be about sunlight striking the river Windrush, beckoning its fish to leap and drawing its current east of England, to the magnificent sea.

Cassian fussed until the bird flew away.

At the height of the baby's fit, the sun broke boldly through the clouds, and a beam sparkled in, casting a round impression on Cassian's forehead. The shine curved symmetrically and tipped into curling points at the cardinal positions.

A fluttering drew Bastian's gaze to the window. There he caught a slight impression of crystal wings shivering against the glass and casting shards of faint light.

Bastian rested his gaze again on Cassian.

The way the sun was shimmering on him—the glow seemed precisely like a Sun Kiss.

The shape brightened on the baby's face for a split second, then vanished.

$\mathcal{B}$astian kissed the place on Cassian's forehead where the Sun Kiss had shone.

He kissed Cassian's heavy eyelids, making them finally close.

He curled Cassian into the cherishing curve of his arm, leaned close to his tiny ear, and whispered to him the story of Aubrey Gyrfalcon and the Golden Moor.

He'd barely made it beyond Aubrey encountering the villagers' doubt when a pellet whizzed over his head from the darkness of the dining room.

Bastian placed the book on the floor and slunk out of the chair with the baby.

He crawled to Cassian's playpen and laid him inside it.

"You don't want to mess with me," he signed, facing the dark dining room. "I've gotten way faster."

He ducked as another pellet blew past.

He slunk to his rucksack and drew out a bright orange racquetball —a Ryudo mortar.

Lucas' pellet gun snapped a third round.

Bastian dodged it, then leapt to his feet. He rocketed through the dining room and sprung into a tight Ryudo leap, hurdling Lucas— loading more caps into his pistol.

Lucas aimed.

Bastian wove, straining to reach the living room.

The rules of Living Room Ryudo were absolute. If Bastian were shot, he'd have to go down and let Lucas claim whatever he wanted from his pockets.

Bastian keyed in on a high ventilation window, open a crack—a most challenging Ryudo target, especially because Mum lost her cool when she caught him pitching in the house.

Bastian whipped the racquetball at the window.

It sailed straight through.

He glanced back at Lucas just in time to catch the sting of a pellet on the dead center of his forehead.

He crumpled to the floor.

Lucas flipped him over with a naked toe.

Bastian tried his best to remain dead, while Lucas leaned over him and fished inside his pockets, but he couldn't stay still. He burst out laughing and rolled away.

Lucas had the eyes of an eagle and outstanding aim. He was almost as bull's-eye a pitcher as Bastian, but he hadn't taken up Ryudo, and now Bastian could out-throw him.

From outside came the sound of footsteps.

Bastian sat up and fixed on the front window.

Lucas knelt beside him and looked where he was staring.

On their porch steps, as stiff and as straight and as perilous as a poleaxe, stood Lady Marrowight.

Naga tore into the living room, his ears flat.

Lucas rushed back through the house, signing, "Red alert!" He knocked over a dining room chair that fell with a smack as he sped to the back porch, to find Mum.

Rhys came down the stairs. "What's going on?"

Bastian pointed at the front door. He hurried to Cassian's playpen and lifted the baby out.

Lucas leaned out the back door and signed to Mum, "She's back."

Rhys went to the front door and opened it before Lady Marrowight.

"Is your mother home?" asked the Lady, holding a large basket.

Her voice was resonant and calm.

It seemed bewitching, how melodic it was—a stark contradiction to her meanness. In knowing what cruel words her voice could produce, Bastian could sense in the calmness a simmering, like a storm seething on a placid horizon.

Her fearsome beauty, too, felt treacherous and contrived, bespeaking a power that sought to control.

Lady Marrowight leaned around Rhys and peered into the house. "I've brought something to welcome her new young one."

"Sure," said Rhys. "Wait here a moment."

Lady Marrowight pushed past him, in.

Naga, his fur billowing, hissed.

Mum lighted into the living room. "Lady Marrowight." She shepherded Naga away. "Ah, how kind." She received the basket.

Inside was a bundle of incense sticks reeking of pepper and rancid perfume, a statue of a jester's head with a sharp chin and a blood-red smile slicing from ear to ear, and a tin of butter biscuits, oozing lard.

Mum, rigidly smiling, hurried the pungent basket to the open back door and set it down on the porch.

Lady Marrowight, her gaze darting like an animal anxious about springing a trap, ventured further in.

She trained her gaze on Bastian.

Beneath her stare, the aching in his chest sharpened.

Naga rumbled a growl.

Mum came back in. "It's so nice of you to stop by to welcome our new son." She eased the baby from Bastian's arms. "This is Cassian."

The Lady looked at Cassian like she was disgusted by him.

How anyone could look at a baby that way, Bastian couldn't comprehend. And there'd never been a more beautiful baby than Cassian. His curls shone as though oiled by olives harvested in the vineyard of a god, and his skin—acorn tan—glowed lustrously.

He hung from Mum's arms, sucking his chubby hand and beating the air with his perfect, plump feet. Were Mum to put him down, it seemed he might dance a reel around a Faerie Fire conjured by his merry eyes.

Lady Marrowight eased yet nearer, drawing Cassian's eyes wide.

She aimed her sharp-nailed finger at his naked stomach.

Cassian drew in his legs and screamed.

Naga hissed.

Bastian heaved Cassian from Mum's hands and backed away with him.

The basket, on the back porch, burst into black smoke.

The smoke didn't lift like ordinary hearth smoke—it shot through the house and slithered into the room like a bundle of eels.

Lady Marrowight tended closer to Bastian, holding Cassian. "Lightless, I shall render you."

The smoke billowed, congesting the room with thick shadows. Tendrils of it twined up the bodies of Mum, Rhys, and Lucas. There was no smell of fire in this smoke—more, it was dank and oily like the fumes from the car crash had smelled. It cast a sense of heaviness. Dread.

Rhys, Mum, and Lucas, all standing perfectly still, seemed stonily asleep on their feet.

Naga, rumbling growls and showing his teeth, stumbled when he tried to move.

Cassian nestled against Bastian and seemed to be dropping into drowsiness.

"A beast, fine for slaughter." Lady Marrowight touched her nails to Cassian's bare thigh.

Bastian, fighting exhaustion, knocked back her hand and shielded the baby's leg.

Lady Marrowight keyed in on *Moor Folk of the English Highlands*, lying on the floor beside the rocking chair. "Soon, Sylphic legends shall fall into death."

Sylphic legends that told of a wight witch. A wight witch who seemed horribly alike to the woman standing before him, while Mum, Rhys, and Lucas stood frozen. Cursed.

Bastian felt fully sentient, although moving was proving difficult. He fought the darkness as he stumbled toward his book. He kicked it out of Lady Marrowight's reach and stood before it, guarding it. Guarding Cassian.

Lady Marrowight rushed at them but stopped. Something seemed to be hindering her.

"Come to me, little one." She drew from the folds of her cardigan her twisted stick. "To run is to die."

"I won't let you touch him," Bastian leaned back but found himself scarcely able to take a single step.

Lady Marrowight struggled forward until the stick's end was pointing not toward Cassian, but Bastian.

Bastian could not move as the stick touched the square center of his chest.

At its contact, his heart set to thrashing.

Bastian knocked the stick from her hand. "Get out of here."

"Stout little thing." She laughed. "Good. Stout hearts make for powerful curses." She reclaimed her stick. "Perhaps you can stave off the blade of a goblin, but you shall not thwart this."

Bastian tried to back up, but his feet would not obey.

Lady Marrowight set into a low chanting that rose into two final, clear words—"Be bound."

She jabbed him in the chest with the stick.

The ache tightened and stole his breath like she'd fired into him a net of metal.

His arms, holding Cassian, went ice cold.

She advanced.

At the thought of her touching Cassian—taking him, Bastian felt a warmth flaring from deeply within him, sending shocks of heat down his arms and legs, loosening them some.

Death-gripping the baby, he tore away, ducking past her. He struggled through the kitchen, making for the basket leaking its smoke.

He stumbled out onto the porch and punted the basket, sending it flying far out into the yard, its cursed elements scattering.

The smoke columns unwound from Mum, Rhys, and Lucas and withdrew out the door like worms backing into their holes.

The metallic grip eased from Bastian's chest like a knife slipping out.

Holding Cassian tightly, he eased back inside.

In the dining room, he dropped to his knees.

Mum, Rhys, and Lucas together roused.

"Thanks for stopping over," said Mum, smiling kindly at Lady Marrowight.

Lucas and Rhys seemed somewhat lost but fully awake.

As if by instinct, they together crowded Lady Marrowight toward the front door.

Naga, snarling, slithered among their legs, his eyes fixed on Lady Marrowight's face.

"Sorry, I don't know what's gotten into him." Mum picked him up and smoothed his fur.

Lady Marrowight hastened out the door and fled down the porch steps.

Lucas glanced back at Bastian and signed, "What in the world are you doing on the floor?"

Bastian signed, "Pygmyweed."

Lucas picked up Bastian's book, its pages wrinkling. "You ought to be careful with this." He smoothed the page showing the witch.

Bastian got to his feet and crammed Cassian into Lucas' arms. "I have to find Pygmyweed." He took the book from Lucas.

"What are you talking about?" Lucas signed.

Bastian glanced up the stairs. "The nursery," he signed. "Take him." He pushed Lucas toward the staircase. "Go. It's the safest place."

Lucas met his eyes. "What's the matter with you?"

Bastian, clenching his chest, signed, "I'll be back as quick as I can."

"Are you all right?" signed Lucas. "Do you need your inhaler?"

"I need..." Bastian stared at Kingfisher's book, at the picture of the witch. "Look, stay with Cassian, in his nursery, until I get back. Don't leave him for a minute. No matter what."

Lucas stared at him. "What's making you look so terrified? Not that horrible woman, I hope."

Bastian didn't respond.

"She really got to you, didn't she?" Lucas glanced at Naga, who seemed more like a silver jaguar at the moment than a housecat, with his hackles spiking, his eyes solid black and still fixed on the front door.

"Naga went wild when she came in," signed Lucas. "If she comes back, he'll alert us."

Bastian hurried Lucas up the first stair. "Just keep Cassian in his nursery until I get back. Promise me?"

Lucas met his eyes and signed, "I promise."

18

Bastian biked through a carpeting of leaf litter, along a path winding through a musty willow wood leading to the Natterjack Lagoon.

He halted by a thick tree at the path's edge and leaned against it. He struggled to breathe.

Whatever Lady Marrowight had done to him, the inhaler wasn't touching it.

Biking all the way to the lagoon—nearly half a mile—in this state seemed impossible. He straightened up, though, and pressed on.

He had to make it to the Natterjack.

Cassian, his family—he himself—needed protection.

He pumped his bike up a small rise and finally reached a stretch of birch trees. From here it was mostly downhill, and just on the far side of the birch grove, the Natterjack Lagoon gleamed.

There, tributaries of the Windrush twined together carrying loads of frog spawn, of dragonfly duns, of imago mayflies, of seedlings to a green gully bubbling with plants referenced by Kingfisher.

Just as Bastian reached the other side of the thicket, a strong wind washed over him—a chilled wind, ozone-heavy like a gale rushing through in advance of a powerful storm.

It inflicted in Bastian's aching chest a sense of dread—like he was sensing the approach of something wickedly Sylphic.

A goblin. A witch.

He crept to a wall of tight bushes and cowered against them.

No goblin manifested that he could perceive.

No footsteps broke the silence of the clearing.

There was no cursed smoke hanging in sight or any sign of an unearthly storm.

All he could see was a bank of sweet-smelling mist slipping in from the south, hanging silvery across the cheering green canopy gently swaying beneath the brilliant blue sky.

The dread skidded off as quickly as it'd come.

The wind calmed, and the sky remained empty but for a few wispy clouds and a harpy eagle, circling low.

Bastian dropped his bike at the edge of the grove and snatched *Moor Folk of the English Highlands* from his rucksack. He rushed to the bank of the Natterjack and there rifled through his book to the section describing the protective charm of pygmyweed.

He fixed the book open atop a boulder using two heavy stones, then splashed into the lagoon's frigid shallows.

A plump Natterjack toad, rife with warts, raised its jowly face out of the water and leapt onto the boulder.

It touched its twiggy fingers to the book as it watched insects drone about its head.

It flashed out its tongue and lashed a dragonfly.

Such a common thing it was—a toad haunting a stream; a simple presence, ordinary with its slick skin, with its lanky feet leaving wet footprints.

And yet in watching it, Bastian could focus on nothing but its hunting eyes.

The terror of what'd just happened to him and his family swelled.

A wight witch had come into their chalet. A wight witch had cast a curse on him and his family. A wight witch had tried to hurt Cassian.

Perhaps he should've told Mum and his brothers what'd happened —that something dreadful and deadly had reached them.

But would they have believed him? They couldn't see Lady Marrowight for the wicked Sylphic thing that she was.

Bastian studied the toad, half-expecting to find a fright of batty wings manifesting from its angular spine.

The toad jumped, speared an unlucky damselfly, then crashed its soppy body onto his book.

Bastian waved at it. "Get off."

The toad sat dumbly, the zipping darts of dragonflies sewing up the air about its head.

Bastian studied the picture of pygmyweed under the fleshy belly of the toad.

The pygmyweed's leaves shone peridot green and were tinged with rubescent bands. They spiraled on a stalk springing from a tangle of feathery roots. A pearl-white blossom, diamondesque and small, peeked from beneath a leaf doublet.

Bastian, sucking ragged breaths, ranged the shady water for the plant while dragonflies dazzled the air, their crystal wings catching winks of sun.

He loosened a stalk from the lagoon's bed and carried it back to the book. He held it beside the illustration.

Though similar, it wasn't the same.

"You're quite a sight for sore eyes," said a familiar voice.

Bastian spun.

Master Sayre.

It was Master Sayre standing on the opposite bank, not thirty yards away. Master Sayre smiling in his weathered way. Master Sayre seeming made of strength. Master Sayre—his mere presence feeling as sturdy as ship wood.

Bastian thrashed through the water across the lagoon to him.

All he needed to say—everything about the storm in the football park and the goblin with the knife and his own stupidity for failing to heed good advice; everything about the wight witch in his book; about the Sylphic water child; about the doctor who'd given him an emblem of dragons; about Cassian—their Sun Child, now born; about Lady Marrowight's cruel words and her stony smoke and her jab to his chest; about pygmyweed and sun dowsing charms—it jumbled all together in a knot in his brain, and he found himself standing stiff in the middle of the cold pool, unable to utter a single word.

"I'm sorry I was away for so long, but it couldn't be helped," said Master Sayre. "You must be chomping at the bit to train."

"There's no time," muttered Bastian.

"But before we get to work, lad," said Master Sayre, "you and I must speak."

As desperate as Bastian was to hear anything Master Sayre had to say, he had not a moment to lose.

He held up the plant. "Is this pygmyweed?"

Master Sayre pointed his wooden yachtsman pipe at it. "You've found a nice sampling of water primrose, but I'm afraid that doesn't share the virtues of pygmyweed."

Bastian slung it aside. "I need pygmyweed." He struggled through the water back to the boulder holding his book.

"What's happened?" Master Sayre waded into the lagoon and followed him to its other side.

Bastian lifted *Moor Folk of the English Highlands*, the toad heavy on it, from the boulder and read, "*Crops of pygmyweed make an attractive hunting ground for toads.*" He lifted the sticky toad and pressed it toward Master Sayre.

Master Sayre cupped his hand and received the toad.

"There—" Bastian abandoned the book into Master Sayre's free hand.

He moved nearer to the bank and ripped a plant growing underwater between two slippery rocks.

"Pygmyweed." He shook off the mud. "I have to go."

"Hang on, that's not pygmyweed." Master Sayre waded after him. "What's this pursuit all about?"

Bastian glanced at the book, resting in Master Sayre's hands. "Protection and dreams."

Upstream, a stone plunked in the water.

Bastian turned.

There, on the eastern bank, in a patch of pale sunlight, knelt a girl.

A girl about his age. A girl bathing round river stones belted with bands of white quartz. A girl in a white dress that cast her as airy and ethereal.

Before her floated a fleet of lily pads, their buds packed and peeking from the water.

Bastian watched her, wondering if she'd dive in and vanish, like the Sylphic water girl from the Natterjack Cave had.

But she stayed right where she was.

She was the loveliest thing Bastian ever had seen.

Her face was fine-featured and heart-shaped. The breeze played at her sweetly curling hair, selecting strands to pull out of her bun and toss about her ears. She was singing softly in a strange language—and the melody, that melody—he'd heard it before.

He recognized it as the sound that'd lilted in the hospital corridor on the night Cassian was born.

The wind seemed to carry her singing and weave it together with a melody a thrush was trilling from some high place.

She flashed her eyes to meet Bastian's.

She kept singing.

"This young lady—Kaliyah—is the daughter of a friend," said Master Sayre, gently letting the toad go in the water. "She'll be staying with Mrs. Sayre and me for a while."

"Pygmyweed." Bastian wandered the water—frantic.

Master Sayre drew nearer to him.

"Lad?"

Bastian slipped on an algae-slick stone and splashed down.

Master Sayre trudged to him and hauled him back up.

Bastian, gasping, clung to his arm. "She came."

Master Sayre steadied him. "Who came?"

"Rhys and Lucas think it's all foolishness," said Bastian. "Mum and Da don't take it a bit seriously." He gripped his chest.

"By the dawn, you're bewildered and freezing," said Master Sayre.

"In the stream—in the cave, things went mad." Bastian struggled through a ragged breath.

"Come, now. Let's move toward the bank." Master Sayre helped him trudge to the eastern shallows.

"I saw things, I felt things," said Bastian. "Terrible things." He scanned the water behind him, murky now from his slip. "And today she came. Meaning to hurt him."

"Deep breaths." Master Sayre guided him to sit on the bank. "Take it slowly. Now—who wanted to hurt who?"

"That Marrowight woman," said Bastian. "If she'd touched him, I… she's worse than crazy. She's—well, wicked. If I hadn't distracted her, taken that strike, I don't know—a baby couldn't survive this." Cradling his chest, he tipped forward. "I might not either."

"Hang on—what strike?"

Master Sayre eased him further away from the cold water and onto a swath of clean grass.

Bastian turned his eyes toward Master Sayre. "I mean to protect the baby. Lady Marrowight saw that. But she also probably saw that I can't." Every inch of his body felt stone cold. "I don't know what's going on." He couldn't stop a trembling setting in.

Master Sayre took off his jacket. "That she could render you like this…we knew she was brewing something, but—"

"Then—you know about her?" Bastian gripped the front of his master's tunic. "Do you know about the Sun Child? About goblins? About the thing in the stream from the cave? Do you know about the boy with the arrows by my house? About the wind chimes, the singing? The drumming? The screaming? The doctor who carries Sylphic relics of dragons?"

Master Sayre held up his hand. "That last one, I know well. Calm yourself, and let's see to you." He snugged his jacket around Bastian's shoulders.

Warmth rose, wrapping him in a scent of tarnished leather and sea brine.

Master Sayre guided him to lie back.

He felt of Bastian's arms, his hands, his chest. "No. Oh, no."

The girl—Kaliyah—stood away from her stones and water lilies and approached.

"It's spreading." Master Sayre glanced at Kaliyah. "He needs help."

"What's spreading?" asked Bastian.

Kaliyah knelt at his side. "This can't be." She laid her smooth hand gently on his chest.

Sopping, breathless, shivering, hardly able to move—it was mortifying for the girl to see him in this state, much less touch him.

Bastian raised up. "You don't have to—"

Master Sayre pressed him to lie back down.

Kaliyah rested her two delicate hands more firmly on his chest. "He's been struck directly."

Master Sayre shook his head. "How could she have slipped past them?"

"Past who?" whispered Bastian.

"To have dodged their watch," said Kaliyah. "She grows sharper, the shrew."

"Can you draw it out?" Master Sayre asked Kaliyah.

Bastian tried to press them to explain what was going on, but he couldn't gather enough air to speak.

"I don't know," said Kaliyah. "It's darker, far denser, than anything I've dealt with before."

Master Sayre tightened his grip on Bastian's shoulders. "Try."

Kaliyah settled her hands again on Bastian's chest. Warmth surged from her fingertips, chasing some of the chill. She closed her eyes, then pressed hard.

Fierce heat swelled into him and flashed down both of his arms. She pulled back.

When she lifted her hands, Bastian found he could breathe steadily.

"How did you do that?" Bastian eased to his elbows and looked down at himself. "What did you do?"

"Hardly anything." Kaliyah looked at Master Sayre. "I've stopped it from spreading, but it's like before—he'll have to heal on his own." Tears filled her eyes. "But how can he? He's got no fortitude."

"Hey," said Bastian.

"He chased it before, to some degree," said Master Sayre. "And so he must keep trying. This could delay our plans, but it by no means destroys them."

"But—you're not going to delay telling him, right?" asked Kaliyah. "You said you'd tell him today."

"Tell me what?" asked Bastian.

"Certainly not, considering the state he's in," said Master Sayre.

"But how else—" Kaliyah began.

"There's no chance he could—"

"No, of course not," said Kaliyah, "but he should at least know what's happening to him."

Master Sayre drew a deep breath, then straightened. "I won't argue about this now, lass." He laid his gaze again on Bastian. "We haven't any choice."

Bastian rubbed at his chest, at the aching chill lingering, though distantly. "What are you talking about?"

Kaliyah stood, facing Master Sayre. "Is he not entitled to know?"

"Why, no, he isn't," said Master Sayre, staring at her as directly as she was staring at him. "Do we have an understanding?"

Bastian eased to sitting up. "Can someone please tell me what's going on?"

Master Sayre looked him in the eyes. "Nothing that we could say will help you at this point." He brought Kaliyah to kneeling again beside Bastian. "Lad, you must recount for us everything that's happened."

19

"*E*verything that's happened," whispered Bastian, holding his chest. "It's been extraordinary."

That Lady Marrowight had inflicted him with this wretched pain; that she'd bound Mum, Rhys, and Lucas with smoke; that Lady Marrowight seemed precisely like the wight witch in his book—Bastian felt he was inhabiting a reality he couldn't parse.

His predicament seemed little different from newborn Cassian's, the baby constantly stark-eyed, as though bewildered each day at finding himself in a strange land.

Master Sayre set his hand on Bastian's shoulder. "Steady yourself." He placed his other hand warmly on Bastian's chest. "And tell us what's happened."

"I can hardly believe it." Bastian stared up at the sunny blue sky. "And yet—I can't deny any part of it."

He recounted the car accident and what he'd seen in the road. He described what he'd sighted by his house that day—a Sylphic boy of some sort shooting flaming arrows at Lady Marrowight. He described Cassian's difficult birth and meeting the A&E doctor who knew Sylphic legends.

And he told them what'd happened today—Lady Marrowight bringing the reeking, cursed basket to the chalet.

Lady Marrowight's bizarre words. Her slithering smoke. The jab from her stick.

When he described it, Kaliyah's hand went to her own chest.

"And since you left the shire," said Bastian, "that's not the only horrific thing that's happened."

He avoided looking at Master Sayre.

"You'll be angry with me, I know. But the night we last were together, I didn't go straight home, like you asked. Lucas and I stayed in the park because—well, I thought I might see something Sylphic. And boy did I ever."

"I know what happened in the park that night, lad," said Master Sayre. "It was foolish of you to fail to heed my cautioning. However, what happened there—and what didn't happen—it shed light on a question that's troubled us for a very long time."

"I don't understand," said Bastian.

"That night," said Master Sayre, "you came under attack from a Sylphic force you know all too well."

"That goblin boy and his blade," said Bastian. "I'm not sure how, but I managed to get away from him with hardly a scratch. Lucas, though, didn't. He's still a little banged up, actually."

He told them of his encounter with the Sylphic water girl in the stream and how he'd relived the night of their fight with the goblin boy.

"I'm aware of what you saw under the naiad's enchantment," said Master Sayre. "She delivered that to you upon my request, to prepare you for a discussion that you and I must have"—he glanced at Kaliyah—"when the time is right."

"The right time is now," whispered Kaliyah, under her breath.

Bastian met Master Sayre's gaze. "Legends coming to life and witches with petrifying smoke; goblins wielding knives; Moor Folk creeping from the throats of caves; promised Sun Children and Keepers—I know every bit of it's true. And yet, I feel like I'm losing my grip. My family certainly thinks that I am."

Master Sayre tightened his jacket around Bastian's shoulders. "It's difficult, no doubt, to accept that there may be elements in our world outside of what we call 'ordinary.' But if you can accept the extraordinary as part of this world, then perhaps Sylphic legends won't seem so far-fetched."

Something within Bastian seemed to loosen at the reasoning. Maybe it was the ache in his chest that slightly was easing.

Or—it more seemed Master Sayre's words had soothed something deeper.

"All these strange sounds and sensations, though—what exactly are they?" asked Bastian. "Music. Rain pattering. Far-off waterfalls. Tinkling bells. Pipes. Bird songs. Chanting. Drumming. Sea waves. And, lately, terrifying things. Like sudden cold winds that seem to pierce to the heart. The ringing of blades drawn. And screaming."

Kaliyah folded her arms. "You don't hear enough. You don't see enough."

Master Sayre cast her a cross glance.

Bastian flipped to the page in his book showing the wight witch. "I find myself wishing that I were going mad. I'd prefer madness to have actually seen a wight witch cast a curse on my family today."

"The wight witch certainly is real." Kaliyah turned to a page holding a drawing of a Sylphic boy in light armor, kneeling on wide vale with fallen warriors and stone statues strewn beneath a coppery sky. "But so is the Sun Child."

Master Sayre took the book from her and set it aside.

"When I pick up on these extraordinary things, I know I'm tapping into the Sylphic Kingdom," said Bastian. "But how could there be an entire kingdom that I can sense, barely—and yet it seems to be no place reachable? Where, even, is the Sylphic Kingdom?"

"Why, the Sylphic Kingdom is everywhere," said Master Sayre. "*Sylphic* refers to the Sun Devaa's immortal people—faeries, dryads, sprites, annwyn, sunwalkers, forest children, oakmen, and the like. They're all around us." He glanced toward the lagoon. "Even now."

Bastian studied the Natterjack where insects were dancing. He glanced at the woodland, swaying in a soft breeze. The sky overhead was a deep ocean blue, and upon it, a curved streak of thin moon was sailing. The stream's moving was lapping the threshold of the black cave in the northern distance.

There didn't seem to be anything Sylphic anyplace.

"Is the Sylphic Kingdom someplace I could actually see?" asked Bastian. "Something I could touch if I wanted to?"

"Yes," said Master Sayre. "And no." He nipped a bouquet of pinwheel phlox growing near and held it before Bastian. "Look closely, lad. And tell me what you see."

The petals were striped in cartwheels of cornflower blue and pure white.

"It's just flowers," said Bastian.

"Look closer."

One of the petals flickered, then moved. A shift in perception, and there lay the camouflaged outline of a powdery-blue butterfly.

The butterfly fluttered its fuzzy periwinkle wings, caught the edge of a lilting breeze, and floated away.

"That's a good deal like the Sylphic Kingdom." Master Sayre handed Kaliyah the bouquet. "And do you see that meadow pipet flittering underneath the gorse thicket, just there? Consider what a snug little chamber that is for the pipet, with its ceiling of petals, its checkers of sunlight, its lushness of green plants, and the rich soil beneath. No faerie's bordereaux could be finer. In the dead of winter, though, upon seeing that chamber, you might say there's nothing but twigs and briars choking a frozen patch of earth. So, the pipet's dazzling hollow fades into invisibility. And yet it remains, only wanting the atmosphere of sun and warm waters and the dawning of spring to draw it out."

Bastian watched the little pipet in his bower, kicking up a plume of dust as he hunted his insects.

"Not all that long ago," said Bastian, "I was desperate to see the Sylphic Kingdom. I thought it was mostly full of goodness. Now, though—it's seeming far more treacherous than good." He met Master Sayre's gaze. "There are other things—terrible things—in the Sylphic Kingdom, even beyond witches and goblins, aren't there?"

"They're called Elemental Spirits," said Kaliyah. "Creatures despising the sun and all virtue. They're destructive. Murderous."

"Come," Master Sayre stood and drew Bastian to his feet. "Let's put you on the Ryudo pitch. After suffering the curse the wight witch laid on you today, Ryudo is all that might deliver you any strength back."

"There's no time for a Ryudo run." Bastian picked up his book. "I really have no time for even this talk." He shrugged off Master Sayre's jacket and gave it to him. "The Sun Child has been born, into my family. I have loads to do to keep him safe."

"There are already charms protecting your chalet," said Kaliyah. "You should stay here and follow Master Sayre's guidance."

"Clearly, my chalet could use more protection," said Bastian.

"The Witch Marrowight may have broken through the chalet's charms once," she said, "but there's no way she could do it twice in a single day."

"My chalet has no pygmyweed," said Bastian. "To keep Cassian safe, according to Kingfisher, I need pygmyweed."

"Ryudo." Master Sayre stood before him. "What are its tenets?"

Bastian let go of a heavy breath. "It's about standing one's ground. Clear thinking and planning in chaos. Throwing true." He glanced over Master Sayre's shoulder toward the lagoon.

"And?" asked Master Sayre.

"And facing opposition square. Agility and creative responses to assaults. Keeping one's eye on the goal." Bastian glanced from Master Sayre to Kaliyah. "Will you please help me find some pygmyweed?"

"You're neglecting the final tenet," said Master Sayre.

Bastian lowered his gaze. "Ryudo is about accepting one's place in the fight."

"In this conflict, at present, Ryudo is your place," said Master Sayre. "You must strive onward, honing these defensive and offensive skills that are, for all practical purposes, Sylphic."

Bastian met his gaze. "Will Ryudo help me keep Cassian safe?"

"It's the only thing." Master Sayre guided Bastian on, toward the Ryudo pitch.

Kaliyah, walking closely beside Bastian, met his eyes. "Elemental Spirits want the Moor Folk defeated so they can bring down the Sun Devaa and crown their own ruler."

Bastian shivered like cold water had splashed him.

"Kaliyah, that's plenty," said Master Sayre.

"They're altogether wicked." She seemed to be avoiding Master Sayre's glare. "There are swamp hags, tangies, spriggans, witchlings, trolls, sloughs, kelpies, minor goblins, dragons—"

Bastian stumbled, his foot catching on an uneven patch of grass.

Master Sayre steadied him.

"Lass, this isn't helping him."

"Actually"—Kaliyah held up a finger—"some dragons. Not all. It's the Elemental Spirits who the Sun Child must fight." She glanced at his book. "But you won't find much about Elemental Spirits in that book. To learn about them, you'd have to read Kingfisher's other book."

Bastian, staring at her, halted.

"What other book?"

Master Sayre stood before them both. "That's quite enough, Kaliyah. Look at how bloodless your words are rendering him."

Kaliyah stomped. "But he hardly knows anything."

"Why can't I know about the other book?" Bastian asked. "Do you think I can't be trusted with it?"

"It's not that, lad," said Master Sayre, "it's just—"

Kaliyah drew a big breath and blurted, "The lost book is said to hold a battle plan and secrets to defeating the Elemental Spirits and their queen—that wight witch, who's worse than anything any Sun Child ever has faced."

She covered her mouth with both hands.

Bastian stared from Kaliyah to Master Sayre.

"Listen to me, lad. The book of which Kaliyah speaks is out of your reach at present. Ryudo is all that will help you at this point." He held Bastian steady by his shoulder. "Ryudo drills chase curses. They're what has healed the injury you suffered last year. And they've strengthened you beautifully, which is how you managed to deflect the goblin's assault on the night that I left."

"If Kingfisher wrote another book," said Bastian, "one about Elemental Spirits, about battle strategies—I need it. Cassian needs me to learn what's inside it."

Master Sayre extended his arm toward the Ryudo pitch. "A short Ryudo course. Two obstacles. One target. Yes?"

Bastian watched the Natterjack Lagoon for a moment, then handed *Moor Folk of the English Highlands* to Kaliyah. He followed Master Sayre onto the Ryudo pitch.

"Today, you'll cast not racquetballs, but Kaliyah's stones," said Master Sayre.

Kaliyah pulled a fistful of plum-sized stones, all banded with quartz, from a pocket on her skirt.

"You've said that Ryudo masters practice with something heavy," said Bastian. "Is this what they use?"

"Masters use something of a similar size," said Master Sayre. "A bit heavier, yes. A bit warmer."

Kaliyah loaded a stone, striped with a thick ring of white crystal, into Bastian's hand.

Bastian took his place at the center of the pitch.

His joints were stiff, and a heaviness had worked its way into his muscles. But as he crouched into his opening stance, he felt a warmth churning deeply inside his chest, as though the heat Kaliyah had pressed into him was lingering there.

"Name my target," called Bastian.

"The boulder, across the lagoon's waters." Master Sayre raised his hand, then dropped it like an axe.

Bastian sprinted across the clearing, making for the lagoon.

His footfalls triggered a series of racquetballs set in catapults that sprung in a sequence driving him off course, to the north.

Breaking past them, he confronted a log that seemed to levitate.

The way this obstacle moved—sometimes up, sometimes down, sometimes straight at him, he could never predict.

It swung in an arc, sweeping toward his feet.

He tagged it with one hand and sprang over it, then set in a sprint toward the lagoon.

The instant he was in range, he stopped and heaved the stone toward the boulder on its far side.

It flew clear over, missing by meters.

The log swept in, knocking him flat.

Kaliyah and Master Sayre ran to him.

Bastian pulled to his knees.

Kaliyah knelt before him and held her hand against his chest. "The pain"—she met his eyes—"has it faded?"

"I don't know. Maybe a little." Bastian glanced at Master Sayre. "Ryudo—can it actually mend all this pain?"

Kaliyah focused on Master Sayre. "Is there any real hope that it will?"

"We always can hope." Master Sayre wrapped his jacket once again around Bastian. "Soon, you'll drill with my own master, and in a powerful way."

"But in the state Bastian was in even before the witch struck him"—Kaliyah tightened her hand against his chest in a protective way—"you said you weren't sure if even your master's methods would work. Should we not give Bastian every advantage we can? Telling him more would surely help."

Bastian of course wanted to understand everything Master Sayre might have to reveal.

But at Kaliyah's words, betraying Master Sayre's uncertainty that healing from this was possible—the bottom seemed to drop from his stomach.

"Come," said Master Sayre, picking up Bastian's book. "Let's find your pygmyweed."

Kaliyah stood and led Bastian and Master Sayre toward the Natterjack Lagoon.

On the bank, she knelt before her pyramid of stones and added to them those she'd carried in her pockets.

Master Sayre set into an exploration of the shallows.

Bastian knelt by her stones and lifted one. "Can I take some of these with me? It might be helpful if I could use them to practice my aim."

"Take them all."

Kaliyah scooped them up by handfuls and helped Bastian load them into his pockets.

When she had him well-weighted with her stones, she stepped into the lagoon and waded to its western bank.

Bastian followed her, feeling some bit of agony watching her skirt and pale, thin legs, tint in the green chill of the lagoon.

She reached underwater and drew out a fleshy plant with a spiraled stalk. She faced him, the eyeleted hem of her dress clinging to her knees.

Bastian received the plant from her.

Master Sayre glanced at the sky—no longer shining, but billowing gray. "You'd best be off." He handed Bastian *Moor Folk of the English Highlands*. "Two days from now, in the sun's early hours, come back to the pitch. You shall drill, finally, with my own master." He looked Bastian in the eyes. "I do believe training with him—engaging in his challenging methods—will chase a good measure of this darkness." He glanced at Kaliyah. "But it's true that I can't be sure how far you'll get."

"Can I know more, then, about what you have to tell me?" asked Bastian.

Master Sayre, his expression compassionate, watched him. "I need you to trust that I'll tell you what I can, when I can."

Kaliyah folded her arms and muttered to herself, "It's not right."

Bastian picked up his bike and walked it to a spindly path, trodden to a dusty smoothness by the slender hooves of deer.

"Lad," Master Sayre called, holding up a silver spool. "The best way to fix a sprig of pygmyweed to a crib is with fishing line."

He tossed it.

Bastian caught the spool, splotched with orange pinpoints of rust from its many visits to the ocean.

He pocketed it, then mounted his bike. He rode as fast as he could manage along the path leading to Kingfisher Chalet.

20

Sitting at the supper table that evening, Bastian could hardly meet the eyes of his parents and brothers.

Watching them smile and talk easy was like seeing them relaxing on a sunny shore, laughing and chatting, while he—on a vessel he couldn't control—was drifting off on a treacherous sea.

"Lady Marrowight came by today, did she?" asked Da, signing. "That must've been interesting."

Just the mention of her name pricked Bastian as a metallic bitterness, like tin foil on the tongue.

He felt desperate to tell them what really had happened. Who she actually was. What she was.

But it seemed impossible that they'd ever believe him.

"Her visit wasn't that bad, to be honest," said Rhys, signing back.

Bastian tightened his hand around his fork.

"She brought Mum a gift," Rhys went on. "It was a rather nice change."

"Lady Marrowight's a maggot and has no business coming around here." Bastian leaned over his plate and speared his Cumberland sausages.

"Manners, Bastian," cautioned Da, slicing the ham shank into cutlets.

Bastian glanced at Lucas, at Rhys, at Mum, all oblivious to having been frozen stony with Lady Marrowight's cursed smoke.

"If you only knew her," he said, signing.

"She didn't speak hurtfully again today, I hope," said Da, his brow raised.

Bastian glanced at the stairs, toward the nursery, where he'd tied the pygmyweed to Cassian's crib.

"She called Cassian a beast."

"Come on, she says enough odd things without your embellishment," said Rhys. "She did nothing but stare weirdly at the baby. Not that I'm wishing to defend her—she's completely lost the plot. But in visiting us today, she clearly meant well."

Cassian's waking cry drifted down from the nursery. He sounded panicked.

Mum rose and went up the stairs.

With the pygmyweed tied to his crib now, decanting what charms it might, had Cassian dreamed?

Maybe he'd seen a battle. Maybe he'd suffered a nightmare of fighting in one and was lying there terrified.

Kingfisher said pygmyweed offered some protection, and perhaps it did. But it wouldn't make Cassian any match for a wight witch.

Mum returned, holding Cassian, and settled gently again in her chair.

"Lady Marrowight does seem to lack sensible boundaries," said Da. "Not to mention tact."

Bastian studied Da—oblivious to anything Sylphic, but for all that, muscled and strong. Smart and kind.

"She thinks she knows everything, but she hasn't a clue," signed Lucas.

Regular people had power, even if it wasn't Sylphic. Regular people had devoted police officers and brave soldiers and brilliant doctors and loving parents and wise teachers—plenty of heroes with strength enough to stand up against evil.

What would actually happen, Bastian wondered, if he did just come clean?

He could tell his family exactly what he'd seen. About all the Sylphic things that'd happened to him. And what Lady Marrowight truly was.

It seemed, actually, that he had no choice but to tell them.

He had to get them to understand what danger they were in—what Lady Marrowight was capable of. What was coming.

Perhaps it wasn't impossible for them to believe him. Maybe, on some subconscious level, Mum, Rhys, and Lucas knew that something non-natural—something dreadful—had happened to them today.

Bastian looked carefully at his parents, at each brother. "Lady Marrowight doesn't just lack boundaries," he said, signing. "And she isn't just clueless. The truth is—she's dangerous."

"She certainly is rude," said Da. "But I daresay, she isn't dangerous."

Bastian opened *Moor Folk of the English Highlands* and held up the picture of the wight witch.

At just glancing at the painting of her angular figure standing on the treacherous cliff's edge, leaning over her cauldron—the chill in his chest that Kaliyah had calmed stirred again.

"Can you not say this is a striking resemblance?" asked Bastian.

Da placed on his reading glasses and leaned forward. "Wight Witch."

Rhys twisted his brow. "Please tell me you're not saying you think Lady Marrowight's a witch."

Mum wrapped Cassian in his blanket and held him more closely against her. "Of course he's not." She studied the book, then studied Bastian. "You're not, my love, right?"

"We'd be better off if you told her not to come around here anymore," said Bastian.

Mum and Da both fixed on him. They seemed a bit shocked by the emotion in his voice.

"We can't risk letting her near us again," Bastian went on, "because—"

The way they were all staring at him—he felt his nerve waning. But if there was any chance they'd listen to him, if there was any chance they could stand all together in the light of this strange, new reality—he had to try telling them the truth.

Bastian took a deep breath, carefully let it go, then laid in.

"Witches are fabled to live in the Wystan Woods," he said, signing. "And it's not just me who knows so. You've all heard the old lore. Legends say that a battle is coming." He glanced at Cassian. "A battle that the Sun Child must win, or else the Sylphic Kingdom will fall."

Rhys and Lucas exchanged glances, like they'd together anticipated this dire moment—Bastian's obsession with Sylphic legends reaching a fever pitch and robbing him, at last, of all sanity.

"But here's the thing." Bastian drew a steadying breath. "It's all true." He leaned in. "I know because I've seen things. I've seen a naiad in the Windrush, underwater, pale as death. I've seen blade-wielding goblins and a Sylphic boy standing by our chalet, shooting flaming arrows at Lady Marrowight. I've seen fiery eyes peering from the dark woods. I've heard things, too. Distant drums. Flutes and pipes. Sea waves. Screaming."

Bastian eyed each of them, watching for signs of fear troubling them as he hit home the terrible truth. "Wight witches and goblins and Sylphic Moor Folk," he said, signing. "They exist."

Everyone kept silent and held so still, it seemed they hardly were breathing.

And then Rhys' somber face crackled into a grin.

Mum and Da together broke into laughter.

Lucas sat back and signed, "I wish I had your imagination."

Mum, subduing her smile, flashed Da a glance the way she did when she was pleased with how cute her little boys were. All of them hated when she did that.

"Place a restraining order if you must," said Bastian, "but do something."

"A restraining order?" asked Rhys, failing at mastering his chuckling. "I don't believe you can place a restraining order because you think someone's a witch."

"Indeed not," said Da. "But I must say, I quite like Bastian's approach to dealing with Lady Marrowight. Making things fun surely takes the sting out of her words. I say, keep that fine imagination stoked."

"But I'm not imagining things."

Da raised his juice glass. "That's the spirit!"

The others joined their glasses to Da's in a toast to Bastian's wild imagination.

Bastian sat motionless staring at their ease, which he had no part in.

Kingfisher's stories were real. Lady Marrowight truly was a witch—a most treacherous wight witch who was coming for Cassian.

The chill in his chest set to aching like a frost had settled inside him.

He pressed at the ache. A witch had done this to him, but his family—they couldn't believe him.

It would be up to forces greater than parents and brothers, then, to deal with the wight witch. It would be up to the Sun Child.

"Why so serious, my love?" Mum cut the last battered banger and divided it among them. "When you next see Lady Marrowight, just laugh on the inside, while on the outside you offer a bit of respect."

"The next time I see her," Bastian signed, "I'll respectfully tell her where she can shove that twisted stick that she carries."

Da smirked. "It is frightfully odd that she carries that witchy old stick." He gave Bastian a chummy nudge. "But let's try to ignore her, my lad. Shall we?"

Outside the window, something flickered—electric blue—over the apple tree.

And then a bright streak, like a shard of pale lightning, seemed to split from an invisible storm and rain down, zapping the tree. Tremors of blue sparks snapped like tiny fireworks in its boughs.

That cold, stormy light awakened a sense of dread in Bastian. It was the same strain of blood-freezing terror that'd gripped him at the sight of the goblin; at the nearing of the witch.

"Bastian?" Rhys bent to catch his gaze.

Da, too, was staring at him. So were Mum and Lucas. No one had eyes on that tree. Of course they weren't seeing this.

The sizzling light burst into a raging blue fire.

Bastian startled at the heat of its flames pressing his face.

"What's the matter with him?" signed Lucas.

Mum rose and stood over him. "Love? Look at me."

All at once, the blue light and the blazing heat vanished.

With its going, the sense of dread eased.

Bastian carefully peeled the breading off a bit of sausage and sailed it through the sea of syrup on his plate, like he'd just needed a minute to think.

"It isn't possible to ignore Lady Marrowight." He looked up at Mum. "She's trouble."

Rhys stood and set to work at his chore, stacking their finished plates. "I expect she'd say the same about you."

21

$\mathcal{A}$fter the kitchen was scrubbed and the garden herbs and root vegetables restrung in their nets, and after the dining room table was set to rights, and after the den was darkened and its fire put out, Bastian settled beside Mum on their back porch swing.

Hanging from the rafters overhead, padded with paisley cushions, the swing was like the pendulous nest of a weaver bird, carrying notes of Mum's cedarwood and coconut lotions. The swing had traveled with them from San Francisco, and it held a place in Bastian's oldest memories.

Mum bundled their sleeping Cassian warmly against them both.

Evening's damp settled as the sky deepened.

Whatever had been in the apple tree had moved off, and its branches were swaying quietly, in their usual way.

Bastian gently moved the swing as he watched the woodland shift from a silent twilit canopy to a choir of blackened silhouettes weaving lullabies out of wind, rocking roosting songbirds into somnolence and shaking little hunting owls awake.

The back door burst open, and Rhys and Lucas followed a swiftly kicked football down the porch steps and over the lawn.

Da bit his wooden calabash pipe and sat before the swing on a log he'd freshly cut. Humming and suckling his pipe, he loosed the tavern-peppery flavors of Cambridge and cured Cavendish as he coaxed a flame to rise inside an oil lantern.

Bastian thumbed through *Moor Folk of the English Highlands*, exploring its illustrations by the cheery lantern's fire while stars, as bright as arrow tips, appeared among the rowan limbs crowning the eastern hill.

The wind picked up and blew the book's pages.

They fell open to a spread Bastian hadn't yet read.

It was a painting of a forest at night, its trees impressed with tiny doors at their bases and lower branches, their latticed peepholes flowing with firefly candlelight.

The text alongside the picture read—

When little lights lay sleeping underneath a waning moon—
    when falcons call and star songs fall,
    attend and rise—alight your eyes.
    Forsake your fear and tarry near
    the goblin's grove; the witch's cove.

When little lights lay weeping underneath an absent moon—
    fear not the tomb. Descend the gloom.
    Make fast your stand. Make still your hand.
    For wise ones claim—in dark's domain,
    the children of the forest reign.

The opposite page showed a black sun blazing over a battlefield riddled with bodies.

The caption read: *The Day of the Dark Sun is foretold to be the day of the coming Sun Child's battle.*

"This battle Kingfisher writes about," said Bastian to Mum, "*The Day of the Dark Sun*—have you ever heard of anything like it?"

Mum studied the picture. "That sun looks, to me, like it's being eclipsed. During a total solar eclipse, the moon completely hides the sun, making it look black, just like that."

"Do eclipses happen very often in Dartmoor?" he asked.

"I'm not sure, love." She handed him her phone.

Bastian typed in the question and learned that a total solar eclipse would be visible in the southern part of England this very year.

On the first new moon of May—read the article—*the moon will roll before the sun, inking it black and casting an unnatural night upon Dartmoor.*

"The first new moon of May." Bastian stared at the baby, nestling against Mum. The tiny baby.

He pulled up a lunar calendar and checked the date. The first new moon of May would occur on May 3rd—only three days off.

But that couldn't be right. Cassian—the Sun Child—was barely more than a newborn.

Bastian searched again and found the very same answer, from multiple sources. He rechecked the details on the lunar calendar, ensuring he was looking at the correct year.

May 3rd of this year was, without question, the date of the coming eclipse. Three days from now, the moon would be new and would ink black the sun, bringing a freak night to Dartmoor.

Bastian tightened Cassian's blanket more snuggly over his small shoulders. He'd imagined he'd have years and years to prepare the Sun Child for whatever was coming. Because—what could a newborn baby possibly do in a battle?

He researched total solar eclipses further. Maybe the one happening in three days wasn't the specific one spoken of in *Moor Folk of the English Highlands*. It could be that many eclipses were forecasted.

But every article he found highlighted how special this year's May 3rd eclipse would be. There wouldn't be another total eclipse visible from Dartmoor during their lifetimes.

A wash of terror struck as Bastian imagined the moon, already deeply waning, day by day diminishing to nothing. A meager three days from now, it would darken the sun and bring battle to these Sylphic lands.

Bastian glanced at Mum, at Da. At Rhys and Lucas. A battle in three days—what would that mean for their family? What terrible conflict was the Sylphic Kingdom bound to suffer?

He rested his gaze on Cassian.

With the moon's disappearance, and a battle in three days—what would be demanded of the Sun Child? What would he suffer?

Bastian straightened some, trying to fend back the horrifying thought of his family, of tiny Cassian, suffering the terrors of an imminent battle.

All day long, Bastian had been watching that waning moon coast, its arc of white seeming like a sail bowed by wind, cruising it fearlessly across the blue sky and through storm clouds.

It was as though it'd been racing to meet what its darkening might bring.

He settled back some at the thought. For the moon—even a deeply waning one, didn't actually symbolize suffering or defeat. Through every one of its phases, did the moon not still serve as a counterpart to the powerful sun?

And tomorrow's moon wouldn't only carry a strengthening darkness—it would also usher in the phase that allowed the mortal and Sylphic worlds to strongly overlap.

Tomorrow's waning moon, though merely a sliver, would shine brashly—the sun casting brilliance to light up its counterpart's rim. That slender moon, though a portent of battle, would also serve as a signal of the secret strength kept by the Sun Child.

Bastian wrapped his fist around the charm the A&E doctor had fastened on him—the Egyptian symbol, the Eye of Ra—an emblem of dragon fire; it, too, a counterpart to the sun.

He steadied as he recalled feeling the advance of the sun's deep warmth, its strong energy—a sensation that'd arisen inside him in the dark early hours of the day Cassian had been born.

Just before Mum had gone into labor, he'd been watching the east, as he was at this moment. The sun, still beneath the horizon, had promised its coming by casting a gilded glow onto the clouds.

The moon had been new that day, in full shadow, its rim barely visible against the pale starry night.

And yet from that climbing darkness of moon, Bastian felt he'd received a touch of the sun's warmth, reflected.

Bastian traced Cassian's tiny, soft cheek.

He touched the place on the baby's forehead where the Sun Kiss had appeared.

A one-month-old baby couldn't do anything in a battle, it was true.

But what about a one-month-old Sun Child?

The wisdom Master Sayre had spoken visited him—that if he could manage to think of the extraordinary as part of this world, then Sylphic realities might not seem so far-fetched.

The bare truth was that the Sun Child kept Sylphic powers of some kind. And Sylphic powers were fierce.

Bastian was fully prepared to take advantage, tomorrow, of the moon's barely-lit form and cast the sun dowsing rite over Cassian. Tomorrow, he'd discover what extraordinary abilities Cassian held.

Bastian found his gaze drawn beyond the silhouettes of his brothers, dribbling the football back and forth at the base of the hill. For high on the hill's top, a flicker of silver was sparking to life.

He almost jumped to his feet at the sight of it—something Sylphic, it seemed, at last. But he held himself steady, aiming not to disturb Cassian, snuggling against him.

He squinted toward the hill and studied the brightening glow.

It looked as though a sphere of light, as big as a football, was hovering inside the rowan berry thicket.

And soon, more lights appeared—lights low and scattered, nestling in the crooks of branches and at the bases of trees.

Bastian stared down at the light-flecked illustration in his book, then looked up again.

The hilltop's woodland was twinkling in exactly the same way as the woodland painted on the page.

As he reread the text beside the painting, one line of its poem seemed to stand out, brightening a touch:

Attend and rise—alight your eyes.

He drew from his pocket the Sylphic scope and trained it on the woodland.

Through the scope, the flickering lights brightened until they seemed to have dimensionality, loosely—like bubbles of shine.

Another line in the book brightened—

Forsake your fear and tarry near
the goblin's grove; the witch's cove.

A rush of warm wind seemed to sweep in an echo of whispering voices.

Bastian received the sounds as a gentle call—the night wind, the canopy brightening strongly now with sharp stars, the forest twinkling —everything nudging him to rise and explore the misty dark.

The mercurial, strong globe of light—hovering slightly higher than the others—rose out of the rowan berry bushes. It drifted away from the thicket and floated down the hill.

It looked as though the night sky had given up one of its stars to sway down to Earth and light up every shadow.

The silver globe floated right between Rhys and Lucas, who kept at their game. The light lilted across the lawn, slipping nearer and nearer to the chalet until it hung gleaming just beyond the porch stairs.

Whatever this light was, it was entirely different from the electric flash that earlier had troubled the apple tree, throwing burning blue flames and inciting in Bastian a sense of dread.

A soft voice from the silver light whispered—"Follow."

And then it drifted away.

Bastian gazed at it as it slipped over the yard and up the hill.

Once again, Kingfisher's book brightened, highlighting a line—

For wise ones claim—in dark's domain,
the children of the forest reign.

What if the Sylphic boy shooting arrows by his house really had been a forest child? And what if this was a sign that one might be near now, tramping along the hilltop in the dark night's domain?

Bastian closed his book and eased away from Mum and Cassian.

"I'm going for a walk," he said to Mum. "To the top of the hill."

"Not tonight, my love."

Bastian faced her. "I must."

Mum stroked his arm. "Don't you think the darkness would trouble you?"

Indeed, on a night like this, with the moon having set, the Wystan Woods were so dark, it was impossible to distinguish the hill's mound from the deep trees.

But that drifting, silver light—how beautiful it looked; how good-seeming.

Bastian's heart quickened at the notion of following something Sylphic and of a virtuous nature—something bearing a light-loving strength; of venturing deeply into the night and exploring a Sylphic place that, for all its darkness and shadows, its hauntings of goblins and witches, was a place where forest children were said to reign.

Mum squeezed Bastian's hand. "Another time, my love."

"Helena," said Da. "He'll be fine."

"It's pitch dark up there," said Mum. "He'd scare himself silly."

Bastian stepped toward the porch stairs as he watched the silver light receding over the hill, where yet more lights seemed to be appearing.

He took a step down the porch stairs. "I'll just walk a bit through the trees on the hilltop."

"It'll be good for him," said Da.

Bastian darted off into the yard before Mum could argue.

He dodged a football pass Rhys nailed to Lucas, then sprinted up the hill.

22

When Bastian reached the woodland beyond the hill's crest, he did find the place pitch dark, but for true golden lights dancing inside the thicket.

The sphere of silver was moving quickly now, levitating far off in the distance. The smaller lights seemed to be drifting with the swift wind more than moving willfully, yet they were keeping a pace Bastian could follow.

From deeper inside the woodland, a quick and resinous music was sounding—like cellos and low pipes, heavy with faint drum strikes that spurred him to run faster.

He couldn't help imagining that this sense of urgency, this excitement, was what Aubrey Gyrfalcon must've experienced, daring the great height of the Golden Moor, drawn there by Moor Folk.

He slipped among thickets of trees, following the lights—all drifting in the same direction, tending toward one another yet never touching, like schooling fish.

The further he moved into the forest, the faster the tiny lights flew.

He drew out his Sylphic scope and tried to close in on them, tried to make out more detail. But the instant he neared any one of them closely enough for a good look, it would fly off or angle back, or simply vanish.

The silvery sphere, though still far off, seemed to have stopped in what looked like a clearing.

Bastian broke into a run with the golden lights—zipping now through a grove of aspens. He raced after them into a pine thicket, its dense carpeting of needles silencing his steps. They twisted him among pathless stands of old oaks, grown thickly and bearded with wood-bristle moss.

Finally, the little lights darted into a starry glade of smooth, gray-skinned beech trees. They swarmed like bees in the center of the clearing.

As Bastian reached them, they lifted into the treetops, then swept high and scattered until he could scarcely tell the difference between gleaming Sylphic lights and bright stars.

He stood still, staring up at them, gripping his book, his heart kicking wild to the cadence of the low music drumming in the woods.

The lights strengthened the shadows of the great trees into dark pools that stretched over the clearing.

Bastian found himself so confounded by the ghostly limbs, so turned around from the sprint through the wild woods, he felt lucky to know up from down. He had no clue which way would lead back to his chalet.

He searched for the silver sphere of light, but it was no longer in sight.

He glanced around the deep forest, examining the spaces between trees for any beautiful Sylphic lights gleaming—or, perhaps, for fiery eyes.

The thought of sighting a goblin here made his breath hitch.

Wisps of clouds swept in overhead, blanketing the stars. Beneath that thick shade, the Sylphic lights in the canopy dimmed.

Without the shine of any light, celestial or Sylphic, Bastian couldn't see his hand before his face.

The whole phenomenon of Sylphic lights seemed suddenly less a marvel and more a trick.

He spun, straining to make out anything in the darkness.

Those lights had felt so pure—but was purity not exactly what an evil, deceptive thing might project? A witch certainly might mislead him, attract him, with such charms.

But the ache in his chest—it felt lighter. It was like engaging with those lights had eased its tightness a touch.

"What are you?" he shouted to the night sky. "Why did you tell me to follow?"

The silvery sphere flared in the canopy.

It drifted from the treetops until it was hovering right before him, at the height of his face.

"We're alone, now, I think," came a whisper from the shine. "You must be quiet, and trust me."

Bastian aimed his scope at the light. "Who are you?"

The scope showed no detail. It just highlighted a vague, shimmering point in the center of the glow, like a bright ember haloed and carried on wind.

"This isn't the question," the voice whispered gently. "The question is—who are you?"

The gentleness of the voice was familiar.

Bastian lowered the scope. "Kaliyah?"

"Yes, it's me," she whispered. "But you must hush your voice."

"Then—you're Sylphic." He backed up. "But how could you be? Or—how is it you seemed human?"

"I can appear as I like," whispered the Kaliyah shimmer. "Now I must be as I am—in Faerie form."

"Faerie..."

"It's possible that I'm more powerful this way."

"As a tiny bit of silver fire?" asked Bastian.

"Is that all you can see? Try looking through Woodthrush's scope again."

Bastian studied her again through the scope. "I can make out your shape, I think. Barely. Your glow—it seemed about the size of a football before. Now there's a faint outline that looks about my size. But all I see clearly is a sparkling flame, levitating."

"I want to try healing you as I am, with my full fire," she said. "When I've done it, you might see things as they are. You might see me as I am. Then you'll be strong enough to hear what I must tell you."

She drew near to him, the heat of her body stinging his face, as though he were sitting too close to a campfire.

"I can't say this won't hurt," said Kaliyah, "but if it works—"

"What's going to hurt?" Bastian lowered the scope.

"You needn't worry—I know exactly what I'm doing," said Kaliyah. "I have experience healing the witch's curses. She just about ruined you, ruined everything. But once we've chased this darkness, you're sure to be stronger."

"What exactly are you planning to do?"

"The darkness the witch has threaded inside you—it's deep," said Kaliyah. "Too deep, and knotted in too complex a way. I'm afraid it's compounded with the old curse her goblin inflicted last year."

"That goblin last year—it was sent by the witch?"

"And today, by the lagoon"—the silver light seemed to be pacing—"when I tried to reach the darkness inside you, I couldn't, really. It was far too deep. I was shocked at finding it so deep. But the problem, I think, was that I couldn't reach it while fleshed. I might be able to now."

"By the lagoon, though, you said I'd have to heal on my own."

"I know, but I hadn't thought of trying it this way," said Kaliyah. "And lucky for all of us, I did."

The heat surged, Kaliyah facing him. Kaliyah close to him.

It was at once wondrous and terrifying being so near to an actual Sylphic being—a faerie.

The pain in his chest, with the heat of her bathing him, felt nearly gone.

But here, in the presence of something truly Sylphic—it struck him that the encounters he'd endured with things Sylphic so far—curses and goblin blades and deadly electric storms and the darkness of sharp-crystaled caves—all of them had ended in anguish.

Bastian pulled back from the singe.

The truth was, aside from her connection with Master Sayre, Bastian had little reason to trust her.

"What makes you think you can help me?" asked Bastian. "I mean, it's kind of you, but—I don't really know you, and you don't know me. Why would you even want to help me?"

"I'll always help you," she said. "Now, do as I say. Lie down."

He pointed the scope at her again. "Did Master Sayre ask you to try this?"

"Look, if you let me do this, I promise to tell you what you must know—what Master Sayre should've told you today."

As disquieting as she was, her form veiled by darkness, by enchantment; as alarming as was the strong heat coming off her, splashing him like flames licking—it was clear that Master Sayre did trust her. By the lagoon, he had asked her to tend him, after all. And she'd seemed to know precisely what to do.

And Bastian couldn't deny that, at her touch, the cold ache had eased; that by her mere presence now, his pain felt lightened.

Bastian set aside his book and scope.

"Please lie back," said Kaliyah. "I'll need you to remain very still."

He settled onto the grass and tilted to lying on his back.

Kaliyah—her shimmery glow brightening some—hovered over him.

His shirt came unbuttoned, as though stirred by wind. The night air cooled his chest.

The flame that was Kaliyah swelled until he could almost make out her face.

A tingly heat singed his chest, her hand pressing. The sensation was exactly what he'd felt this afternoon—a gentle warmth flowing into him from the tips of her fingers.

She pressed harder.

The heat strengthened. Bastian closed his eyes, bearing the burn.

"Almost there," whispered Kaliyah.

The heat sank in like fire shards licking his heart. It escalated to scalding. Burning pain flashed through his body like his blood was on fire.

He shrieked.

"Kaliyah!"—a voice sounded from the edge of the thicket.

The light that was Kaliyah withdrew and flittered up and away.

"What, by dawn's blaze, are you doing?" the voice asked.

Though the words seemed angry, the voice sounded merry. It even struck Bastian as warmly familiar. But whoever owned it was hiding.

Bastian pulled his hands, shaking, to his burning chest. The deep ache was less, but in its place lay a fierce smolder, like he'd landed an angry sunburn that'd sunk into muscle.

"What have you done to him?" The voice sounded close, like its owner was kneeling, leaning right over Bastian.

There was no physical form—only, where the voice was, the stars shone more strongly, as though magnified through a lens.

"I wanted to try healing him again," said Kaliyah—her vague sparkling shape again drawing near. "In Faerie form, I hoped that I could. And I might've managed it if you hadn't interrupted me."

"You've burned him," said the voice.

"Bull nettles, I didn't mean to." It sounded as though she'd stomped the crunchy leaves. "I can fix the burn. I just need moonlit seawater. Bring some. Hurry."

A rustling swept the forest like wind, and then—nothing.

The stars seemed pale after having appeared so strong, so brilliant through the form of that voice.

"Kaliyah?" Bastian whispered to the darkness, his voice shaky with pain.

She brightened, then clarified—in human form—kneeling over him, her eyes shining with concern.

She placed her hands softly on his chest.

He winced.

"I did chase quite a bit of the darkness," said Kaliyah, shifting her hands some. "I think."

At the touch of her warm hands, at their smoothness, their sweetness—Bastian found he couldn't care that she'd burned him. The mere sight of her face seemed to be lessening the stinging.

"What exactly is it that you chased?" Bastian eased up to his elbows. "The goblin, the witch—what did they do to me?"

"The Witch Marrowight wields a form of material darkness," said Kaliyah. "A darkness harvested from shadows beneath tors and mountains, where light has never reached. She manipulates it the way someone might render metal. She can cast curses to command it to move. She can shape it, heat it, freeze it, turn it into smoke—whatever she wants. She's snaked some of the awful stuff into your body, and now it lies stubborn and tangled up inside your heart."

Bastian dropped to lying flat. "She really wanted to kill me."

"When her goblin struck you last year, she did mean for it to kill you, yes. But today, killing you wasn't her aim, we think." She met his eyes. "If it were, I'm afraid you'd be dead."

"I think she came back to my chalet tonight," whispered Bastian.

Kaliyah's eyes widened.

"I saw something terrible and strange," he told her, "something lit blue like lightning—in the apple tree, across the yard from our dining room window. It made me feel dreadful and frozen. It might've been one of her goblins. The pygmyweed, I think, kept it at bay."

"That blue fire was no witch or goblin," said Kaliyah.

"How can you be sure?" asked Bastian. "What I saw in the apple tree—it was terrifying. And I protected Cassian from her today. What if she was coming back for him?" His voice quivered at speaking those words.

"The terror you felt wasn't spurred by her presence," said Kaliyah. "The Witch Marrowight certainly does want to keep you in a state of fear, though. She'd do anything to keep you from realizing—"

"Kaliyah, don't." The voice was back.

It sounded clearer this time. It seemed to belong to an older boy, maybe about Rhys' age. And then, appearing beside Kaliyah as if from nowhere—a silver pitcher smelling of brine.

"Bastian's got to know," said Kaliyah. "If you ask me, it's his right."

"Yes," said the boy. "But this certainly isn't the time."

"What have I got to know?" asked Bastian.

"You'd be doing him no favors," said the boy. "You'd just be adding the shock of it to all this trauma."

"But I'm almost positive that I chased a great deal of the darkness from him," said Kaliyah, standing. "He's ready to hear."

"It isn't that simple," said the boy.

"It's every bit that simple," said Kaliyah. "With the darkness in him chased now to this degree, there's no reason to delay."

"Let's think this through together," said the boy. "Curses get lodged up inside us, right? They get tangled up with weaknesses, engorging them. Before you have any chance of reaching that darkness, Bastian's got work to do."

"But the Day of the Dark Sun is right around the corner," said Kaliyah. "And look at what the Witch Marrowight has managed already. Over the last year, she's struck him twice, in spite of all your protection—"

"Now just a minute—"

"—and if I don't heal the darkness in him now," she said, "if I don't tell him what he needs to know now—who knows what else she might try?"

Bastian sat up. "Tell me what?"

"You'd be placing the whole Sylphic Kingdom in peril," said the boy, "bringing this to light at the wrong time. And need I even mention how furious Sayre would be if he knew what you were up to?"

"Master Sayre trusts that Bastian will chase this darkness himself before the Day of the Dark Sun—only three days away," said Kaliyah. "That's very unrealistic."

"I don't think so," said the boy. "With the day of battle closing in, Bastian will have to chase this darkness very soon. And with what Sayre has planned with his own training master, I trust that he will."

"But if I can just chase it for him tonight, he'll be in a far better position," said Kaliyah. "How is that logic not making complete sense to you?"

"This darkness—it isn't yours to chase," said the boy.

Kaliyah faced the voice directly. "Every passing minute is bringing us closer to the end of everything. And I'm not naïve enough to believe anymore that things will work out if we just trust." She glanced down, her eyes seeming a touch hazed. "I know they won't."

She eased away from the boy and knelt beside Bastian.

"You simply can't tell him," said the boy. "You must drop this."

Kaliyah rested her hand on Bastian's chest in a steadying way.

"If there's something I need to know," said Bastian, meeting her eyes, "please tell me."

"Don't do it," said the voice.

"You're the Sun Child," said Kaliyah.

Bastian sat transfixed, not breathing, staring at the starlight dancing in her silver eyes. He waited for her to break a grin or laugh or say she was joking.

But she only watched him.

The voice of the boy said nothing.

"No, but—" Bastian tipped back to his elbows. "It can't...I'm not—a fighter? That isn't me."

"The faeries have foreseen it," said Kaliyah, sitting back on her heels. "You're our Sun Child."

Her face was solemn, not blithe like it might be if she were trying to prank him. And she seemed too genuine a person to tell a straight lie. She had to be mistaken. Or deceived.

"I've read about Sun Children." Bastian glanced at his book, lying on the cold grass beside him. "I know that Sun Children are born to be brave—tuned to battle. They're fearless. Whatever the faeries have foreseen about the Sun Child—I promise you, it's not about me."

"I've seen it myself," said Kaliyah. "I've dreamed precisely of you, in red armor, on a battlefield, fighting under the banner of the Sun Devaa."

"Dreams certainly aren't precise," said Bastian. "The reality is, I'm no hero. If anyone expects me to hold my own in a fight, they'll be sorely disappointed."

"That's not true," said Kaliyah.

"Let it go," said the boy.

Bastian studied the dark from where the boy's voice was sounding. He lifted his scope and peered through it.

At first, its crystal showed only blackness.

Then after a moment, it presented a pale buzzing, like low television static composing a rough, person-like shape.

Finally, it resolved into a form flickering, a shining face clipping in and out of view.

The boy seemed indeed about Rhys' age.

And he was very alike to the boy Bastian had seen on the day of the accident, standing by Kingfisher Chalet, drawing arrows.

"Who are you?" Bastian asked the shifting form.

"Call me the voice of reason," said the boy.

"What I've done isn't unreasonable," said Kaliyah.

Bastian lowered the scope and stared up at the boy-shaped nothing, his translucent form making the stars blare.

"What if Rhys and Lucas are right about my obsession with Sylphic legends?" asked Bastian. "What if this is what insanity feels like? First hallucinations...now delusions of grandeur—am I going mad?"

"In the best way," said the boy.

"It's not that I haven't imagined being a Sun Child," said Bastian. "At times, I've even wished that I could be like Aubrey Gyrfalcon or Kellyn Woodthrush. I mean, it sounds horrifying, being in so terrible a fight—but the thought of Cassian in the way of danger is far worse. I'm certainly no Sun Child, but I'll not stand by again and watch something wicked try to crush a brother of mine. Being a Keeper is what I can do, and I will do it."

"Cassian isn't the Sun Child." Kaliyah stood away from him. "You are, and I can prove it."

"Bastian is my responsibility," said the boy. "And I say don't meddle any further with him."

"He's all of our responsibility," said Kaliyah.

"Hang on." Bastian shifted to sitting up on his knees. "I'm no one's responsibility."

Kaliyah hauled from the deep pockets of her dress two handfuls of bright, golden gooseberries.

"It isn't going to work," said the boy. "Just standing near him is chilling me to the bone."

"Hush." Kaliyah arranged gooseberries in a ring around Bastian, then met his eyes. "If you've wished for this, I'll make good your desire."

"Wishing is one thing," said the boy. "Taking on the power of the sun is quite another."

Kaliyah drew from her pocket a small branch that shone a soft bluish white in the starry night, its leaf clusters swollen with small, budding apples—green apples that were almost blue, blushing peachy, with streaks of silver dust.

The shimmer and scent coming off them was unmistakable—they were from Kingfisher's apple tree.

The apples burdening the tree beside Kingfisher Chalet were small, their flesh creamy—buttery—holding hints of allspice and cardamom. No one could say what kind of apples they were, and they'd come to be known throughout the shire simply as "Kingfishers."

Da thought they must be something exotic brought from overseas, or a hybrid Kingfisher long ago developed by splicing heirloom strains.

In Kaliyah's hand, softly gleaming, the budding apple switch looked beautifully Sylphic.

"If I were a Sun Child, what would happen at you speaking this charm?" asked Bastian.

"It will be just like your book tells," said Kaliyah. "Infant faeries, called fae, will wake in the seeds of the gooseberries by the light that I'll release from you. They'll rise from their cradles of berries as you call them by name."

Kaliyah opened *Moor Folk of the English Highlands*. A dim glow, lantern-like, shone from her face, illuminating the page.

She raised the apple switch over Bastian.

"Silent suns and sleeping stars
  flying through the storming deep—

whisper to the sleeping faeries
  in the golden berry's keep.

Cease your wheeling and attend;
  tarry not, but take the wing!

Ride the riptide of the west!
  Light them! Let their fair names ring!"

Bastian glanced down at his cold skin.

He looked pale by the shimmer radiating from Kaliyah, but he certainly wasn't glowing with any light released from his body.

He lifted a gooseberry, definitely not bursting with any sort of faerie.

Kaliyah—a look of defeat on her face—lowered the apple switch.

"Since I'm too kind to say, 'I told you so,'" said the boy "why don't we just get on with healing that burn you laid on him?"

He knelt beside Bastian.

The boy's form, though hazy and flickering, now appeared as more than a mere outline.

With his eyes unaided, Bastian could make out that the boy was shirtless and skinny, though muscular, and he was wearing shabby trousers.

He was barefoot, and a bandoleer crossed his chest. From his back hung a bow and a quiver of arrows.

Kaliyah laid her gaze on Bastian's scalded chest. "I did that."

"We'll mend him," said the boy.

She cast the apple switch to the ground. "It should've worked."

The boy set his hand on Bastian's shoulder. "Lie down."

Bastian rested back onto the fragrant grass, dampened with the night's gathering dew.

The nebulous form of the boy pulled Kaliyah to kneeling with him. He eased open Bastian's shirt, dipped his hands in the silver pitcher, and then held them up, dripping.

Kaliyah did the same.

She laid her hands against Bastian's skin, and the boy pressed his hands over hers. She whispered words Bastian couldn't make out— words sounding like the hissing of flames.

She and the boy together pulled their hands off him.

The burning pain faded.

Bastian felt of his chest.

The icy chill, though still present, felt muted.

"Can everyone in the Sylphic Kingdom heal others?" asked Bastian.

"Not by a long shot," said the boy. "All I can do, really, is help. Kaliyah is, well...unique."

Kaliyah lifted a gooseberry between her finger and thumb. "I don't get why it didn't work." She held the berry up to the sky, like she was candling it by a star.

Bastian sat up. "It didn't work because I'm not the Sun Child."

"Are you cross with me?" asked Kaliyah. "That I burned you."

"All you've done is shown me what I'm not." Bastian shrugged. "Any dreaming I might've done about my own bravery, any wondering of what I might be capable, I'm finished with." He opened his book to the spread of the Sylphic boy on the battlefield. "In coming out here, I meant to face the fearful darkness. To answer its call and learn what truths it holds. And I have."

"You think this darkness is fearful?" The boy laughed. "This is cheery and starlit—a beautiful night with frogs singing about it."

Bastian studied Kaliyah's downcast face. "Look, I'm sorry you're disappointed that I'm not who you thought I was. But believe me, you wouldn't want me as your Sun Child."

"That isn't true," she said, still not looking at him.

"I promise you, I'd be less than useless in any battle," said Bastian. "I've had chances to fight for the people I love, but I always freeze up. If I were your champion, I'd just stand petrified as I watched the Sylphic Kingdom crumble. I'm ashamed to admit it, but that's who I am."

Kaliyah turned her gaze upon him. "Sun Children are born brave."

"Then that should tell you conclusively that I'm no Sun Child."

Kaliyah gathered her gooseberries. "Maybe this wasn't the right procedure for the stage he's at. A witch hazel wand might've worked."

"Forget it," said the boy. "You've got no witch hazel, and you're not getting your hands on any."

She eased the berries back into her pockets.

"Given a little time, our world will have its Sun Child," said the boy to Kaliyah. "You'll see."

"Given a little time, our world's going to end." Kaliyah glanced up at the boy. "Are you going to tell Master Sayre I did this?"

"Of course not." The boy crouched before her. "Just promise me that you'll let Bastian be. He will chase this darkness by his own strength—I know it."

Bastian lowered his gaze.

At this point, the ache of this darkness—this curse—felt like a part of him.

Though Kaliyah's efforts did seem to have lightened it, it seemed impossible that he'd ever be free of it.

In Cassian's heart, though, there were no curses knotted.

He picked up the apple switch Kaliyah had dropped.

Tomorrow, he'd perform this rite on Cassian. He'd perform the rite with an apple switch a faerie had used.

Then he'd bring Cassian, tiny and shining—the Sun Child, to Kaliyah and the Sayres. They'd be delighted to see the light inside Cassian wakened, and they could guide Bastian in what he must do to prepare Cassian for the Day of the Dark Sun.

The boy eased nearer to Bastian. "Master Sayre has some Ryudo challenges up his sleeve for you. With what he has planned, there's no way you won't chase this darkness."

"He tells me I'll be training with his own master," said Bastian. "He's spoken often of how difficult his master's methods are—though, he's never said what they are."

"The more challenging you find his methods, the better," said the boy. "Ryudo challenges help us in this way. By them, our bravery rises, our fortitude. The more we ask of ourselves, the more capacity and strength we develop. And Ryudo aside, other challenges will come, in forms that we can't now predict. Your job is to meet it all valiantly with that stout heart of yours. Can you do that?"

"Stout heart."

Hardly. Bastian rubbed his chest.

"Frozen heart is more like it."

A rustling struck the woods like a typhoon had blown in from the sea and was whipping through the trees.

The boy, in a blink, was on his feet. "Kaliyah. Go." He raised an arrow out of his quiver.

From deep in the woods, two blazing eyes shone. A thundering shook from the underbrush.

Bastian, fighting a cold stiffness, eased closer to the boy.

"Bastian," said the boy, "on your feet."

Bastian pushed to standing. "What must I do?"

"Run—fast as you can. Back to your chalet."

Bastian kept his eyes on the disturbance—shaking the distant trees and coming their way.

The darkness in that stretch of forest seemed to be shrouding a force malevolent—a force foul enough to harm not just him, but a forest child. A faerie.

"You just said that I must face challenges," said Bastian.

"Not this one," said the boy. "Not now."

Bastian picked up a heavy stick. "I'm not leaving you alone to deal with this...whatever it is."

The boy glanced at him. "Standing beside me is no frozen fighter."

A roar grumbling from the woods shook the ground.

"You must trust me—do as I say," said the boy. "You must run. Straight home."

"He'll never find his way," shouted Kaliyah, from the edge of the glade. "I'll lead him."

"You split," said the boy. "Call Azdaj to lead him."

Kaliyah set her fingers in her mouth and blared a shrill whistle, then she flitted into a spark and vanished among the high branches.

With Kaliyah's brilliance gone, it seemed all the starlight had fled, leaving the forest desolate. Bastian could no longer see anything of the boy.

The zip of an arrow. The wind of it washing.

A snarl rang, and something heavy fell at the edge of the glade.

A blue snap of fire erupted overhead.

Bastian watched it coast nearer, a deep panic rising in him as it came.

It was the dreadful, electric thing he'd seen land in the apple tree.

"Follow your fear, that blue light," hollered the boy, his voice distant.

The woods quaked, like a goblin—or worse—had made its way to its feet and was charging, breaking trees.

"Bastian—run!" the boy shouted.

Bastian took off.

The blue streak, as it coasted above him, flitted in and out of view like a rogue northern light.

Terror mounded each time Bastian neared it, and the terror itself was, indeed, what he found he could follow, more than its wavering light.

After sprinting what felt like a mile through the dark woods, Bastian caught sight of a treetop, lit up in the distance.

It was his own apple tree—Kingfisher's apple tree—smoldering again beneath dark blue flames.

With those blue shocks of fire raging so close to the chalet, Bastian couldn't imagine how he could get near its door. But after a moment, the fire streaming from the tree drew back and took on an upward-tending shape.

The heat lessened as the fire lightened, casting a gentle glow across Kingfisher's grounds, showing a clear path to the chalet's back door.

Bastian raced across the hill's crest and down it. He sprinted across the empty yard.

The instant he reached the porch steps, the flickering flames in the apple tree vanished, and the whole vale behind Kingfisher Chalet fell quiet.

Bastian ran through the back door and slammed it behind him.

He stared out the window and studied the apple tree, the eastern hill, the rowan berry trees on its crest, and the Wystan Woodland beyond it.

Everything again was pitch dark.

The stars were now all but vanished, cloaked behind gathering clouds.

23

The next morning at dawn, Bastian, holding Cassian, sat down beside his brothers on the front porch steps of their chalet. The sun wasn't even up yet, and the day was already thick with humidity and hot.

The dawn sky was a pale, silky blue, its edges rimmed with steely clouds curling into tips like sea waves.

Bastian and his brothers together watched Mum ease the car away from the chalet, down toward the lane.

Bastian cuddled the baby, sleeping against him, more tightly. Today was the first day that he, Rhys, and Lucas would have full charge of Cassian.

There are things between brothers that parents don't share, and it was thrilling that the four of them would finally be left alone together.

Mum stopped and rolled down the window. "Are you absolutely sure you're all right with him? It's not too late for me to find someone to pop in and keep an eye on things."

Bastian, cradling Cassian, stood. "Mum, we're fine."

Not to mention—today was a flag day for the Sylphic Kingdom. Today, the moon would wane to its narrowest crescent phase, a two-day window that would bring the shift he'd been waiting for—the Sylphic Kingdom manifesting more strongly within the natural world.

Without Mum around, Rhys and Lucas were bound to tire of Cassian at some point.

Then, Bastian could have a moment alone with the baby to perform the sun dowsing ritual.

"Call, should you need anything," said Mum. "Anything at all."

"You're going to be late." Rhys waved. "We've got this."

Bastian drew from his pocket a pouch full of the gooseberries he'd frozen and thawed.

They were plump little globes, perfectly fresh as though just harvested, warm-looking and golden.

They felt full of waiting.

The sun broke the eastern trees and laid its shafts gently over the garden. The light, brushing the baby's face, set to sparkling tiny beads of sweat.

Bastian wicked the moisture off Cassian's soft forehead. It was anyone's guess what he'd look like with his sun blood aglow, after the ritual was complete. Maybe he'd look like a firefly, flickering. Or the whole of him might shimmer, the way Kaliyah had last night. Maybe Cassian—a Sun Child, would shine more strongly than even a faerie.

Mum stopped the car and got out.

Lucas signed to Bastian, "She can't do it, can she? She isn't going to leave."

"She has to," signed Bastian. "She trusts us, right?"

Rhys jogged to Mum. "What's the problem?"

"I forgot to tell you," she said. "The sandwich fixings I prepared are on the bottom shelf of the fridge." Though she was talking to Rhys, her gaze was locked on Cassian—stirring in Bastian's arms.

Bastian gently swayed until Cassian stilled and slipped again into sleep.

"There are peaches and strawberries, and..." Mum seemed on the verge of walking back to Cassian.

Bastian cradled him more closely. He stared lovingly at the baby's closed eyes and stroked his cheek softly, the way Mum did, admiring him.

Rhys rested his hand on Mum's shoulder. "And what?"

"And"—Mum pulled her gaze away from the baby—"those will make a nice, cool snack."

"I know, Mum." Rhys held open her car door. "We'll be all right."

She took a last, somber look at the baby, then offered Rhys a grateful smile as she climbed back into the car.

Bastian waved Cassian's hand to her as she finally drove off.

Rhys faced his brothers and spread his arms. "Gents—the day is ours. What should we do first?"

"Let's walk Cassian to the Natterjack," signed Lucas. "We could explore the cave."

"No way," signed Bastian. "We couldn't take Cassian that far."

"Sure we could," signed Lucas. "It would feel so good today—a nice, cool cave."

"There's no place in Dartmoor darker than that cave," signed Bastian.

"A dark cave's no big deal if we're together," signed Lucas. "We'd of course take a light."

"That cave is full of slick rocks, and it's overrun with sharp crystals."

Bastian slid the gooseberry pouch back into his pocket, next to a stone rung with white—one of Kaliyah's, drawn from the Natterjack not far from the mouth of the cave.

"And Kingfisher writes about goblins living in caves."

Rhys lifted his brow. "I can't believe I'm having to say this to my fourteen-year-old brother," he said, signing, "but—there are no goblins in the Natterjack Cave."

Bastian glanced at him. "You sure about that?"

Lucas stood and signed, "Let's find out."

"A cave—even one with no goblins—is no place to take a baby."

Bastian studied a bundle of gray clouds soaring in low and fast from the north.

"Anyway, it's going to storm."

The dawning sun broke through the hill's taller trees, flooding the weedy lawn with cheerful, new light.

"Any storm's hours away," signed Lucas. "That cave's not far."

"If you want to go, then go," said Bastian, signing. "Cassian and I are staying here."

"But the point of today is the four of us doing things together," signed Lucas. "Anyway, the cave wouldn't be nearly as good without your imagination."

Bastian stared at him and signed, "You mean, if I didn't go, you wouldn't get to make fun of me."

"We'd make fun of you well enough either way." Rhys nudged Bastian. "Come on, show us some Moor Folk."

"Goblins aren't Moor Folk," signed Bastian.

"I don't think we actually have to go to the cave to see goblins," signed Lucas. "Last night, Bastian sleep-talked about goblins creeping out of dark glades. We could go hunting for them in the woods."

"Do what you want." Bastian climbed the porch stairs.

Lucas tapped Bastian's back and signed, "Don't be like that."

"I'm not being like anything," he said, signing. "I just don't want to get caught out in the rain with the baby."

"This isn't like you," said Rhys, signing. "A short walk would be fine for the baby. I'd think you'd be anxious to discover glades haunted by goblins. Or...you're not really afraid of the notion, are you?"

It was clearly a joke, and a jab, but Bastian felt the blood leave his face. He backed up another step.

Watching him carefully, Lucas signed, "You really are afraid from those nightmares, aren't you?"

Bastian signed, "No."

"Whatever we do, it'll be better if we stick together," signed Lucas.

It was true that they ought to stay together. The goblin that'd been in the woodland last night—Bastian had no assurance that it wasn't still out there. It was some comfort knowing the pygmyweed sprig was fastened in Cassian's nursery. But he couldn't pretend he understood how that worked or how far its protection might reach.

Last night, the Sylphic boy might've fought off the goblin and chased it far from the shire. But it was possible the goblin had won.

"Can't we just stay here?" asked Bastian, signing. "I could use some pitching practice."

Lucas glanced at Rhys, who shrugged.

———

Bastian bundled Cassian into his baby swing at the edge of the lawn and played pitcher, while Rhys and Lucas took turns nailing baseballs between two English oaks.

Not ten minutes after they got the game going, though, the sky turned a poisonous green, trnd great raindrops splattered on the yard.

Bastian raced over the lawn and snatched Cassian from his baby swing as an ear-splitting thunderclap bellowed, unleashing a torrent.

Cassian jolted awake and wailed.

Rhys crowded everyone inside.

Naga, soaking, his tail a bushy plume, raced in after them.

Rhys flipped on the kitchen light and handed out dish towels. He wrung Naga's fur dry.

Bastian bounced Cassian and stroked his small back, but it seemed that no comfort could reach him, his hard cry even outshouting the clatter of the storm.

"There, Cassian," said Rhys. "It's just a bit of rain." He handed Bastian the baby's breakfast bottle, only half-finished.

Bastian gently wet the baby's lips with milk. Cassian, softly tasting it, calmed some.

Lucas, rubbing a towel over his head, watched Cassian until his crying quieted into hiccups. "He'll have to get up his courage a bit if he's a Sun Child." He glanced at Bastian. "Won't the Sun Child have to fight in a battle and defend the entire Sylphic Kingdom?"

Bastian coaxed Cassian to take his bottle. "It's going to happen two days from now," he said, signing one-handed. "On the day of the solar eclipse—the Day of the Dark Sun."

"Does the Sylphic Kingdom know that Cassian's only a tiny baby?" signed Rhys. "He couldn't fight a mosquito."

"The Sun Child carries some kind of power or ability that's key to the battle," said Bastian. "Master Sayre says that, although this battle has been foreseen, the outcome is anyone's guess. Apparently Kingfisher wrote another book about this battle—about Moor Folk enemies and secrets to their defeat. But it's been lost."

"Sayre's a great Ryudo Master," said Rhys, signing. "But keep in mind that people around the shire do say he's a touch looney."

Bastian shrugged. "Maybe he just knows things they don't."

"If Cassian's the Sun Child, why have we never seen any Sun Kiss?" signed Lucas.

"I saw one," said Bastian, signing. "I think. But Sun kisses come and go, so it's hard to be sure. And they don't show up on every Sun Child."

"You said the actual way to know is by sun dowsing him," signed Lucas.

Bastian glanced at his rucksack, where lay *Moor Folk of the English Highlands*, beside the apple switch he'd picked up from Kaliyah.

"So?"

Lucas peered out the kitchen window, toward the horizon shining above the hill's crest. "You said you'd sun dowse Cassian when the moon deeply waned. Just look at it."

A faint arc of moon was rising in the blue atmosphere in the east, just underneath the storm clouds.

"Ah, I get it." Rhys snatched the gooseberry pouch peeking out of Bastian's pocket. "This is why you didn't want to leave the house."

"Hey, give those back." Bastian, feeding the baby, couldn't grab them.

Rhys tossed them to Lucas.

"You're going to smash them," said Bastian. "Be careful."

Lucas tossed the pouch on the table before Bastian. A few gooseberries spilled out, shiny and taut.

Rhys picked one up. "It's funny to think of anyone believing that a berry could be supernatural." He popped it in his mouth.

"Leave them alone," said Bastian.

"Don't worry." Rhys ate another one. "These taste ordinary. They must not be the magical variety."

"I am going to try the sun dowsing ritual today," said Bastian, turning away from them some. "Make fun of me all you want. I don't care."

"So, the idea is that you'll do this magical, gooseberry-involving sun dowsing thing," said Rhys, signing. "And then Cassian—a newborn—will somehow be ready to fight in a battle?"

"It's a little confounding, I know," said Bastian.

"Does Master Sayre say what kind of special power Cassian is supposed to have?" signed Lucas. "He can't even keep his eyes open for more than a few hours."

"Once I do the ritual," said Bastian, signing, "I'm certain that more will be clear."

Lucas drew a gooseberry from the pouch. "What are you supposed to do, exactly?"

The way Lucas was studying the gooseberry, the way he was glancing at Cassian—it was the same expression he wore when he read about legendary kings and the histories of wars. Whether he'd admit it or not, Lucas was clearly wondering whether the sun dowsing ritual might really make something happen.

"Kingfisher says that inside gooseberries, unborn faeries—called fae —sleep," said Bastian. "They're said to carry the voices of the Earth itself, and Sun Children can hear them."

"Bloody bindweed!" Rhys studied his stomach. "Does that mean that I just ate a faerie?"

Bastian, casting him a look, opened *Moor Folk of the English Highlands.*

Lucas peered over Bastian's shoulder, while he read aloud—

"When the Sun Dowsing enchantment is spoken over a Sun Child in the presence of Gooseberry Fae, the Child's sun blood will light. The woken Sun Child shall shine and grant the Fae their new names, beckoning them to rise and fly into the Sylphic Kingdom."

Lucas bent closely to Cassian. The baby lay tense, his brow knit, his tiny mouth sucking fixedly on his bottle.

Lucas signed, "He isn't speaking."

Bastian pushed him back. "We have to set the berries around Cassian in a ring and recite the enchantment—*The Song of the Gooseberry Fae.*"

Rhys let out a laugh. "Will faeries burst out of the gooseberries, then, and flit about the chalet?"

Bastian set aside Cassian's empty bottle. "Look, if you don't believe it, why don't you watch?" He heaved Cassian onto his shoulder, snatched the apple switch and his book, and strode to the living room.

Naga followed, prancing behind him. Lucas picked up the pouch of gooseberries and hurried after him.

Rhys stayed behind, shaking his head.

The living room held high skylights and bright windows facing almost every direction.

Brilliant shafts of sunlight were piercing the storm and shining across the tapestry rug.

Bastian laid Cassian in a pool of light, while Lucas arranged the gooseberries in a circle around him. Bastian stripped off Cassian's sleeper.

The baby, nearly asleep, rooted until his thumb slipped inside his mouth.

Bastian handed Lucas the apple switch. "As I speak," he signed, "wave that over Cassian."

Lucas, poorly concealing a grin, lifted the apple switch.

Bastian read, signing along—

"Silent suns and sleeping stars
flying through the storming deep—"

"Now, Lucas," Bastian signed.
Lucas waved the wand.

"Whisper to the sleeping faeries
   in the golden berry's keep."

Lucas swirled the wand over Cassian.

"Cease your wheeling and attend;
   tarry not, but take the wing!"

"Wave the wand like you mean it," signed Bastian.
Lucas waved the wand with everything.

"Ride the riptide of the west!
   Light them! Let their fair names ring!"

Lucas whipped the apple switch in the air.
Bastian and Lucas together leaned over Cassian.
Nothing happened.
Bastian pushed Lucas back to keep his shadow completely off the baby.
Still, nothing.
Bastian trained his Sylphic scope on Cassian. It showed the baby magnified and hazed, breathing softly, not glowing.
Bastian studied his book. "You must not have waved the wand right."
"Or," signed Lucas, grinning, "Cassian isn't a Sun Child."
"Do it like this." Bastian feigned waving the apple switch with more flourish—more like what he remembered Kaliyah doing.
Again, Bastian read, and again, Lucas waved the wand.
Lucas waved the wand sitting, then kneeling, then standing. He waved the wand with his eyes shut, flourishing it for all it was worth, finishing by tracing the outline of the baby.
At the ritual's end, Cassian's milk-stained mouth dipped into a pout, and he howled.
He certainly wasn't glowing.
Bastian picked him up, knocking out of him a burp. "I don't get it."
They'd done everything right.

Lucas sat back, visibly struggling not to laugh.

"What's not to get?" Rhys stepped in and seated himself at a desk where he often worked on his studies. "Cassian isn't glowing because Sun Children don't exist."

But they did exist.

And Kaliyah falsely believed that Bastian was one.

Lucas rested the apple switch on the floor, a slight look of disappointment on his face. It was as though a small part of him really had wanted to discover that Cassian was the Sun Child.

Bastian had to prove that Cassian was the Sun Child, and not just to show Lucas and Rhys that Sylphic legends were true.

If Kaliyah kept up her belief that Bastian was the Sun Child, that would mean she'd expect him to fight in a long-foretold battle—two days from now.

A battle for which he'd have zero Sylphic powers or abilities.

The sun dazzling in through the lifting storm brightened Bastian's hands and arms.

At the feeling of warmth bathing him, an awful thought struck.

What if it wasn't just Kaliyah who believed he was the Sun Child?

She'd mentioned that more faeries than just she herself claimed to have dreamed of this. Maybe there were other Moor Folk—many others —throughout the Sylphic Kingdom, who were equally deceived.

The Sylphic boy hadn't taken a clear stance one way or the other— but it was possible he believed as Kaliyah did.

Bastian fumbled through the book's pages to find the other sun dowsing rite Kaliyah had mentioned—the one involving witch hazel.

"Hey, go easy on that book," said Rhys, opening his laptop. "Master Sayre wouldn't thank you for damaging it."

Surely Master Sayre didn't buy into Kaliyah's belief.

No. If Bastian were the Sun Child, Master Sayre certainly would've told him so—probably back when they'd first met.

And last night, the Sylphic boy had brought up how furious Master Sayre would be, knowing what Kaliyah was up to, hassling Bastian with this dangerous rumor.

"There's another sun dowsing ritual we could try." Bastian ran his finger down the page, studying the details of the rite. "To do it, we'd need witch hazel."

"Do you not feel, even a little, that performing these rituals amounts to a royal waste of time?" asked Rhys.

Bastian absolutely had to run the other ritual and prove Kaliyah's belief false.

He had to prove who the real Sun Child was, to her and to anyone else who might be misinformed.

"We'd wave a witch hazel clipping over Cassian while he's surrounded by stones rung with crystal," said Bastian, signing. "There's a different incantation we'd use."

"Where in the world are you going to get stones rung with crystal?" asked Rhys.

Bastian pulled out the one he'd kept in his pocket. "A friend of Master Sayre's gave me a bunch of these."

Lucas grinned. "Okay, let's try it."

"It's just"—Bastian studied the sketch of witch hazel in his book—"I've never seen witch hazel growing anyplace except in the vale behind Marrowight Manor."

Lucas eased the book closer and studied the picture. "Lady Marrowight does have a crop of that stuff," he signed. "There's a big messy patch of it by her manor's back door."

Going there would be not just terrifying, but foolish—like poking a stick into a snake's lair.

Lucas, standing, signed, "We've snuck into Lady Marrowight's vale before. It wouldn't take a second to clip a switch."

Lucas wasn't wrong that they knew how to sneak onto Lady Marrowight's grounds. And it was true that they'd never been caught. The best way into her vale, actually, led right past the witch hazel crop. If he'd known he needed it, Bastian could've cut a switch on any of the half-dozen times they'd crept in.

But last night, the Sylphic boy in the glade had said Kaliyah, even, couldn't get her hands on witch hazel. Reaching it might be more diffi-cult than Bastian could predict.

But maybe the boy had simply said that to keep Kaliyah from trying to run another Sun Child rite.

"If Lady Marrowight sees you, she'll be after you like lightning," said Rhys, signing.

Bastian rubbed at his chest.

Rhys was more on point than he knew.

But for the Sylphic Kingdom to have any chance in the battle, the issue of the Sun Child's identity would need to be put to rest, and the light in Cassian's blood would have to be woken.

At this moment, Bastian had no idea what powers or abilities sun dowsing might grant the Sun Child. Neither Master Sayre, nor Kaliyah, nor the Sylphic boy had said anything about it.

Maybe they didn't know either. It was possible no one in the Sylphic Kingdom knew.

So, it would be up to Bastian, the Sun Child's Keeper, to find out.

And perhaps he truly could be brave enough to dare the witch's grounds and take what he needed.

The idea of exploring the woods last night—the dark, terrifying woods—should've petrified him. And yet he'd ventured into them.

And though he'd confronted frightful things—that goblin in the glade, and the flash of blue fire in the sky, he'd also discovered the darkness shining with Sylphic lights.

Kaliyah and the Sylphic boy had not been afraid of the darkness at all. The Sylphic boy had even called the dark night *"cheery and starlit —a beautiful night with frogs singing about it."*

Maybe, in accepting the responsibility of being the Sun Child's Keeper, Bastian was finally learning to face his fears. Or, he might be gaining a new perspective on them. The A&E doctor had said that might happen.

And the bottom line was—a battle was going to happen in two days. For it, the Sylphic Kingdom needed a Sun Child.

Kaliyah might not be able to get her hands on witch hazel. But Bastian could.

He clapped his book closed. "Lady Marrowight won't see us."

"Make it quick." Rhys approached and picked up the squirming baby. "And don't get caught." He handed Bastian his phone. "Message me if you need anything."

Bastian carried his book to the kitchen and rested it on the table. He grabbed his jacket, then hurried back and led Lucas out the front door.

From the porch steps, he caught a scent of smoke on the wind.

In breathing it, his chest tightened.

"Do you smell that?" he signed to Lucas.

Lucas shrugged. "It's probably just someone burning yard waste."

A softness brushed Bastian's leg—Naga, twining around his ankles.

"No, Naga, you have to stay here." Bastian stuffed him back inside and snapped shut the screen door. "I can't imagine what Lady Marrowight would do to you if she caught you."

He led Lucas down the front yard toward the lane, until a rapping at the chalet's door made him turn.

Naga, mewing, stretched his silver body up the glass.

He was staring so intently at Bastian, it seemed his eyes were shifting from blue to a vivid silver, like fish scales reflecting bright sunlight.

And beside the door, Bastian noticed a pale light flickering.

It looked, for a second, like the Sylphic boy was sitting there—the boy with the bandoleer and arrows whom Bastian had seen the day of the accident; maybe the same boy he'd seen last night with Kaliyah.

Bastian pulled out Woodthrush's Sylphic scope and trained it on the soft light.

The scope didn't clarify much. In what poor shafts of resolution Bastian could catch, it seemed a Sylphic boy was indeed there, deeply asleep, slumped against one of Mum's planters.

Naga lowered himself to sitting behind the screen door, his tail twitching. His eyes were fixed beyond Bastian, it seemed, locked on the slanting towers of Marrowight Manor, needling through the distant treetops.

Lucas tugged Bastian's sleeve, then signed, "Are we doing this?"

Bastian more closely studied the manor's spires, and there he found the source of the smell. Over its black turrets, a vague plume of dark smoke was curling, just above the tops of the trees.

He aimed his scope at it.

The scope revealed the fume as a material-looking darkness, billowing higher over the trees than it'd appeared with his bare eyes. It seemed to be drifting this way, counter to the wind.

"It must be Lady Marrowight who's burning yard waste," signed Lucas. "If so, she'll be well distracted. It'll be all the easier to slip by her."

In studying the smoke drifting over the trees, Bastian noticed a change in its motion. Snaky tentacles were twining in currents and flowing down into the forest; snaky tentacles like what'd burst from the Witch Marrowight's "gift" basket.

The idea of moving closer to that smoke stood counter to Bastian's every inkling of self-preservation, and he found it difficult to take even one step down the lane. At smelling the vapor, at feeling its crushing effect in his chest, the Witch Marrowight's power felt dreadful and unmatched.

But her power would remain unmatched until Bastian managed to rouse the sun blood in Cassian.

Lucas, watching him closely, signed, "Do you have your inhaler?"

Bastian realized he'd been rubbing at his chest.

"It's in my pocket." He lowered his hand. "It looks like the smoke's drifting east, into the forest. If we stick to the lane, we might avoid most of it."

"Sounds like a plan," Lucas signed.

Bastian led Lucas toward the lane, as Naga scratched mightily at the chalet's screen door.

24

Bastian led Lucas along the lane that weaved from their chalet north, toward Marrowight Manor.

A quarter mile into the trek—halfway to the manor, a glistening from the eastern forest caught Bastian's eye.

He stopped and peered at it through the Sylphic scope.

The scope showed him a vague impression of a boy lying in a high bough of an oak tree. He seemed to be resting back against the tree's trunk, his chin tipped against his chest.

And scattered beneath him on the forest floor—a heap of bright arrows.

The arrows flickered an instant, caught fire, then vanished, their smoke and ash joining the billows moving through the woodland.

Lucas tapped Bastian's arm, then signed, "What are you looking at?"

Bastian started to sign, "Nothing," but—would Lucas be able to see what the Sylphic scope showed? Lucas had seen something in the road on the day of the car accident.

Bastian handed him the scope.

Lucas scanned the woods where Bastian had been aiming. "Everything's so distorted through this thing," he signed. "It's making my eyes water."

"Through it, can you see anything moving in the woodland?" signed Bastian.

"No." Lucas pointed the scope at their chalet, toward the puffs of steam churning from the chimney.

He seemed to be tracing the thatched roof, shining golden in the sun.

"Our chalet really looks like an enchanted house, doesn't it?" Lucas signed. "I wonder if that's how legends get started—people dream up things happening in places that look magical."

The chalet was indeed so stone-cobbled and thatched and nestled in flowering vines that it did seem to have been born in a storybook, spilled off its page, and grown to the cadence of the Dartmoor wilds.

"Or," signed Bastian, "could there be a reason, do you think, that some things look magical?"

Lucas shrugged. "Some magical-seeming things might be based in reality." He handed the scope back to Bastian. "Like—Sylphic legends seem very specific. Almost historical. Kingfisher clearly knew what he was doing, weaving those faerie tales. And the prediction of what's coming—it startles me how detailed it seems."

"Are you saying you think there's any truth to Sylphic legends?" Bastian asked him.

"I mean, Sylphic legends are great, but they're so far-fetched." signed Lucas. "They couldn't be true. Although—I'll give you this—if they were true, they couldn't be more well-documented."

A shrub beside them shivered and broke. Naga raced out of it, his tail a plume of play.

Bastian sprinted after him.

Lucas took a wide angle and tried to herd Naga toward Bastian.

Naga jetted into the woodland and ducked out of sight.

"How could he possibly have gotten out?" signed Lucas.

Bastian signed back. "No idea."

They climbed to the crest of a rise and together looked over the countryside.

From this height, the fields were visible for miles, striped in their yellows and blues, flowing into chestnut groves—tight like bundles of emerald balloons.

Bastian scanned the farmlands for Naga. He looked down the lane both ways, then studied the smoke-hazed woodland.

Just to the north, Marrowight Manor's sharp corbel towers stabbed out of the trees, its crowning ramparts angular and uneven like molars jutting from the mouth of a skull.

The curved spires crooking at the manor's four corners held empty flagpoles that raked the sky with clanging. Besides that, there was no sound, save a distant rumbling of thunder. Even their footfalls seemed dampened by an unearthly heaviness of atmosphere.

Bastian couldn't see Naga anyplace.

"How can we even guess which way he went?" signed Lucas.

"I don't know, but we can't let him get near the manor." Bastian ran down the rise and into the woodland, Lucas following.

Inside the closeness of the trees, the smoke hung heavy. Bastian covered his mouth to try breathing through his sleeve, but—he found he didn't need to. Here, a strange wind was stirring. Wherever they walked, the smoke tendrils seemed to sweep away from them.

Naga still was nowhere in sight.

A little ways to the north stood a hedgerow marking the edge of the manor's grounds. From there, they'd be able to see the whole of Marrowight Manor and its vale stretching.

Bastian hurried to it and peered through a break in the bushes.

The manor's stone walls, though square, seemed to curve in a reptilian sort of way, like they possessed the soul of a dragon, sleeping, curling in on itself, shafting its eyes with a spiked tail that pretended to be a dark poison ivy vine slithering against a charred wall.

Unlike the evenly cobbled masonry of Kingfisher Chalet, the stones of Marrowight Manor looked unstable. It seemed they'd been torn from the earth and stacked haphazardly, like ruins. Though the manor had stood on its vale for centuries, it seemed any push of wind might topple it.

Bastian led Lucas creeping against bristly boxwoods, through hoary weeds glossed with sticky milk, and finally along crops of needle-fingered hollies clawing the garden's edge.

"You got scratched." Lucas lifted Bastian's elbow where a swollen stripe stretched.

"It's fine," signed Bastian.

"You'll be red as a raspberry in a minute," signed Lucas.

Bastian waved for him to follow as he closed in on the manor.

Lucas hung back. "Do you have your EpiPen?"

"Yes," Bastian signed. "Come on."

Sun rays were beaming through clouds moving rapidly in the wind of a gathering storm, but it seemed no light could reach Marrowight Manor. It slept gray on its vale as low thunder grumbled.

A rumbling to match the thunder whispered from the dense overgrowth.

Bastian caught sight of a flash of silver fur and a thick tail—Naga, slinking through the weeds.

He lunged for the cat, but Naga twisted away beneath a low-growing yew.

Lucas pointed down toward the edge of the vale where metal was glinting—animal traps and cages.

He signed, "Watch your step."

On the near side of the vale stood a goblin statue, set in a claw-foot bathtub—upended, making an ugly shrine.

Out from behind it, Lady Marrowight stepped.

She was wearing a long black jacket over a black dress mottled with red embroidery. The jacket was tight around her shoulders and flared at her heels. It looked formal—something one would wear for a dismal and important event, like a funeral. A black sun hat drooped on her head.

Bastian caught Lucas' glance and pointed at her.

A whisper of sound rose—shimmery and barely audible, like fluttering glass wings.

"What's she doing?" signed Lucas.

"I can't tell." Bastian glanced up at the branches of an English oak they'd climbed many times. "Let's get a better look."

They helped one another clamber up until they could see Lady Marrowight clearly.

She was bending over a stony red bowl pronged on an iron pedestal.

She dropped in a palmful of ash and, with her snaky stick, stirred.

Thick smoke rose from the bowl and joined with smoke issuing from four flesh-colored candles posted at cardinal positions around her. She was speaking in a language Bastian never had heard.

A push of smoke curled up and wafted toward him and Lucas. It slipped among the higher branches of their oak.

Out from the woodland, a cluster of twinkling lights darted. They coasted across the vale toward Lady Marrowight and before her stopped, hovering like hummingbirds.

She lifted a knife from beside the bowl and thrust it at one of the lights.

It dimmed and drifted to the ground. All the other lights scattered.

Lady Marrowight kicked the fallen light into a bag at her feet and set into chanting a low incantation.

The music of it was, in a way, sweet—melodious. Bastian might've even regarded her voice as beautiful had the words she was uttering not been so vile.

He couldn't make out much, but he did catch "slaughter," "blood," "filthy," and "wings."

The rising wind flared her jacket and blew her hat to dangling, but the candles did not go out. Instead, their flames swelled as she lifted her hand and raised her voice to shouting.

A punch of wind struck Bastian in the back. He thrust out his arms but caught nothing.

The drop from the tree branch was long enough to dread the hit.

He couldn't twist fast enough to get his feet under him, and he struck the ground sideways.

Lucas hustled down from the tree and knelt over him.

Bastian fought to breathe against a thickness building in his chest.

It seemed impossible that the fall could've been at Lady Marrowight's hand—she hadn't looked up for an instant or betrayed, in any way, that she knew they were watching her. Even now, she was just keeping on with her weird chanting.

Lucas helped Bastian sit up and peeled his shirt away from his shoulder. "You're bleeding."

Bastian glanced at the cut. "It's not bad."

Lucas fished Rhys' phone from Bastian's pocket. He flipped it over to find the screen shattered.

He tried turning it on.

Nothing.

"We have to call it quits," Lucas signed.

They were so close to the witch hazel, though.

And Naga, lost here...

"We can't go home without Naga."

Bastian pushed painfully to crouching.

"And I'm not leaving without the witch hazel."

They snuck on, toward an iron fence jutting from the garden's southern edge. Scaling it was the best way they'd found to get into the vale.

Bastian pulled his way to its top, Lucas beside him. He eased over the fence's sharp spires and dropped to its other side.

Irritation was racing down Bastian's arms, from the scratches he'd picked up. Nicks from nettles on his ankles and shins had flared to a simmering itch.

He eased up his sleeves and studied his skin.

Lucas knelt next to him. "Are you sure you can keep going?"

Bastian pulled his sleeves back down. "We have to."

He slimmed between two twisted rowan berry trees snarling the lawn with knuckled, half-buried roots, their lanky leaves dew-dropped with blood red berries, far bigger than what grew on the hill behind Kingfisher Chalet.

From there, he studied the witch's vale, beginning at her manor on the western edge, along the pine forest lining the northern side, and to its eastern woodland borders.

"I don't see her anymore," Bastian signed.

Lucas peered around him. "She was right by that goblin shrine thing. Where could she have gone?"

Bastian's studied the goblin statue in its weird bathtub monument. Wilted roses were tied in a strangling way around its muscled neck and draped its horns. A long, forked tongue spilled from its fanged mouth.

Bastian keyed in on the crop of witch hazel, growing near the back door of the manor.

On the lawn, between their blind and the witch hazel, lay three toppled stone figures, marble-white, graceful, and tall—like dryads.

Kingfisher had described dryads—tree spirits—as sentries of England's Sylphic Kingdom.

An aspen dryad, slender and long-armed, lay on its face between two others that looked to be the guardians of oaks.

Dozens of other stone statues, no bigger than rabbits, were strewn over the green. They seemed human-like, but for their angular faces.

Sprites.

Lady Marrowight was nowhere in sight.

"It seems Lady Marrowight has trekked off into the woodland," Bastian signed. "The witch hazel is only a short sprint away."

He moved into the clearing, carefully navigating around the statues.

The itching was spreading, now, up his belly, and it seemed to be settling inside his chest as a burn. He tried to breathe deeply but couldn't.

He tripped over a stone sprite and stumbled to his knees.

On the sprite's back lay a divot—an empty place where wings belonged.

Lucas helped him to his feet.

Overhead, sooty clouds blackened the sky. The wind picked up, thickening the ashy air with the smell of petrichor.

Bastian took off running toward the witch hazel bush, as fast as he could, which was not fast, the smoke-laden atmosphere now heavily pressing in.

He skidded to his knees before the witch hazel shrub.

Lucas knelt by him and held a branch steady. "Your pocketknife," he signed, "go."

Bastian drew out his pocketknife. He opened it and sawed at the bend.

"Beautiful, isn't it?" said a melodic voice.

Bastian dropped the knife.

"But the virtues of witch hazel surpass mere beauty." Lady Marrowight was standing right behind them, glowering down.

Bastian snapped off the twig and gently fed it up his jacket sleeve. He turned.

Lady Marrowight's arms and face stood out deathly white against the dark storm building overhead. Her lips were painted a deep blackish red, like wine. Her hair fell to the center of her back in twisting locks.

She glanced at Bastian's sleeve. "So valuable is witch hazel to me that I ensure every other plant, clip, or switch that grows within a hundred miles turns to ash at the touch of night's dark."

From across the vale, the clatter of metal rang—the snapping of a trap.

From it, a cat yowled.

Lucas stood. "Naga," he signed. "You've trapped Naga."

Inside the trap, Naga thrashed.

Bastian pushed to his feet. "That's our cat. We'll just get him and be on our way."

"Fie!" Lady Marrowight cast her arms in the air.

Bastian's knees struck the ground before he knew he was falling.

Lucas tumbled down next to him.

Bastian tried to stand but found his body too stiff to move. He couldn't even take a breath—trying to draw air was like trying to breathe water.

Lady Marrowight spoke on, but Bastian could hear nothing over the thrumming of his blood.

The lawn shimmered, and suddenly everywhere on the vale—sprites were standing. Their backs were blood-covered around the places where wings should be. They together moved toward Lady Marrowight.

As they neared, the details of their faces resolved, showing expressions pained, tears shimmering down every cheek and sizzling into steam as the drops struck the lawn.

The steam assembled into a mist that moved over the grass. Its silver tendrils threaded through Bastian's fingers and wound up his body and against his cheeks.

It was a medium he found he could breathe.

This fresh mist was familiar—he could recall breathing it before, on the night the goblin had struck him in Exeter. As it had then, it eased the constriction in his chest.

Lady Marrowight hauled Bastian out of the reach of the mist, up onto the back porch of her manor.

Lucas stumbled at her other side as though pulled, although she wasn't touching him.

The sprites advanced. As they approached, the shivery sound, the breathable mist, strengthened.

Lady Marrowight stopped. She turned, fully facing her vale.

Bastian hung from her grip, his legs sagging.

The sprites set to chanting music—beautiful and sad sounding, in an unfamiliar language.

Naga's cry rose above the song of the sprites.

Lucas ripped away from Lady Marrowight.

She caught him by the back of his jacket and spoke guttural words.

Her voice rose until it strengthened into a burst of sound that tore over the vale like a sonic boom.

At the blare, Bastian lost all strength. His head cricked against his shoulder.

The sprites seemed to slow. Thunder rumbled.

Naga, his silver fur bristling, his back arched, his claws unsheathed, tore at the door of the trap. He seemed nothing like a housecat—more a tiger.

Lucas, his eyes wide and terrified, glanced around. He seemed unaffected by the blast.

He jerked out of Lady Marrowight's grip.

She snatched him by the shoulder.

Blue electricity flashed from her hand and raced over his body.

He collapsed.

She dragged him close by the hood of his jacket and pulled him to standing. He didn't resist, but just stood by her, his head bowed, his eyes nearly closed.

She crooked her fingers toward the lawn.

Streaks of blue fire roared from her hand, speeding over the grass like a breaking ocean wave.

In a blink, the whole company of sprites—hundreds of them—stood frozen in stone, joining those already petrified and lifeless on her vale.

At a peal of thunder, the storm broke in a torrent. A mighty gale dragged the crowns of the trees skyward.

Lady Marrowight jerked Bastian to his feet and pulled him and Lucas toward the manor's iron doors.

As the doors opened before her, a gush of dank air washed—air that didn't seem breathable.

Bastian tried to step back, to run, but he found himself incapable. All he could do was stand there, struggling to draw air.

Lady Marrowight shoved him and Lucas together inside a parlor that yawned against a dark corridor, its marble floor laid in black and white checks.

Shadows stood against the walls of the parlor like material smoke— smoke taking the shapes of great, muscled forms. Goblins.

Bastian's legs buckled.

He dropped to his knees.

Darkness swelled.

He could only take quick breaths that felt drawn through a pinhole.

Behind him, Lady Marrowight slammed the iron doors.

25

*L*ady Marrowight's hand was a talon on Bastian's shoulder as she forced him and Lucas along the manor's dim corridor.

From someplace below the echoing tiles, shrill sounds grated, like dungeon doors whining.

From outside, strong thunder echoed.

Lady Marrowight drove them at a quick pace, past columns standing as a division between closed doors and branching halls.

No electric lights shone anyplace—not in any of the rooms, and not along any corridor. Instead, torches hung from iron hooks, their flames raging in a cold draft.

In the forest, Kaliyah had "reached" some of the darkness from the curse Lady Marrowight had inflicted Bastian with—the curse that'd compounded with the injury the goblin's blade had dealt last year. But from the sharp ache in his chest, Bastian felt Kaliyah's gentle hands never had touched him. Every breath felt insufficient and icy.

But perhaps Kaliyah had managed to dissipate some of what felt like a knot constricting his heart. If she hadn't, it seemed the manor's chill might've frozen him stony from the inside out.

They came to a place where the corridor widened, and arched openings gaped, one after the other on both sides. Some of the archways led to more firelit corridors. Others opened into rooms.

One room they passed looked like a parlor. Its back wall held an enormous gray stained-glass window.

Through it, weak light was leaking in a mournful, aged way. The room looked like the funeral home where Granddadda's body had rested before it was burned.

A powdery smell of old feathers thickened as they moved deeper along the corridor, and Bastian soon saw why. Room after room held collections of taxidermized animals.

Long-faced bucks stared blankly beneath sets of regal, pronged horns. Eyeless songbirds lay belly-up on tables. From rafters, eagles dangled, frozen in the hunt, their hooked beaks open, their golden talons spread.

Small forest animals littered the rugs and chairs—droop-eared rabbits, foxes with flared tails, tiny field mice, tubby badgers, sharp-skinned hedgehogs.

In one corner sat a stuffed dog, snowy white and ghastly stiff, arranged in a pose of panting.

Then came a room cluttered with iron traps and cages.

Bastian's stomach dropped at the thought of Naga outside on the witch's vale, alone and trapped in a cage drawn from among these.

The next room stood almost wholly dark until a bolt of lightning struck, shocking a cold light through a row of small windows.

The weird light showed a small space piled with bows and quivers. The weapons were smartly crafted, their strings so taut, it seemed they'd sing if plucked.

Bastian glanced at Lucas—wide-eyed and yet seeming to see nothing, placing one foot in front of the other, his breath hanging before him as a mist.

Bastian snatched for Lucas' hand.

Lady Marrowight yanked Bastian so hard, her fingernails pierced his shoulder.

Bastian couldn't draw another breath. His thighs and calves felt weak and on the verge of cramping, no part of his body getting the oxygen it needed. He only stayed upright by Lady Marrowight's grip.

She shoved them through a doorway leading into a kitchen. They collapsed together onto the stone floor.

Lady Marrowight crossed the room toward a set of shelves standing beside an iron stove.

On the shelves, stacks of animal pelts stretched beside long rows of waxy, glass containers. Some of them suspended dead animals in dark green fluid. Others held bunches of feathers.

Still others contained huge insect wings.

Yellowed skulls, some tiny and rodent-toothed, others as big as a bear's, grinned. Cast iron pots and teakettles, their lips grimy, lined the highest shelf.

Bastian crawled to Lucas.

Lady Marrowight retrieved a putrid teakettle and cranked on the iron stove.

She muttered as she set the teakettle atop the blaze.

She twisted open one of the waxy jars, and an acidic stench—cheesy like the rank of old shoes—plumed.

She drained its contents into the teakettle, then drew out her twisted stick and stirred as she muttered strange words.

Bastian grabbed Lucas' arm.

Lucas raised his head slowly. A sense of focus came into his eyes.

He signed, "Where are we?"

"In Marrowight Manor," Bastian signed. He keeled forward onto his elbows.

Lady Marrowight glanced at him but didn't come. She just kept stirring, kept muttering.

Lucas, wrapping his arm around Bastian's shoulders, signed, "Your lips are white."

Bastian couldn't respond. Air was barely slipping through his windpipe.

Lucas pulled up Bastian's sleeves and examined his arms.

Inside one sleeve, he discovered the witch hazel wand.

He drew it out and fed it up his own jacket sleeve.

The witch hazel's flowers no longer looked yellow—they were dinged in shades of gray.

Lucas' hands and clothes, too, looked wan.

Bastian's own clothes had also gone ashen.

The world going gray—this meant he'd soon lapse into sleep.

His doctor had warned what would happen if he fell asleep when he couldn't breathe right. There'd be no waking.

Suddenly, it seemed Mum was kneeling beside him. The fragrances of cedarwood and coconut rose as she rested her arm around his shoulders.

Cassian, lying before them on his play palette, kicked merrily. Bastian cradled the baby's soft foot.

Lucas shook him hard.

Bastian gasped a breath. He felt the cold of the coarse stone floor beneath him and realized Mum wasn't near. He studied his hand, empty of a baby's foot.

He lifted his gaze to Lucas and signed, "Run."

The teakettle screeched.

Lady Marrowight killed the flame and set the teakettle on the floor before Bastian.

She gripped his chin. "How about some tea?"

Lucas pulled Bastian back. "My brother's sick," he signed.

Lady Marrowight poured a greenish-black liquid into a glass goblet rimmed with iron.

The steam rising from the goblet smelled putrid, like old rainwater.

"Get help," Lucas signed. "Get help. Get help."

Lady Marrowight jabbed her twisted stick into Lucas' stomach.

His arms slid to his sides. The focus left his eyes, and his face relaxed into a gentle smile.

Lady Marrowight propped Bastian up against the wall and forced open his jaw. Into his mouth, she poured the stinking brew.

Burning fluid gushed down the sides of his face. Rottenness flooded his mouth.

His racing heart skipped, then slowed, pounding, then easing.

And then he altogether lost the sense of his heart beating.

His struggling body stilled. The dinged shades of his hands and clothes shifted to black.

More hot fluid raced into his mouth and down his throat. His diaphragm convulsed, and he sucked a shallow breath.

He opened his eyes to find Lady Marrowight glowering down at him.

"I'll have that witch hazel back," she said.

"I dropped it," he rasped.

She unfurled her long, white palm. "Now."

"I don't have it." He slumped against Lucas.

She peered down both of Bastian's jacket sleeves—empty.

"Give up your hope in legends, child," said the witch. "Any magic this world holds is dark." She straightened him and held him upright by the chest. "No day can last forever." She poured another swallow of the stinking brew into his mouth. "The sun shall always fade."

That phrase. It was from a poem written in *Moor Folk of the English Highlands*.

Bastian watched her, waited for her to say the rest of the piece. But she spoke no more.

Drawing shallow breaths, Bastian whispered the disregarded words—

"But when it dies, the kestrel cries
that all shall be remade.
I'm wind upon the waters;
I'm light upon the shore.
I laugh at pain, I dance in rain,
I live forevermore."

Lady Marrowight silenced him with another mouthful of the reeking brew.

He found, after that swallow, that the thickness in his throat had almost wholly dissipated.

He recited on—

"See how I've slain the darkness.
See how I've flown its bars.
No longer bound, my heart has found
a dawning night of stars."

Lady Marrowight drew away the goblet. "Darkness cannot be slain. And night shall bind all."

"The night is cheery and starlit, with frogs singing about it," whispered Bastian.

She shook him, making him look at her. "So bold are you to come here, to my vale, to steal my Sylphic charms."

Bastian forced his heavy eyelids to remain open. "The dark night holds forest children, glinting lights, faeries, brilliant stars, shining arrows." Though coming slowly, it seemed his strength was returning.

The witch's eyes narrowed. "You may have grubbed up Kingfisher's lost book..."

Kingfisher's lost book.

Bastian sat up a bit straighter. He watched the witch.

"...but it doesn't matter," she said. "Neither witch hazel nor that book can do anything for you, now that I have you. Your blood shall be my richest potion; your bones, my hard-earned prize."

Bastian couldn't blink. Lady Marrowight thought he'd found Kingfisher's lost book.

That meant—she might know where it was hidden.

Bastian sat all the way up on his own.

"I have found the lost book," he said, watching her carefully. "And you'll never guess where."

"I know where he hid it—the fool." She stood. "He was reckless to bury it in his very own chalet, in his Council Chamber, where he hid from me like a mouse in a hole, guarded by dark enchantments—a mockery of my power."

Kingfisher's lost book, hidden in his very own chalet—the thought struck Bastian as unlikely. He and his brothers had explored every inch of the chalet—if there were any book written by Kingfisher, they certainly would've noticed it. Maybe she'd wrongly guessed it was there.

She stood and set the teakettle back on the stove. "Just a few nights more, and it would've been mine. But no matter. You found your way into his chalet, just as he planned. You have everything he wanted you to have, and yet"—she grinned at him—"I have you."

She lifted her twisted stick and whispered.

It writhed.

Another whispered word, and it shifted into the form of a snake, hooded like a cobra.

Holding the stick's tail, she aimed its head at Bastian's chest. Smoke oozed from the mouth as it reared.

Bastian teetered to standing and pulled Lucas up with him.

Lady Marrowight muttered on in her strange language as the snake's jaws stretched wide, bearing fangs. Inside the snake's mouth, blue flashes trembled, like lightning gathering.

A roar ripped the air as something huge and black skidded to a stop beside the kitchen door, then lumbered through.

A black wildcat, sleek and muscled—a jaguar—wheeled toward Lady Marrowight.

She struck it with a blast of blue electricity from her snaky stick.

The jaguar bit the stick. Wrenched it from her. Cast it aside.

Lady Marrowight's eyes darted between Bastian and the jaguar.

On massive, stealthy paws, the beast cornered Lady Marrowight against the stove.

She snatched an iron skillet from the wall. "You're out of time."

The wildcat snarled.

"The Day of the Dark Sun is nigh. I shall have my way with the Sun Child."

Bastian shouted, "You'll never lay a finger on Cassian!" He pulled Lucas back, toward the kitchen door.

Lady Marrowight slipped along the wall toward them.

The beast, trembling growls, moved between Lady Marrowight and Bastian.

With ears pressed flat against its head, with hackles standing high on its muscled back, it padded closer to the witch.

She swung at it with the skillet.

It lunged, pinning her to the stove.

Bastian dragged Lucas out of the kitchen.

They together raced along the cold corridor.

Every shadow they passed materialized into goblins that seemed made of smoke.

Side by side, they skidded into the checkered foyer. Bastian threw himself at the manor's iron doors.

Two shadowy goblins advanced and reached for them.

Bastian and Lucas together rammed open the doors.

They rushed out and down the back porch stairs. They raced onto the vale.

The shadow goblins didn't follow but rather hung drifting at the threshold of the manor.

Bastian sucked heavy breaths and studied the vale all around.

Its misty air hung in a queer stillness, like the quiet aftershock of a violent storm.

He set into a run, leading Lucas toward the south side of the vale, where the traps and cages were set. They wound among wingless stone sprites. They splashed through puddles and muddy swaths of grass and stopped before the iron cages.

The one that'd held Naga was smashed.

Clouds boiled in from every corner of the sky. They thickened into a green-gray plume over Marrowight Manor.

Lucas picked up an iron bar, snapped off from the cage. He signed, "How?'

Thunder pealed as the dark sky unleashed a downpour.

Bastian snatched the bar from Lucas and cast it away. He signed, "Run."

They raced among the blood red rose bushes edging the vale. Bastian tripped over a hidden trap that snapped, its iron teeth missing his foot by a millimeter. Lucas pulled him upright and on. They together sprinted to the fence.

Bastian stopped before it, cradling the cuts on his shoulder, still bleeding from his fall out of the tree and Lady Marrowight's nails. He couldn't raise his arm without calling up agony.

The manor's door creaked.

Lady Marrowight strode out onto her porch, her eyes fixed on Bastian.

Lucas pulled to the top of the iron fence. He balanced between spires and reached down to Bastian.

Bastian took a step back, calculating the height as he would in a Ryudo course. He ran at the fence and jumped. He caught Lucas' hand, barely.

Lucas heaved until Bastian could gain purchase on the metal and climb.

They scrambled over the fence and dropped. They plowed through the holly crop and the underbrush, tripping past branches and sticks splintered by the storm.

Bastian wheeled to a stop and ducked between two bushes. He sighted the witch rushing their way, kicking aside stone sprites.

There was no sign of the wildcat, but Lady Marrowight's dress was torn, and bloody claw marks marred her white arms.

Her skirt billowing, her tangled hair flying, she cast up her hands and shrieked foul words.

Bastian picked up just one phrase—

"Droning troops with tails of knives, I summon you. Escape your hives!"

A hornet, as big as a bat, swung before Bastian's face. Its bulbous body was white on black—an airborne skeleton. Its steely wings, as shrill as a dentist's drill, screeched.

Bastian grabbed a stick and swung at it.

The creature sidled out of reach, then squealed in and struck a blow inside his wrist.

Fiery poison raged up his arm and into his chest.

Everything went misty as he fell onto his back.

Rain battered his skin.

Lucas knelt at his side.

Bastian could hear nothing above his own rushing blood until Kaliyah's voice washed in.

A hand gripped his leg. A cruel sharpness jabbed his thigh.

He heard himself scream. Felt himself lifted. His forehead fell against a bare shoulder.

Opening his eyes to slits showed him the face of an older boy.

Rhys, maybe?

But no—the boy's hair was cropped shorter, his skin—a deeper tan.

The boy glanced at Bastian with bright hazel eyes. "Hang in with me."

The boy ran through the forest, leaping logs, sprinting up hills while lightning shattered the sky.

The agony from the hornet sting sharpened until the boy with the hazel eyes, and Kaliyah's voice, and Lucas running alongside, and Marrowight Manor, and the echoing ring of Naga's cry, and the wingless sprites, and the grumbling thunderhead, and the whole of the woodland vanished in the roaring fire of a witch's scream.

26

The whistling of a teapot faltered, and soft singing swelled. Sweet scents lifted, of rising bread and brine and freshly cut firewood.

Bastian shifted where he lay—someplace soft and warm.

Moving brought sharp pain racing up his arm.

"You're safe." Kaliyah's voice.

Darkness shifting to pale. His shoulder stinging. His wrist—hot and swollen. A cool cloth pressing his forehead. A soft hand taking his.

The pain retreated to a blunt ache.

Bastian drew a slow breath. Another. He held the air a moment, relishing the stretch of his lungs.

He followed Kaliyah's singing with his eyes half-open until at last he could focus.

Before him shone a latticed window, glittery with sunlight glancing off wings—finches, kinglets, and sparrows fussing at a feeder. He was lying in a dusty beam of sun on a fluffy white bed.

Mrs. Sayre rested the teapot near him, on a bedside table. Beside him, in a birchwood chair, Kaliyah sat gently rocking.

Bastian glanced around. "Where's Lucas?" He tried to sit up.

Mrs. Sayre gently held him still. "Gone home to rest."

"I don't remember coming here."

Bastian glanced down at himself. He was wearing a tunic—too big, cinched at the waist. Master Sayre's.

Mrs. Sayre slipped the cloth off his forehead. "Kaliyah found you in the woods, hornet-stung. When they brought you here, to our cottage, you were limp as a fish. Gave us a fright, you did."

"There was a boy," said Bastian.

"Yes—a friend." Mrs. Sayre removed a melted ice pack from his wrist. "He gave you a shot from your EpiPen, and Kaliyah mixed you some cordial, and now here you are, warm and safe."

"Naga—" Bastian shot up to sitting.

"He's all right." Kaliyah lifted a crystal chalice, latticed in silver like the cottage's windows.

It held a silvery-pale liquid, with three crystal-rung stones tumbling inside.

"Drink this," said Kaliyah.

Bastian rested back. "Why are there stones in it?"

"They're for healing," said Kaliyah.

"Can stones heal?"

"Not by themselves." She pressed the chalice to his lips.

It was water—sweet and lightly scented, like nectar. But it carried an edge of tang. It struck him with a sense of bright camellia petals, and a steadiness issued from a fragrance of sap, as from pinecones. It tasted cool, like morning mist whispering through berry patches.

The pain in his shoulder and wrist lost some of their sharpness.

Bastian took the chalice from Kaliyah and studied its liquid. "What is this?"

"Elderflower cordial," said Kaliyah.

The taste, the smell soothed him. And it seemed to deliver a gentle energy and alertness. Holding it, he let himself relax into the pillow.

Something about the Sayres' cottage seemed to be working on him in the same way the cordial was.

These walls—cobbled of round, granite stones, seemed to cherish. They weren't plastered, but seemed to stand by their own strength, maintaining a heritage of the wild rocks tumbled along Celtic beaches.

Vines studded with emerald leaves and winking white flowers, their petals as delicate as parchment, crept through cracks and trailed along the seams of the stones, up to the thatching.

They seemed to be twisting inward, as though straining away from the sun and toward a stronger, invisible light at the cottage's heart.

A side door swung, and in strode Master Sayre, bringing with him a shaft of daylight and a smell of sea and fish and skies.

He laid down a bundle of neatly folded nets.

"Now, there's our young man." Master Sayre knelt at the bedside. "I'd like to know what happened to you. We gathered from Lucas that the Witch Marrowight caught you in her vale."

Bastian couldn't find the words to respond—everything had seemed like a nightmare. Slowly, though, with Kaliyah's hand pressing his, with Mrs. Sayre bathing his face with the cool cloth, words came.

"We saw her in her vale, standing beside a ghastly goblin shrine," he said. "She was, I don't know, mixing things inside a red bowl. She dropped ashes into it—she seemed to be making smoke. It got so thick, I could hardly breathe. Stone statues lay scattered over the grass. And she spoke ugly words. She had a knife and was slicing up the air."

Mrs. Sayre's hand went to her mouth.

"After that, I hardly can believe what I saw," said Bastian. "Sprites —I think they were sprites—were lying all over the place on the vale. They looked like sprites—the small Sylphic people with wings drawn in *Moor Folk of the English Highlands*. Except, these had no wings. Only nubs." He pushed himself to sitting up a bit higher. "Lady Marrowight caught us, and more sprites appeared, hundreds of them, all over her vale. They were weeping, as though they were in great pain. There was a burst of sound, and then lightning, or something, flashed. Then they all froze stony and dropped onto the grass."

Kaliyah let out a little gasp.

Master Sayre took over holding Bastian's hand. "What else?"

"Lady Marrowight dragged us inside her manor. She forced me to drink something that stunk like a rotten bog, but it somehow helped me breathe better."

Mrs. Sayre hurried out. A door slammed, and it sounded like she was suddenly sick.

"Lady Marrowight spoke of the Day of the Dark Sun," said Bastian. "She said she'd have her way with the Sun Child, and I told her straight that she'd never lay a finger on Cassian. Then, an enormous animal—a wildcat—burst in. It distracted her long enough for me and Lucas to run."

Master Sayre exchanged a glance with Kaliyah.

"We hightailed it," said Bastian. "It was the Ryudo training, I think, that kept me running so hard. Lady Marrowight followed, but by the time she reached the vale, we were already over the fence. She spoke, and a hornet swept down."

Even saying the word "hornet" was great pain.

Master Sayre faced Kaliyah. "I have a hunch it was more than Bastian's work at Ryudo drills that kept him on his feet."

Kaliyah slunk back in her chair.

"In fact, all things figured, lad, you ought to be dead." Master Sayre opened the front of Bastian's tunic, revealing a silver scar on his chest—the imprints of two perfect hands. "Kaliyah, would you like to explain?"

She sat up a little but looked at no one. "So...last night, I led Bastian into the woods. I thought, in my true form, I might be able to draw all that darkness out of him. I know you said to leave him alone, but I really believed I could do it."

"Don't be angry with her," said Bastian. "She was just trying to help."

"Angry? I couldn't be angry," said Master Sayre. "I'm as pleased as a parrotfish, in fact."

He took Kaliyah's small hands in his own.

"If it weren't for your efforts, our world would've been lost this day. Although, another time your rogue willfulness might not be so easily forgiven."

"Can you make sense of anything I told you?" asked Bastian.

"I'm afraid that we can," said Master Sayre, leaning back. "The Witch Marrowight has lived in this woodland for millennia, kept in check by the strength of the Sylphic Kingdom. But lately, she's grown far more powerful, and more ruthless, and cruel."

"Is she the reason those stone sprites had no wings?" asked Bastian. "Did she do that to them?"

"The wings of Moor Folk carry enchantment," said Kaliyah. "Moor Folk use this power to support mortal things in thriving—to call forth good food from the earth; to usher in seasons and temper storms. The witch discovered that, by stewing Moor Folk wings and drinking the brew, she could absorb their power—and by it, access untold capabilities. That's how she manages to wield darkness, among other feats. Apparently, she used some of her brew to revive you."

A cold sweat surfaced on Bastian's skin.

Kaliyah offered him a sip of the petal-fresh cordial. "The witch's aim is to grow powerful enough to overthrow the Sun Devaa."

"But how?" asked Bastian. "The Sun Devaa—isn't he a god?"

"The Sun Devaa, our strong king, is part of the natural order of the world," said Master Sayre. "The witch opposes all nature."

"She's aiming to darken the sun forevermore," said Kaliyah, "which would mean the Sun Devaa's fall. And she's finding gruesome sources of power to fuel her deviousness."

Mrs. Sayre came back in and hovered over Bastian.

She peeled the cooled cloth from his head. She redressed his wrist, grown hotly sore again, with a fresh icepack.

"The witch isn't just powerful, though," said Master Sayre. "She's malicious and destructive—a fact you know well enough." He held Bastian's gaze. "What possessed you to place yourself in such danger?"

"I went to her vale precisely because of the danger that faces us all," said Bastian. "You see—I performed a sun dowsing rite on Cassian this morning, but it didn't work. The Day of the Dark Sun is almost here, and I understand how critical it is for the Sun Child to be ready. I had to get a witch hazel wand so I could run the other dowsing ritual. I've seen, many times, Lady Marrowight's witch hazel crop—so, Lucas and I set out for the manor to take a cutting."

"It was foolhardy to imagine you could outsmart the witch on her very grounds," said Master Sayre. "Witch hazel is a particularly potent herb of enchantment, and the Witch Marrowight has set curses to destroy all but what she cultivates for her own purposes. Even Kaliyah, a specialist in Moor Folk healing enchantments, hasn't meddled in it."

"We did manage to cut a witch hazel switch," said Bastian.

Kaliyah straightened.

"But—we lost it. Still, it was worth trying for. With Cassian's power dormant, with the Day of the Dark Sun just two dawns away, I'll do whatever it takes to see the Sun Child ready for battle."

"Do you really mean that?" asked Kaliyah.

"I thought you'd be pleased by what I was going to do." Bastian glanced at her. "Me, dowsing the Sun Child today. As his Keeper, I'm of course anxious to wake the sun in his blood and see what he might be capable of. I was going to bring him to you, sun-dowsed and somehow battle-ready. But even being a Keeper, it turns out, is beyond me."

Kaliyah rested her hand on his.

"If only I'd pulled it off," said Bastian. "I wanted so badly to make something good happen in the Sylphic Kingdom. I wanted to bring about whatever wonderful powers and abilities are lying hidden in my baby brother. But everything seems so ordinary now. The weeds and stones and switches I thought would empower Cassian...in my hands, they're ordinary. It seems all I'm meant to do is take curses."

Master Sayre's eyes wrinkled with his smile. "Fools who walk the Earth blind may say that the world's an ordinary place which we move through, then leave, without anything mattering much."

"Is it ordinary?" Bastian asked.

"Truly, the world's every bit as ordinary as it seems." Master Sayre leaned in, his eyes sparkling. "And it's every bit as magical."

Bastian gently smiled.

"Enchantment has visited itself upon you," said Master Sayre. "And courage can heal, even more strongly than the hands of a faerie."

"Facing the witch," said Kaliyah, "getting yourself and Lucas out of Marrowight Manor alive—you might've chased her curse well enough to see in yourself what the rest of us see."

Bastian focused on Kaliyah's eyes. "What would you have me see?"

"You already know it," she said.

Bastian slumped back, the ache in his chest suddenly clenching.

For she still hadn't let go of her belief that he was someone he wasn't. He waited for Master Sayre to say something to her, as the Sylphic boy had, to get her to drop this.

But Master Sayre said nothing.

Bastian couldn't let them take him into battle, thinking he had powers and abilities he never possibly could have. He couldn't let them carry on believing he was the Sun Child, when already he knew he would fail.

"Do you want to see clearly?" Kaliyah stood. "Do you want to see things as they are?"

"I already see clearly," said Bastian. "I'm afraid it's you who's in the dark."

"If you doubt that, even a little," said Kaliyah, "close your eyes."

Bastian watched her a moment, watched Master Sayre.

Master Sayre did nothing to put Kaliyah off her pursuit.

And although Kaliyah was looking at him with patience, she also seemed greatly expectant, as though determined to show him what she thought he needed to see.

Bastian let his eyes fall closed.

Kaliyah touched two tiny kisses to his lids.

Heat rose through his body, as the dark behind his eyelids shifted mercurial.

"Look at me," said Kaliyah.

Bastian opened his eyes to find Kaliyah standing closely before him, her face not two inches from his.

Sayre Cottage and everything in it seemed diminished, while she shimmered like a sunrise.

It was as though the person he'd called "Kaliyah" before had been just the shadow of a person; her negative. While here before him stood the solid soul.

"What you see from now on is entrusted to you." Sweeps of light traced Kaliyah's face.

"Your skin—" Bastian rested his fingers on her cheek.

She set her hand over his. "I shall show you my true self. And by knowing me, you'll discover your own heart." She lowered his hand and turned it palm up. "To speak of the Sylphic Kingdom with mortals, with the intent of malice, is treachery. Do you understand?"

Bastian nodded.

"Brace yourself," said Kaliyah. "The binding can be a bit painful."

Kaliyah blew into her hand, conjuring a ball of white light. She pressed it against Bastian's palm.

Bastian flinched at the sting of its heat.

Kaliyah, whispering in her curious language, stirred the globe of light to shine more brightly.

The heat grew almost unbearable but after a moment of great intensity, the light dwindled, and then vanished, leaving Bastian's hand smoking.

The thousand-pointed star—the Sun Devaa's emblem—glistened on his palm. It seemed to be flickering with the beat of his heart.

"My mum was of the Moor Folk—an angel fire faerie," said Kaliyah. "And my da—he was mortal-born."

She took down from the wall a small painting and presented it to him.

The painting showed a faerie—the same faerie drawn on the cover of *Moor Folk of the English Highlands*. Here, though, she was done with more intricate detail.

Her face was heart-shaped, like Kaliyah's, its expression kind. Her eyes were old-as-England blue, like the deep darkening the North Sea's high waves. The faerie was sitting on a rock alongside a large pool in the center of a woodland—it looked like the Natterjack Lagoon. She was resting her hand on the stone's slanting surface. A silver ring, holding a pearl, wrapped her finger. A dimple shone from her chin.

Bastian glanced at Kaliyah, finding that same dimple in her chin.

The artist had drawn the faerie with palpable affection, capturing the gentleness that must've tendered her hands, the love that must've shone from her eyes, and the kindness that must've rested in her heart.

In the corner lay a signature: *M.D. Kingfisher*.

"This ring." Bastian glanced at a pearl ring strung on a leather cord around Kaliyah's neck.

"It's the same," said Master Sayre. "The faerie pictured is Kaliyah's mum, Alura."

He wove his fingers into Mrs. Sayre's.

"We're of the Moor Folk, too. I'm of the annwyn race of the seafaring Moor Folk. Mrs. Sayre is an angel fire faerie, like Kaliyah. When Kaliyah lost her parents, we, along with a few others, were charged with looking after her."

Bastian stared at Kaliyah, at her radiance. "Am I seeing you fully in faerie form—your true self?"

Kaliyah, keeping her gaze on Bastian, took a few steps back. She closed her silver eyes and tightened her hands into fists.

A translucent mist appeared and twined about her feet. The mist traveled up her legs, twisted around her chest, and gathered behind her shoulders, outlining ephemeral shadows that unfurled into solid wings.

Bastian staggered to standing.

Kaliyah's wings, almost twice her height when fully unspun, were veined like butterfly wings, plated like stained glass, colored in the warm reds, stunning corals, and cool blues of a sunset.

The tips of her wings twisted slightly, as though the cosmic artist who'd dreamed them up had laid a final, perfect touch before tacking them to her small shoulders. A silver-blue glow coursed in waves along the latticed channels.

With a breeze drifting through the cottage's windows, her wings filled like ship sails.

Kaliyah's toes lifted. She hovered an inch off the floor.

Bastian rounded her.

She smiled as he touched the back of her neck and followed its curve to the origin of a wing.

The wing's translucent edge felt as solid as crystal. He trailed his fingers across one of the wings' panes, strumming it like a harp. He drew his hand along the rim, angel-feathered and soft as down. Ribbons of light fell where he pressed a blushing pane.

Kaliyah's feet touched down once again. Her wings curled in and vanished.

She lifted her palm, showing Bastian her thousand-pointed star flickering, far brighter than his.

Bastian set his palm against hers. "You couldn't be anything but a lovely faerie child." Tears slipped down his cheeks, and he didn't even care. "What happened to your mum?"

Kaliyah's face dimmed. "The Witch Marrowight wanted her for her wings. She cut off my mum's wings, sending her fading into the Aetherlands. I was a week old when the witch took her from us and locked her in iron."

"She couldn't escape that?" asked Bastian. "With how faeries can change forms—could she not get away?"

"Faeries can't cope with iron," said Kaliyah. "It causes us excruciating pain."

Bastian again sat. "And your da?" He drew her to sitting beside him.

"My da..." She blinked her eyes clear. "My da was Malachi Daoine Kingfisher..."

Bastian tipped back against the wall.

"...the last Sun Child."

Bastian stopped breathing.

Master Sayre handed Bastian the chalice of cordial.

"Years ago, the witch killed my da," said Kaliyah, her voice unsteady.

Master Sayre drew nearer. "By his death, some say a Sylphic prophecy was fulfilled. That it allowed a new Sun Child—a very important Sun Child—to be born." He settled into the chair by the bed. "A Sun Child who could challenge the witch."

At meeting the solemnity on both their faces, a cold sweat pricked Bastian's forehead.

"My da was bound in the knowledge of the Sun Devaa's Sylphic Kingdom." Kaliyah turned Bastian's hand over and stroked his glowing star. "As you've been bound."

She flashed her eyes to meet his.

"You're our Sun Child, Bastian."

"It's impossible," he whispered. "Out of reach."

"Your eyes are destined to see," said Master Sayre. "Your mind is destined to understand. Your heart, for deeds of valor."

"Out of reach..." whispered Bastian. "Yet...I wish it weren't. I see it now—how much I want this. How much I've always wanted it."

"You want it because your heart is true," said Mrs. Sayre. "You're becoming the person you've, deep down, always known yourself to be."

Kaliyah captured his gaze. "As you've cared for your baby brother, whom you thought was the Sun Child, so shall you care for England's Sylphic Kingdom. As you love Cassian, so shall you love all Moor Folk. As you've protected him, so shall you protect us."

Since the moment he first believed Cassian was a Sun Child, Bastian had been desperate to learn what dormant skill or ability might waken in the baby, to keep him safe in the battle; to empower him to defend the Sylphic kingdom.

Waves of relief were striking, now, at realizing that Cassian wouldn't be in the fight.

Bastian clenched his fist around the star radiating from his hand. "What must I do?"

"The Sun Child will lead an assault on the Witch Marrowight, on the Day of the Dark Sun," said Master Sayre. "Though many Moor Folk will fight, only the Sun Child can defeat her."

"Hope shines strongly in the Sylphic lands," said Mrs. Sayre. "Though never have we faced a fiercer tyrant."

"She's hunted me, hasn't she?" asked Bastian. "All the nightmares, the attacks—she's orchestrated everything."

"When you were born," said Kaliyah, "news reached her that a new Sun Child had come into the world, but that he was sick. Whispers rose that you died—that the Sylphic Kingdom was too weak for any Sun Child to survive. A band of forest children made sure those rumors got to the Witch Marrowight. And she believed them."

"The witch's power has grown over these last years," said Mrs. Sayre, "which she took as assurance that she'd ended the line of Sun Children; that the Sylphic Kingdom's fall was inevitable."

A smile lit Kaliyah's face. "But everything she thought was wrong."

"Ay, it was." Master Sayre leaned in. "When the Witch Marrowight discovered that you'd survived, she turned Moor Folk to stone by the thousands. You see, Kingfisher, before he died, spent years researching how he might destroy her. He set down everything he discovered in *Moor Folk of the English Highlands*, and in his other book, which has been lost."

"The lost book," murmured Bastian.

Kaliyah and Master and Mrs. Sayre—they seemed to have no idea where it was.

It seemed none of the Moor Folk knew.

But the Witch Marrowight—she might've actually betrayed its location.

"Much of what Kingfisher wrote of is knowledge that's common to Sylphic folk," Master Sayre went on. "But it's rumored that in his lost book, he hid secrets. Secrets protected by enchantments. Secrets to the Witch Marrowight's destruction."

Bastian sat straighter. "That book—"

"For years, she's aimed to get her hands on it," said Kaliyah, "along with *Moor Folk of the English Highlands*. And she did eventually manage to steal *Moor Folk of the English Highlands*, but we stole it back. She nearly destroyed it, investigating whether it held the secret to her demise that it was rumored to carry."

"And she deduced—rightly—that it does not," said Mrs. Sayre.

"That secret lies in the lost book," said Kaliyah. "Which she arrogantly presumed was too buried in enchantments somewhere in the Wystan Woods for anyone except she herself her to find."

"But she never has been able to find it," said Mrs. Sayre.

"And," said Kaliyah, "she's aimed to make sure that neither would any Sun Child who might come along. She's blighted these woodlands with plants she's made poisonous to Sun Children. We've come to learn that witch hazel might weaken her in some way, or at least serve as a counter-balance to a number of her curses. So she's destroyed all the witch hazel growing or brought to Dartmoor, except what she grows."

"She's hoped to drive us away," said Bastian.

"No, lad." Mrs. Sayre gently lifted Bastian's swollen wrist. "This sting was dealt by a balor hornet—a nasty Elemental Spirit. Bred to kill."

Bastian glanced at the sting. "Then—I could have died from this?"

Mrs. Sayre said nothing.

"Could"—Bastian met her eyes—"could I still die from this?"

Mrs. Sayre just cast a look of sorrow toward him.

"I've seen you, in dreams, advancing on the witch," said Kaliyah.

That wasn't exactly a *no*.

Bastian studied the window, the warm light it cherished, the birds—careless and flittering in the strong sun.

In this place, such a monstrous evil seemed far-fetched.

And storm clouds and cursed smoke and poisoned plants and goblins and witches aside, it seemed impossible for something so mighty as the sun itself to grow frail and black; for the Sun Devaa to weaken; for the Sylphic Kingdom, for all of nature, to falter.

But the Witch's power was so profound, her determination so dark, it was growing clear to Bastian that she could slay even the Sun Devaa.

And if he failed as the Sylphic Kingdom's Sun Child—she would.

A chill swept through the cottage, like a tempest leading a strong storm. The shine on Bastian's hand faded, and the radiant glow the room had taken dimmed until everything looked once again plain.

He sank back against the wall. "But how could it even be possible— me defeating her? The Day of the Dark Sun is just two dawns from now. I'm in no way prepared."

"There, you're quite wrong," said Mrs. Sayre. "Although you haven't been aware of it, you've been training for the Day of the Dark Sun all your life."

"In what possible way am I trained for this?" asked Bastian.

"When I see you on the Ryudo pitch," said Master Sayre, "I see the Sun Child our kingdom needs."

Ryudo was an unusual sport. In Bastian's entire life, he'd never met another person, aside from his private teachers, who practiced it.

Sylphic forces, he now understood, had led him to grow skilled in Ryudo—a Sylphic athletic art form that had primed him for agility and precision, for speed and for strength.

But what could even champion-level agility, aim, speed, and strength do to make him a match for the Witch Marrowight?

And no athletic aptitude could lend him the courage he'd need to be able to face her in a battle.

Bastian's hand went to his chest, aching with the witch's dark curse.

"My own Ryudo master has methods for giving the witch's darkness flight," said Master Sayre. "Tomorrow, you'll meet him. And, with his help, you very well might free yourself of that burden."

Bastian glanced at the Sun Devaa's star impressed on his hand, weakly flickering.

The star on Kaliyah's hand was still glowing brightly, while on his own, it looked as though tendrils of shadows were choking out the coursing light.

"Ryudo tenets and stamina and casting mortars true," said Bastian, "how could that possibly prepare me to fight a wight witch?"

He glanced at his swollen wrist.

"One who, perhaps, already has killed me."

They all simply watched him.

Bastian's hand slid down from his chest. "You don't actually know how I could fight her, much less defeat her, do you?"

"We can't say precisely how you'll do it," said Kaliyah, "but we know that my da spent his life—gave his life—learning how the next Sun Child might defeat her."

"Might?" asked Bastian.

"Master Sayre has known, since before you were born," said Kaliyah, "that to conquer the witch, you'll cast at her something of great power. Ryudo is the best preparation you could have."

"Something of great power," said Bastian. "What?"

Mrs. Sayre set her hand on Kaliyah's shoulder. "Kaliyah is the daughter of Alura, an angel fire faerie, and of a Sun Child. She's as rare as Aubrey Gyrfalcon, for scarcely has sun blood ever blended with the enchantment coursing through Sylphic hearts."

"Angel fire faeries are distantly descended from sea waves and dragons," said Master Sayre. "And by the strength of her heritage, blended with Kingfisher's power—Kaliyah can conjure Faerie Fire. We believe that, in the battle to come, the Sun Child will deal in Faerie Fire."

"Okay, you believe it," said Bastian. "But what's that based on?"

"Faerie Fire is sunlight channeled into a solid form," said Kaliyah. "With it, I can wield an enchantment that heals." She glanced at the scar on his chest. "It has its limitations, but I can do quite a lot with it."

"Do you know how it might end the witch?" Bastian asked.

"As far as we know," said Master Sayre, "Faerie Fire—even what Kaliyah can render—wouldn't be strong enough to even touch the Witch Marrowight. But we also know that Kingfisher, for some reason, believed that it might."

"My da has to be right," said Kaliyah. "Faerie Fire stands in opposition to the witch's dark arts, which is hopeful. I transform light into a material that heals. The witch molds darkness into weapons that destroy. Is that not something?"

"It's not anything unless we discover what your da knew." Bastian closed his dim hand into a fist. "But it isn't just Kingfisher's secret we need."

He met Master Sayre's eyes.

"You needed me powerful a long time ago. The rite of passage Kingfisher writes about—the change that happens at thirteen—I see it now. That's the Sun Child's waking, isn't it? The Sun Child actually coming into power. But the witch damaged me. When the goblin came to Exeter and punched darkness into my body, when the witch shot that curse of dark smoke—they've prevented me from becoming the Sylphic Kingdom's Sun Child."

"You are our Sun Child," said Master Sayre. "And we've received insight enough to know that you have some chance of prevailing in this battle."

Some chance.

"Kaliyah, indeed, has dreamed of you approaching the battlefield." Master Sayre glanced away. "But I'm afraid that's as far as she—or anyone—has seen."

"These Sylphic dreams," said Bastian. "Are they even always right?"

"Well—no," said Kaliyah. "But—"

"Then how can you trust them?" asked Bastian. "How can you trust me?"

Kaliyah took his hand.

Touched its bleak star.

"We trust you because you're alive."

Bastian held the ice closer against his throbbing wrist. "It would take something profound happening for me to even imagine that I could face down a wight witch."

"Profound deeds of valor have ever been part of a prince's journey to his throne." Master Sayre leaned in closely to Bastian. "Fight this battle. End this conflict. Avenge Alura. Be the Sun Child that King-fisher believed you to be."

Bastian glanced at the painting of Alura; at the pearl ring strung around Kaliyah's soft throat.

His own mum wore a ring that was delicate like that, holding a sapphiric stone, as round as a pearl. Tears welled for the sorrow of Kaliyah having no mum, and heat rose from the rancor that Alura's murderess walked free.

He found Kaliyah's silver eyes, shining with tears, too.

Whether he could ever be as strong or as brave as a Sun Child was supposed to be—it suddenly seemed not to matter.

He knew in his heart that he'd do whatever he could to protect the Sylphic Kingdom and its Moor Folk.

He'd lay down his life if it meant making sure the Witch Marrowight could not take another faerie.

"More might've been gained today than chasing a bit of the witch's curse," said Bastian. "As foolish as I was, trespassing to Marrowight Manor, I might've learned something useful. But I don't know. What I discovered—it might not be new information."

"What, lad?" asked Master Sayre.

"The witch mentioned Kingfisher's lost book," said Bastian. "She betrayed that she thinks I've found it. So, I sort of tricked her into talking about it."

Kaliyah jumped to her feet. "What did she say?"

"Her words made little sense," said Bastian. "She spoke of Kingfisher hiding it someplace in his chalet. In some secret place—a council chamber, she said. A place guarded by 'a mockery of her power.' Does that mean anything to you?"

Master Sayre shook a laugh, coarsened by the strong Celtic Sea. "Our Sun Child's not only brave, but quite clever."

Kaliyah snagged Bastian's hand and pulled him running out of the cottage.

27

Bastian and Kaliyah left the woodland and crossed onto the hill behind Kingfisher Chalet.

The back yard was as still as a graveyard and littered with broken sticks and tree limbs. In the west, more thunderheads were mounding.

Lucas stood from crouching behind a rowan berry bush at the hill's crest.

Bastian ran to him, signing, "Are you okay?"

"Yes," Lucas signed. "Or—I don't know. I've been watching for Naga."

"There's been no sign of Naga at all?" asked Bastian.

"You don't need to worry about Naga," said Kaliyah. "He's sure to be all right."

"Did you meet Kaliyah?" Bastian asked Lucas.

"Yes." Lucas waved to her, then signed to Bastian, "Does she know what happened?"

Bastian nodded. "I told her and the Sayres everything."

Lucas glanced through a gap in the rowan berry branches toward Rhys, standing on the porch, bouncing Cassian—wailing.

He pulled Bastian and Kaliyah behind a thicker bush. "Should we tell anyone else about what happened today?"

Bastian glanced at his palm. It looked plain but still felt warm from the star.

He translated Lucas' question for Kaliyah, then spoke and signed, "I think—definitely not."

"For sure not Mum and Da," signed Lucas, glancing at the back porch. "But what about Rhys?"

Bastian spoke his question to Kaliyah.

"Would he understand?" she asked.

"Rhys is our brother—don't you think he ought to know?" Lucas glanced at the sting on Bastian's wrist. "And we have to tell him something to answer for the shape we're in."

Bastian's memory of all he'd seen at Marrowight Manor was vague, some of the details seeming to have faded. Only hours had passed since they'd been on the witch's dreadful vale, and in her horrific manor—and yet the memory of it seemed hazed, like a dream.

"What, exactly, would you tell him?" signed Bastian, watching Lucas closely.

Lucas was quiet for a moment. "I'm not sure how to put it into words. There were odd things, right? On Lady Marrowight's grounds. I remember a storm hitting. She threw us inside her manor, then dragged us down a hall." He rubbed his arm, as if recalling the chill of her hand. "That, I remember concretely. That, and how cold her manor was, how dark. At one point we were sitting in a kitchen, I think—and for some reason, I couldn't move. I may have fallen asleep for a while—I'm not sure. I remember worrying that she was going to hurt you. I remember being afraid. And—I don't know—did she make you drink something? That, I may have dreamed. But I know I saw Naga in a trap. And the hornet that stung you—it was as big as a sparrow." He glanced at Rhys, on the porch. "Do you think Rhys will believe any of that?"

"Do you believe it?" asked Bastian, signing.

Lucas shrugged. "If any part of what I remember did happen, I can't make sense of it. But Lady Marrowight definitely forced us inside her manor, and it was definitely awful. I imagine she'll try to avoid us from now on."

"She certainly won't," signed Bastian. "She believes we have something she wants."

"Do you mean this?" Lucas drew the witch hazel sprig from his sleeve.

Kaliyah's eyes widened. "You got it."

"Do you remember anything Lady Marrowight said to us, when we were in her kitchen?" asked Bastian, signing. "She spoke of a book."

Lucas signed, "Is she after *Moor Folk of the English Highlands?* She's asked you for it before."

"The book she really wants is the other one Kingfisher wrote," signed Bastian. "It's about Moor Folk enemies and the secrets to their defeat. We think it's hidden someplace inside our chalet—in a place called a Sylphic Council Chamber."

"If our chalet had some kind of council chamber," signed Lucas, "don't you think we'd know it?"

Kaliyah eased closer to the sprig of witch hazel in Lucas' hand.

She touched one of its flowers, and the whole sprig revived, its blooms strengthening until it looked as though it were freshly cut, every petal shifting from limp beige to bright yellow.

Lucas' eyes widened.

"It's powerful, isn't it?" Bastian took the witch hazel from Lucas and held it before Kaliyah. "You could use it, I think."

As foolish as it'd been for him and Lucas to have crossed onto the witch's grounds, Bastian found himself so glad that they had. Proud, even, that they had. For daring the witch had meant winning this rare charm for Kaliyah.

She reached for it. "Very powerful." But she hesitated to take it.

Knowing he himself was the Sylphic Kingdom's Sun Child, Bastian felt he had no need any longer for witch hazel. And who knew what a faerie—a specialist in enchantments of healing—might render with this costly charm plucked from a wight witch's vale?

Bastian held it further out to her. "It feels right for you to have this."

She again reached for it but ended by breaking off only a small twig, heavy with flowers.

"It's safer here, on the grounds of Kingfisher Chalet. I'll keep just a piece."

Bastian translated her words for Lucas.

Lucas stared at Kaliyah with the same sense of wonder as when he'd seen the witch hazel revive.

Lucas signed, "I'm not sure how Rhys would take any of this. He'd have trouble believing what we could tell him about what happened today."

Bastian translated.

"Can Rhys be trusted?" Kaliyah asked.

"If he couldn't believe us," signed Lucas, "could you imagine what he might tell Mum and Da?"

The three of them together, through gaps in the rowan berry branches, watched Rhys.

He was pacing anxiously and staring at the woods as he fruitlessly tried to soothe the crying baby.

"We don't have to say anything to Rhys," said Bastian, signing. "If we run into trouble, we can always go to the Sayres."

"We can just tell Rhys that the storm caught us," signed Lucas.

Bastian glanced at his wrist—the knot swollen and purple.

Looking at it dropped the bottom out of his stomach and brought a fresh wallop of pain.

He held up his wrist. "What about this?"

"We could say that a hornet nest blew down, and one stung you," signed Lucas. "I've seen stings on you swell up before. I mean, not like that—but it isn't so surprising that a hornet sting on you would turn vicious."

Bastian translated for Kaliyah.

"That story will have to do," she said. "And it isn't exactly a lie. You did weather a storm."

Bastian led Lucas and Kaliyah down the eastern hill. They crossed over the back yard, carefully navigating among the fallen branches.

Rhys, catching sight of them, hurried down from the porch. "That storm! I was starting to fear you'd been crushed by a tree or struck by lightning or swept into a river." He stopped before them. "Who's this?"

"Kaliyah—she's a friend of the Sayres," said Bastian, signing. "We got caught in the storm, and she helped us. She wanted to see us safely home."

"Kaliyah." He patted her shoulder. "That was kind of you. I was about to have to bring this screaming lad out looking for them."

Bastian relieved Rhys of Cassian.

At finding himself on Bastian's shoulder, the baby relaxed. His crying eased to a moan, and he settled his thumb in his mouth.

Rhys guided them onto the porch.

Bastian, holding Cassian tightly, dropped into Mum's porch swing.

The humidity had drawn Mum's cedarwood and coconut scents from the cushion. He rested his cheek against it and breathed deeply.

He cradled Cassian's plump foot as the clouds thinned and brightened.

Rhys knelt before him. "Bloody bindweed—is that a bee sting?"

"A hornet," signed Lucas. "The storm knocked down a nest."

Rhys studied the purple lump. "I've never seen a sting look like this. Not even on you." He examined the scratches on Bastian's hands and arms, the tears in his shirt and the cuts underneath. "I expected you to come home cold and wet, not beat to a pulp."

Rhys stood away from Bastian and looked him well over.

"Mum's going to murder me."

"That storm tore up the whole country," said Kaliyah. "I think your mum will be glad they made it home in one piece."

"I wouldn't exactly call this 'one piece,'" said Rhys, signing. "What happened?"

Bastian told him that they'd hiked to Marrowight Manor, clipped the witch hazel, then started for home the long way around—from the east, through the woodland—when the storm suddenly hit.

"Nothing weird or awful happened," signed Lucas, glancing at Bastian as if to assure him, *I've got this.* "We didn't see anything extraordinary. At all."

Bastian gave him a small shake of his head.

"It was pretty boring," Lucas went on. "Not creepy and mystical."

Bastian discreetly kicked him.

"Creepy and mystical?" Rhys widened his eyes.

"Lucas is playing." Bastian let out a laugh. "The only creepy thing was Lady Marrowight. She's a fright. We hauled out of her vale so fast, I slipped on grass slick from the storm, and I tore up my clothes."

"No..." Rhys looked from Lucas to Bastian. "You said the storm struck after you left Marrowight Manor."

Bastian and Lucas exchanged glances.

"Exactly," said Bastian, signing. "We saw Lady Marrowight. We ran. It started raining. I slipped. We took the eastern path home. Near the Sayre's, the storm blew down a hornet nest. I got stung. Master Sayre and Mrs. Sayre helped us, along with Kaliyah. We waited there until the storm passed, and Mrs. Sayre took care of the sting."

Lying to Rhys didn't feel right. But telling the truth—this sort of truth—would've felt like trying to convince someone to believe a dream.

"You're not breathing well, are you?" Rhys felt Bastian's chest a moment. "I'll have to call Mum."

"Don't." Bastian stood.

"Why worry her?" signed Lucas.

"She'd think we can't handle being on our own," said Bastian, signing.

"But look at the shape you're in," said Rhys. "A hornet sting. Cuts and rashes everywhere. The asthma getting to you—I shouldn't have let you two go."

"Hornets and storms and scrapes and odd neighbors," signed Lucas, "it's all part of living in the wilds of Dartmoor, right? Mum imagined we'd 'ramble over England like banshees.' Well, today we did just what she had in mind."

Rhys guided them in. "I have to give her a heads up about that sting. Those scratches. If she were to find Bastian like this without warning, she'd have my head. But she can't know that I let you go off sneaking around Lady Marrowight's property—agreed?"

Bastian threw out his fist, initiating the handshake they'd created for pact-making. Rhys and Lucas answered with their fists.

Rhys glanced at Kaliyah. "We'd be better off with your word, too."

Kaliyah covered their fists with her hand and met Bastian's eyes. "Now we're all bound to secrecy."

28

*I*nside the kitchen, Rhys had the television turned to the news.

Bastian, Lucas, and Kaliyah sat down around the table and watched the coverage of the storm's aftermath—rooftops all over England bashed by fallen trees; overflowing rivers swamping farms and homes.

Buildings that'd survived centuries had sustained damage, their windows and walls smashed by floodwaters and blowing debris. An outage map illustrated whole counties without power.

Rhys set a handful of first aid supplies on the table and knelt before Bastian.

"Mum? Are you there?" He held the landline phone close.

"That doesn't even look like England," signed Lucas, taking the baby from Bastian.

Rhys sprayed antiseptic on Bastian's sting.

Bastian bore the pain a second, then twisted away.

Rhys covered the receiver and whispered, "Sit still."

Bastian held his breath while Rhys dabbed the antiseptic onto the cuts on his shoulder and arms.

Kaliyah, catching Bastian's glance, whispered, "Do you have any idea how to reach a basement or attic? Or does your chalet have a storm shelter?"

"We don't have any of those," said Bastian.

"Mum? Say that again—you're cutting out."

Rhys squeezed ointment onto Bastian's cuts.

"The storm brought down some big branches. No, nothing hit the chalet." He covered Bastian's widest cut with a bandage. "We think a hornet nest fell. One got after Bastian. He's okay, but he did need his EpiPen. The Sayres were with him."

Lucas, cradling Cassian, picked up the witch hazel sprig.

"You don't need to come home," said Rhys, cheerfully. "I've got Bastian all cleaned up and patched."

Lucas handed the witch hazel to Bastian, then signed, "Want to try sun dowsing the baby?"

Bastian set the sprig aside. "He's sleeping." He glanced at Kaliyah. "We shouldn't disturb him."

"No, Mum, really," said Rhys. "I know what to watch for. If you were to come home, there'd be nothing for you even to do."

"She's the one who says we need more chances for responsibility," whispered Bastian, signing.

"This wasn't so much an unfortunate accident, as an opportunity," said Rhys. "A challenge of responsibility, really. A test."

"And we passed it," signed Lucas.

"That we passed." Rhys winked at them. "Okay. See you tonight." He hung up, letting go of a heavy breath. "She'll have some time now, at least, to cool off."

"She won't be angry with us," signed Lucas. "That storm wasn't in our control." He pointed to the TV. "Just look at how much worse the destruction could've been."

They together focused on the news, where a helicopter feed was showing coastlines in Wales littered with rubbish from broken ships.

"The Sylphic Council Chamber would be someplace unlikely," Kaliyah whispered to Bastian, "and probably difficult to reach. Can you not think of anyplace odd like that?"

Rhys turned off the news.

Bastian watched him until he'd stepped away into the dining room.

"Upstairs, the chalet has only bedrooms," he signed, whispering. "The rooms are big, but they're simple. And down here, the rooms all connect in a ring. There isn't an inch that we haven't explored."

"Wait."

She stared up at the ceiling, as though listening.

"Are you sure this place doesn't have an attic?"

"The roof is strangely high, I've always thought," said Bastian. "But we've never found a way to reach the space under the roof. Mum and Da say the high roof is just how the chalet vents hot air."

"How big would a Sylphic Council Chamber be?" signed Lucas. "And what would it be used for?"

"What's a Sylphic Council Chamber?" asked Rhys, just coming back in. He set a glass before each of them.

"Just something from Bastian's Kingfisher book," signed Lucas.

Rhys gathered up the first aid supplies and carried them back to a kitchen cabinet.

Kaliyah eased closer to Bastian and Lucas. "According to legend," she said—Bastian translating for Lucas—"the Sylphic Council Chamber is where the Sun Devaa, the Sun Child, and three Moor Folk leaders—the Great Sages—held secret meetings."

She seemed to startle a touch as she looked up again at the ceiling. She stood and walked into the dining room.

"Are we saying too much in front of Rhys?" Lucas signed low.

Rhys turned just in time to catch a glimpse of Lucas' hands.

"All right," he said, signing. "I knew there was something you two were keeping from me." He crossed his arms. "Out with it."

Bastian glanced at *Moor Folk of the English Highlands*, resting on the dining room table.

"The other book Kingfisher wrote—the one that's been lost," he said, signing, "we stumbled on a hint that he may have hidden it in this chalet—in a place called a Sylphic Council Chamber." He picked up *Moor Folk of the English Highlands* and stood. "Kaliyah might have an idea about where that could be."

Rhys watched him a moment. "You're seriously believing this, aren't you?"

Bastian slid the book into his rucksack and shouldered it.

"How can you entertain the idea that this place has a secret chamber?" asked Rhys. "One that not one of us ever has noticed."

"You could help us try and find it," said Bastian. "But if you're going to make fun of us, you can just as well stay here." He joined Kaliyah—standing in the living room now, staring at the ceiling.

Rhys glanced at Lucas. "Well, come on, then," he said, signing. "I'm all for discovering a secret place in this chalet that couldn't possibly exist."

Kaliyah kept her gaze on the ceiling. "There honestly seems to be something above us."

"Maybe there's a mouse in one of the bedrooms," signed Rhys.

Kaliyah squinted, as though trying to decipher what she was hearing. "No—the sound seems more distant than just one floor up."

"But how could we even get above the second floor to find out?" asked Bastian.

A streak of silver leaped between Bastian and Kaliyah and raced through the house.

"Naga." Kaliyah rushed after him. "Of course!"

"He's okay!" Lucas signed to Bastian.

"Why are we chasing the cat?" called Rhys, following them, running.

Bastian skidded to a stop behind Kaliyah in middle of Da's spacious study.

Naga seemed to have disappeared.

Lucas laid Cassian, fast asleep, in his playpen.

Rhys turned a circle, studying the room's corners. "Where could Naga possibly have gone?"

"Hang on." Bastian signed.

Holding very still, he listened.

A Sylphic sound new to him—low, like thunder, or a chorus of drums, was rumbling. It seemed to be coming from someplace straight above.

"What are you hearing?" asked Kaliyah.

"The same thing that you are, I think."

Bastian and Kaliyah together stared up.

The hushed thunder did not sound beautiful, as most Sylphic sounds did.

This seemed more alike to the screaming he'd heard. It seemed to be what might precede screaming.

"What if she knew I was trying to trick her?" Bastian whispered to Kaliyah. "What if she meant for me to go looking for the book here, to lure me to meet something dangerous?"

"I can't say what's waiting." Kaliyah watched the ceiling with bright eyes. "But I don't credit her with a fraction of the cleverness she'd need to tamper with Kingfisher Chalet."

"I would," said Bastian. "She's managed to get inside once already. That we know of."

A muted meow sounded from behind a bookcase.

Rhys hurried to it, signing to Lucas, "Naga's here. It sounds like he's gone behind the wall."

The chalet wall, again, seemed to meow.

"I see a narrow black space." Lucas pointed. "There—in the case behind those tall books."

"How the blazes did Naga squeeze through that?" Rhys unloaded the lowest shelf of books.

Bastian knelt and knocked on the wood. "This feels hollow." He glanced at the others. "It must have a false back."

Rhys helped him remove the upper shelves and shift the panel aside.

Behind it, a shaft stretched.

It led upward, and it was studded with wooden handholds.

Lucas retrieved a flashlight from Da's desk drawer. He knelt before the shaft and shone it inside.

Bastian knelt by him and leaned in.

The beam showed no Naga, but rather a high passageway that vanished around a bend.

The sound of dark drumming, of thundering strengthened.

Bastian reached into the shaft and gripped a handhold.

Lucas held him back. "Are you out of your mind?" he signed. "If you go inside such a narrow, dark space, you'll panic."

The thought of being inside a shaft so dark and constricting that he couldn't move—it stole his breath.

And with those ominous sounds ringing from the void—sounds that the witch truly might've planted to bait him—it seemed not unreasonable that some curse, or something more dreadful yet, was up there waiting for him.

But it hadn't felt like the witch had been trying to deceive him. She'd seemed to legitimately believe Bastian had found Kingfisher's lost book.

She'd been distraught at the idea of him finding it.

And those baleful rumblings Bastian was hearing might mean that the lost book was really within his reach, its secrets waiting; its hiding place coveted and betrayed by the witch.

Bastian threaded himself inside the passageway.

29

Stories he'd read of secret passageways didn't prepare Bastian for what it felt like to be inside a real one.

In books, secret passageways were often described as cave-cool, but this shaft was oven-hot. Sweat trickled down his cheeks, and a musty smell—like cedar steaming in a sauna—thickened the air.

Sheets of cobwebs snagged him as he climbed past gaps crumbly with old plaster. Square nails jutted from the studs, like a seamstress giantess had long ago lashed their chalet together with pins.

He advanced straight up, rung by rung, heat swelling and a heady odor of hot dust pressing him.

With each step he took, a feeling of intensity heightened—like he was sensing at heart level the gravity of what waited here, be it placed by a Sun Child or a witch.

Lucas knocked on the interior wall.

Bastian peered down.

"Is it safe?" signed Lucas.

"I don't know," Bastian signed back. "But it's incredible."

Lucas clambered up into the space. When he drew close to Bastian, he handed him the flashlight.

Bastian climbed a few more rungs, then reached a turn.

He shone the light into it, showing the course of the passageway stretching straight on a few meters, then angling back again over itself.

Rhys leaned into the shaft. "Shout out when you've both reached someplace stable. Kaliyah and I will stay put until we're sure you two won't come crashing down on us."

Bastian led Lucas around the passageway's bend. Where it doubled back, the handholds were spaced further apart. He pulled along them until he reached a wall where the rungs climbed straight up, leading to a large platform, five feet square on a side.

He maneuvered onto it and found he could stand to his full height. Lucas pulled onto the platform beside him.

Bastian studied the next segment, stretching straight up. He shone the flashlight around them.

There, on the wall, not a meter away—a painted goblin leered.

At the sight of it, Bastian tripped back and lost his footing.

Lucas, standing right behind, steadied him.

Bastian raised the flashlight to shine on the goblin.

It was the very same goblin as what was painted in *Moor Folk of the English Highlands*. This was Kek—the Goblin King.

Its eyes flamed. Its muscles bulged. Its gray fangs looked sharp enough to prick. Its clawed hand was gripping a knife.

Though only a painting, it appeared solid and disturbingly lifelike. Its blade somehow seemed three-dimensional, seemed to reach.

Bastian dropped the flashlight.

Lucas snatched for it, but it flickered off and rolled, leaving them in complete darkness—but for a pair of eyes glowing red from the face of the phantasmic goblin.

Bastian crouched and clung to the platform. The chill in his chest deepened and spread through his limbs. He swam in dizziness until he grew aware of how fast he was breathing.

Lucas knelt by him. He held Bastian's shoulder.

Bastian focused on drawing air slowly.

All it had taken was a glimpse of that Goblin King—just an image— for this arresting panic to strike, for the knot in his chest to twist so tightly, it seemed his heart would choke.

But it was no surprise. Though here stood a mere painting of the Goblin King with its hand clenching the hilt of its knife, nothing seemed more absolute than the actual Goblin King waiting for him.

For as surely as the goblin in Exeter had been stalking him, the Goblin King was doubtlessly biding his time for the red day when he'd test Bastian's heart with that blade.

Lucas pounded on the dusty inner wall.

A beam of light flashed up from below—Rhys and Kaliyah, coming.

Bastian watched the flashlight's rays flicker across the goblin painting as Rhys and Kaliyah climbed.

A goblin did not belong in this chalet. Not even in a dark, secret shaft. Kingfisher Chalet was home to Sun Children, and a goblin here seemed a manifestation of a wickedness pervading everything good and peace-loving. With the painting placed here, it felt as if curses, not light, were the material thing.

It seemed the witch's darkness was an unstoppable force, spreading like a poison through Dartmoor, through his chalet, through him.

Bastian's every instinct prompted him to draw back, to climb down. To run.

He struggled away from the edge of the platform and back to the rungs. But there he stalled.

Because he was the Sun Child. And whatever was up here—it was his to confront.

Bastian straightened and faced the painting. He lifted his fingers toward it.

He touched the Goblin King's hand.

Nothing happened.

For all the thing's fright, it seemed to be only a painting.

Although—from around the seams of the wall, he could feel a faint current of heat.

It seemed certain that the painting was hiding something.

Bastian signed to Lucas, "Are you feeling this draft?"

Lucas, his gaze fixed on the Goblin King's face, signed, "Let's go back."

Kaliyah and Rhys climbed the last of the distance and pulled onto the platform beside them.

"Ugh, what a hideous thing." Rhys shone the flashlight straight on the Goblin King and leaned in. "Why on Earth would someone paint something so revolting—and in such a bizarre place?"

The witch had been right that Kingfisher Chalet held secrets. She'd also said that the lost book was kept from her by "a mockery of her power."

Perhaps this goblin was a scarecrow of sorts—a mockery of Sylphic wickedness, protecting the secret to a victory in war.

"It's painted here because it marks a threshold," said Bastian.

"It looks like we can't go on from here," signed Lucas, looking at Kaliyah.

Rhys translated.

"I think that we can." Bastian felt around the painting. "There's a current of air coming from the edge of the wall."

And it wasn't just air.

Something tiny and sparkling was drifting from the wall's seams. The phenomenon was so minuscule—an effect of light that, looking at it directly, he could barely perceive.

It was as though here hung a scattering of tiny, newborn stars that he only could glimpse from the corner of his eye.

"We have to get back there," said Kaliyah.

Rhys felt of the painting.

"That thing's brushed right on the plaster. I don't see any way to reach the other side, short of busting down the wall."

"This chalet was built to withstand," said Kaliyah, her eyes seeming to smoothy follow the lights. "There's no way that wall would crumble. There has to be a way in."

Kingfisher's words—words that had beckoned Bastian to follow the Sylphic lights in the woodland, rose to mind.

Fear not the tomb. Descend the gloom.
Make fast your stand. Make still your hand.
For wise ones claim—in dark's domain,
the children of the forest reign.

Drawing out Woodthrush's Sylphic scope, Bastian whispered those words.

"What's that you're muttering?" asked Rhys.

"A bit of a poem, written by Kingfisher." Bastian lifted the scope.

Through its lens, the form of the goblin shifted.

Light grew around it into a halo, then dimmed.

The terrible shape of the goblin altered into the shape of a person—a smart painting of a clever-looking boy, crouching and plated in red and silver armor.

The low sounds of thunder shifted to a faint chorus of drums and pipes brightened by a quiet, sweet chanting.

The painted boy was pointing right toward Bastian with one hand, while the other was lifted, his palm facing out.

Through the crystal lens of the scope, the goblin's long knife twisted like mist until it was no longer a blade, but a staff resting against the boy's shoulder. A thousand-pointed star strengthened on the boy's palm until it was flickering brightly.

"What are you seeing?" asked Kaliyah.

Bastian handed her the scope. "It's changed to a Sun Child, I think."

She looked through. "That's an image of Aubrey Gyrfalcon." She lowered it. "What could this mean?"

Lucas took the scope from her and peered through.

He signed, "It seems to mean we're on the right track." He handed the scope to Rhys.

Rhys looked through it. "Bloody bindweed—now, that's a neat trick." He handed the scope back to Bastian. "Why's that boy drawn pointing at us, though?"

"I don't think it's us he's pointing at." Bastian slipped out from among them and studied the wall on the opposite side of the shaft. He took the light from Rhys and swept it over the plaster and beams.

From a deep corner, something glinted metallic.

Bastian climbed onto a beam affixed to the wall and shifted nearer to the shine.

There, resting on a small wooden shelf, he discovered a key of tarnished silver, inlaid with blue gemstones.

He carefully lifted it from the shelf.

The shaft set to trembling.

Dust shook from the rafters.

Lucas and Rhys snatched Bastian by an arm each and brought him to standing onto the platform between them.

The wooden shelf, where the key had rested, pulled into the wall.

Ten feet above them, a slab of wood—round, like the covering of a porthole—cut away. The cover sank in and rolled back, revealing a high opening.

The chalet's trembling stilled.

Bastian tipped the light up and studied the chasm.

Wooden beams, thick enough to offer footholds, ascended it in a spiral.

Bastian tested his weight on the first, and it held him.

He climbed up, moving from beam to beam, pushing through cobwebs, until he reached the overhead opening.

To his right, hung the piece of wall that'd cut away. Its backside was riddled with gears like what ticked inside a clock.

His heart pounding, he eased through the round portal.

He raised to his feet and found himself in the garret crowning the pinnacle of Kingfisher Chalet.

Overhead, a conical ceiling stretched. The stone walls were engraved with characters that seemed part of some lost alphabet. The wooden floor lay coated with a thin sheen of dust, laced with the small footprints of a cat.

Dusky light was shafting through the seams of round windows—the chalet's thatching blackening the outer panes of the glass.

One window was open a crack.

Bastian crossed the garret and widened it.

Evening's golden light flooded the space, bright sun rays falling onto a door set in the garret's southern wall.

The door was dark-chocolate-colored and shaped like a cello, narrow through its middle and wide at its base and crown. The door's frame was constructed of gnarly twists of wood. Entwined in the wood were silver sculptures of vines, studded with bright silver flowers.

The emblem of the Sun Devaa—his thousand-pointed star—hung above the door's pointed pinnacle. Above it, an inscription arced, etched in looping cursive:

With key laid in your chosen hands,
with love for Sylphic Folk and Lands,
tread boldly through this wanderer's port
and claim your place within this court.

Bastian's imagination woke, and he could envision the garret full of sprites alighting on gossamer wings; forest children resting their bony elbows on windowsills; dryads peering in through the portholes; faeries laughing; pucks serving thimbles of berry wine.

Lucas tugged Bastian's sleeve, and Kaliyah's.

He signed, "I think we should tell Rhys."

Rhys lifted his brow.

"We need to tell him everything about Lady Marrowight," signed Lucas. "And about what happened inside her manor."

"*Inside* her manor?" asked Rhys, signing. "Oh—please don't tell me you two snuck into that manor."

"We didn't," signed Lucas. "We were dragged. I think."

Rhys looked them each in the eyes. "You have to tell me what happened."

Bastian laid out their adventure in all its terrible truth.

Lady Marrowight knifing the air—cutting wings from the backs of Moor Folk. Naga trapped in the iron cage. Lady Marrowight's piercing grip. The crawling sprites and the curse that petrified them. The icy manor corridor. The shadowy goblins standing like sentries made of smoke.

The hideous brew Lady Marrowight poured down his throat. The snaky staff and how she dazed Lucas with it. The wildcat.

"It sounds mad, I know," said Bastian, signing. "But Lucas saw all of it, too." He drew *Moor Folk of the English Highlands* from his rucksack and handed it to Rhys. "Everything Kingfisher wrote about—it's real."

Rhys, not removing his gaze from Bastian, took the book.

"It's not just Bastian and Lucas who've encountered Sylphic things," said Kaliyah. "I have, and so have Master and Mrs. Sayre."

"I honestly don't know how to make sense of all you just told me." Rhys glanced at the stone wall holding runes, at the finely crafted door, at the thousand-pointed star above it, reflecting the daylight. "But this certainly seems a place Kingfisher intended someone to find."

"Does that mean you believe us?" signed Lucas.

"Let's not go that far," said Rhys, signing. "But your myth is turning out to be surprisingly substantiated."

Bastian startled as his gaze met a pair of blue eyes staring through the round window.

Naga.

Naga leapt through it and scampered into the room. He twisted onto his back in a sunbeam.

He seemed bigger somehow—not physically, exactly, but in some way fiercer. Like he'd just made a kill.

Bastian rubbed Naga's silver belly. "You've known about this place for a long time, I'll bet."

Naga flipped right-side up, then pranced to the small door.

Bastian followed him to it. He touched the thousand-pointed star crowning the door, then traced the sculpted vine down to a handle.

There, a row of blue gemstones glittered, arcing along its curve.

Bastian studied the silver key, its pattern of stones a perfect match to those on the handle.

The key resting on his palm seemed heavy, as though pulling toward the door, desiring it.

Bastian slid it into the lock.

Its mechanism clicked, and the door drifted open.

30

Bastian led the others through the small door, into a dark room as dry and hot as a beach of sunbaked sand, its air tinged sweet by the roof's thatching grass. The still quality of the place made it feel timeless.

At discovering this Sylphic Council Chamber, kept secret within Kingfisher Chalet, shielded by Sylphic puzzles and charms—it seemed certain that only something vastly important would have this degree of protection.

This space seemed somehow the origin of the sounds rising—shivery pipes and hushed chanting, thunder and faint drums—though low, all crystal clear.

It was as though the very wind of the Wystan Woods, ever ferrying Sylphic sounds fabled to carry enchantment, somehow had its origins here.

Rhys caught Bastian's glance. "Are you hearing things?"

Bastian nodded.

Rhys didn't smirk, didn't make fun.

He didn't say anything.

He just placed himself more closely behind everyone.

Bastian shone the flashlight around the space.

The Sylphic Council Chamber was large—as long and wide as the whole plot of the chalet. Rows of rafters sloped up to a high ceiling peak.

At the south end of the chamber stood a circular table with an indigo, spherical gemstone, as big as a basketball, pronged at its center.

Encircling the gem, a collection of small river stones lay, all banded with crystal and arranged so each stripe touched its brothers on either side, forming an unbroken ring of translucence.

Where the flashlight's beam struck the gemstone, light scattered.

Naga leapt onto the table and stretched out before a line of words, inlaid in silver:

Ever shall England's Great Sages preserve peace, ensure harmony, and guide the Sun Child.

Around the table stood five gray-blue boulders, each belted with a polished band of quartz.

Bastian crouched by one and touched the metal shape impressed in its top.

It was the eye emblem, Egyptian—the Eye of Ra; identical to the charm the A&E doctor had given him.

The other boulders, too, each held a silver shape, flawlessly crafted, so smooth it seemed the metal was still in liquid form. The emblems had been inlaid perfectly flush with the skin of the stone.

Beside the boulder with the eye emblem stood one holding a winged sun. Next was the Sun Devaa's thousand-pointed star.

The other two shapes—a sea-blue gemstone set in a weave of metal, and a gnarled oak tree—were unfamiliar to Bastian.

The same five emblems were inlaid on the table's surface, each corresponding to the boulder before it.

Bastian pulled one of Kaliyah's river stones out of his pocket.

Its sedimentary surface felt as smooth as the boulder. A crystal ring identically banded its waist.

He backed away from the table, taking in the whole of the place.

Along the attic's eastern wall stood a row of round windows, smothered on the outside with roof thatching, latticed with lead into diamonds. Bastian lifted a latch off one of the windows and pushed.

It swung outward, taking the thatching with it and saturating the attic with golden light.

The light flooding in spotlighted a flaxen banner hanging at the head of the room.

The banner was trapezoidal, like a sail from a galleon ship. On it was painted the black head of a horse throwing its mane.

Below the painting scrolled a line of text embroidered in an unfamiliar language.

Each letter curled as though inspired by smoke and wind and waves and flames.

Kaliyah came to standing beside Bastian.

She translated—

No day can last forever.
The sun shall always fade.
But when it dies, the kestrel cries
that all shall be remade.
I'm wind upon the waters;
I'm light upon the shore.
I laugh at pain, I dance in rain,
I live forever more.
See how I've slain the darkness.
See how I've flown its bars.
No longer bound, my heart has found
a dawning night of stars.

"What language is that?" asked Rhys.

"It's the language of the stars," answered Kaliyah.

Rhys backed to where Lucas was standing, examining a couple of dusty sets of shelves set against the interior wall. Two trunks rested between them, and above those hung a salt-white fishing net, tacked up with oars.

Keyhole limpets, scallops, solariums, cones, nautilus swirls, and other shells were woven into the net.

The pointed crowns of conches jetted among them, and starfish arms curved through, spangling the nets with starbursts of chalk pinks, dawn blues, and wheat yellows. Strands of seaweed were threaded through the mesh.

"What's all this junk?" signed Lucas, examining the net.

"It's not junk." Bastian drew *Moor Folk of the English Highlands* from his rucksack. "Sea treasures ward off curses and lend power to Sylphic enchantments."

He sat on one of the trunks and read—

"On all sides of England's Sylphic Kingdom lies the mighty, thrashing sea. There's no stronger refuge than the sea and its billionfold peaks of sheltering waves and denizen Sylphic warriors, ranging through bluest currents and riding the great beasts whose thundering voices call out in response to the Sun Devaa's light. Sea treasures carry the protection of the blue countries."

"Bastian—beneath you," signed Lucas.

Bastian stood from the trunk. On its front, a silver nameplate was nailed. It read—*M.D. Kingfisher*.

The others closed in around Bastian as he crouched and unfixed the trunk's heavy latch.

Inside rested a cherrywood box whose cover held a metallic figure of a dragon inlaid. Beneath it, the trunk was loaded with bundles of parchments.

Bastian opened the cherrywood box.

There lay the bleached bones of an animal, nestled in white sand grains, sparkling like stars.

Lucas picked up a bone, still strung to others by tendons. He lifted it until he'd unfanned the skeleton of a large wing.

Bastian dusted sand from the crown of a skull.

It didn't look like any skull he'd ever seen. Its projecting snout was heavy and looked raptor-like—but also somewhat reptilian.

He read the silver inscription on the lid's interior—

"King of beasts and beloved mortal servant of the Sun Child. Ryu, best cherished among Sunwalkers, may your sleep be peace beneath a dawning night of stars."

"What are Sunwalkers?" signed Lucas.

Bastian thumbed through *Moor Folk of the English Highlands* to reach a page holding a drawing of a soaring kestrel—brazen copper-feathered, blue winged, and white-chested.

On the opposite page flew a phoenix, its body and wings striped in vibrant corals and blues, its tail and wing pinions flaming.

He read—

"Sunwalkers are half-mortal, half-Sylphic animal shapeshifters. Some carry immortality, while others succumb to mortal death. All follow the Sun Devaa in the ways of loyalty and kindness."

Bastian set aside the box and explored the parchment bundles beneath. Unrolling the top one revealed it to be a collection of photographs.

Bastian uncurled a picture of a boy, about his age, crouching beside the Natterjack Lagoon.

On the boy's knee sat a toddler, bundled in a glossy yellow raincoat and rain hat. The baby's curls beneath the hat were out of control, and the eyes of both boys were a wash of blue so pale, they seemed the negatives of eyes.

Bastian flipped the picture over—*"Malachi Daoine and Skylar Forrest."* He glanced up at Kaliyah. "Do you know who this baby is?"

"Kingfisher's brother," said Kaliyah.

Bastian studied the picture. "I feel I've seen him before."

"How is that possible?" signed Lucas.

"I don't know," said Bastian. "There's something familiar about him. His eyes, maybe."

"He reminds me a little of Cassian," said Rhys, signing. "Likely, that's the familiarity that's striking."

Lucas drew out another parchment bundle and unrolled it.

He held up before the others a series of charcoal sketches—some of common plants and animals, others of Moor Folk—faeries, dryads, naiads, forest children, sprites, and still more which Bastian couldn't identify.

All were signed, *M.D. Kingfisher.*

Bastian glanced at Kaliyah. "Could this be the lost book? Or pages from it?"

She took the sketches from Lucas and studied them. "I don't know."

Bastian drew out another bundle, near the trunk's base. It was an assortment of bold, oil-pencil drawings.

It included a skeletal bat with the face of a rotten corpse dipping in wails of wind; a dripping swamp hag—fanged, cloaked in a moth-eaten cloth, clawing at a green-grassed bank; a gray, bone-thin horse, blood-dappled, its eyes flaming, galloping through a muddy forest strewn with bodies—wounded forest children, faeries with torn wings, dryads bruised and broken-limbed.

"This seems more like what the lost book would hold," said Bastian, glancing up at Kaliyah. "Enemies of Moor Folk."

Empty quivers hung from the bare shoulders of the forest children, with bows and arrows lying scattered in the mud alongside them, or resting in their still hands. One forest child had his bow raised and was aiming an arrow at the flank of the skeletal horse.

All of the oil-pencil sketches were signed, *S.F.*

Bastian set them aside and lifted a final parchment, lying at the bottom of the trunk.

It was a masterfully rendered sketch of the Goblin King. He was standing on a battlefield and gripping a knife—jagged like a black streak of lightning.

Lucas glanced at Kaliyah. "What are all these terrible things?"

Bastian translated.

"Elemental Spirits," said Kaliyah.

"Can you tell us all you know about this place?" Bastian asked her. "The legends of the Great Sages, and the battles that may have been planned here before?"

Kaliyah stood and moved to the council table. She seated Bastian on the boulder with the winged sun.

Rhys and Lucas sat on the boulders on either side of him. Naga leapt onto the boulder holding the thousand-pointed star.

Kaliyah settled on the boulder carved with the blue gemstone encased in silver.

"The three Great Sages represent different families of Moor Folk who live in England's Sylphic Kingdom," said Kaliyah.

Rhys signed her words for Lucas.

"The emblem of the eye belongs to the Great Sage who represents the Moor Folk of England's moonlit seas, her starry lakes and sunlit rivers. This sapphire sign belongs to the Great Sage of England's tors and heights, its caves rich with mineral veins and jewels shimmering from coarse, rocky places. And the oak is for the Great Sage of the woodlands, vast and wild, full of England's oldest minds."

She pointed at the winged sun inset on the table before Bastian.

"That one's for the Sun Child."

She pointed at the sign before Naga.

"The thousand-pointed star is the signet of the Sun Devaa."

"Are these all different cultures?" signed Lucas.

Rhys translated.

"Precisely," said Kaliyah. "Different cultures that work with one another in harmony. Have you ever noticed that many things in nature are laid out in five points? Like—the structures of pinecones and of flower petals. The three Great Sages, the Sun Child, and the Sun Devaa together reflect such balance. They once maintained peace and promoted harmony between England's Sylphic Kingdom and the mortal world, and they forged diplomacy with the Sun Devaa's other Sylphic Kingdoms. The Sun Devaa and the Great Sages also gave guidance and teaching to the Sun Child."

She pointed to words scrolling around the table's center, which read: *Compassion. Harmony. Teaching.*

Bastian rested his gaze on the dust-caked windows.

Signing, he asked, "If this place is so important, for governance and leadership, why has it been abandoned?"

"The Sylphic Kingdom of England was once the most bountiful of all Sylphic Kingdoms," said Kaliyah. "The trouble began on a day when a wight witch cut the wings off the back of a faerie."

Bastian glanced at the ring around her neck, then lowered his gaze.

"Did the faerie die?" signed Lucas.

Rhys translated and added, "But—Kaliyah, are you all right? This seems to be upsetting you."

"It's fine." Kaliyah brushed the inside of her wrist against her eye. "Faeries are Moor Folk and can't die; they're immortal. But when they grow weary of cares, they drift into a place of peace and eternal light called the Aetherlands. I believe that's what happened to her."

"What happened to England's Great Sages?" Rhys asked.

"Legends hold that the Sun Child, avenging the faerie, waged a battle against the witch. It was a trap. The witch cut those wings to divide the Sylphic Kingdom, and it worked. She convinced many that her power was greater than the Sun Devaa's. She's an ancient enemy of the Sun Devaa, bent on bringing eternal darkness." Kaliyah walked to the open window and gazed out, the evening light shimmering in her hair. "Everything the Sun Devaa stands for—compassion and kindness, balance and wholeness, teaching and wisdom—the witch loathes. For she only seeks power."

"Compassion and balance and wisdom and goodness, though," signed Lucas. "These must be stronger than whatever power the witch claimed to have. The Sun Devaa had to have won that battle."

Rhys translated.

"No," said Kaliyah. "The witch killed the Sun Child in an unnatural way. And she forever banished England's Great Sages, to a far-removed edge of the Aetherlands—a meso-realm bordering a lightless abyss. It's possible to come back from such banishment, but very rare. The few Moor Folk who've returned say a mortal death would've been a mercy compared to the trials they faced in trying to return."

"If the Sun Child is so integral to the Sylphic Kingdom, what happens when one passes away?" asked Lucas.

"Normally, a new Sun Child is born. But when the witch defeated the last Sun Child, she declared that by her great power, she'd extinguished the lineage of Aubrey Gyrfalcon. She asserted that the Sylphic Kingdom was too weak to call forth a new Sun Child; that her power had grown so profoundly that there couldn't be another Sun Child born. Ever."

"So much for Cassian being a Sun Child," signed Lucas.

Bastian glanced at Kaliyah. "It's possible, though, that the witch was wrong."

"The witch vowed that *if* she were wrong, and *if* a new Sun Child were born," said Kaliyah, "she'd kill the child. And that death, she claimed, would definitively mark the end of all Sun Children. She held that such a deed would make her formidable enough to finally overthrow the Sun Devaa. This would mean the end not just of the line of Sun Children, but—everything."

"How could a single Sun Child be such a threat to her, though?" signed Lucas. "What's one person to a witch?"

"The Sun Child bears powers beyond any in the Sylphic Kingdom," said Kaliyah. "But even the strength of the last Sun Child wasn't any match for this witch. After she killed him, Moor Folk started to go missing. And with the Sun Child gone, there was no one strong enough to challenge her. Thousands of Moor Folk have disappeared. Some she's banished to the meso-realm at the edge of the Aetherlands. Many others she's imprisoned in stone."

"So, say the Sylphic witch were to destroy the last Sun Child and overthrow the Sun Devaa," said Rhys, signing, "what would happen, exactly?"

"England's Sylphic Kingdom would fall," said Kaliyah, "and the witch would rise as Queen of the Deadlands. She'd curse the shadow of the moon to forever blacken the skies over England and bleed darkness over the Golden Moor.

"In that lightless, ruined country, there'd be no Sun Devaa to justly lead. There'd be no Moor Folk to care for England's waters and lands. There'd be no Sun Child to defend and protect the Sylphic Kingdom. Everything natural and mortal in England would die."

Kaliyah's gaze trailed through the window, toward the rowan berry trees swaying brightly on the hilltop.

"Flowers would have no sun to reach for. Without Moor Folk to nurture them, crops couldn't rise. Think—lightless seas full of rotting fish. There's be no plankton, no algae, no coral, no kelp forests. There'd be no Moor Folk to temper the forces of nature."

She faced them.

"It's said that the destruction has already begun."

"You mean these storms," said Bastian, signing.

"With the numbers of Moor Folk diminished by the witch, her tempests are tearing England apart," said Kaliyah. "If the Sylphic Kingdom were to wholly fall, the natural world would soon follow."

She drew a shaking breath.

"There'd be no Moor Folk to sing mortal babies and animals into the world, so England soon would be childless. In darkness and anguish, its people would waste. And one dreadful day, all of England would vanish, and the Sun Devaa's other mighty kingdoms over the great seas—his strong mountain peoples, his snow-covered ice worlds, his glorious kingdoms of crystal and sands, his wide countries of plains —everything would fall into darkness."

31

*K*aliyah's words hung heavy as Bastian and his brothers sat in silence.

Lucas and Rhys rose and went back to the parchments. They together looked closely at each of them.

Bastian moved to the wall and unlatched another window, letting in a wash of the early evening's cool.

He peered out to the northeast where beneath a grimy haze, Marrowight Manor's turrets stood, its highest towers punching through the forest canopy.

He drew the Sylphic scope from his pocket and trained it on the manor.

Balor hornets—skeletal-faced and enormous—were droning around its sharp spires. It seemed there were dozens, if not hundreds of them.

Bastian glanced at the purple sting on his wrist. Gray lines had erupted from the puncture point and were threading up his arm.

He adjusted the aim of the scope, training it toward the stretch of the Wystan Woods that stood between Kingfisher Chalet and the Witch Marrowight's vale.

In focusing closely on the forest, he discovered a magnificent effect to the instrument.

The lens of the Sylphic scope seemed to cut right through the woodland, finding eyelets among the weave of tree branches and pulling into very close view the wight witch's vale.

The thought of the Witch Marrowight's dastardly vale sent shivers racing up his spine, and his instinct was to look away from it, to hide.

But he couldn't allow himself the retreat. With the battle only two dawns away, he needed to steel himself to see whatever the scope might show him.

And a close warmth drove further back his distress. For Lucas had approached and was standing beside him.

Bastian swept the scope slowly across the vale and stopped when he located the goblin statue in its shrine.

It looked as weird and as sharp and as foreboding as it had earlier, only now its horns held a heavier burden of black roses.

Bastian caught sight of movement—something closing in on the statue.

He adjusted his aim slightly.

It was the Witch Marrowight. She was pacing among a littering of stone sprites, the stripes of long claw marks now dried and dark on her arms.

She seemed to be fixating on a tender-leafed rose hedge that hadn't been there earlier. The hedge was heavy with bright clusters of blooms, and it seemed to be trying to encroach on her lawn.

Their stalks held blooms of linen whites and sunset corals, buds of cool sapphires and birthday-cake-frosting yellow. They seemed joyful and playful and determined to shine their loveliness on her vale—still smoking from the curses she'd laid.

The Witch Marrowight swung a scythe at the roses, razing them back. As soon as she slashed one, though, another twined in.

It was a heartening sight, that imposing rose hedge, the work of the good Sylphic Moor Folk—faeries, or forest children, or folk of the Annwyn race like Master Sayre, setting loose the plants in their care onto her grounds in a display of defiance.

The witch aimed her fingers at the hedge. Bolts of electric blue fire flashed from her hands and shot into the flowers.

Smoke rose from the smoldering blooms—black now, as though stricken by frost, and lying spent on the ground.

She lifted her gaze from the charred heap and looked Bastian's way.

He tried to duck but couldn't move. He couldn't draw his gaze off her, nor could he lower the scope.

She cast aside the scythe and spread her fingers.

The pain in Bastian's chest went shrill as she lifted her hands, electric blue bands webbing between them.

A heat inside his chest stirred—it seemed it was all that might help him. He focused on that warmth as he watched the witch set to muttering.

With a mighty twist, he wrested away from her gaze and stumbled back from the window.

Kaliyah crossed the attic to him and steadied him. "What is it?"

Lucas took the scope from him and peered through the window.

"Don't." Bastian tugged his arm.

Lucas signed, "What the…?"

Blue lightning tore into the window and struck him.

Kaliyah caught Lucas as he dropped to the floor. Bastian closed the window and locked it.

Rhys rushed to Lucas. "My God—what was that?"

Lucas was lying unmoving, his eyes closed.

Bastian shook him.

"He—he skidded back," said Rhys, glancing from Lucas to the window. "It was like something shoved him. Did you see that?"

Kaliyah held Lucas' cheeks, her hands swelling with light.

"Let go—let me see him." Rhys tried to push Kaliyah away.

Bastian held Rhys back. "She knows what she's doing."

"What's she doing? What's happened to him? Is he breathing?"

Kaliyah's lit hands shone more brightly, casting a silver glow across Lucas' face.

Rhys, staring dumbfounded at Lucas, seemed unable to see the glow.

Kaliyah whispered gentle words in her language—the language of the stars.

Lucas drew a sharp breath and opened his eyes.

"Stay still," said Kaliyah.

"What happened?" signed Lucas.

She smoothed back his hair and pressed her hand to his forehead.

"Did you see what hit you?" signed Rhys.

"I saw Lady Marrowight," signed Lucas. "It looked like lightning streamed from her fingers. My head really hurts."

"He says his head hurts," Bastian told Kaliyah. "What's she done to him?"

"Bring me some sand from Ryu's box," said Kaliyah. "And some seaweed off those nets. Hurry."

Bastian jumped up and dug a handful of sand out of the box.

"Wait—sand and seaweed?" Rhys shook his head. "This isn't a game. He needs actual help."

Bastian stripped a ribbon of seaweed out of the fishing nets and raced back.

Kaliyah guided Bastian to trickle a line of sand into the seaweed. She rolled it tightly and tied it around Lucas' head.

Rhys tapped Lucas' hand, then signed, "Focus on me. Are you struggling to breathe? Can you move?"

Lucas kept his gaze on Kaliyah.

"Lady Marrowight," he signed, "she really is a witch, isn't she?"

Bastian translated.

"A wight witch," said Kaliyah.

"And the Sun Child—she's hunting him," signed Lucas. "Is it Cassian?"

Bastian spoke his words, then signed, "No."

"Does she know who the Sun Child is?" signed Lucas.

Bastian translated.

Kaliyah straightened the seaweed on Lucas' forehead. "I'm afraid that she does."

"Would you feel better if you sat up?" Rhys helped Lucas ease to leaning against the wall.

Lucas signed, "The pain's fading."

Bastian translated.

Kaliyah stood. "You should rest, but you're going to be fine."

"How can you claim to know that?" Rhys stared at her. "What the hell do you think happened to him?"

"Lady Marrowight is a master of pain," said Kaliyah. "It seems she didn't use enough force to injure Lucas, though I've spoken the words to set him to healing if she did."

"You really believe all this, don't you?" asked Rhys. "You actually think our neighbor's a witch."

Bastian couldn't take his eyes off of Lucas, gingerly rising to standing.

"That strike was meant for me," Bastian signed.

And it was Lucas, again, who'd received the brunt of the witch's viciousness.

"That strike might've been for anyone crossing her," signed Lucas.

The Witch Marrowight was absolutely ruthless, certainly.

Her aim, though, was to slay the Sun Child, and by that, to defeat the Sylphic Kingdom, severing its light from the natural world.

But the Witch Marrowight had not slain the Sun Child. She'd succeeded in inflicting her curses upon him, and the agony of those curses was sharp. For this moment, though, this Sun Child was still on his feet.

And this Sun Child had tricked her into giving up what she knew about Kingfisher's lost book.

That book, resting somewhere in this Council Chamber—it kept the secret to her destruction.

Bastian glanced around the room, at the shelves set against the walls—all empty. The book could be hidden anyplace—under a floorboard or inside a wall.

But the second trunk—a place that likely could protect something valuable—was yet unexplored.

Bastian crouched before it.

As he touched it, the drumming sound rose, strongly enough that he could feel it trembling the air.

Kaliyah knelt beside him.

Bastian explored the lid of the trunk for a latch. He drew out the sapphire-studded key and searched the trunk for a keyhole.

There wasn't one.

Lucas signed, "Maybe something goes there." He pointed at the front corner of the trunk, where an oddly shaped recess gaped.

Perhaps he was right. It looked nothing like a keyhole, but perhaps it was one. If so, it would require some sort of object to release the lock.

That this trunk had been built with another puzzle, another layer of protection—a thrill rose at the thought of what it might contain.

"Whatever belongs here will be small—about the size of an apple, it seems," said Bastian, signing. "Let's search around for an object matching that shape."

Lucas went to the nets and examined the sea relics tangled in them. Kaliyah dug again in the other trunk.

Rhys stood, looking lost, in the middle of the room. "How can we search for something without knowing what we're missing?"

The sound of piping, of flutes lifted. The drumming grew stronger. A surging sense of waves strengthened.

Bastian followed the sounds to one of the shelves.

He glanced back at Rhys. "Help me move this."

Rhys took its other end and, together with Bastian, pulled it away from the wall.

Bastian slipped his arm behind it.

Near the wall's base, his fingers slid into a recess.

He glanced back at the others. "There's a gap in the plaster."

Rhys and Kaliyah slid the bookshelf aside to reveal a yawning, apple-sized hole—like a mouse hole, perfectly round.

Bastian shone the flashlight into what turned out to be a deep tunnel.

Something was in it, about a meter back. Though the flashlight's beam was falling right on it, the thing reflected no light.

Bastian threaded his hand into the hole.

His palm fell on something cold, made of metal.

The drumming ceased.

He gripped the thing. Pulled.

A jab to his finger.

He dropped it and jerked out his hand.

A bead of blood slid down his finger.

He reached back inside and scooted the thing toward them.

Easing it from the wall, he found it to be a heavy statue—a goblin.

Kaliyah drew back. "It's of iron."

The goblin statue wore a spiked bandoleer. A pair of pointed horns crowned it. Tusks projected from its lower lip, and its mouth was turned down in a grimace.

Its eyes were two sunken, blank holes. It was positioned in a crouch, as though ready to strike. A drop of blood hung from its knife.

The silence the Sylphic Council Chamber now held was stark—it brought Bastian to realize that for years, Sylphic sounds had been with him almost unceasingly, as constant as his own breathing. At their very quietest, even, they'd been like the ringing hum that swells in the absence of noise.

Now, though, there remained not even the sound of silence.

And then another, different rumbling rose.

Naga—growling, spitting, charging, hissing.

He pounced and knocked the statue away from Bastian.

He clamped his jaws on the statue's neck and pummeled it with his back feet, his claws fully advanced.

The fur on his spine standing tall, his tail an explosion of silver, Naga batted the statue a few meters away, then leapt onto the trunk's lid and watched it.

The statue lay on its side, rocking longer than it ought to have moved. The blood drop slipped down its blade.

Then the statue suddenly stilled.

Bastian stroked Naga, smoothing his rumpled fur.

Naga stood on his hind legs, pressing his paws to Bastian's chest, rubbing his whiskered cheek on Bastian's wounded finger.

Bastian reached for the statue.

Kaliyah held him back.

"That's an icon of the Goblin King—a relic that belonged to the witch, now stolen. Don't touch it more than you must. The thing's cursed."

Bastian carefully lifted it, avoiding its knife.

He crouched before the trunk.

The sound of drums trembled once again, softly—hardly more than a breath.

Bastian glanced at Kaliyah, kneeling beside him.

"I hear it," she whispered.

"You hear what?" asked Rhys.

"A sign that we might've found what we're looking for," said Bastian.

He set the goblin inside the trunk's recess.

Bolts clinked. Naga jumped off the trunk as its lid lifted.

Bastian and the others together stood and backed away from it.

Inside the trunk, there rested a jumble of metal and leather plates— parts of a suit of armor.

Each armor piece was polished mirror-bright. Crimson leather pads were stitched tightly to the steel with white cords. Silver buckles hung from them.

Bastian lifted a piece. Tried it on his arm.

It fit perfectly.

Beneath the armor, he found the trunk empty.

And yet—the trunk's interior base was much higher than the floor.

Bastian trailed his fingers along the base's edge until they landed on a divot.

He pulled, and a false floor came away.

Beneath it, half-buried in sand, there rested a large book.

It was bound in dark leather. A blue stone mounded from a metal inlay on its cover. The stone was like half a moon, as big as his fist, rising from a ring of gray metal. It was sapphiric—the same kind of stone as what studded the Sylphic Council table.

The stone shone the same oceanic blue of Naga's eyes. Of his own. Of Cassian's. It was netted with crystals the texture of cirrus clouds, blown by winds into transparency.

The ring Mum wore was made from a jewel like this. The stone on the book, its familiarity, called up a wave of impressions—Cassian's birth; the sparkling Windrush; Kaliyah's river stones; the Sylphic Kingdom's Great Sages—exiled and missing from this Sylphic chamber; Alura's pearl ring.

This book's connection to Bastian felt familial; ancestral. And it confirmed what he already knew but now felt to the level of bone.

He indeed was the Sun Child, and he had a vital role to play in the Sylphic Kingdom's destiny. In the world's destiny.

On the book, above the stone, scripted in silver calligraphy, scrolled the words—

Dark England: The Beauty and Terror of Elemental Spirits of the Isles, by M.D. Kingfisher and Forrest Skylar.

32

*B*astian and Kaliyah trekked over Kingfisher Chalet's dusky grounds, Bastian carrying *Dark England: The Beauty and Terror of Elemental Spirits of the Isles.*

At the foot of the hill, Bastian stopped. "Are you sure it's safe, us carrying this to Sayre Cottage? Maybe Master Sayre should come here to see it."

"That book holds enchantments," said Kaliyah. "I can feel its charms of protection. They're making a bubble around us. No one could unlock that trunk but a Sun Child, I'm sure of it. And now that you have this book, no Elemental Spirit could claim it. The book's safe, and it'll keep us safe, too."

"Safe."

Bastian gazed toward Marrowight Manor where something was on fire, bleeding black smoke into the failing twilight.

"Nothing is safe."

Kaliyah stared with him toward the smoke. "She's preparing."

A sliver of crescent moon, shining over the trees in the west—faint though it was—seemed to be shafting down onto the Wystan Woods.

Bastian peered at the setting moon through Woodthrush's scope.

The lens pulled the moon's craters closely into view, and the dark side encroaching looked fierce. At the sight, the gleaming moon seemed not merely waning, but fading out.

Dying.

He turned aside. "I think the book should stay here." He carried it beneath the limbs of the apple tree. "The witch told me she was close to getting her hands on it. What if—despite its enchantments—she now can?"

"She saw you in the Sylphic Council Chamber," said Kaliyah. "She likely believes that you've already read the book. I'm sure she's changed her strategy."

Bastian laid the heavy book on the grass. "Then we should definitely open it here. Read it right now."

"You must wait for Master Sayre to help you."

Bastian studied the hill and the woods beyond them; the trail that wound half a mile to Sayre Cottage.

He could think of nothing but the goblin that'd hunted him inside those woods last night, when Kaliyah had beckoned him into the dark.

The day he'd received *Moor Folk of the English Highlands*, the goblin stalking him had caused the car accident. And it was certain that, whether or not the Witch Marrowight had changed her strategy, she coveted *Dark England*.

"Master Sayre saw my da fight the witch." Kaliyah gestured for him to follow her up the hill. "Whatever teachings this book holds about the battle, Master Sayre will best know what to make of it."

Bastian stared at the book, meant just for him.

Its blue stone seemed to draw him, like a cool wave coaxing him toward the ocean.

"I have to see what's written here. Right now."

He knelt before the book.

As he opened the cover, Kaliyah eased to sitting beside him.

The first pages held the names of Elemental Spirits—hundreds of them written in tiny print:

Alastor...Bodach...Djinn...Dragon...Goblin...Kelpie...Tangie...Warg... Wight Witch...

"This book is enormous." He glanced at Kaliyah. "Is there any way to know, or even guess, where your da's teaching on the battle might be written?"

Kaliyah drew a deep breath.

She blew against the pages.

They fanned, showing frightening images—Elemental Spirits— painted one after another, on every page.

At the book's center, the pages fell still.

What was written there seemed of little importance.

It held just a few sentences describing an *Oillipheist Dragon*, with comments about the qualities of murky water bodies most attractive to the Sylphic beasts.

Bastian tried to turn the page, but he couldn't.

He peeled at the page's edge, but from this point on, they seemed as tightly lodged as a block of wood.

"Guarded secrets." Kaliyah sat back. "With any trace of dark enchantments nearby—of curses, they won't open."

"That means"—Bastian stood—"something Elemental is nearby."

He pulled out Woodthrush's scope and peered into the woods.

Kaliyah stood and lowered the scope from his eye. "The something Elemental nearby is you."

"What?"

"The darkness the witch shot into you—this book won't open its secrets to you until that's gone."

Bastian shoved the book toward her. "Will they open for you?" He backed away.

"It's unlikely."

He backed further away from her, from the book. "Try."

Kaliyah knelt and set the book before her. She pulled at the stuck pages but couldn't release them.

She blew on her hands, lighting them to a soft glow. She laid them on the book's gemstone. On its cover. She rested them on the stuck pages. On the book's spine. On its gilded edges.

The pages beyond the center remained fixed.

"We have to tell Master Sayre." Kaliyah stood. "Keep the book here if you'd like. I'll fly."

The thought of her leaving—of her leaving him alone with this book of wicked things; alone with the horror of smelling the witch's black smoke; of knowing alastors and goblins and tangies and dragons were coming for everyone Sylphic and everything mortal—for him—he couldn't bear the thought.

He pulled his gaze down from Kaliyah's bright face.

Kingfisher's dark work, he'd found. But it remained locked beneath his dim hands.

Everything evil described in *Dark England* would indeed be swiftly coming. And here, at this critical moment, he was proving to be the disappointment he'd imagined he would be.

He dropped to his knees.

"Don't despair." Kaliyah rested her warm hands on his shoulders. "My da boasted great confidence in the next Sun Child."

"Your da didn't know me."

She crouched and met his eyes. "But I do."

The sickle moon slipped out from behind a cloud, dusting the forest to the west and glittering the landscape. Pale ribbons of moonbeams lilted through the apple tree, dappling Kaliyah with droplets of silver.

Rhys and Lucas rushed out of the chalet and sprinted across the lawn, passing a football, their figures silhouetted against the darkening evening.

It seemed as though everything Sylphic they'd seen and learned had drifted to the perimeter of their minds, dream-like.

"Are they forgetting what we've just seen?" asked Bastian. "What we've just done?"

"It's difficult for mortals new to encountering the Sylphic realm to make sense of it," she said. "Rhys and Lucas will likely remember today as meaningful, but as the hours pass, they'll lose the sense of why. If they learn to see more, the details of today may come back to them. It seems Lucas, though, can already see quite a bit."

Bastian pointed Woodthrush's scope at Kingfisher Chalet. He could just make out the round outlines of thatching that camouflaged the windows of the Sylphic Council Chamber. He trained the scope on Da—sitting on the porch, cuddling Cassian.

Mum was standing inside at the window, in the butter-bright kitchen, finishing the dishes. She dried her hands, then came outside. She settled into her porch swing and took the baby.

Bastian and the others had barely had time to shroud the entrance to the shaft before Mum and Da came home.

Mum had taken a serious look at Bastian's scratches, his sting, but she did, in fact, adopt the approach of thankfulness that their injuries hadn't been worse.

She was pleased at Rhys' management, and she was impressed at how clean and rested and well-fed they'd kept Cassian.

Bastian stared at his parents, at the baby nestling in Mum's arms. He waited for the tranquility of the sight to slow his heart.

It didn't.

Mum and Da, strongholds of protection, could do nothing about the threat that was coming.

And whatever strength he himself harbored to combat it, whatever bravery or ability Kaliyah and Master Sayre claimed to see in him, he couldn't detect.

He was a Sun Child, useless, standing beneath a moon failing, broadcasting the report through the wide Sylphic Kingdom that the Day of the Dark Sun was drawing very close, and in its wake would come the end of their world.

"Should we find a way to make Mum and Da take the baby away from here?" asked Bastian.

"There isn't a place on Earth the Witch Marrowight won't touch." Kaliyah watched Bastian a moment. "Even if your mum and da could understand what's going on—even if they were to stand with you on the battlefield—they could do nothing."

Bastian laid his hand on the cover of *Dark England*. "I know."

He opened it once again on the grass before them and flipped through the pages he could access.

Each included a drawing of an Elemental Spirit followed by a description of its powers and tendencies.

He found the page entitled—*Wight Witch*.

The drawing presented a woman looking neither young nor old, wearing a ragged dress, standing on a craggy hill.

Her long hair was drawn whipping around her in a rage of wind. She held her hand, sprawled like a spider, over a red bowl, darkly shining like molten rock. Her skin was so pale, she was dead-looking. Her eyes were no color at all—just two iron-gray bullets.

Her eyes weren't as frightening, though, as her smile—a twisted and satisfied leer, like she was brewing something deadly and enjoying it. Her eyes seemed to follow him, their chill drilling into him.

Kaliyah set her arm around Bastian's shoulders and read aloud—

"Wight Witches are among England's oldest Elemental Spirits. They are cunning and resourceful and will go to any length to achieve their aim. Most are recluses, but there have been cases of Wight Witches banding together in covens.

"Wight Witches meddle little with the mortal world, but mistake not their isolation for peace. There's nothing deadlier than a Wight Witch with an ambition."

Bastian's hand went to his chest.

Kaliyah tightened her arm around his shoulders.

She read on—

"As cruel as they are, though, as terrible as the curses they conjure, Wight Witches are not without weaknesses. They fear fearlessness and will try every means to keep their subjects terror-stricken and groveling.

"Things that absorb sunlight—sun-loving plants, dragon fire, warm stones, star-sparkling rivers—these, a Wight Witch finds intolerable, and they might temper her power."

Bastian straightened. "These insights—could this be what Kingfisher meant for us to know?"

"This is all common knowledge, and fairly general," said Kaliyah. "Wight witches vary in temperament and power. The one we're dealing with is absolutely lethal." She cast a look of confidence at Bastian. "But it doesn't matter. She can be undone by a Sun Child."

"But can she be undone by *this* Sun Child?" Bastian stared at the stars, growing blotted by smoke.

With the smolder from the Witch Marrowight's manor drifting thickly now overhead, the dark night felt material.

He slipped *Dark England* into his rucksack, alongside *Moor Folk of the English Highlands*.

Kaliyah picked up Woodthrush's scope. "Tonight, the Moor Folk are reveling—celebrating their hope in the battle." She touched his hand. "Now that your Sylphic star is alight, you'll likely be able to see them. Want to try?"

Bastian glanced at the star on his hand, barely glowing.

She stood. "I think it might help you." She took a step back toward the hillside.

Bastian shouldered his rucksack, weighted with his two books. He tried to sense the charms of protection Kaliyah said she felt in *Dark England*, but he could feel nothing.

He trekked beside Kaliyah up to the dark crest of the hill.

33

When Bastian and Kaliyah reached the top of the hill, the wind shifted, bringing a resin-scented breeze that pressed the witch's smoke back north.

The sky's clearing unveiled the bright rim of the thin crescent moon.

It seemed like a sail on a seaborne galley ship, blown to billowing by solar wind.

The west, though it yet glowed by twilight, cradled a company of strengthening stars.

Kaliyah helped Bastian climb onto a boulder resting at the hill's top.

She guided him to watch the deepening Wystan Woods where vague forms—mere impressions of movement—were drifting between the still trees.

Bastian drew Woodthrush's Sylphic scope from his pocket and trained it on a slip of stream bending into the thicket.

The soft water shimmered with the toe touches of a thousand flower faeries lifting from marsh blossoms up into flight.

Their figures were as slight as drops of rain, their movement over the stream as smooth as swooping chimney swifts. They swirled together like a murmuration of starlings, their cheeks lit with bright dimples. They together plunged into the sheen of water, then all at once burst out again, like sparks scattering from a fire.

As they took to the sky, each tiny figure composed a cell within the body of one magnificent whole: a flowing creature of moonlight, its graceful rise broadening until a wedge of the night sky shone silver.

They grazed the high atmosphere, letting down a curtain of glistening mist until a breeze collectively toppled them back to the Earth.

In training the scope on individual faeries, Bastian could make out their hair, shining in shades from bright blonde to strawberry to oaken to jet.

Their eyes sparkled as lively as hearth flames—some blue, some green, some black, some golden brown, and some silver.

He traced the flight of one faerie, rising with the poise of an ice dancer.

She wore fitted wraps of leaves woven into a short dress corseted with stitching that twinkled like rain-spattered spider silk. Her skirt, scalloped at the hem, billowed with cereus flower petals and glinted with shining seeds.

Down feathers softened her feet, and her iridescent wings were shaded in blues, greens, and silvers. Shining stitching divided the wings into plates, like stained glass.

At another sweep of wind, the whole cast of faeries landed at once in the stream, shimmering on it like rainfall.

"Are there always this many faeries in the Wystan Woods?" asked Bastian.

"They come out in companies this grand just for special occasions." Kaliyah pointed to a distant glade. "There—a forest child dances with a wood faerie."

"A forest child." Bastian aimed the scope and concentrated on a streak of shimmering motion until it resolved.

The forest child—thin and as tall as Rhys—was dressed in rough-cut slacks and nothing else. The smile brightening him seemed years beyond his youthful skin.

His dancing was all stomps and turns, while the wood faerie contributed smart footwork and pirouettes.

"Can you hear the music?" asked Kaliyah.

In focusing on the whispering wind, Bastian could make out a trace of sound.

Though vague at first, the harder he listened, the louder it swelled, and soon he was bathing in the pealing of bright pipes and the strike of plucky guitars and the strong reports of skin drums.

"Their dance is called *The English Saltarello,* or *Sun Child's Dance,*" said Kaliyah. "It's a dance of hope." She slid down from the rock, then kicked off her sandals. She reached for Bastian.

Bastian jumped down beside her.

Kaliyah cast up her arms and brought them down again. She swirled away, then back, in perfect synchronization with the wood faerie. She pulled his hands down sharply at the pounding of the drums.

"When you hear the drumbeat, stomp your foot." She demonstrated. "Then turn, stomp your other foot, then take my waist and lift me to the other side." She spun back in front of him.

Bastian listened for the drum and tried to stomp on cue. Kaliyah laughed but carried on, turning him by the shoulders when he should be facing the other way.

As they danced, the brightening starlight seemed to forge a sense of hope. The starlight rang of the twilit atmosphere; of the forest—blue beneath the waning moonshine; of gentle clouds carrying nourishing rain; of tender plants reaching for light; of Kaliyah pirouetting, as sweet as a dandelion seed carried on a summer night's wind.

The starlight stitched the moment into his heart as one that he'd carry forever.

At a lull in the music, they climbed back onto the boulder.

Bastian opened *Moor Folk of the English Highlands* and turned to a section that detailed the many tribes of Moor Folk. He alternately explored the book and peered at the woodland through the Sylphic scope.

In a nearby clearing stood animals that, at first, looked like common rabbits, fawns, and foxes. Soon, though, he realized they shone. Annwyn ladies holding baskets were strolling among wild strawberry brambles in a grove. Dryads stepped from the trunks of trees and waved their graceful arms as they danced softly away, into twilight.

"Is it possible that I'm seeing everything you can see?" Bastian lowered the scope.

"There." Kaliyah directed him to look toward a stream. "A naiad floats on her back, leading a pack of turtles to a mat of river barley."

The naiad was the Sylphic water girl—the strange and wondrous creature who'd led Bastian into the Natterjack Cave.

"I know her," said Bastian. "That's the naiad Master Sayre sent to show me the vision."

"She's called Leif," said Kaliyah. "She's the daughter of the Great Sage who guided the Sylphic tribes of high places and tors, and their cavernous roots. She wears the jewel of her tribe."

Bastian found clasped around her forehead the same kite-shaped, water blue jewel she'd worn on the day he encountered her.

"And there," said Kaliyah, "just at the brink of the hill, there's a family of rain angels, singing."

The rain angels looked somewhat like faeries, but they were more nebulous—their outlines composed of miasmic traces of light.

It was their song, Bastian realized, that offered the undercurrent to all the music sounding in the forest—its clarity, its innocence, its harmony raising a flush of shivers on his skin.

"On the edge of the woodland," said Kaliyah, "just before that brink of tall trees, an oakman is speaking to his birds."

Bastian trained the scope where she was pointing. "What's an oakman?"

"They're brothers to the woodland. Guardians of its animals and plants. Oakmen are part of the *compassion* of England's Sylphic King-dom, caring for every living thing. But most of all for the small ones—insects, mice, and songbirds. Though, they also keep safe the strong ones—badgers, raptors, foxes, bucks, and the like."

Bastian traced his scope over the oakman, from his cap—comprised of acorns—to his bare and muddy feet.

His vest and trousers were cobbled of moss and leaves, some fresh, others curling with time.

He was gesturing to a rapt audience of tufty nightingales occupying every nook of an elderflower bush.

"It looks like he's using sign language," said Bastian.

"He is," said Kaliyah. "Oakmen can't hear."

Bastian lowered the scope. "Are they born deaf—like Lucas?"

"Legends say the sense of hearing distracted them from senses more important to their work. So, over time, their hearing has dimin-ished. No eagle has a sharper eye than they. They're also highly percep-tive—they can see straight into the heart and know what someone needs."

Without the scope, Bastian could just make out a vague flickering.

With the scope, he could follow the movements of the oakman's hands—but the signs he was using were unfamiliar.

"Can you understand what he's saying?" asked Bastian.

"A little," said Kaliyah. "The nightingales before him are young. He's explaining about the revelry. He calls it 'a merry Sylphic celebration, and a sign of the Sun Child's triumph.'"

Bastian lowered the scope from the shining oakman.

This world of Moor Folk felt so rich; the Sylphic Kingdom—a magnificence.

And the survival of every faerie, every oakman, every naiad, every plant and every animal—every Sylphic being here—depended upon him.

A strong flash of blue and orange fire springing from a clearing made him jump.

Bastian aimed his scope at the blaze—a roaring bonfire.

Four older-looking boys were sitting on cut logs surrounding the bonfire and singing terribly while one plucked a messy tune out of some kind of hand-cobbled guitar.

They were bare-chested and wore tattered trousers. Their hair stood in rough-cropped projections, and their skin was smudged with streaks of earth, like they'd been rambling for hours and hours in the wild and were due for a bath. Three of the boys were as skinny as saplings, while the fourth had a brawny build.

One stomped the ground to the guitar's tune while another pretended to be a wood faerie, dancing a clownish, blasphemic variation of what Kaliyah had performed.

They shrieked laughter and toppled, hauling themselves back onto their logs and reviving themselves with shining liquid dribbled from four glassy mugs.

They seemed like simple campers having a roaring good time—boys a little older than Rhys—but for the wings projecting from their shoulder blades.

Their wings were short, transparent, and sharp-tipped, their rims gleaming darkly silver.

They looked like oakmen, a little. Or perhaps—forest children.

"What are they?" asked Bastian. "Are they oakmen? Or could they be—are they forest children?"

"Yes," Kaliyah whispered. "Forest children are the princes of England's Sylphic Kingdom. Our knights. Oakmen care for the woodlands. Forest children look after all of us."

No face had ever held more mirth than these, and it was contagious.

Bastian laughed as he watched one of the boys pick up a loaf of bread. He was licking his lips, readying for a giant bite, when another boy raced by and swiped it.

The first hauled around the fire after him, weaving in and out of the surrounding logs until he had the legs of the thief firmly in his grasp and pinned to the ground.

A third moved in and plucked the bread from the downed boy and divided it with the fourth, sitting on a broad stump and shaking his head.

The fourth boy stood and opened a kettle hanging over the flames. He ladled its brew into the mugs, then dropped a small stone into each of them.

The scent of the brew drifting was bright and strong. It smelled buttery, with cool traces of lemon, of mint. Bastian could almost taste it —a warm sweetness, like a beam of sun drawn from a twilight-striped sky.

"What are they brewing?" he asked.

"Marigold cordial, for joy," whispered Kaliyah. "They're celebrating the battle—the win that's to come."

Bastian lowered his gaze. "Isn't it a bit early to celebrate?"

"They share Kingfisher's confidence in you." She rested her hand on his shoulder. "My confidence."

Bastian aimed his scope at the fourth boy, stirring the kettle of cordial.

That boy stood taller than the rest, and a steep cowlick of black hair stood from his forehead. His face wrinkled about the eyes—bright hazel eyes—and the bridge of his nose was shallow, its tip small. There was a peculiar familiarity about him.

Bastian leaned in.

Shifting unbalanced him, and he cried out as he slipped off the boulder and landed in a tuft of crab grass. He recovered his scope just in time to see the merrymakers evaporate in a whorl of mist.

The revelry's music dissipated into a whisper of night wind and the raspy lullabies of locusts.

Bastian lowered his scope. "Why did they leave?"

Kaliyah shrugged. "Forest children can be skittish." She jumped down.

Bastian eased to standing. "There's something that I want to ask you, but—will you promise to be honest?"

She looked at him straight. "I'll always be honest with you."

"All these Moor Folk are celebrating a victory they believe in, but—are there any who doubt?"

"Why is that something you want to know?"

"I knew it." Bastian stowed his scope. "Of course some Moor Folk doubt me, and probably it's the more reasonable ones. The battle's going to happen the day after tomorrow, and I'm a whole year behind in preparing for this."

"You may not have been on track a year ago, after your setback in Exeter," said Kaliyah, "but you're right where you need to be now."

The look on her was bright peace. Tracing her features, Bastian could find no fear at all.

"How can you be so confident?" he asked her.

"I've told you," said Kaliyah. "Faeries dream of what hasn't yet happened. I've glimpsed the battle, as have many others."

"But you can't be sure of the win that everyone's prematurely cele-brating."

She said nothing.

Bastian slid *Moor Folk of the English Highlands* into his rucksack, next to *Dark England*.

"I must go to Master Sayre," said Kaliyah, moving toward the wood-land. "He'll have some ideas about how you might unlock *Dark England*—I'm sure of it. In the meantime, try your best to find sleep."

At the edge of the clearing, she turned and waved, her small hand barely visible—shining as though catching traces of starlight.

She shifted to a glimmer of twinkling light and slipped away into the trees.

34

As Bastian neared his chalet, thunder rumbled, and the wind lifted and cooled.

He turned up the collar of his jacket and cut through a patch of high weeds.

Despite how cold he was, despite how sharply the ache from the curse was chilling his chest, he couldn't help wondering whether all he'd seen tonight might truly be some sort of assurance that he could fight the wight witch. And win.

Maybe it was the fragrance of the marigold cordial lingering in the breeze. Maybe it was the steady surety he'd felt in Kaliyah's confident words.

Or maybe the grandeur of faeries and forest children dancing, of oakmen and naiads and animals reveling—of so many believing in him —had given him the sense, for an instant, that victory was possible.

He glanced up at his chalet, at the concealed windows of Kingfisher's Sylphic Council Chamber.

There, the witch hazel sprig they'd won rested, along with a collection of crystal-rung stones—everything he'd need for a sun dowsing ritual.

What would happen if he were to sun dowse himself this night? Master Sayre and Kaliyah seemed to believe it was only through Ryudo that he could chase this curse.

What if, though, they were wrong?

Maybe he, on his own—using Kingfisher's enchantments—could chase the curse. Maybe on his own, inside Kingfisher's Sylphic Council Chamber, he could awaken his powers.

Shining then, he'd race to Kaliyah, to the Sayres, bearing *Dark England* with its mystery unshrouded—the key to defeating the witch.

Any Moor Folk who caught sight of him brightly running through the woodland would know that their Sun Child was brave and strong and ready, and rumors of his waking would spread.

Anyone who, this night, might be afraid would feel emboldened, despite that a battle was coming—as he himself would.

Master Sayre would help him plan the witch's downfall, and they'd prepare for a fight that would already be won.

Bastian ran up the back porch stairs and into the chalet. He sprinted to Da's study and moved the books they'd placed to conceal the passageway.

Naga jumped down from a windowsill and watched him.

Clutching his rucksack, his two books inside it, he slipped into the dark passageway and climbed, Naga following closely at his heels.

Though he carried a small flashlight in his rucksack, trying to hold it while climbing felt chancy. Rather, he navigated his way by feel.

As he neared the upward stretch of the passageway, the fire of the painted goblin's eyes shone strongly enough to cast a red sheen onto the platform, and beyond it.

By that uncanny light, he carefully clambered up the final series of beams and pulled himself into the garret leading to the Sylphic Council Chamber. He hurried to the small door and unlocked it.

Naga pushed in before him and trotted to the table. He leapt onto it and sat on the spherical gemstone, as though keeping watch.

Bastian pried open each window along the chamber's eastern wall, letting the starlight shafting between clouds cast a sheen of fair light in the room.

He pulled Woodthrush's scope from his pocket and studied the hill.

Faeries, their wings catching winks of stars, were floating among the twisted rowan berry trees.

The strains of pipes and drums that'd danced on the wind during the revelry still sounded, but distantly.

He could yet hear the rain angels singing.

He gathered the crystal rung stones from the table and picked up the witch hazel wand from the shelf where he'd left it.

He sat on the boulder bearing the emblem of the winged sun and arranged the river stones in a circle on the floor, linking their quartz rings.

He unloaded his flashlight and two books onto the table before him. He opened *Moor Folk of the English Highlands*, trained his flashlight on the page, and read—

"Starlight burning, sunlight churning,
in the darkness, Earth is turning."

He waved the witch hazel wand over himself, letting down a shower of pollen.

"Worlds are winging, thrushes singing—
bend to hear the sunrise ringing."

He waved the wand.

"Out of mire, light the pyre!
Make this Sun Child shine like fire!"

He struck the wand in a circle above his head so wildly, a rain of petals dropped.

A slight tingling awoke in his chest.

He laid down the witch hazel and opened his shirt.

He waited.

Watched.

There was no sign of any glow.

He turned off the flashlight and stared at his chest, at his palm.

Both remained cold.

Unlit.

The room chilled as a breeze dropped from a fresh storm cloud.

The light of the few surviving stars winked out as thunderheads sailed in like a fleet of dreadnaughts. Silence swallowed the room as cold air pressed in from the mounding storm.

In that quiet, that darkness, the ache in his chest felt choking.

Naga broke the silence with a low growl.

He jumped down from the gemstone and dashed to one of the windows. He stood on his hind legs and peeped out.

Bastian followed him and peered out the window through Woodthrush's scope. He scanned the dark hill and the deep woodland further east.

The revelry seemed to have evaporated the way the forest children had. The only thing at all visible was firelight piercing the northern horizon—flames and smoke rising from the grounds behind Marrowight Manor.

The way the landscape blared black, how it was backlit by that line of low fires from the witch's vale, it looked like the pretty countryside had gotten an infection that'd erupted into a canker. The manor's pinnacles pierced the sky like stingers.

"Kaliyah's dead wrong," said Bastian. "They all are." He stroked Naga. "The Sylphic Kingdom has no Sun Child."

Thunder bellowed—shuddering the chalet, and lightning webs burst.

Bastian drew back his hand at feeling Naga's shoulders grow tense.

Naga loosed a fierce growl and tore out the window. He scaled down the thatching, and in a blink, he was gone.

The silence that followed grew troubled with a disturbance of screaming—distant and shrill.

Sweat pricked Bastian's face, and his hornet sting sweltered. He rubbed his arms, hives rising from the witch hazel dust and from trekking through the weeds.

In a moment of silence between thunderclaps, Cassian's cry floated up from his nursery.

Could Cassian be feeling the terror Bastian was confronting? Could he sense that the world was rocking this night on the brink of an ill-fated war?

Bastian left the Council Chamber and climbed down the passageway. He eased back into Da's study and watched the hall for Mum or Da coming to look in on Cassian. Their bedroom, though, remained dark.

He covered the shaft's entryway and crept upstairs. He slipped into Cassian's nursery and turned on a low lamp.

He found the baby red-faced, his raspy wail seeming to come from a place of deep dreaming.

Bastian reached into the crib and worked his finger into the baby's balled fist.

Cassian's scrunched face relaxed.

Bastian gently lifted him and cradled him closely.

Cassian—snuffling, warm from his fit—cinched in his pajamaed legs and cocooned against Bastian's chest.

Thunder sounded distantly, the storm flying fast away now, echoing low from the west. With the battle so near, who knew but that the pygmyweed, hanging dry on the crib, had compounded with the storm's wailing and brought Cassian terrible dreams.

Bastian snapped off the Pygmyweed and pocketed it.

He bundled Cassian and carried him downstairs. He opened the back door and stepped out onto the porch, into the storm-cooled night.

Thick clouds skating off left the sky ablaze with sharp stars. The smoking streak of the Milky Way arced, its edges aglow as though backlit by candles.

Bastian wiped away tears shimmering on Cassian's cheeks, then buckled him into his baby swing. The porch's baby swing always set him straight to sleep, and after a moment, Cassian was snoring.

Bastian dropped into Mum's swing and gently rocked, fiddling with the parched sprig of pygmyweed cascading out of his pocket.

***

Sometime later, Bastian startled awake, not to the warning bell of a crying baby, but to the sparkle of a laughing one.

A boy was crouching on the porch before Cassian, feeding him spoonfuls of liquid out of a crystal chalice.

Bastian nearly tipped out of the swing.

The boy seemed not to care that Bastian had woken, nor that he was gaping at him—the boy just went on cooing to Cassian as he dribbled another measure of fluid into the baby's mouth.

Bastian widened his eyes in a struggle to make out whether this was a dream.

The boy looked about Rhys' age, but he seemed both older and more childish.

His skin held the tawny glow and perfection of Cassian's, but his face was wise-eyed, and his wavy tousles of brown hair carried streaks of silver.

The boy glanced at Bastian and smiled.

"What a good brother you are to see that your babe gets a night of stars from time to time."

His voice was windy and husked.

This didn't seem real—and yet the scorching sting on Bastian's wrist and the itching on his ankles and arms seemed to confirm that it was.

Bastian approached the boy. "Who are you? And what's this?" He snatched the chalice.

The sloshing fluid smelled sweet. Three stones tumbled at the chalice's bottom.

Cassian babbled and reached.

The boy took the chalice back possessively. "It's naught but honeysuckle cordial, brewed with a splash of a special enchantment—won by my own cleverness, I don't mind saying."

He gave Cassian another healthy swallow.

Cassian kicked in delight. The boy patted his curls.

Bastian rubbed his eyes. "This feels like a dream."

The boy helped himself to a long sip of cordial, then tipped to sitting on the porch stairs, leaning against his sharp elbows. "All of it's a dream, no doubt." He gazed at the stars lighting the dark eastern hill. "Every stone a memory, and every stone a lie."

Bastian looked crossly at him. "What's that supposed to mean?"

The boy chuckled. "If you don't know, then I'm afraid there's no hope for us."

Bastian looked at him sidelong. "Who are you?"

The boy stood and politely faced him. "Have you no guesses?"

Bastian considered him, beginning at his bare and muddy feet, rising to his rough-cut, dirty trousers, to his bare-chested, bony frame; his sly grin and gleeful eyes, to his tousled locks of mottled hair.

"I've no idea."

The boy set his fist against his hip. "Well, if I'm to be honest, I haven't any idea either."

"You don't know your own name?"

"Oh." The boy chuckled. "I'm called Gray Jay, but knowing the name isn't the problem. The trouble lies in knowing truly who one is." He rubbed his angular chin. "I haven't quite worked that out yet."

Bastian unfastened Cassian from the swing. The baby blew a doublet of happy mumblings.

Bastian cradled him. "He seems better."

"That'd be the enchantment we boiled in the cordial," said Gray Jay.

"Who's *we?*"

"The boys and I."

Bastian studied him a moment. "Why are you here?"

"Yeats had it, you know," said the boy. "Without mortals, the Moor Folk would be naught but shades, floating sadly through the Sylphic Kingdom." He settled onto the top porch stair. "And without Sun Children, why, there is no Sylphic Kingdom."

Bastian situated Cassian again in the swing and sat next to the boy.

"This really feels like I'm dreaming," he said. "Dreaming of talking with Aubrey Gyrfalcon or Kellyn Woodthrush." He leaned in a bit. "Are you a Sun Child?"

Gray Jay laughed. "Why, no, I'm no child at all. I've reached at least a thousand years."

Bastian jumped. "A thousand years?"

"Well, I was a thousand, and then some, last I counted." Gray Jay tapped a finger to his temple. "But that's been some time ago." He swished the cordial around the stones and took another sip. "Sun Children carry the blessings and curses of mortality. We forest children carry the blessings and curses of time."

"So—you're a forest child? For real?"

Gray Jay pinched him.

"Ow—" Bastian yanked away.

"Ask your arm to tell you if I'm real." Gray Jay cackled and drummed his feet on the porch.

"How do I know you're not something wicked, trying to trick me?" asked Bastian.

Gray Jay set the cordial aside and stood on the porch. He squeezed shut his eyes and clenched his fists.

In a burst of light, a pair of shining wings erupted from his back.

Bastian stumbled down the stairs and landed on his backside on the lawn.

Gray Jay's wings were like those he'd seen on the boys around the campfire. They resembled triangular moth wings but looked to be made up of metals and lights rather than the tiny scales of insect wings. Yet their translucent panes carried the same sheen of iridescent blue cloaking the butterflies that flitted through the Wystan Woods.

Gray Jay opened his eyes and relaxed his hands. The wings scrolled into him like smoke until they lay closely against his back, hardly more noticeable than a skinny boy's blade bones.

He clapped, delighted. "Why, if that didn't make you as pale and stun-faced as the moon." He guided Bastian to sitting on the porch steps and leaned kindly over him. "Here you are." He wrapped Bastian's fingers around the chalice of honeysuckle cordial and helped him drink. "We can't have you fight the witch when you can't even fight the weeds. This draught will make a peace between your body and the plants she's set against you."

The brew smelled like summer wind, filtered through a honeysuckle vine.

As Bastian swallowed, he was shaken by the recognition of what a hummingbird might experience, dipping its tongue down the throat of a flower.

His itching dimmed, and a delicious relaxation started at the level of his skin and sank deeply in, loading him with sleepiness. The burn of the hornet sting cooled.

———

WHEN HE AGAIN OPENED HIS eyes, Bastian found himself lying crookedly across the porch swing beneath a dove gray, pre-dawn sky.

He pulled up his sleeves and examined his arms.

His hornet sting was still a nasty whelp, but all the hive bumps had vanished.

In the silver east, gray clouds advanced. The wind picked up and lifted the heavy canopies of trees throughout the grounds and atop the hill, rocking them like ships.

Bastian moved to Cassian, sleeping peacefully in his swing.

He unbelted the baby and carried him inside.

He shut the door just as a shock of lightning stabbed beyond the hilltop.

The peal of thunder shaking the house seemed fiercer than what could come from any natural storm. Heavy raindrops battered the windowpanes.

Bastian carried Cassian upstairs and tucked him into his crib.

He shuffled to his own room and tied the pygmyweed sprig to its headboard.

He climbed inside his sheets and tried to access a sense of peace by recalling the sound of the forest child's laughter and the shine of starlight on his wings.

But he couldn't get warm, and no peace could reach him. He lay shivering as thunder rattled the windows.

He thirsted for a draught of honeysuckle cordial brewed with a forest child's enchantment.

35

When Bastian next opened his eyes, a fan was whirring sun-steamy wind through his bedroom, knocking the pygmyweed he'd tied against his headboard.

Lucas, across the room, was crying out in his sleep.

Bastian jumped out of bed and went to him.

He gently shook him.

Lucas opened his eyes and sat up some. "I had an awful dream," he signed. "It was so real. Lady Marrowight had you. I dreamed that the weird shock that hit me yesterday hit you instead. You were laid out flat on her vale."

It seemed Kaliyah was right about Lucas, that he had learned to see quite a bit of the Sylphic realm. He apparently recalled at least some of what'd happened at the manor, and in the Council Chamber yesterday.

"You weren't moving," signed Lucas. "You weren't breathing."

Bastian watched his brother, trembling with the aftereffects of the witch's strike.

"Is it cold in here?" signed Lucas.

Bastian glanced at the beam of sun streaming in. "It's sweltering."

Lucas shivered.

Bastian turned off the fan. He pulled the quilt from his own bed and tucked it around Lucas.

From the nightstand, he lifted the strip of seaweed—laden with Kaliyah's healing sand, and tied it again around Lucas' head.

"Is this how you've felt all this time?" signed Lucas. "Something wicked really did strike you in Exeter, didn't it? That night—there really was some dreadful thing in our room."

"A goblin," signed Bastian.

Lucas signed, "I see why you're plagued with bad dreams."

Bastian's dreams this night certainly had been terrible. Through the early hours, the wind had been a wail, its siege snapping small branches that battered the chalet.

He'd dreamed of the witch advancing with an army of sword-wielding goblins and gigantic hornets. All that'd divided Bastian from her was the black wildcat, growling, pacing, watching her with its icy blue eyes.

"Don't worry about me," signed Bastian.

Lucas glanced at Bastian's arm. "That hornet sting looks hideous."

Overnight, it'd swelled to a throbbing welt that covered the whole inside of his wrist.

"I'm sure it looks worse than it is."

"And I see how your chest is hurting you." Lucas pushed to sitting up a little. "Isn't there anything to be done?"

"I'm not sure," signed Bastian.

"And the Sylphic battle forecasted to take place during the eclipse—it really is going to happen, isn't it? Last night's moon was barely a line in the sky."

"Try not to worry." Bastian coaxed him to lie back down. "Just try to sleep. I'll find Kaliyah."

BASTIAN LIFTED HIS WIND JACKET, then stepped out onto the sunny porch.

He trekked through the limb-littered yard and climbed the eastern hill.

To the north, Marrowight Manor's spires bit into the sky like a jagged rock rising from a stormy gray sea. Its fires were now smoldering, giving it the feel of a camp of troops sleeping fitfully in the unrest of the battle's eve.

Then drifting in—a scent, sweet and summery. Ripeness, like a berry thicket.

Bastian moved toward a motion in the forest.

Kaliyah slipped out from among a stand of thickly grown oak trees. Her eyes were trained on the ground as though she were searching for something.

She was wearing dark denim overalls, their legs rolled to the patches on the knees.

Her wheat-golden hair cascaded halfway to her elbows, the front brushed back in a braid. But the curls at her temples had rebelled and were floating toward the sky, making a golden crown.

Though she appeared entirely human, Bastian could not unsee the traces of exquisite light dusting her frame, marking her as the faerie he knew her to be.

She was carrying a reed basket heaped with what she'd gathered from the forest.

It looked like it held wild strawberries, fresh leaves, shining acorns, and crystal-banded stones.

Kaliyah wandered nearer to Bastian, stopping now and then to collect a seed or a mushroom.

Bastian started to call out to her, but—watching her, a faerie in human form harvesting goods from the woodland like a bee visiting wildflowers—it was too magical to interrupt.

After a few moments, she glanced up and met his eyes.

She ran until she was standing before him. "I told Master Sayre about *Dark England* and its sealed pages."

"Lucas," said Bastian. "He—"

Kaliyah took his hand and guided him on toward the trees. "To open the book, Master Sayre says you must chase every bit of the dark curse."

Bastian glanced back toward the chalet. "Lucas seems to be—"

"Today, you'll practice Ryudo with Master Sayre's own teacher." Kaliyah drew him into the copse of oaks. "With what he's planned, you're sure to chase the last of the darkness—I just know you will."

Bastian drew his hand out of hers. "Lucas seems feverish." He stopped. "I'm afraid it's some effect of the strike that he took yesterday."

"Bull nettles." Kaliyah set down the basket. "I wasn't done gathering. Will you take that to Mrs. Sayre on your way to the Ryudo pitch?"

Bastian glanced at the basket. "Why are you collecting berries and seeds?"

"We might need them tomorrow."

"For the battle, we're going to need strawberries? Acorns?"

"Some of our forest children have made a discovery," said Kaliyah, in a low voice. "The witch plans to brew a curse of some kind on the battlefield. We don't yet know what—they haven't managed to get close enough to her manor to see what she's doing. We have some guesses, though, and I'm collecting what we might need to counter it."

Bastian lifted the basket. "Is there anything I can do for Lucas?"

Kaliyah hurried toward Kingfisher Chalet. "The best thing you can do for him—for all of us—is to drill for what's coming." She slipped through the rowan berry bushes and disappeared down the hill.

Bastian carried the basket on into the forest.

He followed a path that wove to a knee-deep crossing in the Windrush, then hiked through a wild stretch of woods. Finally, he reached the edge of the birch copse surrounding Sayre Cottage.

The hearth smoke piping from its roof was a translucent thread—the dying remnant of a fire that seemed not to have been tended since nightfall.

Two ancient towers of oaks, their trunks thick, their branches gnarled, flanked the cottage like sentinels.

East of Sayre cottage lay a fenced meadow where a stable nestled.

The stable looked ancient, like it had roots in the middle ages; like it'd climbed out of the earth on stones that'd endured a millennia of standing in England's sun and rain.

In the stable lived the Sayres' Friesian draft horse.

The horse was as black as the North Sea at midnight and bigger than any horse Bastian ever had seen. He fittingly carried the namesake of Egypt's Sun God—

Ra.

Bastian and his family had visited the Sayres' stable when they'd first moved to Dartmoor. Bastian had touched Ra's high, bristled nose and fed him a handful of timothy grass.

Before him, the great horse had knelt.

"Can I ride him?" Bastian had asked Master Sayre. He'd ridden horses before, but never one so big, nor so handsome.

"He's fit for a prince," Master Sayre had said, helping Bastian climb onto Ra's back.

The stallion had carried Bastian in a trot, then in a gallop, arcing wide around his meadow.

Though the speed was maniacal, Bastian felt locked together with the animal, as though they belonged to each other.

He'd felt Ra to be so skilled a steed that it seemed impossible for him to let his rider fall.

On his stable door hung a sign with a verse painted on it.

This had perplexed Bastian at the time, but he now recognized it as straight out of *Moor Folk of the English Highlands*:

See how I've slain the darkness.
See how I've flown its bars.
No longer bound, my heart has found
a dawning night of stars.

Ra was trotting at the meadow's edge, throwing his kingly head, his nostrils sculpted like a chessboard knight's. He was all majesty with his glossy chest, his muscled, midnight flank, and his showy, kinked forelock.

He seemed strong enough, old enough, to have truly been ridden by armored princes.

Being near the horse stirred a sense of bravery in Bastian.

The company of one seeming so battle-wise cast a feeling of having brothers and sisters in arms—friends who knew what was coming and would stand by him anyway.

Bastian uprooted a handful of timothy grass, then climbed onto Ra's fence.

Ra came running.

He lowered his nose to reach Bastian's hand.

Bastian stroked Ra's cheek as the great horse peered through the shanks of his forelock, his eyes casting light like polished steel.

Bastian climbed down from the fence and followed the Sayres' garden path.

The Sayres' garden, cherishing all corners of the cottage, seemed still in its infant state of spring—untouched by the scorching heat, the curses, the terrible storms that were troubling Dartmoor.

The pathway, cobbled of honey-silver limestones and cascading with white-and-ruby freesias, leaped over a trickle of the Windrush, then swept to the front door of Sayre Cottage.

As Bastian climbed the porch, blue delphiniums and sunset-colored honeysuckles twining up an arched lattice turned toward him, as though inspecting him. Against the porch, morning glory petals untwisted before him as though opening to the sun.

Bastian lifted his hand to knock on the arched door, but it drifted open on its own.

Inside, the lush of sugar baking into creams and cakes blended with the scents of loam and elderflowers. The poignant taint of salt and seaweed on a rack of Master Sayre's coats struck Bastian with the sensation that a rocking sea swayed just outside.

The bed Bastian had recovered on—Kaliyah's, presumably—perched under a wall of bright windows at the back of the kitchen. Oil lanterns hung merrily at the room's corners, awaiting dusk, and logs crackled in the stone hearth. Silver-gilded wine racks stocked with narrow-waisted bottles crept up either side of the fireplace.

Atop the mantel rested a row of pan flutes, and on the floor beside the hearth, a child-sized cello leaned against a silver stand. Bastian could almost hear the thoughts of the instruments, silently reflecting the dance of the fire as they dreamed of melodies that'd echoed inside their wooden skins—even last night, perhaps.

Here, in this charming cottage, it was difficult to believe a battle was coming. Here, it was hard to imagine that unless he managed to access the courage to confront the Witch Marrowight, unless he chased the dark curse from his heart and learned how to defeat her, even this lovely place—flourishing and fragrant with flowers, built with good earth and sound stones and strong vines—would be tinder to burn in the black smoke and flames of the witch's foul ambition.

Beside the fire, Mrs. Sayre was rocking in a chair sculpted from birch saplings and twiglets.

She was softly speaking to herself and seemed wholly immersed in her handwork. Firelight flashed on the silver needles she held, guided by her nimbly knitting fingers.

Her creation was draped on her lap, her homespun yarn the color of sun-bleached bone.

"Mrs. Sayre?" Bastian placed the basket on the floor. "Kaliyah asked me to bring you this."

Mrs. Sayre looked up from her work. "Ah, Sun Child. Come. Let's see if this fits." She held up a knitted cuirass.

"Where's Master Sayre?" he asked.

"On the water, bringing in Folk from the coast, and fishing for sea charms. He won't be back until nightfall." She helped Bastian off with his jacket. "This is best worn against skin."

Bastian removed his shirt. Mrs. Sayre fixed the cuirass over his head and fastened it.

In her lap, it'd looked like a heap of knitted yarn. On him, it looked like looped chain mail, perfectly fitted to his form.

"May this keep you intact for your drills today," she said.

"Intact?"

She glanced at the sting. "I've some cordial that you're to drink." She went to a teakettle set on a potbelly stove that was practically in the living room. "Orders of Master Sayre's teacher."

"His teacher—is he here?" asked Bastian. "I can't wait to meet him. I've been looking forward to training with him for months."

"This is your lucky day, you might think, to train with that fellow— one practicing Ryudo a sight longer than Master Sayre. A sight longer than anyone, actually." Mrs. Sayre stirred the contents of the teakettle. "Ryudo, one could argue, originated with him. His teaching style, however, is"—she overpoured a chalice full of brew and handed it to him—"well, you'll want that."

Bastian sniffed it. "Honeysuckle cordial?"

"No, honeysuckle is for healing. This is elderflower cordial—for courage."

Bastian took a swallow of the brew—light and sweet, like nectar. It was the same draught he'd tasted when he woke yesterday after the ordeal at Marrowight Manor.

Its bite lent the sense that it was laced with light itself. And its scent—fresh like cool earth—brought a wash of energy and alertness.

"Considering what you'll be facing in drills today"—Mrs. Sayre smoothed and squared the cuirass on him—"well, drink up."

He stared at her as he finished the cordial. "What will I be facing?"

She patted his shoulder. "I'd best let Doctor Skylar answer that." She received the chalice from him. "Now, be off."

BASTIAN JOGGED to the Ryudo pitch to find at its center a man standing, whistling a fair tune—sweet, like a distant nightingale trilling.

In the air right above the man, a rippling darkness hovered. It looked slightly solid in places, but then would flicker back into translucency, like an airborne mirage.

The man drew a fist-sized dark rock from a pouch on his belt. He cast it straight up.

When the stone reached the pinnacle of its arc, it burst into flames and exploded in a rain of cinders.

Bastian, nearing the man, slowed.

He'd seen this man before.

The curls twisting out of the man's topknot; the kind face—it was the doctor who'd spoken to him the night Cassian had been born.

And then a fresh recognition struck.

Bastian stopped.

Mrs. Sayre had called this man *Doctor Skylar*.

Those bright eyes. The curls.

The name scribed on the photo of Kingfisher and his brother had been—*Forrest Skylar*.

The bright-eyed doctor waved him over.

As Bastian approached, he found himself unable to look away from this doctor—by all counts remarkable, Kingfisher's brother—despite that the terrifying thing in the air was taking on an electric blue glow.

Bastian stopped before the doctor. "At your hospital, you told me you only dabbled in Ryudo."

"These things are relative," said the doctor, seeming unconcerned that the rippling dark and blue something was hovering slightly nearer.

"Mrs. Sayre said you've studied longer, even, than Master Sayre has," said Bastian. "That Ryudo originated with you."

"Am I proficient? Passable, perhaps," said the doctor. "Am I as good as I'd like to be? Not even close. As far as engendering the sport—yes, I like to think I had a hand in it."

"I'm guessing you know who I am," said Bastian. "I mean, besides that I'm the kid whose brother was born the night we met."

Doctor Skylar, keeping his eyes fixed on Bastian's, bowed. "You're our Sun Child."

Bastian held still, at a loss for how to respond to someone bowing to him. After a moment, he bowed back.

Doctor Skylar raised him to standing straight. He pulled back Bastian's shoulders. "Let me see your opening stance."

Bastian crouched into it. "Are you something Sylphic?"

"Only by association." Doctor Skylar squared Bastian in his pose. "By the dawn, you do have some power, if we could just get it out from under that darkness."

"Are you really a doctor, too?"

"Best method of making one's way in the world if you ask me. Although, I find great pleasure in Ryudo, not to mention stewarding... well, something indeed Sylphic, which shall be your challenge. But we'll get to that."

"My challenge?" asked Bastian.

Doctor Skylar guided Bastian out of his stance. "You'll face something terrible today. Something wonderful." He gestured to Bastian's chest. "May I see to you?"

Bastian moved closer to him.

Doctor Skylar settled his hand on Bastian's chest. Winced.

"It shows some strength, by the way, that you're able to bear this as well as you do."

He shifted his hand an inch and concentrated, his expression deepening some. He let Bastian go.

"Bearing this darkness," said Bastian, "I'll be no kind of Sun Child."

"You've found *Dark England*, I understand," said Doctor Skylar.

"Which you helped to write, I've gathered. Have you known, all this time, where it was?"

"Kingfisher—perhaps unwisely—squirreled it well away from everyone before he died. But he did, after all, manage to see it into your hands, and that's something. I, for one, didn't doubt that he knew what he was doing. By the book's darkness, may light yet shine."

"But the most important section," said Bastian, "the section intended specifically for me, for the Sun Child—I can't open it. Do you know what it says?"

"Unfortunately not," said Doctor Skylar. "I mainly contributed illustrations. It was my brother who developed the secrets it conceals."

"Master Sayre believes I won't be able to open the book until this darkness is chased." Bastian lifted his wrist before the doctor. "This curse."

Doctor Skylar studied his sting. "I practice medicine for a living, seeing all manner of pain. Yet that welt makes my legs ache."

Doctor Skylar seemed very kind, but also matter-of-fact. If anyone could tell Bastian whether he had no prayer of defeating the witch, it seemed Doctor Skylar would shoot straight.

"Do you think I'm likely to fail?" Bastian asked him. "That I'm not who the Sylphic Kingdom needs? If you're to be my training master, then you might as well know—I have sound reasons to doubt."

"Today shall give you a trial on that score," said Doctor Skylar. "And perhaps a solution. For in facing this challenge, you might very well chase that darkness. Something Elemental pressed it inside you, and so—it's quite likely—only facing something Elemental will break it."

"Something Elemental." Bastian staggered a step, his mind's eye flashing with the red ember glow of a goblin's glare, his knees weakening by the terror that washed.

"I've faced Elemental Spirits before. Goblins several times, and even the witch. Yet—I still carry this curse."

"And by those encounters, insight has dawned," said Doctor Skylar. "When the goblin seized upon you and your brother in the park last month, we learned that the darkness in you had weakened considerably since that first encounter in Exeter. It was your light, your power shining through, which held him back."

"And it seems the Witch Marrowight figured that out," said Bastian, rubbing his chest. "She's managed to complicate things. What if I can't chase the rest of this darkness?"

"Let's not think on that yet."

"How can I not think on it?" Bastian held Doctor Skylar's gaze. "The fate of the world depends upon me facing her tomorrow—and I'm not a safe bet."

"A wight witch is one thing, but doubt is a far fiercer opponent," said Doctor Skylar. "This, truly, is what you must chase."

The thing overhead had coasted to the edge of the Ryudo pitch.

Glowing slightly blue, it lost altitude and crashed into a copse of trees, its landing bending their limbs and leaving their boughs quaking.

Bastian stared at the trees but could make out nothing in them save a vague shimmer of blue. "What is that?"

Doctor Skylar stared at the disturbance.

"Sun Child, meet Azdaj."

Bastian pulled the Sylphic scope from his pocket.

Doctor Skylar stopped him. "Best to not look on him until you've had a run with him."

Without any scope, Bastian couldn't make out the shape of the thing—Azdaj, seeming to rise out of the trees. He could only mark the evidence of its passing—splintered saplings, crushed bushes, ripples of blue lightning.

The fear that seized him in watching the quivering blue darkness take to the air and approach—it was deeply felt and familiar.

On the night Kaliyah had lured him into the dark Wystan Woods, something from this strain of dreadful had been perched in the apple tree beside Kingfisher Chalet, shedding shocks of blue lighting exactly like what now was coursing against the bright sky.

That night, it was the terror of this creature that'd guided him home.

"You've seen him before, yes?" asked Doctor Skylar.

"He led me, once, out of the dark woods," Bastian—close to hyper-ventilation—whispered. "This terrible something—it seems it could've killed me."

"Yes, that's true. But for all his teeth and his fire and his rage, Azdaj is a pretty decent guy."

Teeth. Fire. Rage.

Bastian glanced at Doctor Skylar. "Then, that night—why didn't he kill me?"

"He'd already feasted."

"And today"—Bastian swallowed hard—"has he feasted?"

"No." Doctor Skylar reached into his pouch and drew out a round rock, the size of his palm and banded with crystal.

"Take your stance."

Staring at the blue flashes snapping, the ache in Bastian's chest swelled until his heart felt encased in iced metal, shards of the dark stuff piercing him from within.

"I have no mortar," Bastian whispered.

"For your first run, your objective is merely to stay on your feet; to remain breathing." Doctor Skylar backed off. "Take your stance."

Bastian, his knees trembling, crouched into it and faced the terrible something.

Doctor Skylar whistled a musical trill and heaved the stone in a high arc toward Bastian.

The terrible something charged.

The terrible something flickered from nothing into a streak of blackish silver; from nothing into iridescent waves rippling with dark-ness; from nothing into lit, silver eyes; from nothing into a snouted, reptilian streak of fire, moving faster than anything Bastian ever had seen.

Bastian dropped to his knees.

The rock swept right over where his head had been.

There, it lit with blue fire scrolling from a heavily fanged mouth.

Bastian covered his face and contracted into a ball as the air around him flushed hot, then cooled.

He glanced up to see the glowing blue of Azdaj swooping into the sky above the woodland and leaving a trail of dark smoke.

Bastian uncurled.

An inch from his face lay the stone, smoking.

Its crystal ring shining was no longer white, but a deep bluish silver that danced, like the stone's heart was on fire.

He lifted and studied it a moment, then slid it, piping, into his pocket.

It seemed Azdaj was wheeling in the sky, readying to return.

"Again," called Doctor Skylar. "Take your stance."

Bastian tried to stand, but the ache in his chest brought on a fit of coughing, and he couldn't straighten. He stayed where he was, on his hands and knees.

Doctor Skylar jogged to him. Leaned over him.

"Recite for me the first tenet of Ryudo."

Bastian struggled to kneeling and looked up at Doctor Skylar's face —a face that, though compassionate, seemed not to care at all that he felt nearly dead.

"Did you teach Master Sayre Ryudo this way?" Bastian whispered.

Doctor Skylar lifted his brow. "The first tenet."

"Facing opposition square," said Bastian, lowering his gaze. "Standing one's ground."

"And the last tenet?"

"Finding your place in the fight."

"Right, so..."

"But I barely could think, much less respond to that thing, rushing at me, and engage."

Bastian glanced around them at the Ryudo course and could no longer see anything rippling with light or glowing blue.

"We often find challenges difficult because of a flaw in perspective," said Doctor Skylar. "You won't know the rewards of courage until you're willing to embrace the risks of failure and pain."

"I know more than a little of failure." Bastian rubbed his chest. "And pain."

"Think of that ache as a weight on a bat. Imagine how much stronger you'll be when you're free of that agony."

"What, exactly, is Azdaj?" asked Bastian.

Dr. Skylar glanced at the pocket of Bastian's cargo shorts where the Sylphic scope rested.

"Take a look at your opponent."

Though Bastian could see nothing unusual on the Ryudo pitch, he knew precisely where his opponent waited. A dread chill, like an icy sea wind, was drifting from the north.

He raised the scope toward it.

Dark smoke. Silver smoke. Light blaring out of the smoke. Brightness shifting to flames like petroleum fumes lighting.

Then out of the fire stepped a large, lizard-faced creature with rippling black scales, its eyes shining like hot silver stars.

Iridescence flickered the sunlight glancing off the scales plating Azdaj's body—glowing as though the skin underneath was forged of white-hot embers.

"You have"—Bastian found little air at his disposal to shape into words—"a dragon."

"Dragons, though Elemental Spirits, can carry loyalty for the Sun Devaa," said Doctor Skylar. "Azdaj is one of these."

Facing the dragon was like facing a lion on fire, its eyes the epicenter of the blaze.

Two great, batty wings blotted the sunlight around it. A long, horned tail lashed like a whip.

The beast wasn't as gigantic as Bastian had imagined a dragon might be. But for something this terrible, this fierce—being the size of a lion was plenty big.

Azdaj spread his wings. Snapped his jaws. A hood of skin flared around his face like the collar of a frilled lizard. He widened his silvery eyes, flashing blue.

And in those eyes, Bastian saw more than the reflection of the fire leaking from Azdaj's mouth.

He felt arrested by the dragon's gaze as in it he saw an image of himself, grounded and unconscious on the Ryudo pitch. He saw an image of Azdaj, forked tongue unfurled, licking blood from Bastian's broken body.

The vision in the dragon's eyes shifted to a panorama of the Wystan Woods, serene under twilight's gentle blush.

A flash of blue fire vanquished that scene, and the dragon's eyes filled with an image of stars shining over a nightscape of tors and moorlands, their heights passing swiftly beneath his great wings.

Azdaj turned away and set to pacing, scraping his claws on the turf like a bull.

Bastian snapped out of what felt like a trance.

"His eyes," said Bastian. "In his eyes, I saw something—like visions. Dreams."

"That's how dragons communicate," said Doctor Skylar. "That, and the branchial fringe around the face. They can position that hood and angle their cranial spines to express their intent."

Bastian studied the fanned skin framing the dragon's face.

It no longer was flared but rather was gathered mainly up, pointing at the sky.

"What's his intent now?" asked Bastian.

"This is hunger," said Doctor Skylar. "A thought of taking to the air in pursuit of food."

"And his eyes," said Bastian. "By those visions, what was he communicating?"

"Dragon eyes hold memories of what they've sighted," said Doctor Skylar. "They can transfix an onlooker, enchanting them to see what the dragon has experienced."

"I saw myself unconscious," said Bastian. "And him—feasting."

Doctor Skylar nodded. "And sometimes, they hold images of their longings." He drew out a lava rock and pitched it toward the dragon.

Azdaj swooped near and caught it in his teeth. He crunched it to bits as he wheeled away to the back of the pitch.

"At a glance, you might feel that a dragon is your death," said Doctor Skylar.

"You're not kidding," said Bastian, his eyes on Azdaj's fangs, visible despite the distance dividing them.

"But the truth is—that dragon is your pathway to strength."

For Bastian, though, just keeping himself standing while looking at the dragon was a feat. "I feel no strength."

Doctor Skylar secured Bastian's gaze. "Facing down that Elemental Spirit is the only way to access the secret which my brother so carefully protected." He drew another stone, crystal-ringed, from his pocket. "Are you willing to confront this?"

Bastian again studied the dragon through the scope.

The shape of Azdaj's wings brought to mind the skeleton in King-fisher's trunk—Ryu, a Sunwalker.

"Is he the same sort of creature as Ryu?" Bastian asked.

"This is the child of Ryu," said Doctor Skylar. "Ryu faded, years ago, but left a clutch of eggs. Azdaj was the firstborn."

"I saw Ryu's remains—in the Sylphic Council Chamber," said Bastian. "They were much smaller than Azdaj."

"Azdaj, like Ryu, takes the form of a harpy eagle when material." Doctor Skylar's gaze traveled back to the dragon, whom he watched with great love. "Although, he prefers this ethereal state. It gives him so much more liberty. And he does relish setting things on fire."

Azdaj took flight and coasted overhead.

Doctor Skylar fell into his shadow.

"Mind yourself, Bastian—he's well-allied to us. But for all that, he does carry fire, a mouthful of fangs, and claws that need trimming. He is capable of accident."

Bastian backed away, the aching cold in him rising. It seemed to be coming from not just his chest, but from his whole body, every nerve prickling. If dread could be physical pain, this was it.

A light flickering at the edge of the Natterjack Lagoon drew Bastian's gaze down from the dragon.

There, Kaliyah eased to the earth—shifting from a sparkle to her human form.

"Come to wish our champion well, have you?" called Doctor Skylar.

"Keep back," called Bastian. "There's a dragon on the pitch."

"I know," she called. "I could see him from your chalet."

She sprinted across the pitch and stopped before Bastian.

"Is Lucas all right?" he asked, keeping tabs on the shadow, the terror, of Azdaj.

"I repeated the charm," said Kaliyah. "He was well enough when I left to take on Rhys in a football skirmish." She glanced at the sky. "Mind if I watch you battle your dragon?"

At the notion of Kaliyah watching this—Bastian felt in the same instant, both stronger and weaker.

"Have you faced Azdaj before in Ryudo?" asked Bastian.

"I'm nowhere near ready," said Kaliyah.

"How long have you practiced?"

"All my life." She backed away.

"In mastering this power, may the darkness inside you blow to ash," said Doctor Skylar. "And may the Sylphic Kingdom receive its Sun Child." He met Bastian's eyes. "Take your stance."

Bastian crouched into it.

Doctor Skylar held the crystal-banded stone high.

Bastian tried to gather enough breath for what promised to be a long sprint, but he couldn't get enough air.

"Wait," he called.

Doctor Skylar set to whistling beautifully. He launched the stone straight at Bastian.

The dragon took off in a swift lumber.

Bastian kept himself facing the galloping dragon. Azdaj's eyes—his most visible feature—seemed locked on the stone.

Bastian held his position as the stone coasted mere inches above him.

The dragon leapt into flight and soared straight over Bastian's head, blasting the stone with blue fire, dropping it at Bastian's feet.

He skidded in a fiery crash-landing alongside the edge of the pitch.

Looking on him now, Bastian could make out more of him: large, webbed wings—wildly flapping; a long, sweeping tail; the rippling darkness of his flanks; smoke billowing from his nostrils; the frill around his face broadening and slackening in turns.

"I can see him," said Bastian. "Or, at least flashes of him."

"That would be the light inside you gaining some ground," said Doctor Skylar. "Again."

Bastian picked up the smoking stone, its crystal aglow with blue flames.

"I don't know if I can handle that again."

But the icy ache in his chest did feel weaker.

He slipped the stone in his pocket beside the first one.

Doctor Skylar drew out a third stone, rung with quartz, and handed it to Kaliyah.

"Light that for us, would you?"

Kaliyah held the stone between her palms and blew into it.

The crystal striping it lit to gold.

"Your target," said Doctor Skylar, "is the Natterjack Cave. Your mortar—Kaliyah's stone."

"But the dragon is trained to go after the stone," said Bastian. "If he sees me holding it, he'll go after me."

"This is, of course, the point," said Doctor Skylar.

"But when he jets his fire at the mortars, they fill with flames," said Bastian. "If he does that to me, what will...actually, no. I don't want to know."

Doctor Skylar backed away from him.

Kaliyah, following Doctor Skylar, tossed Bastian the lit stone.

It was piping—just a degree below unbearable.

The rippling shade of the dragon coasted to the middle of the pitch. Light and darkness together trickled over the grass, and their blades blew as though above them a thunderstorm were hovering.

Bastian could just make out the whole of the dragon, pacing. He could feel hot smoke washing, smell its cinders.

The air trembling off the creature was spinning a fresh scent, too, as though silent, ozonic lightning were cutting the atmosphere.

Bastian measured the weight of the stone.

"Your opening stance," hollered Doctor Skylar.

Bastian crouched into it, but a cramp in his thigh troubled him. "Wait."

Doctor Skylar trilled a bright whistle.

The dragon set into a raging run.

Bastian jogged until the cramp worked itself out.

He leapt over a log and sprinted toward the lagoon, but the dragon drove him the dead opposite way.

Each time Azdaj neared, Bastian's blood ran cold, and he stumbled.

Keeping himself on two feet was the first trick, but he soon got a feel for the weaving patterns of the dragon and dodged him.

Finally, he made his way near to the water.

A zap of heat struck him.

He skidded across the grass and twisted onto his back, his shoulder blazing with pain.

"Get back on your feet," shouted Doctor Skylar. "On your feet!"

Bastian couldn't imagine doing anything of the sort—keeling over and dying seemed about all he could manage.

The icy ache was pounding in his chest so hard he could barely draw breath.

But in trying to right himself, to stand, he surprised himself to find that he could.

"Quite excellent," Bastian heard Doctor Skylar say to Kaliyah.

"I've never seen anyone pick up a dragon's tricks so quick," she replied.

Azdaj, chuffing, landed. Reared.

Bastian set into a sprint, but his foot caught on a root, and he dropped.

Azdaj sprang into a run.

A bracing for death.

Bastian shielded his face in his hands, every inch of him anticipating a burn of electric blue fire and trembling with an upsurging wish that death by dragon would be quick.

Azdaj landed right by him. He nosed aside Bastian's hands and snorted smoke.

From the dragon's mouth spun a fine tongue of fire. It struck the stone in Bastian's hand, turning its band from bright gold to a smoldering bluish orange.

Though Azdaj had set fire to only the stone, his gaze betrayed a bloodthirst Bastian only ever had seen in wildcats in sanctuaries, and in Naga from time to time.

Though the dragon was standing still, it seemed certain that one false move might provoke him to cook anyone lying helpless before him —even a Sun Child.

Before Bastian could think how to move, Doctor Skylar had taken Azdaj by the sharp, high ridge of spikes jetting at the back of his head.

Bastian slipped the third piping stone into his pocket.

Kaliyah, her eyes shining, hauled Bastian up. "Best him, and you'll find healing. Best him, and like a metal made strong in blue fire, you'll rise ready to challenge the witch."

Bastian cradled his shoulder, throbbing from where Azdaj's flames had struck him.

Kaliyah took a new stone from Doctor Skylar and blew its crystal golden. She placed it in Bastian's hand.

Bastian, taking his stance, felt he'd recovered his full strength. More than his full strength.

Doctor Skylar and Kaliyah backed away.

Bastian dandled the hot stone, his eyes fixed on the Natterjack Cave.

The thought of a stone on fire in that cave felt releasing. With the stone's faerie light almost burning his skin, flashing heat up his arm and into his chest, he felt—for the first time—a Sun Child.

A Sun Child built to wield terrible power.

"You can do this," called Doctor Skylar.

Bastian held the burning stone close to his chest, his fingers just tapping the cool earth.

Doctor Skylar let go of the dragon.

Bastian could perceive Azdaj clearly enough now to find elegance in the sweep of his terrible wings.

Bastian sprang to the right, barely dodging a shaft of fire straight off. Not a bit touched him, but the air shook with its punch.

Azdaj wove wild.

Bastian read the pattern and leapt, wheeled, spun to avoid each bolt of fire. He reached the clearing's edge. Angled back. Raced for the Natterjack Cave.

Azdaj sped overhead, blocking his path with a wave of blue fire.

Bastian dodged it, just catching a slight zap again on the shoulder. He tripped to a stop. Feigned turning back.

Azdaj followed.

Bastian cut away and rushed at the cave.

Azdaj beat his wings, managing an unwieldy turn toward Bastian.

Bastian sprinted. Skidded to a stop.

Cocked the stone. Cast it.

The stone, its crystal ring throwing golden light, rocketed at the cave in concord with the black shade of Azdaj coasting overhead into towering pines, his branchial frill pressed tightly against his neck.

The blazing stone soared into the mouth of the cave, shimmering its wet interior.

Doctor Skylar hollered, and Kaliyah whooped.

Bastian watched the cave as the lit stone sank deeply inside its darkness. It seemed to land, projecting a burst of bright light.

The shine illuminated, at the cave's throat—a figure.

By that flare, Bastian captured the gist of the figure's face. He glimpsed a pair of fiery red eyes. Eyes that seemed fixed on him. Eyes that seemed to be challenging him.

A wave of chill washed him.

Kaliyah was crying his name and clapping, but he couldn't heed her, or even look back. He couldn't take his eyes off the face in the cave.

The flare dimmed, and then finally vanished, leaving the cave in absolute blackness.

Doctor Skylar approached from behind, his footfalls gentle on the grass.

"In the cave—is that what I think it is?" asked Bastian.

Doctor Skylar rested his hand on Bastian's shoulder. "Stepping into that cave is entering the heart of England's Sylphic Kingdom. It reveals us—our most terrible trials. Our most damning weaknesses. Our deepest wounds. Our greatest strongholds of courage. It brings our true self to the surface."

Bastian laid his hand on the three stones, smoldering with dragon fire, inside his pocket.

"I just faced a dragon, and yet—I fear this more."

He could see it all in his mind's eye—blood wetting Lucas' face; the goblin lifting a gleaming knife; Lucas unable to stand; Lucas unmoving.

And through it all—Bastian had been overcome by his own weakness.

He could think of nothing but how it'd felt to lie on the ground petrified, wholly incapable of fighting, while he watched Lucas bleed.

"You feared Azdaj, and yet here you are," said Doctor Skylar.

"Confronting my most damning weaknesses..." Bastian peered up at Doctor Skylar. "He'll dismantle me."

"Healing comes from dismantlement." Doctor Skylar let go of him.

Bastian studied the dark cave but hesitated to approach. For although this way might indeed lead to healing, it also led straight to a battle.

Kaliyah took hold of his hand. "I'll go with you. As far as I can."

Bastian pressed her fingers.

They together stepped into the lagoon and waded to the mouth of the cave.

Passing its shadowed border was like passing the threshold of death.

Darkness swarmed them as though the air were materially black. It thickened until he could no longer see Kaliyah.

It deepened until he no longer could sense whether she still held his hand.

36

Bastian stood in the utter darkness, metering his breathing. He was standing too deeply inside the cave to see any daylight.

When it came to confronting the goblin, would he run? He tried to imagine himself standing face to face with the creature—tried to imagine himself holding strong at its approach, the way he'd squared against Azdaj.

He couldn't even visualize it.

Whole worlds depended on this, on him finding healing and courage in facing his fears; in discovering his true self.

And yet here, on the brink of determining who he truly was, he felt paralyzed. This was the airless place of dread he'd inhabited from the moment the goblin had first struck him; from the second Lucas had hit the ground until Bastian could reach him and see he was breathing. This was the place of blind grief he'd entered the night Granddadda died. This—the terrible waiting while Mum was unstable; the uncertainty of whether Cassian would be born alive.

He felt for Kaliyah's hand.

It seemed she'd utterly vanished.

Bastian steadied himself against the cave wall.

The crystals growing on it felt massive—far longer and sharper than when the naiad had drawn him here.

He eased away from the wall, drawing a distance between himself and the tips of the crystals. He glanced back at the cave's opening.

He turned back. He searched in the darkness until he felt a course of boulders that seemed they would lead back to daylight.

But just as he set his foot on it, a flicker of a thought touched him.

It was a memory. The memory of holding Cassian for the first time.

On that day, he'd promised to be Cassian's protector.

"I'm just a kid—I'm no champion," Bastian whispered.

He was a kid who was afraid of the dark. A kid who feared bullies. Goblins. Wight witches. And, though a Sun Child, trembling.

He was no warrior, primed to defend a kingdom from a tyrant—it was true.

But he was a brother.

If the Sylphic Kingdom fell, so would the mortal world. And soon in that darkness, Cassian, too, would die. Lucas. Rhys.

His heart thrashing, Bastian faced the dark throat of the cave.

He took a step deeper in.

The black air, its dank cold, swallowed him as though a door behind him had shut.

Before him—around him—a low, green light swelled.

He found himself in the forest clearing, in the football park. It was nighttime, the darkness cut weakly by the park's field light. He was holding a football.

The sky was choked with thick thunderheads, visible only by lightning bursts. Around him, a cold storm wind was lifting. Beside him, Lucas was kneeling, tying his shoe.

"Hey bastard!" shouted the voice from the misted forest.

The goblin boy strode into the glow of the field light.

He looked—just like last time—almost identical to the bully from Exeter. Only this time, Bastian could handily perceive that the boy's body was shifting in and out of the shape of a goblin.

Bastian nudged Lucas.

Lucas slowly stood.

The goblin boy, his fists balled, crossed the grass.

Lucas pushed Bastian behind him and signed to the boy, "Leave us alone."

"What was that you said to me, gimp?" The boy jabbed Lucas' shoulders.

This was the moment when the goblin boy had punched Lucas in the face. When he'd gone after the Sylphic scope. When he'd thrown Lucas against the rubbish bin. When he'd unsheathed the knife.

Bastian keenly remembered the sickening feeling of fear striking so sharply as to keep him petrified, hardly able to think or move.

But now his muscles flickered, warm and waiting. A simmering heat seemed to be steadying his heart.

Bastian pushed between the goblin boy and Lucas. "He said to leave us the hell alone."

"Well, aren't you smart," said the goblin boy, leering at Lucas, "to be able to talk at all."

"Get away from us," Bastian shoved the goblin boy.

He hardly budged.

"It must be awful." The goblin boy grinned. "Having a brother like him."

Bastian took a high swing.

The goblin caught his arm and twisted until Bastian spun, shrieking. "I'll break your arm. I'll make you a gimp, too."

Lucas edged around Bastian and shoved the goblin hard enough that he let Bastian go.

The goblin rammed his shoulder into Lucas and lifted him, squirming. He carried him toward the rubbish bin.

Bastian started to run after him but paused. The sickening feeling was again taking hold—the feeling of powerlessness to stop the dangerous strike to the head Lucas was about to suffer.

Bastian's gaze fell on a smooth stone, the size of a seagull's egg, lying on the grass before him.

Picking it up, he found it was banded with crystal.

It was the Ryudo mortar he'd cast into the cave.

The goblin boy, his arms constricting Lucas' legs and neck, turned. "You going to let me do this, bastard?" He walked on toward the rubbish bin. "Maybe you'd secretly like to be rid of him."

Bastian rolled the stone in his hand, testing its weight and feeling of its fire.

"Everyone loyal to you is going to die anyway," said the goblin boy. "Let's have him be the first."

Bastian drew a slow breath. Focused.

"What's it going to be?" The goblin looked back. "Him or you?"

Bastian whipped the stone. Fast and straight.

It struck the goblin boy square in the throat.

He stumbled. He plopped onto his rear, choking coughs.

Lucas jumped away from him and ran to Bastian.

Bastian stood staring at the goblin boy, struggling to get to his feet. He could hardly believe he was seeing the goblin boy downed; that he was feeling the warmth of Lucas standing—unscathed—by his side.

He'd done it.

He'd kept his focus, his courage, his strength. He'd kept Lucas clear of a thrashing that seemed inescapable.

His chest felt on fire with strength.

Bastian pulled Lucas further back as he screamed, "Come near us again, and the next one will crack your bloody skull!"

KALIYAH'S VOICE ROSE, singing in her faerie language a song that seemed to be of clouds on seas, of starlit skies, of the thrush's lullaby, of hushed twilight woodlands, of misty tors, of waterfalls softening into streams.

A shining haze washed over Bastian like a dousing of quicksilver, and at its touch, his muscles slackened.

He rested in the dark on the tail of her song until he was aware of nothing except his own easy breathing and the gentle beating of his heart.

His mind flooded with visions, like memories—memories that didn't belong to him.

A muscular man standing before the Witch Marrowight on her smoking vale. The ground fluttering with severed wings.

The witch raising her crooked hands.

The man answering with blue dragon fire, raining.

Webs of lightning streaming from the witch's fingers and striking the man.

The man vanishing into smoke.

37

*B*astian found himself lying on a patch of tender grass, alongside the stream gliding out of the Natterjack Cave.

Dew had stained his arms and legs cool. Above him, stars glimmered in an indigo sky.

Seeds and spore and lichen dust were floating in the wind, glinting in the starlight shafting down.

He sat up.

These were the Wystan Woods he knew, and yet they were changed. They were richer. More solid.

His perception of them seemed to have deepened, like when he'd seen Kaliyah with wings.

The trickling water murmured in the Windrush's stream like a child's laugh. There seemed to be words in the wind.

Faerie lanterns glistened at the base of every tree, spraying cones of light onto their boughs.

Kaliyah approached from behind and rounded him. Her wings were unfurled, their rims coursing silvery blue. Shimmering swirls streaked her face.

She led him past Doctor Skylar, standing still.

He seemed somewhat transparent, his skin softly glowing, like a star tempered with mist.

Kaliyah drew Bastian to the Windrush's bank.

Never had the water looked so clear.

The stream carried no storm current, no rage. It only flowed gently along its southwesterly course, leading to the Natterjack Lagoon—shining in the distance as though lit from within.

Pebbles on the stream's bank glistened like jewels, each one of them rung with a belt of quartz.

The lily pads edging the stream were in full bloom, but rather than holding flowers, they each held a flame. The Natterjack toads leaping among them left frosty toeprints—remnants of the handling and care they received from the Moor Folk.

In a clip of light, Kaliyah vanished.

A blink, and she'd shifted to tiny—no bigger than Bastian's hand. A white dress, fitted to her like a glove, seemed woven of spider silk and nightingale feathers. It shone as though tanned from the skins of summer clouds. Her skirt looked sewn from orchid petals studded with dew drops. Her curving locks glittered.

She flitted to his hand and kissed the balor hornet sting on his wrist.

Its searing eased.

She lighted on his palm and there came to rest.

On the still water's surface, within Kaliyah's light, Bastian saw his face reflected.

His nose still held its freckles. His hair still stood in rumpled, twisting peaks. But it was gilded with streaks of platinum, like Gray Jay's. He was wearing the armor plates he'd found in the Sylphic Council Chamber.

Kaliyah flitted up and gestured for him to follow.

She guided him into the stream's shallows and toward the mouth of the Natterjack Cave.

The cave's walls, their heavy crystals, glowed beneath the lanterns of fireflies.

The fear Bastian normally suffered here was gone. Even its memory felt distant. The aching knot in his chest, although it seemed still to harbor a sliver of ice, of dread toward the witch—it also held a relieving sense of openness. Light shining where a very long night had persisted.

Kaliyah pointed him toward a bed of moss between the two boulders, as spherical as Earths. "Lie down."

He lay on the springy moss and found himself soothed by its groundedness, by the scents lifting of cool water, of night winds, of succulent reeds.

Kaliyah spun like an ice dancer in a web of light, and as she slowed, she grew again to his size. She seemed at once both young and old, like she was in the middle of a thousand years of childhood.

She washed his sting with luminescent water rippling in a basin hewn from crystal. She pinched at tender places on his wrist, exhuming thorny poison slivers. Each needle excised made him cry out, but relief followed. Finally, she pulled away.

Bastian studied his wrist, brightened by her light.

The spidery bruising had vanished.

Kaliyah set her hands on his shoulder, where Azdaj's flames had struck him. From his skin, dark smoke drifted, like she'd doused a brooding fire.

She rested both of her hands on his chest.

Light streamed from his chest, from between the plates of the armor, and from the Sun Devaa's star on his hand.

The light coursing from his palm shone far more brightly than it had inside Sayre Cottage, though it still seemed weak compared to Kaliyah's shine.

"What is this place?" whispered Bastian.

"You know it as the Natterjack Cave," she said. "Moor Folk call it Chrysalis."

Wind rustled the trees outside the cave's starry opening.

"He comes." Kaliyah shifted to tiny again. "I was bidden to bring you to him. Wait here until you're called."

Bastian eased among the crystals reaching from the water's boulders, following them to the cave's entrance.

He gazed after Kaliyah's tiny trail of light, weaving along a corridor of the Wystan Woods.

She vanished into a density of trees.

A boy-like figure came into view near the lagoon's western bank.

Through the mist rising from the stream dividing them, Bastian could just make out the tip of a bow reaching from a bandoleer strapped to his back. From his shoulder hung a handful of feathered arrows bundled inside a quiver.

The boy had almond-shaped eyes, their blue catching glints of stars. His fair hair was tousled, his jawline sharp, his skin bronzed. His armor was identical to Bastian's.

As the boy advanced, Moor Folk and animals slipped from the woodland's shadows, onto the open trail.

Among them were slender dryads, nimble-winged sprites, stout wood nymphs, silver-breathed foxes, bright-eyed eagles, acorn-capped elves, shimmering flower faeries, and brazen forest children.

A wildcat, blackly silver and studded with moon-gray rosettes, appeared on the western bank.

He fixed his eyes on Bastian and rumbled a gentle, entreating growl.

Bastian recognized at once that this was his call.

He stepped into the water and cautiously approached the creature who was, without a doubt, the wildcat who'd saved them at Marrowight Manor.

The wildcat turned aside and approached the boy with the arrows, now standing on the bank. He lay down at the edge of the water before the boy, making himself a statuesque bundle of paws and mighty legs, wrapped inside a thick tail.

The boy stood still in the stream's shallows.

He seemed to be carefully studying Bastian—standing thigh-deep in the middle of the stream.

"What's your name?" the boy asked, in a voice so raspy, it could've been taken for wind.

Bastian tried to speak but couldn't.

The boy advanced further into the water. "Have you lost your name?"

"Knowing the name isn't the problem," Bastian whispered. "The trouble lies in knowing truly who one is."

The boy lifted his chin, giving Bastian a sly look. "My father shall name you."

The wildcat dipped his face in the stream. Silently lapping, he kept his bright eyes on Bastian. When he lifted his head, he'd amassed a silver-water beard, the way Naga did when he drank.

"Can you tell me who you are? And"—Bastian glanced at the wildcat—"who he is?"

"I'm Aubrey Gyrfalcon. And this fellow, we call Gambol—a Sunwalker. You named him Naga."

Gambol butted his huge head against Bastian's palm. He twisted onto his back in a shallow stretch of water and pushed his great paw toward Bastian.

Bastian caught the black paw. Looking into the wildcat's deep eyes, he found the gaze of his friend.

"Kaliyah said she was bidden to bring me here," said Bastian. "Why?"

"Only my father can speak to that." Aubrey glanced over his shoulder. "And now he comes."

Gambol righted himself and shook, showering Bastian with chilly water drops.

Aubrey backed among the Moor Folk. Gambol nipped Bastian's hip and shepherded him back inside the cave.

Bastian crouched on a rock at its mouth and studied a fair brightness lighting the distant woods.

Gambol laid his heavy head in Bastian's lap as Bastian stroked his cheek, river cool.

Kaliyah, tiny, alighted beside them.

The pillar of light advanced until it shone among the gathered Moor Folk.

Aubrey Gyrfalcon's magnificent father, Lord of the Sylphic Kingdom, stood bare-chested and wide-eyed, his muscled frame a dark copper. His curling, dark-golden hair was piled into a knot atop his head. The Sun Devaa's eyes shone the same blue as Bastian's.

Bastian tried to stand, but Gambol held him back with a heavy paw.

"None may stand in his presence without his bidding," whispered Kaliyah. "Don't try."

In one hand, the Sun Devaa gripped a walking staff—the very one Bastian had found in the woodland.

He stepped to the edge of the water. "Welcome, Sun Child."

At the Sun Devaa's voice, the whole forest seemed to rustle, the world bowing a bit.

The Sun Devaa nodded toward Aubrey, prompting him to move into the deeper middle of the stream.

Aubrey reached his hand to Bastian.

Gambol nudged Bastian off the rock and into the water.

The Sun Devaa folded his arms as Aubrey guided Bastian to approach.

"Sun Child, your name is Brave," said the Sun Devaa. "Like Aubrey, you have a destiny to render." He cupped his hand around the top of the staff and breathed light onto it.

The light crystalized into a blue gemstone. The staff's glassy shaft transformed into silver.

Bastian's body warmed—all but the dead center of his chest. His skin glowed.

"Fear no longer keeps you," said the Sun Devaa.

"The dark curse that the witch placed, though," said Bastian. "The pain—it's not fully gone."

"Her darkness is fractured. You've the strength, now, to shatter it."

"How?"

"Let go of your fear, Sun Child. It holds no power over you."

Despite all that Bastian had managed with Azdaj, with the vision of the goblin, he hadn't yet managed to deal with the Witch Marrowight. The fear of her still felt strong enough to overpower him.

"I'm not sure that I can let go of my fear." Bastian met the Sun Devaa's eyes. "A witch waits."

"And to her grounds, you shall carry my light. You shall bear my strength into battle, and you shall end witches, or worlds." The Sun Devaa waved the scepter, bringing a gust of storm wind.

Rain swept down in torrents, battering the Natterjack and its Windrush's stream, hammering the cave's mouth and muddying the woodland trails.

The Moor Folk and animals scattered—feet tramping, wings beating, hooves thundering.

Bastian struggled to stay upright, but he couldn't fight the strength of the turbulent water.

Aubrey and Kaliyah pulled him out of the stream. They together fought their way to a sheltering boulder on the bank of the rainswept Windrush.

When Bastian again opened his eyes, he found himself lying on a patch of grass alongside the shore of the Windrush, his clothes warm and dry.

Above him, a brilliant night sky shone.

A Natterjack toad, staring at him eye-to-eye, croaked from the starlit bank.

Bastian startled to sitting.

Before him stood Kaliyah, Doctor Skylar, and Master Sayre—all of them gently glowing.

Bastian rubbed his wrist, no longer aching.

The sting had vanished, leaving just a small silver scar.

Moving felt strange—his arms and legs, his stomach and chest, were tight and warm.

Looking down, he found himself sheathed in a slim layer of muscle that hadn't been there before.

Wearing ordinary clothes felt unfitting—he missed his armor.

"See, you are brave," said Kaliyah, her smile brightening with her wings.

"I understand that we have a Ryudo champion," said Master Sayre.

Bastian glanced down at his palm.

"But do you have a Sun Child?"

His thousand-pointed star seemed barely to be simmering in the deepness of the night.

"In the cave, in the Windrush—was that some kind of dream?" asked Bastian. "I met Aubrey Gyrfalcon—he must've died ages ago."

"Aubrey lives," said Kaliyah.

"How is that possible?" asked Bastian. "A new Sun Child can only be born if the ones before have died, right?"

"Aubrey is like me—half-mortal," said Kaliyah. "He's the child of the Sun Devaa, and he inherited his da's immortality. Long ago, he relinquished his reign as the Sun Child to serve as Prince of the Aetherlands. He joins his da at important moments."

"The Sun Devaa—I've never seen or imagined anything like him," said Bastian. "He's so strong. Why won't he just deal with the witch?"

"Strong, the Sun Devaa certainly is," said Master Sayre. "But like the rest of the Sylphic Kingdom, he'd be just a shade without mortals. As our Sun Child, you own the responsibility—and power—over what threatens the Sylphic Kingdom."

"I understand that the Sun Child's responsibility is mine," said Bastian. "But the power of the Sun Child isn't. The Sun Devaa told me that darkness—that fear—has no power over me. But he was very wrong." Bastian showed them his dim palm. "Deeply inside, I can still feel the chill of fear."

Doctor Skylar knelt beside him. "May I?"

Bastian nodded.

He unfixed the front of Bastian's shirt. Felt of his chest.

"How much is left?" asked Master Sayre.

Doctor Skylar met Master Sayre's gaze. "It's like his heart's made of ice."

"But the Sun Devaa said the darkness is fractured," said Kaliyah. "Can ice not be broken?"

Bastian glanced at her. "The Sun Devaa said I have the power to shatter it. He told me to let go of this fear, but all that was cryptic. I certainly don't know how."

Doctor Skylar tightened his hand against Bastian's ribs. "Concentrate on any heat that you feel inside, however small."

Bastian focused on his chest, where Doctor Skylar was pressing. There was a flicker of heat beneath his hand—like a glimmer of a sunset on cold water.

"Imagine that heat flowing," said Doctor Skylar. "Down your arms and into your palms."

Bastian closed his eyes. Tried.

Concentrating on the heat, it did seem to stir.

He visualized it coursing through him, channeling into his palms.

He opened his eyes.

The thousand-pointed star on his hand brightened an instant, then sputtered. Then it went wholly dark.

"In the cave, it did light—somewhat." Bastian glanced at Kaliyah. "Did I imagine that?"

She touched his wrist—healed. "Everything you experienced was real."

"Even in that sacred place—Chrysalis, I felt the magnitude of the terror that waits." Bastian cradled his chest. "Does our hope rest on nothing?"

"My brother had visions of your power," said Doctor Skylar. "I'm certain that the victory he perceived, you shall bring to pass."

"You say that, and yet"—Bastian held up his unlit hand—"the dark book with its secret for ending the Witch Marrowight—I can't open it. Without knowing what your brother wrote there, I will fail."

"Think of all you've accomplished," said Kaliyah. "Can you not imagine going still further? Growing bold enough, brave enough, bright enough to prevail?"

"The prophesies speak of a battle," said Bastian. "A battle where I might...where everyone might..." He glanced away. "The Sun Devaa himself said that I'll either end witches or worlds."

"I, for one, know you can defeat her," said Kaliyah. "Do you not, even a little, believe you can shatter that darkness inside you?"

Bastian pushed to standing beneath the blazing stars, beautiful—but for all that, wheeling to bring the night's end.

"Not by dawn." He glanced at each of them. "But if it brings you comfort to think so—I won't speak of this further."

He crossed the starlit stream to its shadowy western bank.

"Where are you going?" called Kaliyah.

"To my brothers," said Bastian. "Hours are all we have left before the eclipse. I need to be with them."

She started to follow.

Master Sayre held her back. "Leave him. He needs time."

"But he's right," said Kaliyah. "He hasn't got any time."

3 8

———————

astian came home to find Lucas sitting in the living room, waiting up.

He still had the kelp tied around his head.

"Kaliyah said you were in for some kind of intense Ryudo challenge," signed Lucas. "How'd it go?"

"To be honest..." Bastian crashed down onto the couch beside him. "Actually, don't ask."

Lucas glanced out the window. "I watched the moon set while I waited for you. It was so bright and clear—but for all that, it was just a thin line." He met Bastian's eyes. "When the moon rises again, it'll be gone, won't it? In full shadow."

"The moon," signed Bastian, "the Sylphic Kingdom. The mortal world. Everything." He glanced at the black window, empty of the moon. "That light, disappearing—it means the beginning of the end."

Saying it out loud, Bastian found he could barely grasp the concept —his world, all worlds, destroyed.

And yet this is what would happen.

Only one final sunrise, one moonrise, remained.

"Everything won't be lost," signed Lucas. "Not if the legend plays out the way Kaliyah believes it will. She really trusts the Sun Child."

Bastian drew a deep breath and let it go. "She really does."

He rested his hand on his pocket, loosening the three stones fed with dragon fire, their burn a mild sting on his thigh.

"But who is the Sylphic Kingdom's Sun Child?" asked Lucas. "Where is that child?"

Bastian met his gaze. "I'm not sure that there is a true Sun Child."

"But—what would that mean for the battle tomorrow? A witch will be waiting."

"It means an easy win for the witch." Bastian pulled a hot stone from his pocket and watched its dragon fire flickering.

A memory flashed of the vision he'd seen in the cave—a man standing before the Witch Marrowight. Just one man. Between the man and the witch, fire had flared, exactly like what Azdaj threw.

The witch had lifted her threatening hands, and the man had answered with blue fire.

Bastian leaned forward, studying more closely the stone.

Dark England referred to dragon fire as "a witch's bane."

"The battle would be an easy win for the witch"—Bastian turned the warm stone over in his hand, its glowing ring casting pale tendrils of blue light—"unless there isn't any battle."

"What are you talking about?" signed Lucas. "Hasn't a battle been foretold?"

Bastian stood. "The battle isn't the only thing that's been foretold." He rushed toward the study, then held up and glanced back. "Tell Mum and Da I've spent the night with the Sayres."

He rushed to the passageway and pushed open the panel. He carefully replaced it behind him, then climbed the handholds by feel.

The darkness, the close air of the shaft didn't trouble him at all.

Because dragon fire—it was a witch's bane.

He pushed up onto the platform, then leapt up the rafters without giving the goblin painting as much as a glance.

Kingfisher had foreseen that defeating the Witch Marrowight involved the Sun Child casting something of great power.

Bastian, though damaged by curses of darkness, though rife with fear of the witch, was the Sun Child Kingfisher and the other Moor Folk had foreseen. And Bastian, the true Sun Child—though he was a broken light, a weak star—he carried a pocketful of dragon fire.

He'd take her on tonight.

Alone.

He climbed into the garret and hustled through its small door. He rushed to *Dark England,* lying on the Sylphic Council table.

He laid his hand on the packed center pages meant to open at the touch of the Sun Child.

They didn't budge.

"No matter," he whispered to himself, flipping to a section he could open, on wight witches—the piece that held all the insights he needed.

He reread the paragraph about "banes" of witches—

Sun-loving plants. Star-sparkling streams. Warm stones. Dragon fire. Fearlessness.

He slammed closed the book.

Maybe bravery wasn't a character trait so much as a craft. He'd desired, for so long, to be brave. Fearless. Strong. Perhaps these qualities were skills to be practiced and used, developed and exercised; not gifts that one might or might not have been born with.

He drew out the three piping dragon-fire stones and laid them on the table.

The light they cast was a roiling light, fearsome and weird—like the warm light of a brazen sunset piercing its flashes of gold through the blue of a turbulent storm. They brightly illumined the Sun Devaa's banner.

It would certainly be an act of fearlessness—nailing these warm stones, fished from a star-sparkling stream and packed with dragon fire, straight at the head of the witch.

This night, he'd defeat the Sylphic Kingdom's deadliest enemy, and not because he felt brave. In all honesty—he was terrified. He'd defeat her because he was choosing to do a brave thing.

He fed *Dark England* into his rucksack. He knelt before the trunk and hauled out the pieces of armor it held.

He stripped off his clothes, down to his boxers and pulled his legs through the undercoverings. He plated his shins, thighs, and hips with the bright silver and red guards.

A flickering flashed in the window.

An instant later—Kaliyah was standing behind him.

"What the blazes are you doing?" She glanced at *Dark England*, peeking from his rucksack. At the armor, sprawled everywhere. At Bastian, dressed to the waist for battle.

Bastian pulled a set of arm shields from the trunk. "You should be with the Sayres."

"And you should be trying to rest." Kaliyah drew nearer to him.

"Today, I faced off with a dragon," said Bastian. "Alone."

"You're not actually thinking of—"

"And today, I re-lived the night that I squared against that goblin. On my own, I kept my brother safe."

She placed herself between him and the trunk of armor. "Please tell me you're not up to what it looks like you are."

He rounded her and stood over the trunk. "But in all this, I've been fussing at the fringes. What I've not done is—on my own—faced down the witch."

"You have faced the witch on your own," said Kaliyah. "At her manor, you crept close enough to her that she caught you. Cursed you. Poisoned you. And look at how you ended up."

"How?" Bastian, staring at her, fixed an armor piece over his bicep. "Weak?"

"Think about what it's taken for you to overcome the darkness she dealt."

"I haven't overcome it." Bastian lashed tight the cords of one of the gauntlets on his forearm.

"If you're foolish enough to venture again—alone—to her grounds, you're opening yourself up to a world of hurt, and more curses."

"I'm used to dealing with curses," said Bastian, knotting the gauntlet's cord.

"And you'd be delivering victory right to her." It seemed Kaliyah was blinking back tears. "Bastian, she'll kill you. Where does that leave the rest of us—we who will stand by you in battle?"

Bastian knelt and slid on the other arm pieces. "There's not going to be any battle."

Kaliyah pulled him to standing before her. "You're our Sun Child. We need you. The Sylphic Kingdom needs you. The whole world does. I..." She glanced down. "I need you."

"Yes, everyone needs me," said Bastian. "And since this is my fight, I'm handling it my own way. I might be a Sun Child, but I'm an aberrant one. And so maybe this plays out in an aberrant way—in a way no one expects, least of all the witch."

He glanced at his rucksack, holding *Dark England*.

"Even if I can't reach the secret your da meant for me to read, he's still told me plenty."

Kaliyah stomped. "This isn't how it's supposed to go. My da tried to defeat her alone, and he's gone. With what little you know, on your own —you haven't a chance."

"Dragon fire is a witch's bane." Bastian lifted and held before her eyes a lit stone. "I have dragon fire, mingling with the Faerie Fire from your own hands. Kingfisher foresaw me casting such power."

"But he saw nothing about you doing this alone," said Kaliyah. "None of us have."

"I might have no hope of calling up the light that a Sun Child carries." Bastian fisted the stone. "But I'm hell on a pitching mound."

She took the stone from him and laid it aside. "The secret that *Dark England* keeps—I believe my da died to bring it to us. Should you not wait and see what might happen? Maybe the dawn will deliver new insights that we didn't expect. It has to, in fact, for your victory to come about—and so it certainly will."

"I once heard you say that you don't trust things to simply work out," said Bastian. "That's why you took things into your own hands, in trying to chase this darkness from inside me."

"And I failed," said Kaliyah. "But your battle—I've glimpsed. In my dreams, I've seen you facing the witch, surrounded by thousands of Moor Folk—your friends. And anyway, I might've been wrong about believing that things don't work out. I hope I was wrong. If we trust that good will prevail, it just magically might."

"Are you hearing yourself?" asked Bastian. "You want us to just stand around and wait for something magical to happen?"

"You can't blame me for it." She tossed up her hands. "For dawn's sake, I come from a magical kingdom."

"Well, I don't." He went back to the trunk of armor and knelt before it. "Where I come from, tyrants crush you unless you stand up to them. I'm ending this. Before dawn. And I'm doing it alone."

Kaliyah stared at him, her expression hardening. "You say this battle is yours alone. But battles aren't ever fought alone. Least of all this one."

Bastian pulled the last pieces of armor from the trunk.

She moved in. "That screaming you've heard—Bastian, those are the voices of Moor Folk trapped in the witch's dungeons, kidnapped to weaken your army."

Bastian threaded his arm through a shoulder plate.

"And last night, after the revelry—did you hear them?" asked Kaliyah. "Voices crying with fright."

He yanked tight the cords.

"Last night, the witch's goblins swept through the hillsides," said Kaliyah. "They took hundreds of us."

Bastian fastened on himself the other shoulder plate.

"And that brew that Gray Jay gave you to fight off the curses in the weeds the witch planted," said Kaliyah. "Where do you think he got that? It was brewed from the witch hazel piece that you took, spoken over with words he risked everything to steal, straight from the witch's book of curses."

"Gray Jay has helped me, no doubt," said Bastian. "But no cordial, no forest child could help me now."

"You aren't getting it," said Kaliyah. "It's taken his band of forest children months of tracking the witch, of spying on her, to collect all the words of that charm. Seven forest children are stone, now, so you could be clear of that curse when you fight beside me and Master Sayre and Gray Jay and the rest of the Moor Folk tomorrow. Don't you see that this conflict involves a whole kingdom?"

Bastian saw red with the thought of it—forest children turned to stone for his sake.

He adjusted the shoulder plate. He'd end the witch before the new moon crept above the horizon.

And tomorrow when the worlds woke, there'd be no battle crying, no blood. No witch. Just a bright sun and a new moon eclipsing it swiftly then streaking away, never to trouble the Sylphic Kingdom again.

"Not one more scream will I hear," said Bastian. "Not one more creature, Sylphic or mortal, will she touch. It's for a whole kingdom that I fight."

He slammed closed the trunk.

"This night, I hunt a witch."

Kaliyah snagged his arm and held him closely before her. She rested her hands on his chest, letting them find their bright imprints, laid there to heal him.

"I'm part of this," she said. "Why are you refusing my help?"

Her silver eyes, staring into his, carried the beauty of ten thousand starry nights.

They provoked an impulse to pitch a scalding mortar at the dead core of a target; to square with a dragon; to mount his bike and dash through the dark Wystan Woods to a witch's lair.

"I don't want you to help me." He slipped his hands around the back of her warm neck, into her silken hair.

Tears filled Kaliyah's eyes as they flickered between staring into his own and gazing at his lips.

He gently pulled her close. Kissed her forehead.

"I want you to live."

She jerked away from him. "Bull nettles." She rifled through Bastian's clothes and pulled out the cuirass Mrs. Sayre had made. "You must wear this." She tugged it over his head and set to fastening the buckles around his ribs.

Bastian touched the pearl ring resting against her throat—the ring passed down to her from Alura. "That she took your mum—I ache." Kaliyah's mum—the first victim of the witch. "I swear to you, she'll pay."

Kaliyah unfixed the ring's leather cord from around her neck. "This pearl was collected by the last Sun Child from the Sylphic Blue Countries. If you must have this fight, then bear into it Kingfisher's gift to my mum." She tied it around Bastian's neck. "And may it be some protection."

Bastian lifted the final piece of armor and buckled it over his chest. He shouldered his rucksack, bearing *Dark England*, loaded his pockets with the three piping stones, and slipped down the passageway.

39

*B*astian mounted his bike and charged down the lane leading to Marrowight Manor.

Dark England, in his rucksack, seemed heavier than all the armor plates fastened to his body combined. But it felt like a greater armor. Though he couldn't sense the book's enchantments, he pictured himself riding inside its bubble of light—the protection Kaliyah had described. He pictured it as a force that could deflect spears and arrows, impenetrable to goblin blades.

In the northern sky, an eerie glow hung. It was as though all around Marrowight Manor, a fire was blazing.

As he neared, the smoke thickened. Ash and cinders drifted in the hot wind. He kept a close lookout for anything Sylphic—any Elemental Spirit that might be on watch and could catch him; or any Moor Folk who might try to stop him.

The whole Wystan Woods, though, seemed silent and empty; tense —as though everyone normally here were distracted this night, preparing for the onset of the long-dreaded war.

He cut to the woods and rode until the thicket offered no more trails wide enough for a bike.

He abandoned his bike in the last clearing before the manor's brambly outskirts and advanced on in a run.

He made for the oak he and Lucas had climbed.

When he reached it he surveyed the woodland and found it still empty.

He scaled the oak's branches to their highest point, from where he could see the witch's whole vale.

The edges of her grounds were smoldering, the perimeter bushes and spruces on fire. It seemed she was clearing the battlefield of these plants—sun-loving.

The interior of the vale stretched vast and empty, but for the goblin shrine. All the stone sprites, all the statues of dryads were set in long rows edging her grounds—petrified monuments to her power.

Though the whole vale felt thick with threat, with heat, with smoking curses—there were no goblins, nor any other Elemental Spirits in sight.

Bastian drew the three stones, piping hot, from his pocket. The thought of striking anyone, even the Witch Marrowight, with a stone dense with dragon fire seemed horrid. In battles he'd read about, the stronger army customarily offered a defeated enemy a chance to surrender.

He clutched the stones, their scalding heat, their lightning blue glow betraying their colossal power. Perhaps he should offer the witch an opportunity to back down.

She'd know at a glance, surely, that these stones held dragon fire. She truly might back off.

And if she didn't, then, with this witch's bane—a flame she'd have no hope of extinguishing—he'd set the whole vale, the whole manor on fire.

One by one, he loaded the stones back into his pocket.

The first stone would be for the manor, to draw out the canker it concealed. The second, for any interference that might divide him from his target. And the third—if it came to it—for a witch's head.

He climbed down the oak and ran to the iron gate. He scaled it and landed silently on its other side.

He peered between two rowan berry bushes and studied the vale.

It still looked vacant.

He raced into it, past the traps, past the witch hazel, ragged by the manor's back porch. He skidded to a stop at the dead center of the vale.

He cocked his arm way back and cast a stone straight at a window on the manor's first floor.

The stone flew true and smashed in.

Dragon fire—plumes of gold and silver and blue—burst from the window and blew out every pane on the ground floor.

The iron doors blasted open, and out came the Witch Marrowight, blue fire and black smoke billowing behind her.

She didn't seem troubled by the incineration. She seemed hardly even to notice it.

"Come to give yourself up, have you, Sun Child?" called the witch, over the roaring flames.

Bastian raised the second stone.

"Are you enough of a fool to think you can actually touch me?" She stopped halfway between the flaming manor and him. "There's not an ounce of strength left in that cold heart I gave you."

"I've come to finish this," Bastian shouted.

"Alone?" She scoffed. "Maybe your deaf brother isn't the stupid one."

Bastian gripped his stone. "You see—I have fire from a dragon. It's you who'll give up if you don't want to burn."

She buckled in laughter.

"Back down." Bastian couldn't help the tremor that came into his voice. "And I won't hurt you."

She grinned broadly. "Our battle, Sun Child, is ordained to take place after daybreak, when the new moon is high. Shall we not have it?"

"Our battle is now." He stepped nearer to her. "Unless—you surrender."

"Well, I'm no great upholder of tradition." She, too, eased in. "If you prefer, I could put you in chains where you stand. Like a little beast slated for slaughter, you'll be. A fine ornament for your pitiful Moor Folk friends who in anguish will look upon you, come dawn and despair."

"You can't come near me," shouted Bastian. "I'm protected."

"By what? Sylphic charms?" The bemused smile left her. "Child's play."

She looked to the northern edge of her vale.

From the shadows, where she was watching, two glowing, red eyes manifested.

"Bind him," said the witch.

The shadows amassed into the muscled form of a goblin.

This goblin was huge—not as big as how Kek, the Goblin King, was described—but far stronger-looking, far more deadly, than any Bastian had yet encountered.

The goblin drew a jagged black blade.

Bastian staggered. "Call him off, or...or I'll finish him first."

The witch's eyes lit with pleasure.

The goblin strode nearer.

Bastian launched the stone straight at its thick body.

It flashed blue on the goblin's muscled stomach, then vanished.

A shiver of shock ran through Bastian. It was like the goblin's darkness had swallowed the stone, the strength of its dragon fire immediately quenched by what seemed an older, deeper, more formidable power.

"I'm protected..." Bastian stumbled a step back.

The goblin stopped straight in front of him, its red eyes glowering down.

"Sylphic armor," murmured Bastian. "Sea charms from Sylphic blue countries. Bubbles of light."

The goblin clutched him by the throat. It raised him until they were eye-to-eye.

Bastian clawed at the goblin's hand, but it wouldn't loosen.

He kicked frantically but touched nothing. He couldn't breathe, couldn't fight.

He couldn't reach the last stone in his pocket.

"Take care not to kill it just yet," said the witch.

The goblin glanced at her but didn't heed the command. It was like he was craving to finish the job—the murder that Bastian had thus far evaded.

He gripped Bastian's throat tighter.

A blast of fire erupted beside the witch.

She dodged a flaming arrow impaling the ground at her feet.

A fiery arrow lodged in the goblin's neck.

He dropped Bastian.

Bastian, choking coughs, scattered back.

A rain of arrows littered the grass around the witch—a rain so thick, arrow shafts snagged her skirt and kept her pinned where she stood.

The goblin swatted at arrows flying—arrows driving him back toward the witch.

The witch struggled to break free of the web of fletching but she seemed hardly able to take a single step.

Bastian checked around the edges of the vale but could see no source of the onslaught of arrows. Nothing at all moved in the darkness of the forest, in the haze of the smoke.

Until—near the manor, Bastian sighted four figures slipping out from among the trees.

They had to be forest children, judging by their silhouettes—high bows on their backs; quivers stocked with feathery arrows.

They crept inside the manor's open back door, the dragon fire there less, but still licking the walls.

The arrows flew on, and the witch kept on zapping them into ash, but she was hardly keeping up.

Bastian pushed to his feet. Drew out his final stone.

He studied the position of the witch. The witch who desired the end of the world; the witch who'd murdered Kingfisher and cast Alura to the Aetherlands, orphaning Kaliyah; the witch whose goblin had drawn blood from Lucas; the witch who'd turned thousands of Moor Folk to stone; who'd planted a curse of darkness in his very heart, arresting his courage and rendering him impotent as a Sun Child.

Raging heat churned deeply inside him.

A feeling like fire billowing rose in his chest and flashed down his arms.

The stone in his hand sputtered and sparked, then erupted like a burning sun.

Bastian aimed, mightily cocking his arm. He whipped the stone at the witch.

Her hand, quick as lightning, reached.

She caught the stone right in front of her face.

Her dark laughter sounded as she swung the flaming stone in an arc, conjuring a sphere of fire around her.

The arrows reaching her now skidded right off those flames, the dragon fire swelling into what seemed like a shield.

Bastian, stumbling, guarded his face from the firestorm.

A hot burst ignited the air, and he felt his body lifted and thrown back.

He opened his eyes to find himself lying on the grass, licks of fire flashing around him. He couldn't tell up from down and could hardly move.

It seemed he was lying inside a halo of blissful sunlight.

"*Dark England*," he whispered. "Its bubble of light—I see it."

Suddenly standing over him were Master Sayre and Doctor Skylar.

"That's no book's charm." Master Sayre sat Bastian up.

He was right.

This light was coming from no book, no stone.

It was shining through Bastian's armor plates, straight from his skin.

"It's happened!" Bastian lifted his palm—his thousand-pointed star there flickering so brightly, he couldn't look straight at it. "I can finish her." He met Master Sayre's eyes. "What do I do?"

Master Sayre and Doctor Skylar took him by an arm each and hauled him back.

"No." Bastian tried to twist away from them. "Let go, you must let me. This is my fight—I must face her."

"You have, and you've made beautiful work of it," said Master Sayre.

"She still stands." Bastian fought them. "Let me finish her."

"You've run out of dragon fire, thank the dawn," said Doctor Skylar. "Stay close to me and brace yourself."

"There must be stones on the vale." Bastian frantically searched. "A plain stone to the face would do damage to even a witch."

"We've brought something a good deal better than stones," said Master Sayre.

Doctor Skylar whistled beautifully.

Azdaj streaked in from above.

The Witch Marrowight raised her arms and cast a streak of lightning at the dragon.

Azdaj slithered around the strike.

At its burst, the sky shifted to red, as though it had ignited the clouds.

Bastian spotted something moving inside the iron doors of the witch's manor.

It was the forest children.

Their four shadows crept down the manor's smoldering porch and slipped along its edge toward the northern forest.

"Hold steady," called Master Sayre.

Azdaj unloaded a stream of fire on the witch.

The witch seemed to struggle a moment in the burn, but when Azdaj let up, she rose tall.

She churned what had lit the ground into a great globe around her —a wheel of dragon fire streaked with blue and with silver and gold, like a sphere of blown glass.

She flared her hands.

Dragon fire arced into the sky.

"No." Doctor Skylar pulled Bastian behind him.

Fire streamed everywhere.

Master Sayre and Doctor Skylar, covering their heads, crouched over Bastian.

And then Bastian found himself suddenly washed by cool air.

The knit cuirass wrapping him seemed to be conjuring wind, keeping the flames at bay.

He glanced up to see Azdaj levitating in the sky, just above the witch.

It seemed she was keeping him in a helpless hover by his own fire, spat back.

"How do you like that, traitor?" she screamed.

A fresh rain of arrows struck the vale around her, and she let go of the fire.

The patches of grass that were burning blew out at the touch of the arrows.

Azdaj tore away from her and flew straight at Bastian.

Doctor Skylar yanked Bastian to his feet. "Hold your stance."

Bastian watched Azdaj come, smoke leaching from his mouth, a rage of blue fire streaming in his wake.

Azdaj sank his talons into Bastian's chest plate, and in a blink, he was soaring into the clear night air, flying east into a country of starlight.

Master Sayre and Doctor Skylar, from far below, kept their eyes trained on him as he and Azdaj soared higher.

Master Sayre and Doctor Skylar—still standing on the vale with the witch...

"Azdaj," called Bastian.

The dragon looked down at him.

"Go back. We have to go back for them."

Azdaj just arced into a faster flight.

He slithered high over the night woods, leaving the smoking vale far behind and coasting into the clear freshness crowning Sayre Cottage.

The dragon dipped low and dropped Bastian in the center of the Sayres' garden. Then he again took flight, striding high, cutting the shape of a dragon out of the starry night sky and streaking from time to time in a blast of blue flames.

Kaliyah burst out of Sayre Cottage and raced to Bastian.

40

*B*astian lay on his back, on the cool grass of the Sayres' garden. A bright heat was flashing over him, but not in a dragon-fire sickening way.

It felt nourishing. Morning sunlight.

He felt Kaliyah kneel beside him and take hold of his shoulders.

"Are you hurt?" asked Kaliyah.

He tightened his fists. The warm heat—the great brightness, scrolled inward until it was surging just in his chest, leaving his body night cool.

"Thank the dawn, you're safe," said Kaliyah.

And that he was.

Safe, and at peace.

For here he was with Kaliyah, in the Sayres' lovely cottage garden, while the forest children he'd seen, and Master Sayre, and Doctor Skylar, were still trapped on the witch's flaming vale.

"Dragon fire—the book called it 'a witch's bane.'" Bastian shrugged off his rucksack without meeting Kaliyah's eyes. "I thought I'd found a way to defeat her. But the dragon fire—it didn't touch her. She even took control of it and threw it back at us."

"A cunning witch she is," said Kaliyah, yanking at the ties on Bastian's shoulder plates. "To wield dragon fire—I've never heard of any Elemental Spirit trying to pull off something like that." She eased Bastian's armor off his body, piece by piece.

Bastian stopped her before she pulled off the undercoverings. Beneath those, he was wearing only boxers.

"Take them off yourself, if you'd rather," she said, "but I must have a look at you."

The rising sun hanging just beneath the horizon was casting a red glow against the brightening east. In that weak light, Kaliyah looked pale.

In mere hours, the risen sun would meet the dark moon—a shadow come to wage a battle of its own on the grounds of a darkening sky. Perhaps Kaliyah—never fearful—was now afraid of what the eclipsed sun might mean.

Bastian slowly pulled out of the undercoverings.

The shame of wearing just boxers in front of Kaliyah was nothing to the shame of having crossed her warnings only to have miserably failed.

She looked him over roughly, like she wanted to keep some distance from him. "There are no burns, no serious cuts or bruises on you."

She drew *Dark England* from his rucksack and handed it to him. She set to work, loading the armor pieces inside the rucksack.

"You're angry with me."

Bastian lowered his gaze.

"I was so stupid."

"You weren't." She glanced at him. "Well—you were. But some good may come of it."

"You would think that," said Bastian. "You, who are prone to believe so implicitly in me. When it came to it, though, you doubted me."

She kept at her work, neatly situating the armor pieces to fit in his rucksack.

"Even though you were justified," said Bastian, "I can't believe you told Master Sayre and Doctor Skylar where I was going. I meant to fight the witch alone. Did you not get that? Now, who knows what's happened to them? They might be—"

"I didn't tell them." Kaliyah finally met his eyes. "The forest children saw you leaving your chalet. They said, from the look on your face, from the dragon fire fumes pouring out of your pocket, it was very clear what you were meaning to do. Rather than stop you, though, they drew up a plan to use your assault as a distraction to get into the witch's manor."

Bastian's mind flashed with the memory of the dragon fire sweeping over the vale, overpowering everyone.

"That curse she's been stewing for the battle," said Kaliyah, "they know she's been preparing it in her kitchen. They've tried to get in, several times, but they've found no way. And so they've had no chance to discover what she's planning—until tonight."

"They shouldn't have followed me—those forest children. Master Sayre. Doctor Skylar."

Kaliyah gently guided him to his feet and shouldered his rucksack. She wrapped her arm around his waist and led him down the stone pathway to the door of Sayre Cottage.

Inside, Mrs. Sayre was kneeling before the hearth, throwing sparkling sand onto its blaze.

Bastian placed *Dark England* on the kitchen table.

Kaliyah abandoned his rucksack beside it. "Is there news?"

Mrs. Sayre peered at the blaze. "Azdaj lifted Master Sayre and Doctor Skylar from the vale. Whether they were injured in the fire, I don't know. The forest children, I can't see."

"The witch's battle plan, the curse she's been stewing—do you think they found it?" asked Kaliyah.

Mrs. Sayre studied the hearth. "There's been too much dark smoke about. I wasn't able to see their faces clearly or determine if they were carrying anything."

"And how about the Witch Marrowight?" asked Bastian. "Did they kill her?"

Mrs. Sayre, watching him, stood. "Kaliyah tells me you feel this fight belongs to you."

She brought him a clean change of clothes—those he'd worn when he'd arrived at Sayre Cottage, hornet-stung and soaked to the bone.

Bastian took them and eased them on.

"And the crux of this fight is indeed yours, Sun Child," said Mrs. Sayre. "None have the power that you wield. Any other attempt to end the witch would finish with the death of the poor champion."

A pounding struck the door.

Kaliyah rushed to it and opened it.

Outside, there stood a forest child—bruised and scraped, breathing like he'd just sprinted a mile.

It was the forest child who'd come to Bastian in the night, following the reveling—Gray Jay.

Leaves were tangled into his hair, and his chest and arms were streaked with mud. His ragged trousers were torn, their edges singed. Blood smeared him from cuts on his arms and legs. One of his shins was badly gashed.

A bandoleer stretched across his chest, holding a bow buckled high on his back. An empty arrow quiver dangled from his hand.

Kaliyah pulled him in. "Where are the others?"

Gray Jay, seeming to be in some shock, just stood at the threshold.

Mrs. Sayre hurried to the window at the back of the cottage. She snipped a honeysuckle cutling from a vine growing up the pane and dropped it into a boiling teakettle. Kaliyah scurried to a cabinet and raced back with a pot. She knelt before Gray Jay.

From inside the pot shone autumn's maple leaves—orange and red and golden. They looked succulent—just fallen.

She selected a red one and pressed it to his worst wound, on his shin. She cleared blood off his leg with a yellow one. When she pulled the leaves away, Gray Jay's leg was clean, his cuts scabbed.

Bastian moved a stack of Mrs. Sayre's quilts off the couch. Kaliyah pulled Gray Jay toward it.

He resisted. "Someone else needs tending more."

He whistled out the door.

Two more forest children, as tattered as Gray Jay, slipped from beneath the low branches of an oak, at the edge of the Sayres' garden. They, too, wore bows and quivers, slung on bandoleers.

Atop their shoulders, they carried the body of a fourth forest child who appeared to be sleeping.

Or—dead?

Bastian, staring at them, slipped to the door's threshold.

"These are the Wystan Boys," said Kaliyah, standing closely beside him. "They're the bravest children of the forest. Gray Jay leads them."

The forest child on the right—the shorter of the two—was stocky, with sandy-blonde hair, bleached like he spent every day on a beach.

The other one—muscular and thin—seemed familiar. A steep cowlick of dark hair projected from his forehead. The bridge of his nose was shallow, its tip small. He looked sinewy and quick, and his skin was a deep bronze. His almond eyes shone hazel.

Kaliyah pointed to the shorter, blonde forest child. "That's Lox, and that's—"

A flock of birds erupted from the oak.

Gray Jay pulled Bastian and Kaliyah away from the threshold and behind him.

The two forest children held steady beneath the oak. They turned away, studying the woodland behind them.

Small nubs were visible beneath their shoulder blades—stowed wings.

"That's Kosa they're carrying." Kaliyah moved to run to them.

"Easy, love." Gray Jay caught her. "They can manage him."

Gray Jay glanced around the cottage. When his gaze fell on *Dark England*, resting on the table alongside Bastian's rucksack, he seemed to relax some.

Bastian and Kaliyah moved out of the way as the Wystan Boys rushed Kosa in.

Kosa's breathing was coming in shaking fits.

His legs, bare beneath the knees of his trousers, were ripe with bruises, and bloody scrapes stained his arms. A gruesome swatch of burned skin marred his chest and shoulder.

His face was waxy, and gray rings circled his eyes, like he was wrestling through a dangerous fever and losing.

Kaliyah quickly looked him over, examining for an instant each injury.

From beneath the couch, she pulled a bag and unzipped it.

A tumble of butterflies fluttered out.

She caught them and settled them, one by one, on the burn crossing Kosa's chest. The butterflies uncurled their spindles and tapped Kosa's skin.

Kaliyah rummaged inside the bag, pulling out pinecones and acorns, conifer needles, oak leaves, and dried flowers. She unwound a length of kelp.

Mrs. Sayre set a basin on the floor and poured water from a pitcher over the kelp as Kaliyah held it, until it was malleable. They laid it across Kosa's forehead.

In a flurry of hot wind, the cottage door flew open. Master Sayre and Doctor Skylar burst through and slammed it behind them.

Mrs. Sayre rushed to them. "Bless the dawn—are you hurt?"

"No," said Master Sayre, "thanks to these lads, and Azdaj."

A shadow washed the windows—Azdaj, taking flight.

Bastian silently moved away from the commotion and stood in the shadow of a bookcase.

No thanks would be offered to him.

He'd meant to end this conflict by dawn, and here was the dawn brightening the cottage—the last dawn. He'd meant to do a courageous thing, but he'd managed just to be reckless. The witch yet lived, and a forest child lay horribly injured by the dragon fire Bastian had given her.

This was his fault.

The teakettle whistled. Mrs. Sayre poured from it a chalice full of the honeysuckle cordial.

She hurried it to Kaliyah.

Kaliyah pulled three river stones from her bag. She whispered over them, then dropped them in. She stirred them with a birch twig, then spooned a bit into Kosa's mouth.

Using the cordial, she carefully bathed his burns, the butterflies floating up and out of her way, then lighting back down.

Kaliyah whispered a soft song to Kosa in words Bastian could barely make out—

Light to summon waters flowing;
  light to still the night wind's blowing;
  light to break the husks of old stones;
  light to shaft through sleeping cold bones.

Sleeper, wake to see the sunrise.
  Stir to hear the starling's dawn cries.
  Sleeper, rend the bonds of yarrow;
  wake to raise your feathered arrow.

Kaliyah laid her palms—softly glowing—on Kosa's cheeks, sending ribbons of light wavering across his skin.

With her fingertips alight, she touched the bleeding scrapes on his face, his arms, his shins.

His cuts dried.

His bruises shrank like evaporating water puddles.

Kaliyah inched her glowing fingers along the edge of the burn on Kosa's chest.

Just ahead of her bright fingertips, his skin knit, finishing to the same acorn brown as the rest of him, only lightly bruised.

Color washed into Kosa's face, and soon he was breathing evenly.

Master Sayre released a heavy breath. "After Azdaj took us, what happened?"

"We'd just finished scouting the manor when she spotted us," said Gray Jay.

"She bridled that dragon flame," said Lox, "and a lick hit Kosa square."

He set his fingers against Kosa's cheek.

"One minute, he was at my elbow. The next, he was tumbling along the ground, screaming. Gray Jay managed to pull him out of the fire, and thank the dawn. A blink longer, and he would've been stone!"

"Did you discover the curse she's concocted?" asked Doctor Skylar.

Gray Jay turned his gaze onto Bastian. "Ay."

Mrs. Sayre unfolded a blue and ivory quilt, made soft by feathers stitched into the batting.

She tucked it snuggly around Kosa.

She poured the last of the honeysuckle cordial into three chalices and handed one to each of the other Wystan Boys.

Bastian found that he couldn't draw his gaze off the tallest forest child.

He studied the forest child's hazel eyes until, finally, recognition dawned.

This was the boy who'd carried him to Sayre Cottage, after he'd been stung.

And this was the boy he'd seen standing alongside Kingfisher Chalet, the day he bought *Moor Folk of the English Highlands*.

This boy, he'd seen by the campfire during the revelry.

But not only that.

Bastian steadied himself against the bookcase.

For this boy's face, he'd known all his life.

This forest child was the boy who'd cared for Bastian when he was tiny.

It was this forest child who'd taught him to pitch, to love baseball.

Bastian slipped out of the bookcase's shadow.

Gray Jay, still watching him, lifted his chalice and waited for his Wystan Boys to follow. "To the Sun Child."

The Wystan Boys raised their cups to Bastian, then quaffed their brew.

Bastian took a timorous step forward. "Dom?"

The tall forest child with the hazel eyes smiled. "Hello, Sun Child." He opened his arms.

Bastian rushed to him.

He threw his arms around the forest child.

"Would you look at that." Dom patted his back. "The Sun Child carries memories of me."

"I could never forget you," said Bastian. "In our chalet, we've got pictures of you hanging up."

"Do you, now?" Dom blushed a bit.

"Did you know, back when you used to take care of me, that I was the Sun Child?"

Dom guided him to sit at the dining room table. "After Kingfisher disappeared, we Wystan Boys were charged to watch for the next Sun Child." He sat beside Bastian. "Faeries predicted that the child would be a boy, and that he'd be born in Exeter the April that you came. We sun dowsed every newborn in the boroughs. Finally, I found you—deathly sick. Some of the Moor Folk feared that you'd perish. That we'd have to wait for another Sun Child. But I knew you'd live. And when you did, since it was me who found you, I got to keep you."

"Keep me?"

Dom leaned back. "Ay, I was the Sun Child's Keeper. I was charged to look after you."

He accepted more honeysuckle cordial from Mrs. Sayre.

"You and I would play until the stars were out. Me and the Boys used to set you aglow and put you in the middle of our camp, in the place of a fire. I'd whisper you stories of valor beneath Exeter's twilight, then lay you down beneath your pygmyweed cutlings."

Dom sipped his cordial.

"Many a gooseberry fae you called forth."

Bastian absently accepted a chalice of cordial from Mrs. Sayre.

"You were a good dreamer from the start," said Dom, "and took to my teaching like a froglet to the Windrush."

"Did you live in Exeter?" Bastian asked Dom. "*Do* Moor Folk live in Exeter? And what about when we moved to San Francisco? I remember you visiting there, too."

Gray Jay chuckled. "Forest children have wings, Sun Child. We can shoot off when the sun touches the Earth, and fly to Egypt and back before its crown dips beneath the Celtic Sea."

"It's been so long since we were together," said Bastian. "I wish you'd been around."

Lox, giggling, stood.

"Dom's been around."

He sidled toward a trunk in the corner and opened it.

"You've seen him quite recently, in fact."

"Oh?" Bastian turned.

Dom joined Lox by the trunk.

Together, sniggering, they dug into it.

Dom turned and leapt into a slant of light.

He wore a frizzled wig, thick glasses, and a set of snaggled teeth.

On Dom's bandoleer, Lox had pinned a name badge—upside down.

Bastian startled, spilling his cup. "Esmerelda?"

Dom bowed. "Esmerelda, at your service, Sun Child."

Bastian staggered to standing, spilling Dom's cup, too. "It was you who sold me *Moor Folk of the English Highlands?*"

"It was our honor to see the book into your hands after we won it back from the witch," said Gray Jay. "She stole it, following Kingfisher's death. It was one of many prized things she took."

Lox tossed a small sack to Bastian. "There's your birthday money back."

Bastian didn't even try to catch it.

"Were you there, in the bookshop, too?" he asked Lox. "Kosa? Gray Jay?"

"We were in the storeroom," said Lox. "Keeping the shopkeeper charmed."

"And I've seen you before," said Bastian. "All of you. During the revelry—by a bonfire in the woods."

Dom took off the pieces of his costume and set them aside. "There hasn't been a day when you weren't under my protection. We've done our best, keeping the witch at bay. Though—there've been times when we failed you."

"You couldn't fail me," said Bastian. "Not ever."

"All I've wanted was to protect you," said Dom. "Watching you dare the witch's grounds this night was the hardest thing I've yet had to do."

"I really thought I could handle her." Bastian lowered his gaze. "I see, now, how foolish I was."

"That was no foolishness," said Dom. "It was bravery. And destiny."

"It was the onset of the prophecy," said Gray Jay. "The prophesy that will be fulfilled when you stand on the battlefield this day and fight —our Sun Child. The night's confrontation was the dawning of your reign."

"And may your reign be a long one!" Lox raised his chalice, then knotted his brow, as though in some doubt.

"In crossing onto the witch's grounds this night," said Dom, "you broke a curse that's kept us far from her manor and long in the dark."

A cry rose from the couch—Kosa, waking, seemed troubled by pain.

Kaliyah soothed Kosa's forehead and whispered again to him.

"That he was so badly hurt," said Bastian. "That's my fault. I meant to deal with the witch on my own."

"Kosa's sacrifice was his choice." Gray Jay approached Bastian. "And it wasn't for nothing."

Dom took a skin flask off his belt. He sipped from it, then poured a draught into Bastian's cup.

"Before today, we could only discover bits and pieces of what the Witch Marrowight was up to," said Gray Jay, "only hints of what sort of foul curse she might be planning to brew for the battle. Now, though, we know her full strategy."

Bastian sniffed the liquid in his cup—elderflower cordial.

"Drink that, lad," said Dom. "You're going to need a kick."

Bastian swallowed some.

It gave him the buzz of strong coffee, but he didn't feel scattered, like when he sipped from Da's espresso cup.

He felt focused and sharp.

"In Exeter, at your birth, the witch tried to kill you but failed," said Gray Jay. "We've imagined, all this time, in all her attacks, that she wanted to simply finish what she started. But now we know the truth— that she wants you alive."

"Has she not sworn to kill the next Sun Child, though?" asked Bastian. "Wouldn't my death solve everything for her?"

"Your death alone, no," said Gray Jay. "The witch has indeed been mastering a new curse—one most dreadful. And today, in the dark before dawn, through the diversion you so boldly crafted, we discovered it."

"So, she means to curse me, but not kill me?" asked Bastian.

"Oh, this curse would kill you," said Gray Jay. "But it would go beyond merely killing you. It would drain the Sun Devaa of his power and transfer it to her."

"During the battle," said Dom, "the witch aims to brew the curse right in the center of her vale."

He emptied the cordial into Bastian's cup, then capped his flask. "To do it..."

Dom waited for Bastian to swallow all of the cordial.

"...she needs the heart of a Sun Child. Fresh and beating."

41

Bastian dropped against the back of his chair. Since he'd discovered the truth of who he was, he'd imagined he was doomed to fail. But he'd never considered what failure precisely would look like.

The idea of falling into the witch's hands, of being mutilated, of enduring such incomprehensible pain, of dying in front of everyone who needed him to live—it brought shadows into his vision.

But the horror of the witch's plan, of his own death, didn't stop there. The Witch Marrowight would use his death to rock the foundation of the Sylphic Kingdom itself.

By it, she'd rob the Sun Devaa of his power and break the balance that all worlds—Sylphic and mortal—depended upon to survive.

Dom rested his hand on Bastian's shoulder. "We're with you."

In Dom's eyes, Bastian saw a tender care he'd known from his earliest memories.

Dom was with him.

As were the other Wystan Boys. And the Sayres, Kaliyah, and Doctor Skylar would all stay by his side. Along with many other Moor Folk—those hundreds upon hundreds he'd seen at the revelry, and more still—the Sylphic Folk Master Sayre had rallied from the coast.

In the battle today, they would certainly follow him as far as he had to go.

Their sacrifices, though, would not be rewarded.

Unless Bastian managed to find a way to defeat the Witch Marrowight, those who died today on her vale would be like the first tumbling stones that broadcast a landslide; the onset of a pitch night that never would break into dawn.

Kaliyah, now, though—even after seeing Bastian fail, even after seeing Kosa burned and cursed—no longer did she look pale or afraid.

And it seemed that her father, Malachi Daoine Kingfisher, had been equally fearless in this war. He, even at the moment of his death, was said to have remained certain that the Witch Marrowight would fall on the Day of the Dark Sun.

Bastian pulled near *Dark England: The Beauty and Terror of Elemental Spirits of the Isles.*

"If the witch has a plan, so must we."

Dom flipped through the book until he reached the page showing the Goblin King.

"That's who'll first defend her."

Bastian cracked his neck, stiff from the goblin lifting him. "Goblins, I've dealt with."

A doubtful expression crossed Lox's face, like he perceived a great distance dividing the goblins Bastian had dealt with and the Goblin King.

Gray Jay turned pages to another illustration showing a huge, decrepit stallion.

"She also keeps a Kelpie."

The Kelpie's head was skeletal, its eye holes flaming, its ragged mane and tail hanging corpse-gray, its rotten skin a sickly green. It seemed a frightful nightmare, long dead, summoned back to range the lightless moors.

"The Witch Marrowight. The Goblin King. A kelpie," said Bastian, his voice hitching. "Okay."

"Many others want to see her rise," said Gray Jay. "The tribes of swamp hags, tangies, spriggans, trolls, sloughs, and minor goblins, to name a few."

"And they'll have weapons," said Lox.

He lifted a fire-stoking stick from the hearth and brandished it like a sword.

"The Goblin King wields the Lightfighter. A blade of darkness, forged of ore and shadows sapped from caves beneath mountains, never touched by the sun."

"What weapon does the Kelpie use?" asked Bastian.

Lox paused his feigned assault and lowered the stick. "The Kelpie is a weapon. The oldest myths name him *Bonecrusher*. His rage and ragged hooves are legendary."

Bastian lowered his gaze.

"You're not alone in this fight," said Gray Jay. "We'll do all we can to protect you."

"How?" Bastian asked.

Dom pulled a handful of slender, polished twigs from his quiver.

They looked finely crafted, as though Dom had worked their smooth shafts to lustrous, making them perfect for flight. Each was tipped with a dark-metal arrowhead, sharpened to gleaming. White and gray feather fletching plumed their polished shafts.

Bastian took one, his heart sinking. "Is this all you've got?"

"We'll keep you well clear of Elemental Spirits," said Dom, "so you can face the witch."

Bastian touched the biting tip of the arrow. He drew away his finger, a dark drop of blood on it.

"What if I get hit with one of these?"

Dom flashed his brow. "Forest children are practically born with bows and arrows in our hands." He nodded at Lox.

Lox lifted his bow off his back. He drew an arrow and aimed it at the front open window.

Before Bastian could blink, the air thwished, leaving the bow singing and the Wystan Boys hollering and racing out the door.

Bastian sprinted out after them and looked to where Dom was pointing.

Lox had threaded his arrow through the missing eyelet of an oak and into a swollen tree scar, shaped like a heart.

Bastian pulled the arrow down from the tree.

Not a feather was ruffled.

He laid the arrow in Dom's waiting palm. His cheeks and hands felt bloodless.

Dom loaded the arrow back into Lox's quiver. "Not to worry, Sun Child. We'll have our eyes on you."

"So, your whole plan is to help me get close to the witch?" asked Bastian.

"That's right," said Lox, "so you can do her in." He double punched the air.

"Do her in." Bastian stumbled to sitting on a log. "Even if I had any idea of how I might bring her down, I'm not sure if I could. Last night, though I faced her, I couldn't even conceptualize actually killing her. It was out of desperation, not decision, that I cast that last stone."

"You certainly can't kill her," said Master Sayre. "Elemental Spirits, like Moor Folk, are immortal. Your task, Sun Child, is to end her tyranny—to bind her and deliver her to the Sun Devaa for justice."

Bastian glanced at his palm, shining.

Kaliyah, holding *Dark England*, stepped from among the Wystan Boys. She laid the book on the grass before Bastian.

Dom glanced at the book's blue jewel. "Lay your light on that stone, Sun Child. The darkness inside you, you've chased. May you now learn the secret that Kingfisher kept for you."

Bastian flexed his hand. He concentrated until he felt a keen warmth rising in his chest.

He channeled it into his hand and rested his palm, radiant, against the blue stone.

White smoke drifted from the book, and then came a burst of wind that staggered them together back.

The pages flew open, cutting right into those that'd been sealed.

At the dead center of the book, the pages stilled.

Bastian eased close to it.

He discovered the pages before him wordless and bracketed by the curling bodies of painted dragons.

Doctor Skylar, Kaliyah, the Sayres, and the Wystan Boys knelt around him.

Bastian watched his palm as the star quivering there brightened. He rested it on the blank page.

There, words appeared, like a galleon ship manifesting from mist.

He glanced at the others.

They all seemed, still, to be watching the book closely, waiting for something to happen.

"There's writing here," said Bastian. "Are you not seeing this?"

Dom shook his head. "Those words are meant for you, Sun Child. What you do with them is your choice. Speak them aloud if you wish. Or keep them in silence."

Bastian read aloud what he saw—

"The Witch Marrowight, thinking herself clever, ordained the Day of the Dark Sun as the day of her foretold battle, for the powers of Moor Folk wane without sun.

But may her day deliver her doom.

My daughter, child of an Angel Fire Faerie, gifted with sun blood passed to her from my line—she bears the rare talent of conjuring Faerie Fire, an art almost lost in these twilight days.

In the hands of a Sun Child, Faerie Fire can bind what is Sylphic in stone."

"That's how you'll imprison her." Kaliyah leapt to her feet. "We knew my da learned you'd throw something at her—something of great power. This is it! Together, Bastian—we can do this."

Bastian read on—

"Wight witches, though, cannot be bound in this way."

Kaliyah stilled, whispering, "Bull nettles."

"The Witch Marrowight, of all wight witches, harbors unmatched strength. Faerie Fire, even if cast by my own hand—a Sun Child's hand —cannot touch her.

But Faerie Fire conjured on the Day of the Dark Sun is another matter."

Kaliyah, the Wystan Boys, and the others leaned in.

"When the black shadow moon veils the day, the Sun Child must face the witch. For only in the bleakest moment of the eclipse will the sun's corona—the power and crown of the Sun Devaa—shine from the darkling sky.

Faerie Fire, strengthened by coronal light, can bind even a Wight Witch in stone."

Kaliyah stared at the book, at Bastian's bright hand. "On this day, when the strength of the Moor Folk falters—still, there will be light."

Bastian read on—

"May the tyranny of the Witch Marrowight be so ended, and may she face justice. Victorious, then, shall the Sun Child stand beneath stars ablaze in midday.

If the Sun Child fails—if he perishes, so shall the Sylphic Kingdom and all mortal lands. For no other Sun Child will rise, and the Witch Marrowight shall name herself Queen of the Deadlands."

Gray Jay gently laughed. "The witch will fall by fire conjured from the Sun Devaa's very crown."

"And on the day she herself chose for battle," said Dom.

"Unless..." Bastian couldn't remove his eyes from the words—*if the Sun Child fails—if he perishes...*

Dom closed the book. "I've been training that pitching arm of yours since the day you could grip a ball. Faerie Fire, in your hand, shall be wicked."

Kaliyah cupped her hands in a sunbeam. She blew at the light, conjuring a roiling globe the size of an apple, rippling with silver-blue flames. She shifted it into Bastian's hand.

It was the weight of one of her river stones and piping hot, like the stones loaded with dragon fire had been.

He dandled the sphere of sunlight in his palm as he stood.

Gripping it, bearing its heat, felt like a key slipping into its lock.

A sense of wholeness settled. A tapping into the true self.

Bastian rolled the fire from hand to hand. "It feels liquidy. What's it made of?"

"Faerie Fire—Sundrops—are beads of sun plasma, cooled by the breath of a faerie," said Dom.

"During the eclipse, I won't have full sun," said Kaliyah. "The dimmer the sun gets, the smaller the Sundrops will be. Your aim will have to be precise."

"I'll bet all my arrows it will be." Dom crossed to the other side of the yard. "Throw that at me, Sun Child." He pounded his chest. "Fast and straight, just like I taught you."

"Will it turn you to stone?" called Bastian.

"That's exactly what it'll do." Dom smiled.

Bastian lowered the Sundrop. "I can't."

"Not to worry—you'll be able to mend me," said Dom, "right as rain."

"I wouldn't know how to mend you."

"Kaliyah will teach you." Dom clapped. "Let's see what you've got. Think of me as your Ryudo target and pitch that light. Hard as you can."

Bastian glanced at Kaliyah.

She nodded.

Bastian studied Dom's position. He measured the distance between them; focused on the strength of the wind. He gripped the Sundrop as firmly as he could.

He cocked his arm and let it fly, fast and straight.

The Sundrop struck Dom in the chest.

He collapsed. Blue and orange flames encased him.

Bastian rushed to him.

The fire rapidly died, leaving tendrils of smoke snaking around Dom's body, paling his flesh to a marbled gray stone.

"What have I done?" Bastian crashed to his knees beside Dom.

Doctor Skylar knelt, too. "Nothing that can't be undone."

"But how can he breathe?" Bastian bent over Dom's stony body. "Dom can't breathe."

Kaliyah crouched. "He doesn't have to breathe. He's lost in a deep, enchanted sleep."

"Lost." Bastian's eyes clouded. "Dom can't breathe, he can't breathe."

Kaliyah held Bastian's cheeks and eased him to looking at her. "Try to focus."

Bastian blotted his eyes on his arm. "I can't."

"Yes, you can. Begin by closing your eyes."

Bastian shut his eyes, tears wetting them.

Kaliyah pressed Bastian's palm with its shining, thousand-pointed star against Dom's rigid chest.

"Think about the light in you," she whispered. "Do you feel its heat surging in your heart?"

Bastian lent his mind to the warmth throbbing in his chest, moving like quickening breakers behind his ribs.

"Visualize that heat channeling along your arm and into your palm," said Gray Jay. "Just like when you opened *Dark England*. Just like when you cast your dragon stone at the witch."

Bastian tried.

Heat coursed along the inside of his elbow and flushed hot in his fingers.

"Open your eyes," said Kaliyah.

His palm was glowing white.

Beneath it, inch by inch, Dom's marbled skin was shifting back to flesh.

A moment more, and Dom was supple and sun-kissed, breathing steadily.

"Dom," said Bastian. "Can you hear me?"

Dom blinked his eyes open and tried to sit up. He teetered back.

Bastian caught him.

Dom weakly smiled. "That's cracking aim."

"Are you hurt?" asked Bastian.

Dom sat straight. "I'm right as rain." He shook stone dust out of his clothes. "Strike the witch like that, and we'll have ourselves a battle won."

Gray Jay studied the blue of the eastern horizon. "The dark moon— it rises."

Bastian glanced to the west where, behind the woodland, King- fisher Chalet rested, a warm swirl of hearth smoke curling above it.

"Can I—"

"You'd like to visit home," said Dom.

"To see my brothers," said Bastian.

"It won't be the last time," said Kaliyah.

"Go," said Gray Jay. "Say what words you must. Then suit up in that armor. Meet us at the border of the witch's vale by midday."

"How will I make it there without getting caught?" asked Bastian. "Surely, she'll have the forest watched."

"We'll see that you have cover, to home and to battle," said Dom.

"And in the battle, I'll be your guide," said Kaliyah. "I'll bear your Faerie Fire, and I won't leave your side." She touched her ring, Alura's ring, strung around Bastian's neck. "As much as this battle is yours, it's mine."

Bastian unfixed the pearl charm tied to him. "Together, we'll finish what your da began." He fastened it on Kaliyah. "Together, we'll end the Witch Marrowight."

42

The walk from Sayre Cottage to Kingfisher Chalet was a mere half mile—and yet trekking through the woodland this day, Bastian felt it to be much further.

He found himself unable to move quickly through any part of it. Rather, he took his time, savoring the moments he had in this lush, bountiful forest, untouched by any curse laid by an eclipsing moon's shadow; blissful in what might be the woodland's final hours of thriving under the Sun Devaa's reign.

Bastian stepped into the shallows of the Windrush stream, flowing gently to the Natterjack Lagoon. He held still in the water, admiring the glimmer of the sun in its ripples.

Small bleak fish brushed his ankles with their bony tips of fins, and just under the surface, silver flickering minnows held themselves in rows like saluting troops, flaring their glistening tails.

He moved further into the crossing, but a glitter in the water halted him—a girl's face.

It was the naiad—Leif—who'd guided him into the cave on the day Cassian came home.

She was lying on her back on the bed of the stream, gazing up at him. She drew her hand—slender-fingered and cool white—through the water.

She pulled from her tendrils of hair a marsh marigold. She raised it out of the water and handed it to him.

Bastian took the flower and kissed it.

Two blue pebble tears tumbled down her cheeks.

In the trees above the stream, winged animals—swifts, robins, hawks, bats, thrushes, owls, warblers, and many others—alighted.

As Bastian passed through the shallows and onto the shore, the flock took to the air, washing him with a turbulence of wing-spun wind. He strode up a trail flanked with forest animals—foxes, deer, rabbits, groundhogs, and field mice.

When he came to a buck, old and antlered, he paused and knelt without quite knowing why.

The buck laid his broad horns gently on Bastian's shoulders.

Bastian gazed up into the buck's great brown eyes, all heart, until he stepped away, following his doe and small fawn into the woods.

From the thicket to the north, a gentle singing was sounding. There were no words in the music—it was a hummed lullaby, and more poignant than any Sylphic music he'd yet heard.

He took a step down the trail the buck and his family had walked.

The further he followed it, the more voices he heard—voices rising in powerful, close harmonies that brought a shivery tingling to his skin.

Rounding a tight cluster of mesquites showed him the source of the singing.

It was sounding from a summer gooseberry glade, their berries reaching the peak of ripening.

Bastian approached a near bush and knelt. He gently took a cluster of gooseberries into his hand.

At the heart of each berry, a silver star seemed to be shining.

Gooseberry fae.

The Sun Devaa's thousand-pointed star on Bastian's hand brightened, and from every berry, he could feel each faerie's name rising to his consciousness, as though he'd known them all his life.

He focused on a single gooseberry, resting highest atop the cluster.

"Cerylia."

The skin of the berry parted, and out floated the tiny star, its shining points clarifying into perfect, miniature arms and legs.

The gooseberry fae, no bigger than the tip of his little finger, rose until she was hovering at the height of his face.

She wore the slightest dress—a lacing of what seemed made of feathers and sunbeams.

She opened her eyes, yawned and stretched, then searched the sky.

A seagull swept down from flight and coasted close.

She caught his mantle feathers and sailed with him up and away, until both the brightness of the bird and the brilliance of the faerie faded into the distance.

With Cerylia's disappearance, the gentle lullaby strengthened. It was as though the others in the cluster Bastian held were aching to be born into the Sylphic Kingdom with her.

Bastian, holding the cluster closely, knelt.

"Bliss," he whispered. "Araxia."

Two gooseberries split, and from them, two tiny stars lifted.

Bliss, an especially golden, gossamer-winged fae, came out spiraling and shot to the sky as though she'd join with the sun.

Araxia clarified into a translucent, gray form—her face streaked with a glittery, silver cast.

She had no wings, and her body seemed to share some lineage with dolphins, so smooth did she seem.

She slipped away from him, her movements that of a swimmer. She caught the wings of a passing dragonfly who ferried her in a streak of iridescence toward the Natterjack Lagoon.

One of the gooseberries in the cluster was not only shining, but shaking, as though the fae it held couldn't bear its confinement for a single moment more.

"Nyx," said Bastian.

And in a blink, Nyx was born, not even waiting for his gooseberry to split, but bursting out by the sharpness of his shine alone.

Nyx shivered as his arms and legs clarified, his new skin seeming mottled. It was as though a blue star's shine had been frozen in frosty streaks of air that clung to him.

He dropped like a stone to the earth by Bastian's foot.

His brow crossed, he crawled under a fresh leaf and drew it around himself like a cocoon.

Bastian studied the domed shelter, shining a muted blue.

"You seem afraid of the daylight," he said.

Nyx scooted his leaf cocoon backwards until he was tucked tightly inside it, resting under a shrub.

The singing of the choir of gooseberry fae grew yet stronger, but Bastian couldn't heed them and stood up and away.

For was he not calling them into a kingdom whose end might be imminent? Perhaps Nyx knew that. Maybe all of them did.

He glanced around, finding the woodland vacant. There were no animals, even, anywhere in sight. He slipped away from the gooseberry glade and wound back along the trail leading west, toward his brothers and Kingfisher Chalet.

He crested the eastern hill behind Kingfisher's grounds to find the chalet with its doors and windows wide open, inviting in the breeze.

He glanced at the star on his palm, seeming to shine almost as strongly as the sun. He clenched his fist, drawing its heat deeply in— stowing it for release at the moment in battle when he'd cast back the measure of light he'd been given.

He sprinted down the hill, across the back yard, and up the back porch stairs. As he rushed to the back door, he knocked over Cassian's empty swing. He righted it and ran inside.

He found his brothers in the living room, Rhys coiling the cords of his amp, Lucas selecting comic books from a pile.

Rhys looked up. "How are the Sayres? Readying for an Earth-ending battle, I guess?"

"I thought we agreed to ease up on teasing him," Lucas signed to Rhys.

Bastian glanced around. "Where's Cassian?"

Rhys drew a piece of guitar sheet music from a folder. "We just settled him on the back porch. We're gathering some things to do out there. Want to come?"

Bastian stepped back. "You left Cassian outside?" he signed. "Alone?"

"Just for a minute," Lucas signed back. "He's fine. He's in his swing."

Bastian signed, "He's not in his swing."

He skipped into a run.

Rhys and Lucas dropped everything and rushed after him.

Bastian scanned the yard as Lucas and Rhys skidded to a stop before the empty baby swing.

"Oh, my God," signed Lucas, staring at the swing. "We have to call Mum and Da."

"No way," Rhys said, signing back. "Cassian's got to be here, some-place. Maybe he somehow climbed out of the swing?"

"He can't climb," signed Lucas.

Bastian gazed at the spires of Marrowight Manor, punching blackly through the trees.

"She's taken him."

"Who's taken him?" asked Rhys.

Bastian raced inside and to the study.

Lucas and Rhys ran after him.

Bastian unshrouded the hidden shaft and crawled in.

Rhys caught his ankle. "Cassian's not in the attic."

"Of course she'd fight dirty." Bastian's voice came panicked as he pulled himself up into the shaft.

"Bastian, look at me," said Rhys.

Bastian met his eyes.

Rhys held his gaze. "I need you rational right now."

"I'm being rational." Bastian shook him off. "Just follow me. I'll explain everything."

***

BASTIAN DUCKED through the Sylphic Council Chamber's small door, Rhys and Lucas tailing him.

The crystal-belted river stones were still sitting on the floor, ringing the boulder embossed with the winged sun. Beside the stones lay the witch hazel wand.

Bastian opened a window and trained his scope on Marrowight Manor.

There, dozens of minor goblins were walking the grounds, carrying spears. Above the vale, the sky was teeming with balor hornets.

Bastian shifted the scope and found the shrine of the Goblin King.

His heart clenched.

For before the shrine lay Cassian, red-faced and screaming, his tiny hand gripping the tip of the statue's sharp sword.

The Witch Marrowight was standing over the baby, her hand crooked. Black vines were creeping from the stone goblin's fingers and twisting around Cassian's body.

Bastian dropped the scope.

Lucas signed, "What is it?"

Bastian couldn't speak. He only could point out the window.

Lucas picked up the scope and peered toward Marrowight Manor.

His jaw dropped open.

Rhys took the scope from him and aimed.

He sucked a breath. "Bloody bindweed—she's got our baby!"

A flash streaked over the trees on the hilltop—the flight of a faerie.

Bastian took back the scope and followed the faerie's bright trail until she disappeared among a row of oaks standing just south of the witch's vale. A limb shivered at her landing.

He focused closely on the tree.

Its branches were crowded with forest children, their bows drawn. One of the forest children eased to the end of a branch and trained an arrow on the witch.

A goblin, standing beside the witch, lobbed a long spear.

The oak trembled, and from it, the forest child fell, the spear sticking from his stomach.

Bastian, his hand trembling, lowered the scope.

"She wouldn't hurt Cassian, right?" signed Lucas.

Rhys threaded his fingers into his hair. "Lady Marrowight freaking took someone's baby—our baby."

"I mean, she's unhinged," signed Lucas. "But even a nutjob wouldn't hurt a baby." He glanced from Rhys to Bastian. "Right?"

The Witch Marrowight had cut wings off sprites and other Moor Folk. She'd locked faeries in iron and cast dryads and forest children in stone. She'd set a cursed hornet on Bastian, poisoned him with hexed plants, and sent her goblins out as assassins.

She'd murdered Malachi Daoine Kingfisher, and today, she—with her own curse-wielding hands—meant to kill Bastian and destroy the Sun Devaa, bringing death to all worlds.

"She'll stop at nothing," signed Bastian.

Lucas signed, "What are we going to do?"

"We'll have to go get him," said Rhys, signing. "There's no question about that." He squinted out the bright window. "But why the blazes would Lady Marrowight have taken him?"

"That, I can tell you." Bastian glanced at his hand, at the Sun Devaa's star—barely visible. "But for you to understand, there's something I need to show you."

He lifted his palm, aiming its shine right at Rhys and Lucas.

They together stared at him.

Bastian closed his eyes and concentrated. Heat swelled in his heart. He pushed it into his hand. He opened his eyes.

Light was streaming from his hand, brightening his brothers' troubled expressions.

Rhys lifted his brow. "Is something supposed to be in your hand?"

Bastian looked at his palm, gleaming silver with light. "Can you not see the star?"

Rhys took his hand. "What star?"

Bastian signed to Lucas, "Go and get *Moor Folk of the English Highlands*. We need the dowsing charm."

Lucas darted off.

Bastian gathered up the crystal-rung stones. He sat in the middle of the floor and arranged the stones around him, their quartz rings touching.

"It's happened," muttered Rhys, pacing. "You've honestly cracked. We've got a bloody disaster on our hands, our baby brother kidnapped, and you're sitting in the middle of a circle of stones like a lunatic." He wiped sweat from his face.

Lucas raced back in, holding the book.

"The witch hazel sun dowsing ritual—find it," signed Bastian. "Rhys can wave the switch."

Lucas picked up the witch hazel switch and demonstrated, flourishing it over Bastian. He handed it to Rhys.

Rhys loosely took it. "Do you two not get what's happening?"

"Trust me." Bastian nodded at Lucas.

Lucas signed—

"Starlight burning, sunlight churning,
  in the darkness, Earth is turning."

Lucas elbowed Rhys.

Rhys limply waved the witch hazel. "We're wasting time."

Lucas signed on—

"Worlds are winging, thrushes singing—
  bend to hear the sunrise ringing."

Lucas glanced at Rhys.

"You've both lost it, do you know that?" He waved the witch hazel.

Lucas widened his stance and signed boldly—

"Out of mire, light the pyre!
  Make this Sun Child shine like fire!"

Bastian's white T-shirt warmed and brightened, then a burst of light shot from his chest.

Rhys and Lucas staggered back, shielding their eyes.

Rhys ducked into the light and grabbed Bastian's arm. He studied Bastian's hand, blaring light.

He peeled off Bastian's shirt.

The epicenter of the glow outlined the prismatic shape of his heart, the silvery light wavering with its beat.

"Blazes," signed Lucas, "you're the Sun Child!"

He set his hand over Bastian's chest and watched the light shimmer through his fingers.

Bastian worked the heat back through his body until he felt it tingling just deeply inside his chest.

Rhys sat back on his heels, managing no words.

Bastian stood.

"Lady Marrowight is a wight witch," he said, signing. "She wants to destroy England's Sylphic Kingdom, and all mortal lands. During the eclipse, I must lead the Moor Folk in an effort to stop her. The Sayres are Sylphic. So's Kaliyah. There are four especially brave forest children called the Wystan Boys, who are like knights. Together, we discovered the key to defeating the witch, and we've formed a battle plan. We have to get Cassian away from that vale."

"Lady Marrowight couldn't—" began Rhys.

"Not Lady Marrowight," said Bastian, "the Witch Marrowight."

"The...witch," said Rhys. "Why would she take Cassian?"

"To divide my focus, I imagine," said Bastian, signing. "If I'm after Cassian, I'll be easier to catch. During the eclipse, she plans to brew a curse that'll transfer the Sun Devaa's power to her. Doing so will destroy the Sylphic Kingdom and all that it protects. And it will end the line of Sun Children. To do it, she's got to..."

He drew a deep breath.

Let it go.

"What?" signed Lucas.

Bastian signed, "She's going to try to cut out my heart."

Rhys and Lucas glanced at each other.

Bastian pulled his brothers close and told them all that the Sayres and the Wystan Boys and *Dark England* had taught him—about the witch, about her allies, about Kingfisher's secret to defeating her, and about how death would rain down in all worlds if he failed.

Bastian opened his rucksack and pulled out the pieces of armor.

Rhys and Lucas helped him fasten them over his shins, thighs, arms, and shoulders.

Rhys cast aside the knitted cuirass.

"I need that," said Bastian. "It's saved my life once already."

Rhys held up the leather and steel chest piece. "This is far stronger." He knocked his knuckles against its metal. "But perhaps even this isn't sturdy enough. If it's your heart she wants, we'll have to protect your chest. How could we strengthen this?"

Lucas sat up from digging in the trunk. "Will this work?" He lifted a hammered plate of steel, with strips of metal projecting like ribs from its edges.

Rhys worked the open side over Bastian's chest, so the metal plate was guarding his heart.

A vibration shimmered in the metal. It brightened to a glowing orange, then sizzled to a burning white.

Bastian clenched his eyes, steeling himself against the singe.

When the metal dimmed, Rhys pressed around the edges of the piece. Not a bit of Bastian was burned, and the piece lay fitted perfectly against him.

Bastian fastened the knitted cuirass over it.

Rhys closely watched as Bastian fixed the leather chest piece tightly over the cuirass. The expression on Rhys was one of admiration, and fear.

Fully clad, Bastian felt more like Aubrey Gyrfalcon than the boy his family knew him to be. The armor felt right—light. In it, he felt he could run a hundred Ryudo courses. Outmaneuver dozens of dragons. Strike any target.

He felt like himself—the Sylphic Kingdom's Sun Child.

In place of any fear troubling his mind, a single, resolute vision settled: Kaliyah's Faerie Fire streaking from his hand and striking the Witch Marrowight—the Elemental Spirit seeking to overthrow the Sun Devaa and destroy everything mortal and Sylphic, sun-loving; the Witch Marrowight—the wicked enchantress keeping Moor Folk imprisoned in iron, in stone; the Witch Marrowight—Alura's murderess; the Witch Marrowight—a destroyer of Sun Children; the Witch Marrowight—Cassian's kidnapper.

43

Bastian, clad in his armor, together with Rhys and Lucas, hustled up the lane leading to Marrowight Manor.

"If this face-off is going to happen during the eclipse," Rhys said, signing, "you won't have much time."

"I read that the eclipse will last just seven minutes," signed Lucas.

Bastian glanced up at the eastern sky, where the new moon—scarcely visible—was climbing. "Seven minutes is an awfully long time to square with a witch."

Rhys signed, "Lucas and I will be with you."

"No way." Bastian stopped. "I'll have the Wystan Boys and the other Moor Folk by my side. Your job is to get Cassian and get out."

"We're not leaving you in a fight by yourself," said Lucas, signing.

Rhys stepped nearer to him.

Bastian glanced at each of them. "You don't know what the witch is capable of."

"It doesn't matter," signed Lucas. "We're going to stay with you."

"This battle is Sylphic," said Bastian, signing. "Getting Cassian to safety has to be your priority. If you were to stick around, I wouldn't be able to focus. You'd only be helping the witch." He threw out his fist. "I need you to trust me on this."

Rhys glanced at Lucas, then added his fist.

Lucas completed the pact.

Bastian signed, "No more speaking. Only sign."

379

He started on, but Rhys grabbed him.

Above them, nine eagles, flying low, streaked in a triangular formation. They all seemed to have their eyes trained on Bastian, Rhys, and Lucas.

Then came a line of four coasting falcons, then owls winging past in clusters by the dozens. Following them came a collection of nightjars streaking in, their flight patterns jerky and anxious, as though they were impatient for the moment they'd touch down on the witch's vale. Then came birds of all sorts, by the hundreds.

A company of tiny songbirds split from the flock and swooped down, fluttering to land among branches at the edge of the woodland. They peered inquisitively at Bastian as he passed, seeming eager to get a glimpse of their champion, their Sun Child.

Foxes slipped among the tree trunks and neared the edge of the lane, watching with keen eyes as Bastian and his brothers walked on. Field mice were skittering about in the leaf litter, and from bushy haunts and holes, hedgehogs and badgers ambled near.

Even beetles, perched atop boulders, raised onto their prickly back legs.

Some of the animals were girded in blue, red, and silver plating. Others bore black flags embroidered with the Sun Devaa's thousand-pointed star.

Bastian, with his bare eyes, could see everything Sylphic, it seemed. He caught glimpses of oakmen slipping through the woodland, hooking seashells and weaving kelp into the animals' armor.

Then, forest children came into sight, along with faeries, sprites, dryads—and still others Bastian couldn't name. The forest children wore no armor and carried bandoleers, bows, and quivers. The faeries were clothed by their origins—some evidently of flowers, woods, or rivers, but others, Bastian couldn't identify.

He glanced at his brothers. "In the woodland—what do you see?"

"So many animals," signed Rhys, staring as they walked along the tree line.

"Just animals?" signed Bastian.

Rhys signed, "Some of the animals are shining."

"And there are other things shimmering," signed Lucas. "Glowing things—walking among them, tending them, it seems."

Rhys, staring hard at the woodland, signed, "What could that brightness possibly be?"

"Those are oakmen," signed Bastian.

Rhys squinted and signed, "Why can't I see them more clearly, as you two apparently can?"

"It takes experience to learn to see Sylphic things," signed Bastian. "When Lucas and I snuck to the witch's grounds, there were plenty of Sylphic things around—Elemental Spirits in her manor and Moor Folk on her vale. From that, and from what's happened since, Lucas seems to have gained some sight."

One of the oakmen faced them. His form flickered a moment, then stood out clearly from his shine. It seemed he was aiming to make himself more visible.

"Wait—there." Rhys pointed, then signed, "I think I see—is that one of the oakmen?"

The oakman caught Lucas' gaze, and then gestured with his hands.

Lucas eased to the edge of the trees. "Is he...signing?"

"Kaliyah said oakmen lost their hearing long ago," signed Bastian.

"What's he saying?" asked Rhys.

"The signs are different than what we use," signed Lucas. "But if I were to guess—I think he wants something...the rising sun...then, brightness, or glory. Victory, maybe? I think he's saying something like —'may light prevail.'"

Bastian signed back to the oakman, in the gestures he'd used, "May light prevail."

The oakman signed something else and pointed to Marrowight Manor. It, too, was no sign Lucas and their family used, and yet Bastian easily comprehended the gist—"Give her hell."

Bastian guided Rhys and Lucas on through the outskirts of the woods, to the grounds edging Marrowight Manor.

When they reached their climbing oak, Bastian signed for Rhys and Lucas to scale it.

Rhys pulled himself up to a high branch. Lucas followed.

Bastian started after them but stumbled at sighting two eyes suddenly gazing down from the oak's gnarled trunk.

The tree's bark resolved into the face of a woman—a dryad.

A limb, curved like a shoulder, dipped before him.

He climbed on.

The dryad lifted him into the thickest part of her bough, just below Lucas and Rhys—both staring wide-eyed at the tree moving.

"Can you see Cassian?" Bastian signed to them.

"No," signed Lucas.

The dryad's leaves shuddered in what seemed a shushing whisper.

The near trees, the brush, and the bushes in front of them parted, creating a sightline toward the closest edge of the witch's vale.

And there lay Cassian.

Cassian, his curls billowing, his tiny hand clinging to the iron leg of the goblin statue, was babbling merrily. Black bands, like sticky weeds strung from the goblin statue, were clinging all over his sleeper.

Bastian studied the thicket of bushes near the manor, through which he and Lucas had crossed to sneak in before.

There were no Elemental Spirits lurking near that part of the thicket. Only a line of statues—stone Sylphic creatures, petrified by the witch.

The boughs of trees lining the southern edge of the vale looked crowded with forest children and shone brightly with the light of perched fairies.

Bastian tapped his brothers' legs, then signed, "There, through the bushes, you can cut your way in. Hide, and wait for my signal."

Lucas pointed wildly at the vale.

Rhys and Bastian both focused on the witch's grounds.

A minor goblin, its eyes trained the baby, was lurking at the edge of the vale. The goblin glanced around, then hobbled near to Cassian.

Bastian flushed hot. He eased to a lower branch.

The dryad held him back with a thin limb.

"Little monster," croaked the goblin.

Warm light scrolled into Bastian's palm as he imagined finding a fallen branch and casting it at the goblin's head.

The dryad pulled her limb more tightly around him.

Rhys and Lucas both reached down and held onto Bastian's shoulders. Their eyes were hard-trained on the vale, on the goblin, it seemed.

Bastian backed against the dryad's trunk. They were right. He'd be no use to Cassian, to the Sylphic Kingdom, to anyone, if he fumbled into getting caught before the battle had even begun.

The goblin squatted, placing itself eye-to-eye with Cassian. "What an ugly thing you are."

Cassian lay still on the turf, staring wide-eyed at the goblin. After a moment of intense absorption, he squealed a laugh.

The goblin uncurled its purple forked tongue.

Cassian stuck out his tiny tongue, too.

The goblin bore its maw of pointed teeth.

Cassian giggled but stopped in a startle at the manor's heavy door creaking.

The goblin backed away from Cassian and fled into the shadows.

Gripping her crooked stick, its fanged head rearing, the Witch Marrowight strode onto the vale.

Her cold eyes were dead fixed on Cassian.

Cassian twisted away from her and screamed.

Bastian glanced up at Rhys and Lucas. "Go."

The two of them climbed down past him and ducked into the underbrush.

44

Bastian shimmied down the oak and crept to the iron fence dividing the woodland from the witch's vale.

Scaling the fence seemed to bear some risk, but this entry point was much closer to Cassian than any other.

And in the trees all around, forest children were perched, some watching him and some watching the witch. They might be able to offer him cover.

As he laid his hands on the gate to climb, out of the brush slipped a fox. He wore no armor, and his fur was hazed brown with dirt.

He pawed at a shallow ditch hollowed out under the iron gate. He glanced at Bastian, then crawled through.

Bastian knelt and studied the opening. Though it was narrow, he found it deep enough for him to fit. He crawled into it and eased underneath the gate.

Once on its other side, he crouched and peered at the brush to the east.

There grew a crop of prickly vines that Rhys and Lucas were cutting with pocketknives and easing through.

Bastian scanned the vale.

The Wystan Boys were standing at even intervals on the far eastern edge.

The four of them held arrows fitted to their bows, their bows resting steady in their hands.

Around the Wystan Boys milled hundreds of Moor Folk—other forest children and faeries; oakmen and animals; long-limbed dryads—humanesque when parted from their trees, and naiads dripping with the leavings of their rivers.

Gyrfalcons, seagulls, and harpy eagles clad in plated harnesses were wheeling overhead, bearing shining faeries.

The woods behind the witch, to the north, stood rife with red-eyed goblins and tattered swamp hags.

Three minor dragons—smaller than Azdaj, but still the hefty size of hyenas, were lashed to trees with what looked like cords of lightning.

Other Elemental Spirits, too shadowy to make out, walked among them, their footfalls disturbing a greenish glow seething low to the ground—the manor bleeding a poisonous fume into the woodland.

Above the northern thicket, balor hornets swarmed.

The tension of the impending battle, the movement of metal and hooves, the shushing of forest children shifting in the treetops, and Cassian's lonely cry—it altogether echoed in a despairing way, like winds drifting at the lead of a deadly storm.

Master Sayre and Doctor Skylar stood behind the Moor Folk army, both of them gripping Azdaj's cranial spines.

The dragon, flashing black and silver, huffing sparks and smoke, was watching the witch with narrowed eyes.

His branchial frill stood out rigidly around his face, the meaning of it clear—he was on the hunt.

Kaliyah, her brilliant wings flared, was standing beside Dom.

The witch, hooded and cloaked, reached the center of her vale. She lifted her twisted stick.

The footfalls and rustling in the woods quieted, leaving the air ringing only with Cassian's wail.

Gray Jay met Bastian's gaze. He tightened his arrow against his bowstring.

Bastian sprang from the thicket and sprinted for Cassian.

Arrows whooshed, and the voice of the witch rose, screaming curses.

Bastian locked eyes with the baby.

Cassian reached.

A spear punched the turf between them.

Bastian leapt over it and raced on, finally crashing to his knees before Cassian.

He studied the webby bindings clinging to the baby's clothes. They seemed a cross between black poison ivy and metallic spider webs. Bastian ripped them, his heart thundering.

No sooner could he shake off one, though, but two more would shoot out and snag Cassian's sleeper. Bastian tore the sleeper off him and cast it away.

The vines hung in the air a moment, as though bewildered—then they one by one snapped onto Cassian's diaper.

Bastian pulled the diaper off and covered the baby's bare skin, guarding him with as much of his armor as he could. He scanned the trees for Rhys and Lucas.

The hedge they were easing through was catching on their clothes, hooking them in place with sprouting thorns.

Bastian glanced around for Kaliyah.

He couldn't find her in the crowd rushing onto the vale.

But there was the witch. The witch—coming.

The vines stood at bay in the air before Cassian, as though responding to an unspoken command. They one by one coiled away.

Rhys and Lucas finally cut their way clear of the hedge. They crept along the edge of the vale and slipped behind a thick oak.

Lucas, his clothes torn and showing cuts, leaned out and signed, "Quick, bring him."

Bastian readied to run with Cassian, but a chill stayed him. And then a cold shadow swallowed him.

Towering over him, his horned head blotting the sun, stood the Goblin King, Kek.

Kek stood seven feet high, at least. Over his shoulder hung an iron bandoleer loaded with flashing strips of blue lightning. He glowered down, his small red eyes flaming. Gray saliva slipped down tusks jutting from his underbitten mouth.

Bastian lowered Cassian to the ground.

He slid the baby behind his legs.

A storm of arrows sang in.

Bastian cowered, readying for their bite—but when he opened his eyes, he found himself untouched.

A cage of arrows—forest children's arrows—stood around Cassian.

Kek drew a shaft of cursed lightning from his sling. "Child of the Sun—you will curse the day your eyes opened on the miserable Sylphic light."

A troop of Moor Folk—Gray Jay leading—rushed the vale, making for Bastian.

Behind them ran Dom. And beside him—Kaliyah.

Dom skidded to a halt and snatched Kaliyah's arm, keeping her clear of an onslaught of spears.

A siege of bat-winged tangies, their faces pale, their eyes bug gut-yellow, their ragged clothes sodden with blackish-brown fluid, rose from the northern woods and swooped overhead. They pelted down shards of ice.

Kek lifted his snapping blue curse.

An arrow shrieked an inch from Bastian's ear. It lodged into Kek's lightning bolt, dousing it.

Kek ripped out the arrow and snapped it.

Straight, true arrows extinguished dozens more of Kek's electrified curses.

Kaliyah and Dom rushed nearer but halted before a band of swamp hags, gripping daggers.

Dom shot several of the hags, but more advanced.

Kaliyah tried to dodge among them, but she couldn't break through their line.

Kaliyah wasn't able to reach him.

Kaliyah bore his sole weapon, and she couldn't reach him.

Bastian stared up at Kek.

Dark metal hoops studded his lip. An obsidian ring pierced his nose. His greasy hair stood in a knot. He seemed like the damned spirit of a Samurai warrior. His black eyes looked rage-filled.

The dreadfulness of those eyes, or perhaps some curse they were dealing, kept Bastian unmoving.

The tenor of the sunlight twisted as the moon lay its blade on the rim of the sun.

Kek released Bastian's gaze and glanced at the sun, as though feeling its weakening.

Arrows flashed toward him swiftly, but he handily deflected them, turning them to ash, one by one.

Bastian glanced around at the chaos raining over the vale.

Spears and knives were flashing everywhere. A fresh wave of Moor Folk, led by Kosa, was entering the battlefield.

The witch, bearing a pleasant expression, was watching the Goblin King fight back arrows as though they were insects.

She held Bastian's gaze a moment, then looked up at her Goblin King.

She called to him, "Get on with it."

Kek jerked, and a dark sword slid from a sheath strapped to his arm.

The serrated blade loomed as black as pitch. Ebony smoke drifted from it like steam leaching from dry ice.

The sun did not glint off this blade—the terrible weapon Lox had described.

This was the Goblin King's Lightfighter. In a halo around it, the daylight seemed vanquished.

Bastian stared up at the Goblin King.

As Kek lifted the black blade, Bastian's limbs tended numb, and the clatter of the battle dimmed. He could sense nothing but the sound of Cassian cooing from within his cage of Sylphic arrows.

Powerless, weaponless, Bastian waited for the strike. All he could manage to plan was how he might shield Cassian with his body once the Goblin King struck him down.

Kek swung the blade mightily, lodging it in Bastian's chest plate.

Bastian sank to his knees.

The leather of his armor disintegrated, leaving the blade wedged in Mrs. Sayre's cuirass, covering the steel shielding. Black smoke needled in through the holes of the cuirass and between the steel ribs of the chest plate.

Bastian fell to his back, twisting beneath the agony of what felt like a thousand icy needles piercing him.

A barely imperceptible shade, a deepening shift in the blue of the sky, told of the sun's slipping another degree behind the moon.

Kek dislodged the Lightfighter and lifted it to deal the blow that would slice Bastian's cuirass and split the steel guard; the strike that would cleave Bastian's bones, bearing his heart for the witch to collect and dismantling all hope.

Breathless, Bastian readied himself for death.

But against his thigh, something brightened. Something bearing a trembling heat. A round warmth.

Bastian clawed for it—Kaliyah's Sundrop, but his reaching fingers pressed it away.

Something moved behind Kek.

Rhys.

It was Rhys, slipping in from the brush, his gaze darting between Bastian and Kek.

He was pale as with fear; as though he could perceive well what was happening on the vale.

Kek held still a moment, then turned. His eyes narrowed at Rhys. He drew another curse, flashing electric, from his bandoleer.

A tempest of arrows sang in as Kosa and his troops neared.

A knot of tangies swooped around Kek like a shiver of airborne sharks, taking the arrow strikes and vanishing.

Kek lobbed the electric curse toward the woodland at Rhys.

It struck Rhys in the belly, and he fell back onto the grass. Black smoke drifted around him.

When it blew clear, it showed Rhys' body, fully shifted to stone.

Lucas jumped out of the brush and raced to him.

Bastian slid toward the Sundrop.

Reached.

Balor hornets swooped in, their stingers dripping black fluid.

Two Sundrops sailed in, fashioned by Kaliyah and cast by Dom, it seemed.

The Sundrop struck the center of the swarm, and the hornets scattered like firecrackers.

Kek again faced Bastian and drew his Lightfighter.

The thwish of an arrow.

Kek staggered.

Another bright arrow whined in, missing Bastian's cheek by a millimeter.

It pierced Kek's blade.

The Lightfighter flickered, then disintegrated.

Kek swiped the weapon's hilt, and a new blade shot from the sheath.

Another arrow screeched in, lodging deep in the metal. A dozen more arrows pierced it.

The sky darkened another degree as the moon crept onto the face of the sun.

Bastian hardly could move and could draw air just in feeble gasps as he watched Kek rage, the Lightfighter's blade evaporating and reforming, again and again.

The satisfied expression left the witch as she struggled to move through the falling arrows dividing her from Bastian and Cassian.

Bastian, blinded with agony from the pain of moving, reached for the Sundrop.

He grasped it and—mustering a shred of strength—lifted it.

He aimed it. Pitched it.

It struck Kek in the throat.

Kek staggered.

His Lightfighter dimmed.

The smoke needling into Bastian's body withdrew. His eyes cleared, and he breathed freely.

He pulled to his knees and lifted the two Sundrops that'd disrupted the hornet swarm and dropped by him.

He lobbed one, striking Kek between the eyes.

In the roar that followed, he pitched the third into Kek's open mouth.

Red light poured from Kek's body.

Smoke twisted up his legs in a cyclone.

The swirl of black connected with the horns of the goblin statue, and the statue sucked in the churning smoke.

A wind lifted, thinning the dregs of the fume into a black haze—all that remained of the Witch Marrowight's Goblin King.

The witch looked on, wide-eyed. She stumbled back a few steps, chased by arrows.

A troop of minor goblins raced in and stood guard around her.

Bastian crawled to Cassian and reached inside his shelter of arrows. He touched the baby's soft head as he watched Kaliyah race to him across the cleared field.

Bastian reached for her hand and pulled her to kneeling as the sky dimmed.

"The moon," said Kaliyah. "It's advancing."

Bastian pointed. "So's the witch."

The Witch Marrowight, hooded, her midnight cloak dragging, her position defended well now by a line of goblins fending off arrows, approached.

She snapped, and out of the mist seething in the northern forest, a huge, ragged horse appeared.

It was deathly pale, skeletal, and eyeless—her Kelpie.

The Kelpie was as big as a bull Asian elephant. Its coat hung dusky, like the beast had risen from an ash heap.

Its body was missing skin in places, showing bloody muscles and bones. Its huge head loomed, more skull than face.

Kaliyah blew into her hands, quickly spinning dozens more Sundrops—now just the size of elderberries. She set each of them on the ground behind Bastian.

The Kelpie—*Bonecrusher*—scraped its cracked hoof across the ground.

He charged.

A growl thundered from the shadows of the Wystan Woods as the great Sunwalker Gambol bounded onto the vale and plunged his thorny claws into the Kelpie's shoulders, dragging it down.

More minor goblins and the three minor dragons sped onto to the vale, leading a hoard of tangies.

The tangies rushed in and divided Kaliyah from Bastian.

Arrows kept the tangies from Bastian, but Kaliyah, they snatched.

One of them raised a twisted stick and jabbed her in the back, between her wings. In a flash, she was tiny and flittering.

They brought out a small iron cage, caught her, and snapped her inside it.

She screamed, steam rising where her skin touched the iron bars.

Dom raced from his blind, unleashing a rain of arrows on the tangies, on the Kelpie.

He rushed toward Bastian.

The Kelpie staggered and backed into the shadowy edge of the vale.

Gambol wheeled toward Gray Jay, Lox, and Kosa—the three of them surrounded by goblins flashing spears, all dodging the spouts of fire from the three minor dragons.

"Kaliyah," Bastian, shouted, running for her. "I'm coming."

Dom caught him. "Let the Moor Folk see to her. Your business is with the witch."

The witch was enclosed by a company of goblins, their spears raised in a synchronized line, making an iron shield.

Though she'd lost her Goblin King, she was watching the battle with some indifference. It was as though she were still fully confident in her Kelpie, in her army.

Her gaze traveled between her troops—succeeding in driving the forest children back—and the diminishing sun.

"She's stalling," said Bastian to Dom. "We have to get closer to her."
He knelt and gathered a handful of Sundrops.

He led Dom in a run at the witch.

Dom shot arrows before them, clearing a path. But for every meter they gained, they lost two.

A stallion's deep-throated whinny rang in the shifting light.

Ra, his black mane streaming, broke through encroaching tangies, through goblins, through swamp hags, through the minor dragons—disrupting their fire and sending them off into flight.

He stilled before Bastian.

Dom heaved Bastian onto Ra's broad back. He gathered Kaliyah's remaining Sundrops and piled them into Bastian's hands.

"It's your world and ours you now hold in your hands, lad." Dom closed his hands around Bastian's. "Fast and straight."

Bastian piled the Sundrops before him on Ra's back.

He held on to Ra's mane and spurred him to race at the witch.

The Kelpie tore in from the shadows.

Bastian locked his thighs against Ra's flanks and gripped his shining mane. He'd felt before that he and this horse were meant for one another. Now he knew that they were.

The two great beasts—the one the servant of the Sun Devaa and the Sun Child, the other allied with the witch—clashed like storming waves.

Bastian ducked low against Ra's back as the mighty stallion righted himself and rounded the vale in a gallop that brought him within striking distance of the Kelpie.

Bastian launched a Sundrop.

It flew through a hole on the Kelpie's forehead—a vacancy where a star should've been.

The Kelpie vented a scream into the unnatural dusk.

Light poured from its body. Smoke twined around its legs and encircled its withers.

In a blink, it was petrified—a marbled stone statue of a rearing, hellish stallion.

Bastian lifted his gaze to the sky.

The sun shone down weirdly, in a bent way—a dark golden scythe.

He grasped Kaliyah's Sundrops, no bigger now than peas.

Bitter laughter issued from where Cassian lay in his shelter of the Wystan Boys' arrows.

The witch, her hooded cloak leaching dark mist, had managed to slip to the baby and was bending over him, muttering.

Lightning crackled between her raised fingers.

Bastian spurred the stallion.

Ra charged, carrying Bastian into throwing range.

He let fly a fistful of Sundrops that rained over the witch.

She stumbled back, screeching.

Bastian wheeled, then guided Ra to stand facing her, a few dozen meters away.

As the light from the Sundrops dissipated, the witch uncowered.

Though her black cloak was smoking, she seemed untouched.

From beneath her hood, the witch trained her cold eyes on the army of Moor Folk, fighting through the tangies that were her last line of defense.

She swept her arms in wide circles, churning smoke and blue fire. She screamed a chanted curse as she cast the fire in an erupting shriek over the vale.

Faeries crashed down, fluttering on singed, blackened wings. Bucks bearing forest children tipped to their sides, braying.

Forest children dropped their bows and cried out as sonic blasts and blue flames washed the vale. The Wystan Boys, among their troops, sank to their knees.

Ra reared.

Bastian, clinging to him, lost almost all of the Sundrops.

One forest child—Kosa—seemed to have forced his way to standing in front of the other Wystan Boys and was leaning into the wash of electric air, his guarding arms parting it.

When the smoke cleared, the Moor Folk army was a stone army, but for the Wystan Boys and a scattering of oakmen and other Moor Folk nimble or lucky enough to have dodged the assault.

Azdaj crooked to standing and tried to take flight—but his wings appeared stiffened, and he couldn't rise.

The witch spun to face Bastian. A lunatic smile leered from beneath her cloaking hood.

"Fool of a Sun Child," spat the witch.

Bastian had only two Sundrops remaining.

He lifted one—now as small as a river pebble. "Back off from Cassian."

The witch threw back her hood. "Or what? You'll pepper me with your little faerie lights?"

She wheeled her arms and summoned bolts of cursed electricity to her hands.

Bastian pulled back his arm to launch a Sundrop, but the witch was a quicker draw and struck him in the chest with a spear of blue lightning.

Ra planted his hooves, and Bastian clenched his knees, fighting to stay mounted.

He dropped the bead of light as electric ropes bound his arms behind his back.

The witch pointed her sharp finger at the faltering sun—little more than a twinkle in the platinum sky.

"Your army is stone. The strength of your great sun is gone." She crooked her hands.

Movement, from the side of the vale, caught Bastian's eye.

From the far eastern edge of the battlefield, Lucas was running.

The sonic blast hadn't touched him.

Lucas hurdled the petrified bodies of Moor Folk, the madness of his sprint delivering him straight through the clawing arms of tangies and goblins.

Spears and knives slashed at his arms and clothes, but he didn't slow. His face was rage, and his eyes were fixed on the witch.

The four Wystan Boys, all on their feet and running, lent their arrows to Lucas' aid, clearing his path of Elemental Spirits, delivering him between Bastian and the witch.

Lucas skidded to a stop midway between them.

He signed, "Stay away from my brother."

Lucas—no.

Bastian tried to free his hands to sign, but they were bound too tightly—with every slight movement, the electric ropes shocked him.

The witch cackled. "Little hero." She eased closer to Lucas. "Have you not learned the immensity of my power? Perhaps you couldn't hear me say—*No day shall last forever. The sun shall always fade.*"

Her legions laughed with her and eased down their weapons.

"Or, perhaps you're more stupid than deaf," said the witch.

A small Sundrop lay twinkling in the grass beside Lucas' foot. He bent down and lifted the tiny light. He studied its glow, coursing over his hand.

His glance flickered to the sky, as though he were studying it, feeling for the direction of the wind. He rolled the Sundrop in his fingers.

A hint of a smile came to Bastian as he watched Lucas gather an understanding of the Sundrop's density and weight.

Lucas fixed his eye on his target.

The witch gathered her cloak and donned a mock frown. "Mercy, oh, don't throw it!"

Her legions laughed.

She gathered up her long cape as though readying to flee. "A faerie light in the hands of a deaf child might be enough to cut the tail off a rat."

Lucas pulled back his arm and launched the light.

It arced and struck the witch in the eye.

Screeching, she clawed at her face.

Light flowed in tears from her damaged eye.

The electric ropes binding Bastian's hands loosened.

He struggled his hands free, but he couldn't release the bindings twisting around his body.

He searched Ra's mane for Sundrops.

Scraping his nails into Ra's coat, he found a meager few, hot like pinpricks, as small as sesame seeds.

The witch spun her hands around her face, generating a mask of smoke. When it dissipated, she had again two undamaged eyes.

She crooked her hands, and from her fingers, streams of fire poured over Lucas.

The fire roared for an instant—and then Lucas stood frozen in stone, in a posture of defense.

Tears of light again dripped from the witch's eye. She generated a new mask of smoke.

When she stepped out of the smoke, she seemed whole again—but somehow off-balance.

Dom, Gray Jay, Kosa, and Lox all crept nearer, easing among the bodies of the downed Moor Folk.

The witch lifted her hands, leaching smoke. "Your army is weak, Sun Child. Your sun dies in darkness."

From the edge of the field, Azdaj roared, spitting fire. He shook ashy sediment out of his wings, then lifted to the air, churning wind, sputtering in an off-kilter flight toward Bastian.

The witch cast a stream of lightning at Azdaj, and another at the encroaching Wystan Boys.

Azdaj, his wings limp, spun down and crashed into the northern forest.

The Wystan Boys together stumbled to their knees.

"The sun shall always fade," said the witch, smiling at the smoke rising from a copse of broken trees cradling the downed body of the dragon.

"That's a lie," said Bastian. "Light prevails over even the deepest night. Kingfisher knew it, and so do I."

The witch scoffed. "Kingfisher was mad." She flung a dribble of light off her face. "His miserable life lay in my hands. Maddened by fear, he begged me for mercy—as should you."

"You granted him no mercy," shouted Bastian. "You killed him."

The witch lifted her face, her eye draining light.

"I did not."

She swiped smoke across her eye, clearing it.

"Kingfisher pleaded for exile, and I granted it. He was worth far more to me alive, for why end one Sun Child, when the sun I can slay?"

Kingfisher...the witch had just claimed that he wasn't dead.

Bastian gripped Ra's mane, holding the horse steady, facing her.

The witch paced nearer.

"Kingfisher selfishly chose exile in exchange for agreeing that I and the next Sun Child would battle on a day when the sun would be darkened by the moon. Fool! The Day of the Dark Sun—today—is the day of the Sun Devaa's weakness."

She glanced at the sky.

"And today"—she raised her arms—"is the day of my dark power fulfilled."

The sky went sepia.

Lightning rippled across the witch's arms. She crooked her hand, and smoke poured from her fingers.

A cauldron, as big as a back yard swimming pool, materialized out of the smoke.

Thousands of wings bobbed in a sooty roil of fluid, their filigree silver and golden tips surfacing as she stirred its smoking green liquid with wind.

"What a cruel sovereign is the Sun Devaa for sending children to fight his battles," said the witch.

She flicked a finger, and Bastian's damaged cuirass and chest piece together ripped and fell away.

Dark smoke wheeled around Bastian. Bound him.

The light glowing from his chest flickered low in the dimness of the strange daylight—the sun all but vanquished by the moon.

The witch conjured a crackling bolt of blue lightning. "The sun will go, each night it will go. And this day when it goes, it will not shine again." She cast the lightning at Bastian.

The bolt struck, splitting his chest open.

Bastian slipped off Ra's back and landed hard on the turf.

"Fools and babes." The witch spun, shouting over the battlefield, "Behold—"

The moon advanced.

"—the death of the Sylphic Kingdom's last Sun Child, and the passing away of the Sun Devaa's frail Moor Folk Realm. My strong reign as Queen of the Deadlands begins!"

The moon closed in—its final assault on the sun.

Bastian's chest, cold and open, trickled blood and light onto the shadowy grass.

The witch faced him. Lifted her arms high. Crooked her fingers, calling for lightning.

None came.

She raised her arms higher and shouted into the wan sky.

Nothing happened.

She screamed curses, but no power answered her call.

A racing darkness crossed the battlefield.

From where they knelt, the Wystan Boys hollered as a dreadful bleakness—the raging cone shadow of the moon—swept the land.

At last, the body of the moon spread itself fully over the sun.

But the sun—that near star that the witch believed to be dead in the sky...wasn't.

The sun's silver corona flared, shining like a seam of crystal around a river stone.

The Wystan Boys whooped as the sun's light strengthened into a fiery crown—the crown of the Sun Devaa: a solid ring of light and power, flashing brilliance.

The smoking bindings dissipated from Bastian's body.

Stars burst in the daytime sky, engorging the scattered Sundrops until they were as big as oranges.

The witch stared down at her hands—forceless and leaking residual smoke like a quenched fire.

She lifted her gaze to Bastian, her eyes tracing the blood streaming from his chest. "You're going to die, Sun Child."

Summoning what warmth, what sun blood would respond to his call from where he lay, Bastian concentrated on calling light from his broken chest into his hand.

"You can still beg for mercy," said the witch.

Bastian felt he was drawing all the heat, all the life from his body, and gathering it into his palm.

"You need only ask," said the witch, easing back.

Bastian's thousand-pointed star flickered, then shone.

He sat up.

"I hold power over your death," said the witch, "and can stop it."

Bastian grasped a Sundrop and hefted it. "Not one more scream will I hear."

"Kingfisher was piteous and foolish," said the witch. "But you're strong, Sun Child. You're cunning. Will you not seek my favor?"

Gripping the roiling globe of Faerie Fire, Bastian gathered his feet beneath him and stood. "Not one more creature, Sylphic or mortal, will you touch."

"Is your life worth so little to you?" The witch's gaze was fixed on the fire in Bastian's hand.

Bastian drew a smarting, steadying breath as he measured the distance to the witch.

"Here, in your final moment of choice," said the witch, "will you not seek my help? You can yet deliver yourself."

Deliverance. Truly, this is what Bastian ached for.

"It's for a whole kingdom that I fight." Bastian cocked his arm and pitched the light, fast and straight.

The witch's eyes widened at the streaking Faerie Fire, a mortar of colossal power conjured by the child of her old adversary, and cast by his successor—a fastball spinning, throwing flames—blue, gold, and silver.

"But I, Empress of Darkness..." she muttered. "I was to be Night's Fearsome Queen."

In a burst of blackened soot and a scream, the Witch Marrowight vanished into the weird light of the afternoon night, leaving a smoking, obsidian statue.

45

*B*astian twisted onto his back. The light of ten thousand stars shone down by the darkness of the eclipse.

As the coronal crown of the Sun Devaa blazed, so the light in Bastian's heart flashed from his chest and glittered from the star on his hand.

The cauldron the witch had conjured dissipated, bursting into hundreds of wings.

They darted everywhere, fluttering onto the backs of stone statues that melted into living, breathing sprites, faeries, and forest children.

All the Moor Folk on the battlefield who'd been confined in stone together roused. They helped one another to stand and brushed dust from their skin.

Some of the wings flew to Marrowight Manor, clattering at its doors and windows, smashing them.

A murmur rumbled as hundreds of animals sprang from the manor, followed by waves of forest children and faeries, pale and bruised from lying in iron dungeons.

Kaliyah and the Wystan Boys raced to Bastian. Lucas, holding Cassian—together with Rhys, followed behind them.

Bastian glanced down at the hot blood and golden-silver light seeping from his chest.

Kaliyah knelt beside him. "Don't move."

"The forest children, the sprites and the faeries she took," Bastian whispered. "All the Moor Folk cast in stone—are they released?"

Lucas and Rhys crashed down beside Bastian and stared at his chest—at the blood on him.

Bastian struggled to keep them in his sight. He worked to conjure a way to speak to them of light, of love, of brothers, of what matters, when words falter.

"Tell Cassian," Bastian signed.

Rhys spoke with Kaliyah words that Bastian couldn't make out. Dom and Gray Jay appeared beside him and each held down one of his shoulders and hips.

Kaliyah lifted her hand, softly glowing, and soothed tears off his cheeks that he hadn't felt fall. She trailed her fingers down his chest and rested them over his heart.

There, light met light.

Coolness flowed from her fingertips as she slipped them inside the agony of sliced skin, of split bone, and touched his heart.

He jolted at a flash of great pain, but Gray Jay and Dom kept him unmoving.

Kaliyah drew her fingers across the rift in his heart, weaving it closed. She traced her fingers back and forth over his gashed ribs, mending bones and muscles, layer by layer, and finally sealing his skin.

When she lifted her hand, the pain dissipated, and the faculty of breathing returned. The vale smelled no longer dank, but as fresh as spring's first sun-warmed day.

Blossoming plants, succulent vines, glossy shrubs, and trees burgeoning with berries and flowers and acorns and seeds advanced over the threshold of the witch's grounds, shafting the scents of petals and water and soil.

Shriveled buds rained from the blood black rose bushes, and their thorny vines burst into blossoms—silvery, like stars climbing out of the earth.

In mere moments, the whole of the vale shifted from a battlefield to a peace-bearing, succulent meadow.

Dom, cradling Bastian's shoulders, eased him to sitting. "England's Sylphic Kingdom stood on the brink of everlasting darkness." He glanced at the span of stars shining in the midday dark; at the blaze of the sun's sharp corona. "You, Sun Child, have guided us into this—our Dawning Night of Stars."

The calls of pipes and the thunder of skin drums swelled as Moor Folk throughout the surrounding Wystan Woods chanted songs of the fall of the Wight Witch and the triumph of the Sun Child.

"This day will not be remembered as the Witch Marrowight's Day of the Dark Sun," said Gray Jay, "but as the rise of the Sylphic Kingdom's Sun Child and his Dawning Night of Stars."

Bastian slipped his hand into Kaliyah's. "In the heat of the battle, the witch spoke. Your da—she told me that he wasn't killed. She said that he chose exile. Exile in exchange for agreeing that she and the next Sun Child would battle on this day."

"He knew," said Kaliyah, tears rising into her eyes. "He knew you would bring her down."

"Aye, and she was wholly in the dark," said Dom. "She thought she had this battle won."

Gray Jay lifted Kaliyah's chin and brushed the tears off her cheeks. "There now, little faerie. Your da lives. England's Sylphic Kingdom is indeed blessed, for two Sun Children light our days."

"How is that possible?" asked Kaliyah. "Where could he be?"

Dom tipped his chin toward a beam of light trailing down from the darkling sky. "The Sun Devaa may tell us." He guided Bastian to his feet. "He summons you. Go with Kaliyah."

46

$\mathcal{K}$aliyah guided Bastian away from the witch's vale, to the south. They together trekked up a sweeping crest of a desolate moor, dotted with curling ferns.

The sky, deeply blue, shone with gilded silver clouds.

Bright corals and indigos streaked the horizon on all sides, as though the sun were rising and setting at once in every direction.

The ground sparkled with lichen capping small stones and silver ivy weaving among thick mosses, from whose green, tiny white flowers reached.

The groundcover smelled richer than even the timothy grass in Ra's meadow, and its fragrance swelled the air with an atmosphere of twilight.

Kaliyah drew from the earth a white flower and held it before Bastian. "Drink of the Sun Devaa's heights."

A drop of nectar trickled from the throat of the bloom. The reflection of the colored clouds shivered in the droplet until Bastian set it on his tongue.

Its taste triggered the feeling of running toward a person more beloved than anything; of waking up to realize that a holiday's begun.

In taking in the rich air, Bastian felt he'd never drawn a full breath until now.

Gambol advanced up the slope of the moor and came to standing beside him. He licked the dregs of nectar off Bastian's finger.

Bastian picked another flower and milked a shimmering dewdrop. He held it to Gambol.

The great Sunwalker licked it, his silver eyes closing.

Bastian stroked Gambol's great forehead, shining with a silver star, and caressed his soft ears.

A silhouette approached them—a figure backlit by bright clouds, coasting low. Aubrey Gyrfalcon.

Aubrey wore a battle helmet and held a bow and a quiver of arrows.

"Welcome to the Golden Moor," Aubrey called, his arms outstretched, "the heart of England's Sylphic Kingdom—now your kingdom." He glanced from east to west. "All this you see, from far to wide—it is your title." He stopped before Bastian. "You stood your ground, Sun Child. You are *Brave*. The songs of England's Sylphic Kingdom have sounded within you from your birth, and you've answered with tremendous valor."

A distant drumming echoed, and then came a whispering of chimes, shimmering like a rushing of wings.

The drumming complicated into a percussive chorus as other drums, sounding from other directions, strengthened in syncopation. Raspy pipes flared, joining the song.

And then came voices—whispering voices singing words seeming from Kaliyah's language. Words that, beyond any doubt, were of profound joy.

Warm light swelled, and with it came crowds of Moor Folk, climbing the rise.

They parted, creating an aisle leading to a place on the moor's pinnacle where the light shafting from the horizon shone brightest.

There, backdropped by the brilliant sky, stood the Sun Devaa.

Aubrey and Gambol took their places beside him. Ra, whinnying, crested the hill and stood near.

Kaliyah and Bastian together approached the Sun Devaa.

The Sun Devaa lifted the lichen-covered walking staff he held.

He blew into the vacancy at its top, and a translucent jewel, toned blue, like the deep North Atlantic, materialized.

The tips of the jewel's casing shifted to shining silver and wove along the shaft until the whole of it had transformed into a kingly, metal scepter, veined with wood.

"On this day, you've met your destiny." The Sun Devaa lifted the scepter and rested its gemstone on Bastian's shoulder.

"May your reign be one of peace," said the Sun Devaa, "and may you ever be blessed with Dawning Nights of Stars, our Brave Bastian Goldcrest—Sun Child of the Moor."

Bastian knelt.

The Sun Devaa touched the scepter to Bastian's other shoulder, then drew it away. "Rise, Sun Child."

Bastian stood and accepted the scepter from the Sun Devaa's outstretched hand.

He started to speak, but at meeting the Sun Devaa's striking eyes, he held still.

"Fear not to speak to me," said the Sun Devaa. "Long are the years that we shall share council."

"Kingfisher—the last Sun Child," said Bastian. "We've thought he was dead, but the witch said he was exiled. Is that true? Is he alive?"

The Sun Devaa, his blue eyes shining starkly against his umber skin, shifted his gaze to Kaliyah. "England's Elder Sun Child walks the Earth yet, and still breathes mortal air."

"How is it, then, that I was born a Sun Child?" asked Bastian.

"Kingfisher accepted exile so that you—one who could overthrow the tyrant wight witch—would come forth. Kingfisher's destiny was to position her for defeat, and now his destiny has carried him onto the sea, and beyond the sea."

Bastian met Kaliyah's gaze, then watched the Sun Devaa. "Will he ever return?"

"It may be that two Sun Children could one day stand together on the Golden Moor. But a great many things would have to transpire to usher Malachi Daoine Kingfisher back from exile."

The chorus of drumming rose.

The space before Bastian shimmered.

In a brush of light, the Sun Devaa and the Moor Folk vanished, leaving Bastian standing on the high hill behind Kingfisher Chalet, beneath a simple afternoon sky, Kaliyah holding his hand, Lucas cradling Cassian, Rhys standing behind them all, his hands on the shoulders of his brothers, and Naga—small and silver, twining about their ankles.

47

On the evening following the battle, the sky rang clear and blue, and the silvery sun shone mildly as it drifted down a golden-crowned western sky.

Bastian held Cassian tightly as he climbed up the back porch steps of Kingfisher Chalet, the baby tired out from sitting in his lap, watching Rhys and Lucas dribble a football.

Bastian lifted *Moor Folk of the English Highlands* from a log and opened it. He showed Cassian the painting of the forest children standing in battle ranks—the four faces of the Wystan Boys, among them, now clear to him and cherished.

Rhys and Lucas carried on with their game, practicing trick footwork and nailing the football between the oak saplings.

Bastian settled into the porch swing with Cassian.

A pair of crystal wings fluttered near, catching the colors of the sunset, as a faerie—no bigger than a swallowtail butterfly—drew close.

Kaliyah.

She lilted toward their chalet, her wings shivering like a hummingbird's as she finally arrived, hovering before Cassian's eyes, captivating him. Kaliyah's summer-tanned skin set off the white of her skirt—woven from the palms of water lilies and the shed wings of annulet moths.

She kissed Cassian's forehead, leaving a shimmer of silver, before settling onto Bastian's hand.

Cassian giggled and reached for Kaliyah's wings.

"Can Cassian see you as well as I can?" asked Bastian.

"All babies can see the Sylphic Kingdom," said Kaliyah. "But at a year old or so, they forget how."

Bastian soothed the baby's cheek. "There's no turning back from here, is there?"

Kaliyah rested her chin in her hand. "Do you want to turn back?"

"Since I first learned Kingfisher's legends, I've dreamed of being a part of the Sylphic Kingdom."

He closed *Moor Folk of the English Highlands* and studied its resplendent cover—the painting he now understood to be of a Sun Child—Kingfisher himself, and Alura.

"But Mum and Da will never understand who I am," said Bastian. "And I'll have to go back to school in a few weeks. I'm not sure how to pull off being both a Sun Child and an ordinary kid."

"All the Sun Children who came before you lived the double-life you're beginning," said Kaliyah. "The Wystan Boys will teach you."

"I wish I could learn from other Sun Children how to manage."

The light in Kaliyah's wings dimmed. "If only my da were here. He could show you."

Cassian touched the picture of the Sun Child and squealed in delight.

Kaliyah, carried on the baby's laughter, fluttered into the air. She again settled down and stilled her wings.

Bastian held Cassian's gaze. "You were a brave baby yesterday."

Cassian crammed his fingers into his mouth.

Bastian cuddled him more tightly. "I'm sorry that you were afraid."

Cassian grabbed his feet and wrinkled his bright eyes.

"But you weren't all that afraid, were you?" asked Bastian. "You can't even walk, and you're a goblin fighter."

Kaliyah crept onto Cassian's chest and peered at his face. "I see the glistening of stars inside your eyes, Cassian. And so, I shall speak to you a blessing—

> *"Drift in dreams of chasing stars.*
> *Take any path that you would choose.*
> *May dreams design within your heart*
> *a love for light you'll never lose."*

Mum and Da, returning from an evening stroll, climbed the porch stairs.

"But it's such a shame about Lady Marrowight," said Mum.

"Indeed." Da took off his satchel and sat on a log. "I wonder if she'll renovate."

Bastian exchanged a glance with Kaliyah.

"What happened?"

Da pulled out his reading glasses. "Your mum and I ran into the local land inspector. He was called to investigate Marrowight Manor after a dozen golden eagles were seen flying out of its windows." He drew a journal from his satchel. "The inspector found the place in wretched shape, infested with woodland animals—field mice, all kinds of birds, hedgehogs—even a few bucks."

"He declared the place 'unfit for occupation,'" said Mum.

"Its stone walls are apparently unsound," said Da. "He called it 'a miracle' that they hadn't caved in. Especially considering the variety of wildlife that had somehow pressed in."

Rhys stopped the ball with his foot.

Da stifled a laugh. "Inside, they even found fox droppings."

Cassian set to fussing.

Mum received him from Bastian and took his place in her swing.

"Can you imagine?" asked Mum. "Foxes just wandering through your home? The inspector said Lady Marrowight never reported a single thing. But there were the droppings, clear as day in the dining room."

Rhys and Lucas came to the porch.

"And here's another tidbit for you," said Da, signing. "Mr. Brighton said that yesterday, his lost dog came running home from the direction of Marrowight Manor. You lads remember her, I expect? A fluffy white Samoyed pup. Why, she's been missing for months."

Bastian glanced at his brothers, then asked, signing, "Where's Lady Marrowight?"

Mum, busy with soothing the baby, answered absently, "The inspector found a letter tacked to the door from a distant relative of Lady Marrowight's—an Esmerelda somebody—who said Lady Marrowight had retreated to her home in London for a respite."

Rhys signed Mum's words for Lucas, then asked, "Did the letter say if she'll come back?"

"It's doubtful," said Mum. "The manor needs an enormous amount of work. Lady Marrowight may prefer to find a different estate."

Lucas tugged Bastian's sleeve, then signed, "Someone's coming."

Bastian stepped down from the porch and stood with his brothers.

It was a man approaching, from a northern trail of the Wystan Woods. The man's curly blond hair was fixed in a knot atop his head. He had a trim blonde beard, and his sleeves were rolled high over his muscled arms. He was whistling beautifully.

Doctor Skylar.

Da stood.

Doctor Skylar, carrying a package, glinted a small smile toward Bastian.

"Well, my!" Mum scooted to the edge of her swing. "Are you not the very doctor whom we met at the A&E department last month?"

"Ah!" said Doctor Skylar. "I thought you two did look familiar."

"Is there something we can help you with?" asked Da.

"I'm new to the shire. Just took a cottage down the way. I've brought a package that was misdirected." He studied the label. "It's addressed to"—he flipped the package over—"someone called Bastian Goldcrest."

Bastian accepted the package—unmarked. "Do you know who it's from?"

Doctor Skylar shrugged. "Sorry, lad, I couldn't guess."

Lucas took it from him and examined it.

Doctor Skylar smiled kindly at Mum and Da. "You folks have a pleasant evening."

Da waved with his reading glasses. "Welcome to Dartmoor." He settled back down.

Once Doctor Skylar was well out of earshot, Mum said, "Bastian—that was the very man Da and I told you about. He's the doctor we met on the day of the accident—the Sylphic legend enthusiast."

"You don't say," said Bastian, signing.

He, Rhys, and Lucas together watched Doctor Skylar retreat into the woodland shadows, shafts of twilight shimmering along his path and glinting off the bright silver-blonde of his corkscrewing hair.

"I think I recognize that man—from the battle, it seems," Lucas signed, low, to Bastian and Rhys. "Or—do I?"

Rhys discretely signed, "Why in the world would an A&E doctor have been there?"

"He isn't only a doctor," signed Bastian, glancing from Rhys to Lucas. "That's Forrest Skylar—Kingfisher's brother."

Lucas shoved the package into Bastian's hands. "Blazes, open it."

His brothers staring, Kaliyah fluttering by his cheek, Bastian tore off the wrappings.

Inside lay a blue leather book, its silver-gilded edges shimmering in the fiery sunset.

Kaliyah shot away like a spark and darted over the eastern hill and into the Wystan Woods.

Bastian dropped to his knees.

Lucas and Rhys crouched beside him.

Bastian raised the book before his eyes.

The sunset glinted off the silver lettering of the title:

Sylphic Blue Countries: Exile and Adventure in the Kingdoms of the Sea, by M.D. Kingfisher.

THE END

ALSO BY TRICIA D. WAGNER

A STARRY-EYED BOY.
A CRYPTIC MAP. A MYTHICAL TREASURE.
WHAT PERILS AWAIT IN THE CHASING OF DREAMS?

"WAGNER HAS A BEAUTIFUL AND POETIC WRITING STYLE WHICH SERVES TO ENHANCE THE DESCRIPTIVE DETAIL SHE PROVIDES TO HER NOVELS. THIS GIVES HER BOOKS A WHIMSICAL AND OTHERWORLDLY QUALITY THAT SUPPORTS THE FANTASTICAL ELEMENTS WITHIN THEM. READERS WHO APPRECIATE THOUGHTFUL NARRATIVES THAT FOCUS ON THE HUMAN CONDITION WITHIN THE CONTEXT OF CHARMING AND MEMORABLE STORIES WILL QUICKLY FALL FOR THIS SERIES AND ITS IMMERSIVE QUALITY.
THE MEDICAL AND SCIENTIFIC ELEMENTS FOUND WITHIN THIS BOOK HELP READERS PUZZLE OUT THE QUESTION OF WHAT IS TRUE IN SWIFT'S WORLD ALONGSIDE THE LEGEND AND LORE. THIS IS A SATISFYING SERIES THAT WILL SPEAK TO YOUNG ADULT READERS AND ADULTS ALIKE."
- MARY R. LANNI, MLIS, REVIEWER, *REEDSY DISCOVERY*

"AS SWIFT LIVES UP TO HIS NAME AND HIS FAMILY LEGACY, YOUNG ADULTS RECEIVE A FAST-PACED FANTASY THAT WILL APPEAL NOT JUST ON THE ADVENTURE OR FANTASY LEVELS, BUT IN MATTERS OF THE HEART AS THE YOUNG STRUGGLE FOR INDEPENDENCE AND ACTION IN THE FACE OF PARENTAL RESTRICTIONS. TRICIA D. WAGNER'S ATTENTION TO PAIRING PSYCHOLOGICAL STRUGGLE WITH THE ADVENTURE OF FINDING A PROMISED TREASURE CREATES A STORY THAT PULLS ON THE EMOTIONS OF YOUNG READERS AS IT SATISFIES THEIR DESIRE FOR ACTION AND ADVENTURE."
- D. Donovan, Senior Reviewer, *Midwest Book Review*

FREE EBOOK

ABOUT THE AUTHOR

Tricia D. Wagner is an award-winning novelist, poet, and short story writer. She grew up in Amarillo, Texas, chasing storms, riding stallions, sojourning through painted canyons, disappearing into floating mesas under starry skies.

She now lives in Rockford, Illinois (though the truth is, she's a citizen of a dozen fictional countries.) Tricia works in education and lives day to day wonderstruck but luckily can feel her way about this terrifying, beautiful Earth through writing.

Tricia has pieces published in the *Write City Magazine*, *Chicago Newa*, *Word of Art 3D*, *Literary Yard*, and *Midwest Review*.

To learn more about Tricia, sign up for her readers' club, and hear about upcoming releases, visit:

www.TriciaWagner.com

AUTHOR'S NOTE

I love connecting with readers and writers. If you're interested in stories, then you're a kindred spirit to me, and I have lots more in store for you. To quote another kindred spirit in writing, Jedi Master Stephen King:

"Writing is magic, as much as the water of life as any other art. The water is free. So drink. Drink and be filled up."

If you're interested not only in stories, but in story creation, visit my website and sign up to receive a FREE **'Story Kickoff Character Worksheet.'**

I designed this tool for that first moment of getting our feet wet at the brink of a story.

To get your free worksheet, visit:
www.TriciaWagner.com